Resurrecting Mars

by brandon spacey

Resurrecting Mars

by brandon spacey

Copyright © 2013 by brandon spacey
and SpaceBrew Publishing.

All Rights Reserved.

spacebrew.com

Cover art and photograph by brandon spacey.

Resurrecting Mars is a work of fiction. All characters appearing in this work are fictitious. Any resemblance to real persons, living or dead, is purely coincidental.

Second Edition

Novels by brandon spacey

Callie Simmons Novels

book 1: Midnight's Park
book 2: Resurrecting Mars
book 3: Into the Darkness
book 4: Red Bell

Shawn Stedwin Novels

book 1: A Flutter in the Window
book 2: Hello, World

Standalone Novels

Shedding Sadness
Chasing Comets

For Callie, my stellar princess.

| **CHAPTER** *one* |

jackpot

Donnie Oliver stood leaning against the large doorway of the machine shop, a cigarette dangling between his fingers. The wind blew his red hair about and his eyes made fluttering slits against the Arizona sun as he reached for his shades. With his other hand he wiped his forehead and flung small droplets of sweat against the slick concrete floor. A Hummer stood idling in the bay behind him, making small puddles of its own as the air conditioner condensed precious water. It was mid-May, but the non-winter months didn't really stand up and differentiate themselves much in the desert. It was either stifling hot or it was winter.

Donnie stood six-foot-two and weighed a little over two-hundred pounds. He was thick and stocky, in pretty good shape, but would burn like bacon if he stayed in the sun too long. His light complexion simply refused to allow a tan. And he had long ago accepted that he would never look like a magazine model. He crushed the cigarette out with the toe of a dirty brown boot and dropped the butt in the can beside the door.

Once inside the Hummer, he pulled the brake release and slid out of the bay with a trailer in tow behind him. In the trailer stood a long crate full of nitrogen bottles, all of which had just been re-manufactured and refilled with fresh product. He would run them to the warehouse where they would be stored high in the racks until the company's next deployment mission.

The company was the Oliver Company, and their product was satellites. Some of their clients included GlobalTel Worldwide, National Geographic and the United States Military. Donnie's older brother, Samson, had founded the company with some of these in mind, knowing there would be a healthy demand for satellites in the coming years. After winning the contract with GTW in early 2002, it hadn't taken much to persuade Donnie to leave his current career. The contract involved deploying sixty satellites over the next ten years, and had put the Oliver Company in the top 100 richest businesses in the United States.

Donnie had been an astronaut at NASA for the last eight years, coming straight out of the Air Force where he had been a captain and a pilot of the YF-22 prototype. Working on such highly classified projects in the Air Force had bought him that coveted seat on the Space Shuttle for the next several missions. This translated easily to his new role at the Oliver Company, where he not only served as Chief Operations Officer, but also the Chief Deployment Officer. Every satellite went up on a shuttle he piloted.

His brother Samson had attained his master's in robotics, and had the technical know-how to build the satellites as well as the robotic arms and machinery used to deploy them. Samson also ran the business.

As he pulled onto the steel ramps and into the warehouse, the truck and trailer squeaked and groaned. The warehouse looked from the outside like a fortress. In the past couple of years, the Oliver Company had done much expanding to support its new roles. The warehouse had not been rebuilt, but rather remodeled, with insulation panels and steel siding on the outer walls, and a system of tracks and cranes within, for hoisting heavy equipment. It was the very definition of technology and the implementation of it.

Along the north wall were a dozen models of new technology satellite systems. The satellites were not antiquated, nor were they collecting dust. In fact, they were bought and paid for by various companies and ready to be deployed. The company cycled the satellites at the rate of about one unit every one to two months. They stood housed in air-tight crates to keep them safe from the elements. Built in vacuum-tight labs, the satellites had to be maintained with the strictest of precaution against even the tiniest of outside influences, like dust.

Along the other three sides of the warehouse were storage racks, loaded with high-tech motors and generators, telescoping robotic cranes and other space-worthy equipment and machinery ready for the next lift to the ISS. All of them were in vacuum-tight crates just like the satellites. Being based in the desert of Arizona made it especially hard to keep the equipment clean. There were no racks in the center of the warehouse, as that was where the shuttles would be parked for loading. The crane that hung from the ceiling could easily access everything on the outer racks and run it to the middle of the floor to drop it in the cargo bay.

The racks and shelves were perpetually filled with product and the Oliver team cranked out new technologies for new clientele. With such purchases as the GlobalTel Worldwide corporation had made, the Oliver Company was on its way to the financial establishment it would take to begin deep space exploration. Donnie's lifelong dream of setting foot on Mars would perhaps soon be realized. He had once said, "The Universe has a heartbeat. And I want to take its pulse"

The tires squeaked on the clean concrete as Donnie wheeled the truck to a stop beneath the arm of the resting crane. He stepped out onto the floor and lit a cigarette as he made his way to the control room where Thaddeus Cloys awaited him. Cloys was smiling, wiping his hands on a dirty rag.

"We got a problem, boss," Cloys said. His voice was uncommonly deep, and belied his personality. He was meek as a lamb with a huge heart and a love for all that lived, but at first sight, one would be led to believe otherwise. He stood almost six and a half feet tall, weighed close to 350 pounds, and was built like a professional wrestler. His dark brown skin contrasted against a perfect set of bright white teeth as he smiled.

"Oh yeah? What's that?" Donnie couldn't help but smile back.

"I guess you ain't talked to Samson, yet, right?"

"No, I haven't. What's the news, Thad?" replied Donnie.

The big man's smile broadened. "Looks like someone wants an ST-95," he said, and his grin was so wide Donnie thought it would surely split his face.

Donnie frowned and pulled his head back. "And that's a problem?" It was uncommon that the company sold the ST-95 model satellite, but when they did, it was a good month for everyone. Bonuses would surely betide those involved in the arrangement. The satellite was efficiently reproducible, and could be manufactured for relatively cheap. But even the base model sold for almost seventy-million dollars. Donnie had been waiting for some time for this news, and knew that once they sold the next model they would be within reach of their Manned Mission Series.

"Well, we're gonna have to build one," Cloys said quietly, still smiling.

Donnie punched his shoulder as he caught on. "Excellent. Excellent news, Thad! Who wants it?"

"I'm not sure, but I think I heard him say RRC," Cloys said.

Royal Research Corporation was not in the satellite business – at least not since Donnie last checked. He ran his fingers through his thick hair, crinkling up his face.

"Lemme guess. They want the R-ten-eleven refit package. Right?" Donnie smirked.

"No, boss. That's the best part. They want it vanilla." Vanilla was the company slang for plain, or 'no refits.'

"What? They'd be useless!" Donnie scoffed.

It was true. The ST-95 unit maintained a constant link with the Oliver Company's Satellite Tracking System via the proprietary comm-chip, and had several fail-safe systems that ensured they would never lose control of it. But even with these expensive luxuries, it was useless without a refit package. There were four add-on bays for modules such as spatial photography, weather recognition and forecasting systems, and spy systems – all of which the Oliver Company manufactured. Without a refit module, it would be like sending an incredibly sophisticated automobile into orbit.

"That's what they said, and hey – that makes our job easier!" Cloys said, nodding his head.

"Hmm. I just don't understand. Sounds like they want to cannibalize it. Use it for parts. Or steal our technology," Donnie thought aloud. "What'd Sam say?"

"He's all go, boss," Cloys said expectantly.

Donnie grunted. "Well hell, I guess that's good news then. Never sold a unit without the brains though." He started back for the Hummer, which sat patiently awaiting his return, door standing full open. "You wanna pull these nite bottles for me?"

"Sure thing, boss," Cloys said, returning to the control center.

On the way back to the machine shop, and short the weight of the nitrogen bottles in the trailer, Donnie dialed his brother's office on the wireless phone.

"Oliver," Samson said.

"Just wondering what your plan is here, Sam. Cloys tells me you authorized the sale of an ST unit, which I completely understand at the exorbitant price you settled on. What I'm having trouble with is…"

"Is why they want it with no brains. I know," Samson said, cutting him off. "It baffles the ever-living shit out of me. But they made the offer, and

Hastings is on a plane right now, on his way to sign the contract. I didn't want to argue semantics. They know what they're getting."

"That's the thing," Donnie said. "Do they really know what they're getting? It's like a lawnmower with no blade."

"Yeah, yeah, we went over all that. He insisted, and wants it within six months. Can we do it?" Samson puffed his cigar.

"Oh most certainly we can do it. I just wanted to hear it from you. This thing really is for real."

"This thing really is for real, Donnie."

"Good God almighty. I'm so excited I could piss my pants," Donnie explained.

"Well, hold off on that, I'm going to need you to meet Hastings and go over the contract with him," Samson said.

"When's he getting here? He'll need a ride from the airport I assume?"

"Yeah, but that's taken care of. Just meet him in the yard office around 3:30."

"Will do. So one more thing, Sam. This obviously provides us the funds to put us on track to start thinking about…" he was cut off again.

"The Manned Mission Series. You bet. Mary is already setting up a board meeting next week." A slight pause followed, and both men silently let the good news settle in on them. "Good stuff, eh?"

Donnie chuckled. "Damn good," he said and hung up.

The yard office was plain and functional – a break room with a television hanging in the corner. It sufficed as an office amidst the other facilities, all of which were littered with tons of high-tech machinery and equipment. A cheap fold-up table stood proudly in the middle of the room, and a countertop ran half the perimeter, where it ended at the refrigerator.

Donnie Oliver stepped in letting the door slam behind him. His hair was windblown and his eyes were not adjusted to the weak artificial light of the office. Jonathan Rodgers and Gregg Hastings sat at the table awaiting his arrival, Jonathan mashing the buttons on a remote control trying to find something on the television.

"Gentlemen," Donnie said, nodding at the two men, and Hastings rose to his feet. His respect for the Olivers was evident in the eager look on his round face. The company was constantly in the news, and had been applauded and awarded on numerous occasions. Oliver fetched a bottle of root beer from the fridge and pulled a chair out with his foot as he shook hands and met eyes with Hastings.

"Donnie Oliver!" he said, excited as Hastings was about this meeting. *This is the deal of a lifetime*, he thought – and not for the first time. "How are you? Was your flight okay?" He plopped into the low-back chair and scooted himself into the table, pulling hard from his root beer.

"I'm doing great, Mr. Oliver; it really is a pleasure to meet you," Hastings said, straightening his tie as he seated himself. "My flight was great. I slept most of the way."

Oliver smiled. "Good deal. You want a root beer?" he asked, turning to point toward the refrigerator.

"No, no thank you," Hastings said, waving his hands dismissively.

"Well, I guess you are just dying to see this contract then, are you not?"

"Oh absolutely, Mr. Oliver…"

Oliver cut him off, "Donnie, please."

"Donnie. I am – we are ready to do business with you. I just have a couple of questions, if you don't mind."

"No, please, go ahead. I would expect nothing less," Donnie said, clasping his hands comfortably behind his head, leaning back in his chair. The chair squeaked loudly, as if to indicate it wouldn't last much longer. He frowned and leaned closer to Rodgers. "Have these chairs replaced," he said quietly. He then pushed on the table and said, "Table too."

Rodgers nodded quietly and made a note on a small pad he kept in his breast pocket.

"Well, first of all, we have questions about the range of the units. How far can they go before the outbound transmission is lost, for instance?" Hastings asked, sliding his hands on the table.

"It's really indefinite. It's got a digital repeater behind it; so technically, you could still talk to it even if it left its orbit. All the ST-95 units have redundant radio connections with our intercepts, so you have global control and constant connectivity."

Hastings furrowed his brow slightly and spoke slowly, "Forgive me, I'm not very technical."

"That's okay. Here, I'll show you." Oliver stood and walked over to the white board, and started scribbling pictures on it. "Here's the Earth, and forgive me; I'm no artist," he said. "This here is your satellite. And over here and here and here we have intercept satellites. They receive and forward your signal for you when your satellite is eclipsed. With one intercept at every trisection of the planet, we never have an outage. You have constant and total control of your unit. Now obviously, if this is to be in geosynchronous orbit, none of that will matter anyway. It's really basic technology, but it's there nonetheless. And it's redundant. There are two nodes on every satellite. If one goes out, you have the other."

"I see," Hastings nodded. "That's good. And the other question is a little deeper, I'm afraid."

"Shoot!" Oliver encouraged, snapping the cap back on the colored marker and returning to his seat.

"How much power do these engines have? I mean as far as propulsion, and will they ever run out of gas, so to speak?" Hastings asked.

"I'm sorry, Mr. Hastings, I was under the impression your team had read up on all the specs sheets before you flew out here."

Hastings waved his hands again before he spoke, his face red. Donnie was almost embarrassed for him, as he had flown out here unprepared. He had either not been briefed properly, or really didn't know what he was getting into, Donnie thought. Donnie's heart sank as he realized the prospect this could present. If they hadn't truly reviewed the material, and truly didn't know what it was they were buying, then it was very plausible that the deal wouldn't even happen. No one wanted a useless satellite.

Hastings finally spoke after gulping back his hesitation. "No, no, no, we did! I'm just curious, really. My own personal interest is all!" He tried a smile.

Donnie Oliver smiled back at him, no less wanly than Hastings's had been. "I see. Well the satellite is completely solar-powered – as are most that are currently in orbit, whether it's one of ours or not." Donnie silently vowed to maintain his cool, and folded his hands in his lap. *Who the hell were they to send an amateur out to try me?* "The propulsion systems are minimal, just enough to straighten their orbit or relocate for better resolution – all depending on what you're looking for. But I assure you they will never 'run out of gas'."

Hastings nodded, then scratched his head. Oliver's thoughts crept quickly back to his original train of thought. *Never send a boy to do a man's job. Or rather, never send a plumber to do an electrician's job.* Oliver realized it wasn't necessarily Hastings's fault, though. It did, however, severely impact his impression of the Royal bunch. Maybe Hastings was a contract. An outside lawyer here to do their dirty work.

"And these run on the same communications channel as the rest of your units, I assume?" Hastings said, looking at Donnie.

Donnie looked over at Jonathan, then frowned and cleared his throat. After sitting still for a long moment, Donnie finally spoke. "I'm not sure how this has any bearing on your contract here, Mr. Hastings. That's proprietary information, and should your company attempt to overcome that circuit or tamper with it in any way, they would be in breach of contract. In a nutshell, if that comm-circuit is overridden or bypassed, we will effectively soft-lock the unit."

Hastings nodded slowly at Donnie, never breaking his eye contact. "Sure. Sure. Okay, so you have the documents then?"

Donnie breathed in deeply and sat staring at Hastings for a period in which an uncomfortable silence ensued. He then retrieved the documents from a briefcase sitting beside his chair, and placed them in a neat stack on the table. The signing was on.

Julia Callahan and Mark Bragg sat patiently watching as coordinates changed on the monitor. They were trying to get a better look at a blip Mark had noticed on the radar, but it was too far away. Julia pulled her hair back, holding it tight behind her head and sighed loudly. Mark looked at her, leaning back in his chair, face tortured by a hard frown.

"All right, let's put in the chords from the other angle. See if we can look at it from the other side," she said, letting her hair fall and rubbing her face. "This could be mechanical interference. It could be anything."

"Do we have anything out there that far?" Mark said. They had been at it entirely too long, and were both in need of a break. But something like this didn't happen often, and the excitement of discovery far exceeded the desire for slumber.

Julia was training Mark. She had been at the company for almost ten years, and had recently requested a new hire she could train to replace her. She was planning to move on in a couple more years. Mark was a sharp protégé, and caught on quickly – relieving her more stress than she would have thought possible.

"Of course. We have Star Seeker out there," she reminded him.

"Ah yeah, that's right – on its way to Neptune," said Mark. "We just have to turn it around, yeah?"

Julia smirked at him. "Well not the whole thing, dummy. Just the telescope."

"Yeah, that's what I meant."

"Uh huh."

Mark logged onto the satellite control terminal and began keying in coordinates and commands. "Of course there is the chance that we'll have planetary eclipse or something else in the way," he said. Julia thought he might be trying to regain some of the intellectual ground he had just lost to her.

"That's pretty unlikely. Space is just that. A whole lot of empty space," Julia said scientifically. "We should actually have a pretty good line-of-sight, but we'll have to figure out exactly where the object is in relation to Star Seeker."

"Shouldn't it just be the exact opposite coordinates as these here?" Mark said, again digging himself a hole.

"You're assuming it's straight out from us, and that object is exactly between us. That's a little remote, chief."

He sighed and furled his mouth, turning back to the monitor. Julia patted him on the shoulder as she stood up. He began backtracking, reversing the coordinates and working away from Earth, trying to find the object from the last known position of Star Seeker. He could get the telescope to rotate and bring it within a few thousand kilometers, and fine-tune it from there, hopefully without a lot of effort.

He keyed in the rough changes, which would start moving the telescope to point back toward the Earth. It would take almost forty minutes to respond, as Star Seeker was nearly twenty light-minutes away. It would take twenty for the signal to reach the satellite, then twenty for the return trip of the image. He stood up stretching, then excused himself to the restroom.

Star Seeker – an Oliver-built model – was a deep space telescope, and had the capability to record many variables in its vicinity, and could store up to ten terabytes of images. It was programmed to take one picture every hour, or anytime it detected movement relative to its constant motion. This made for some exquisite captures of comets and other anomalies in its field of vision.

After forty-five minutes, Mark and Julia returned to the satellite console to have a look at the return. The image in the corner of the screen that represented the satellite and its position started moving. A series of image refreshes followed, each one indicating a slight change in the telescope's position, as it wheeled nearly 180 degrees on its x-axis.

Mark pounded a few more commands into the terminal, and the numbers and code changed rapidly on the readout screen. The image they were seeing was full of stars, like a cloud of spectral dust. Julia cooed at the sight.

Mark turned to face her, looking her up and down quickly. He had met Julia at a Meeting of the Minds – a seminar hosted by the Houston Astronomical Society – and had taken an instant liking to her. She had spoken intelligibly in a room full of profound geniuses, and it had made his head spin. He guessed her IQ was dangerously close to 200.

Julia had graduated from Pennsylvania State with a Master's in Cosmology and Astrophysics, then went on to get her PhD at Michigan State University in General Astronomy. She was well known in the scientific community, but had taken this job as Lead Trip Coordinator – a rather humble and lowly position considering her knowledge. Her company had constructed an observatory on the south end of the building for deep space exploration, and had named her Head of Discovery. She had been passionate about her details for many years, but had finally resolved that she was only seeing a limited section of space because of her location. She wanted to move to Alaska so she could see a different section for a while.

She stood with her hands on her lower back, stretching and popping it as she stared at the screen.

"Back hurts again, huh?" Mark asked, raising his eyebrows, then turning back to the console. "Aren't you a little young to be hurting like an old woman?"

She slapped his shoulder. "Yeah, yeah, rub it in. I'm not as young as you think," she assured him.

He turned around again, frowning. "Actually, I think you are. You can't be a day over twenty-five."

"Ha!" Julia choked, and laughed out loud. "Thank you, but yes I can be. And am! More than a few days

I'm afraid." Then she quickly changed the subject, pointing at the console. "Hey pull up a visual on that."

Mark followed her order and brought up the image display from the deep space scope. But the view was a rather disappointing solid black, with only a few specks of white spattered about.

"Did you put in the right chords?" she asked him, leaning in closer. 'Chords' was their technical slang for coordinates.

"Well, yeah. These coordinates should – in theory – be almost the exact polar opposite of the ones from Hubble 9. You want to check my work?" he asked, looking over his shoulder at her serious visage, furrowed again in concentration.

"Well, you've been known to folly a number or two, Bragg," she said. "But no, that looks right. 'Cause that's Mars there, right?" She was pointing at a tiny dark spot on the screen – a void of stars.

"Umm, yeah. The vector of this line-of-sight may be skewed slightly, but if that's Sol, that definitely has to be Mars."

Again, Julia stood up straight. "Yeah. That's what I was afraid of. It's right the heck in the way."

"Uh, yeah. That's exactly what you said. Miss 'that's pretty unlikely'. What was all that about empty space?" Mark said, smirking at her.

She chewed her lip and raised her eyebrows. "Aw, who cares anyway? Star Seeker's too far away. All we would see is an inconclusive speck. But darn it, Mark – something is out there!"

"For once, Julia, I am forced to concur. It's got a sheen like a star, but it's too small to be a self-sufficient luminance," he said, rubbing his stubbly chin. "Still, it may be a rock with a nice smooth angle."

"Nah. Impossible. The consistency of its luminescence is too sustained. It's either metallic or on fire. I'm willing to bet my bonus on it," Julia said quietly. "Good find though, Mark. You should dig in to that. Try to get something out there to get a closer look at it. You may shortly have something named after you."

Mark laughed uneasily. It felt good to be assured by someone of her expertise, but at the same time, it seemed too good to be true. How could he have beaten her to it? She had said before, "The sky's too big for one man." No one could find them all. Even still, he wasn't quite so confident yet to accept credit for something of such great meaning. He had found several comets and named them – everyone had. But this was too close to home to go unnoticed. This was between home and its next neighbor.

He spun in his chair and stood, stretching his arms above his head. Julia smiled at him, her eyes meeting his. Mark had blonde hair that brushed against his brow, and a carefree attitude about it that contrasted his personality. He was a perfectionist in most cases, never sloppy about his work. But his hair wasn't a bother.

He towered over Julia; a half-foot taller and easily seventy pounds heavier. Mark was thick through the chest with arms to match, and a tight stomach. He was a good-looking guy. But to Julia he was a subordinate; a co-worker. The last thing she wanted was to spend her home time with someone she spent all day with at work. Not that she had much of a home life, being so devoted to the company.

The company was Privatized Spatial Services, a space traffic control facility, much like that of airports. When the exploration of space became popular within the private realms, the government had ultimately determined there was a need for such, and for obvious reasons. There were several such facilities around the globe as privatized space travel was becoming more and more popular. Not to the extent that normal air travel had come by any means, but enough people with enough money had become interested, and the dangers of satellite collision or close encounters with other private ships – or even airplanes – were present indeed.

In addition to the government-controlled space traffic control centers, there were several private ones that would sell their services to large companies that did a lot of space flight. A company that sent a hundred trips into space a year could get better attention from a private STC facility. The private firms were of course networked with the government ones, and ultimately under the control and mandate of the FSAA (Federal Space and Aviation Administration) just like the government-run facilities. But with paying clients, they could provide more personalized service, which included continual traffic monitoring as opposed to that traffic being passed from station to station as it moved about.

Other features of the private and very expensive traffic control agencies were better takeoff windows and quicker clearance times. Instead of waiting until the government was ready to clear a takeoff, the company could pretty much determine its own time based on a schedule provided by the traffic control agency. This schedule followed the normal guidelines in that it looked for weather, satellites, aircraft, and opportune time slots. All in all, it was much easier to get a shuttle into space with a private agency, and the most advantageous component of a private agency's services was that the government didn't get involved in the cargo.

"Wanna smoke?" Mark said to Julia.

"Sure," she said, and followed him out the back door. She didn't actually smoke, but oft times went outside with the smokers because otherwise she would forget to take a break.

Complete with signatures, the contract was ready for implementation. All that was left was fulfillment and requital. Donnie Oliver returned to his office in the back of the machine shop. A stark contrast to the concrete and machinery of the rest of the warehouse, his office was insulated, sound-proofed and luxurious. Though he hardly ever spent time there anymore, he had furnished it fairly heavily. He had thrown in a couch and television for good measure.

Upon logging into the network, he scanned the contract and saved it to the file server, then picked up the phone and called his production team to order. "We have 180 days to build an ST-95 unit. No refits." He had been asked to repeat that last part. "No refits."

It was a bright light for the Oliver Company's future, and Donnie couldn't help but smile every time he thought about it. The board had come to meeting that next week and called to order the first of the official Manned Mission Series, which would send a deep space explorer shuttle to Mars with a full crew and a load of miscellaneous equipment that would spur a series of tests on the Red Planet's surface. The launch date was set for February 9, just eight months away. For the first time ever, human beings would set foot on Earth's second-closest neighboring planet, and would carve their names in the world's history books.

The shuttle in which they would be traveling was one of the largest in their fleet. Donnie Oliver had conceived its propulsion system in a dream. He had jumped out of bed upon waking and revolutionized space travel in one quick swoop. He had been dreaming of a propulsion system powered by antimatter inductors like the ones used in Star Trek. With the progression of technology reaching impossible peaks in the early twenty-first century, physicists had learned to collect and store antimatter in penning traps. These were essentially electromagnetic vacuum batteries that kept the antimatter from coming in contact with other matter particles.

In that no scientist had yet learned where they could find antimatter – and it was assumed that there was none in existence, nor had there been since about a tenth of a second after the Big Bang – they had to produce it. As stated in Einstein's theory of relativity, matter is a very concentrated form of energy, thus energy and matter can be transposed. By crashing ultra-high-speed particles into a sheet of nickel, the energy behind this speed is transformed into matter. Matter cannot be created without creating antimatter though, and vice versa. As soon as the matter-antimatter particle pair is created, the antimatter is pulled into the penning trap for storage. If this antimatter particle were to come in contact with the matter, it would disappear in a flash of energy.

The only problem with creating antimatter was that to collect enough to be useful, it would take millions of years. It took about a year to produce a raisin-sized chunk of antimatter weighing about a gram at a cost of about eighty-million dollars. This tiny chunk of antimatter would power a 100-watt light bulb for about three seconds. This ridiculously expensive energy was impractical and could only be stored for a few months in a penning trap anyway. It would take at least a kilogram of antimatter to power a spaceship to Mars and back, and as it was generally thought to take about three months to get to Mars, the crew would run out of fuel before the halfway point and never be able to get back.

For an antimatter propulsion system to ever work, something would have to be revised. Donnie's dream had given him an idea that had done just that. With the stroke of a marker on a whiteboard at three in the morning, he had shown his half-drunk, half-sleeping, very agitated brother how they could overcome the antimatter deficit.

The only problem with his resolution was that it was dependent on splitting antimatter particles. He hadn't known this wasn't possible. In the end, and with the help of a third party, they had come up with a new way to reproduce their resources. In essence, this was the act of catching particles in more than one place at time, and copying them in the act. Tapping the resources of other unreachable dimensions had appealed to all parties involved.

Quantum Mechanics as a science was still in its infancy, and no one was sure if any of this theoretical babble would even be worth pursuing off paper. On paper it looked exquisitely plausible – even simple, if you knew the science. After Donnie had sufficiently explained his approach to the attack, they had agreed to meet the next day – at a more reasonable hour altogether – to discuss it further, and with this third-party scientist who had much experience with quantum mechanical exploration and experimentation.

In Samson's executive office, the three of them had gathered around the mahogany round table with high hopes and optimistic expectations. Callie Simmons, an old college friend of Donnie's from Arizona State had come with little knowledge of what the meeting would entail. Donnie had flown her down from Maryland for the meeting.

"Thanks for coming out on such short notice, Cal. Basically what we need here is affirmation. I hope, anyway," Donnie said.

"Well let's hope I can provide it. Forgive me for being unprepared – I wasn't really informed what this would pertain to…" she trailed off, staring at Samson.

He waved his hand dismissively leaning back in his leather chair. "Not an issue. Your flight was okay, I suppose?"

"Fantastic. I fly quite frequently now days, so I'm kind of used to it. Seems like these days everybody wants me somewhere other than where I am. But you know, it goes with the territory, I guess."

"So you're not with RRC anymore?" Donnie asked.

"No, I left Royal about two years ago. Now I'm a public face for Bohr Enterprises. It's not bad, I just sometimes miss the lab," she said, staring at the table, where she could see an almost perfect reflection of the ceiling in its sheen.

"That's a career move," Donnie reminded her. "Well all I wanted to do here was run some ideas by you and find out if they are even plausible. If not, then we need to find out how to make them more plausible, or scrap it completely, as the case may be. Either way, I think we may be onto something pretty serious here, and need to know if we've both run off the deep end."

Callie nodded, pursing her lips. She was being paid twenty-five thousand dollars for sitting at this table with them – a meeting that would last no more than seven or eight hours. She was always well paid for her two cents' worth.

"What we're proposing here is a propulsion system powered by antimatter, to put it simply," Donnie said. He twirled his pen in his fingers and leaned back confidently in his chair.

"Star Trek revisited," she said with a smirk.

"Now don't knock it so fast!" Samson said. "There's an idea here that you might be essential in helping us to bring to light." He paused a moment, then added, "Plus, it came to Donnie in a dream."

Callie laughed out loud. "Well most of his best ideas came to him that way. I think I can save you some time here, fellas. It's plausible that you could propel something with it, but it would require a super abundance of something that could cost trillions of dollars to produce." She crossed her legs and straightened her skirt, then noticed Donnie hiding a smile behind a closed hand. "Or have I not done my research?"

"Well we'll see. My thought here is that we can utilize some sort of quantum machine to split these things and make them more abundant. They can be split, can't they?" Donnie asked.

Callie leaned back in her chair and blew a stray lock of hair out of her eyes. "Nope. Antimatter is subatomic. It's a single particle. To try and split it would annihilate it," she said.

Donnie sighed heavily, staring at the ceiling. "Well, shit. That was over too fast."

"Well, now wait a minute though," Callie said, holding up a finger. "We're not through here. I like what you said. You said a 'quantum machine'. A quantum computer indeed could be the answer."

Samson twirled his pen, frowning. "Elaborate, please. I think we may be a little behind you in the physics department."

Donnie had studied astrophysics quite a bit, though he had never finished college He grasped most of it pretty well when it was explained to him. Samson, though, had never strayed too far from his robotics books.

"Well if we can somehow find a way to capitalize on the wave function, we might have an answer." She chewed on her knuckle for a moment, staring at the table, then stood up and picked up a red dry-erase marker. "I do have some experience with a quantum computer, but getting a hold of one now might be a task."

"You've used a quantum computer?" Samson said, clearly impressed. "I didn't know those even existed yet."

"Uh, yeah. They do. I did a little – well, I... I've messed around with one a little bit." She walked over to the whiteboard, popping the cap on the marker. "It just wasn't for the same application, but whatever, right? This is all theoretical, of course," she said, pointing the tip of the marker at the words she was speaking, "so there are no guarantees, but welcome to science, right?"

She then proceeded to draw out the idea she had for bringing their dream to life. The math meeting lasted nine hours, only breaking once to have Chinese food delivered. Callie had explained to them the principles of quantum mechanics, and speaking until her mouth was dry, she had brought them to understanding of her idea, which was – to say the least – very 'out of the box'.

Callie's idea was to catch subatomic particles while they were sleeping. "In quantum mechanics," she said, "we measure the movement and speed of these particles with a wave function. Inasmuch as science can prove our theories, the wave function has proven to us that these particles can exist in two locations at once. The idea here is that if that is possible, it is entirely possible that once the antimatter half of a particle has ceased to exist in one of those locations, it is prospering in another dimension, doing the same thing all over again.

"Now. If we can copy these things while they are hopping, we have effectively doubled our resources. Now multiply this by macro scales and we are exponentially creating particles in exponentially multiplying locations. After twenty orders of magnitude using this application, we would have a billion particles. Twenty-one, we'd have sixty-four billion. It'd be like one to the sixty-fourth, then sixty-four of those ones to the sixty-fourth. And you see the pattern."

"So we are not only doubling our resources, but also doubling the number of locations they are doubling in?" Donnie asked.

"Well, doubling isn't the right word. It's finite, but can grow infinitely large very quickly. We are talking macro multiplication here. Exorbitant exponentiation. And this is with every cycle. The only problem is rounding up the product," she said in response.

Donnie was still thinking math when he replied, "Rounding it up to what?"

"Rounding it up period. Gathering it. Collecting it all. Once we have produced it in all these other 'theoretical dimensions', we need to have to have a way to retrieve it all. I think I have something that will take care of that. You'll need the tech department to build you a machine that will plural these buggers though," Callie said in closing.

Her application of the science had been magnificently complex, but through slow steps, she had shown them exactly what to build. In effect, it was a glorified quantum computer that had roots in other dimensions. Superstring theory was the desired science in her application, as it involved ten dimensions – nine spatial and one of time. Working with one-dimensional elementary particles, and correlating their interactions, the new machine would have to put tracers on these particles, like leashes. If a breadcrumb trail could be left in the wake of their dispatch, then in theory, the particles could be reeled back in after they had split and done their part in the process. Callie had dried two red markers in expounding her theories on the whiteboard. She had made it up as she went along, basing her thoughts on sciences of which she was already sure. And Pluraling, as a science in and of itself, was born.

It took two and a half years to modify an existing prototype quantum computer and get the science of Pluraling down to a task, but execution was now a flawless function of the machine.

Needless to say, Callie hadn't taken the return trip to Maryland to return to work at Bohr Enterprises. Her return to Maryland a week and a half later had only been to collect her personal things and break the lease on her apartment. She was moving to Arizona to fulfill her new role as Chief Technology Officer of the Oliver Company.

The hot air blew dust in Donnie's eyes as he paced outside the warehouse, cell phone tight against his ear. His conversation with the journalist had been in progress for almost thirty minutes, and showed no signs of slowing even now. He had seen many press conferences and television cameras, being interviewed about his mission to Mars. He had been on 60 Minutes two nights before, and was now preparing to have the camera crews from Discovery Channel move in. The camera crews would be filming everything from conception to departure, from the time they left Earth to the time they returned, and interviewing all the key personnel for a special two-month television series. The only secret the Oliver Company would be keeping was its antimatter drive. Though it would make everyone rich beyond calculation, they kept it under lock and key.

The steel door on the side of the warehouse opened, and Jonathan Rodgers stepped out into the June air. He made the motion of covering the mouthpiece of the phone to buy a moment from Donnie.

Donnie widened his eyes and covered the mouthpiece.

"They're here, boss," was all he said, then nodded and stepped back into the warehouse.

"Okay. I need to get off the phone now. Can we pick this up later?" Donnie asked the magazine writer. After a moment, he hung up and entered the warehouse. People were running around in a frenzy to get things straightened and ready for television crews. The overhead bell was ringing, which meant the phone was ringing. Mop buckets were scattered about the concrete floor, and wet floor signs lurked in wet spots in an organized randomness.

Donnie walked quickly to his office in the back corner of the building as the phone continued to ring. Shanna King, his young assistant, rushed up to meet him and handed him a clipboard with papers needing signatures, talking a hundred miles an hour. That's how Donnie liked it. She had learned quickly to speak fast lest she be interrupted by something else entirely. If she was interrupted, it was likely Donnie wouldn't get back to what she had been saying, and all would be lost.

"Samson called. Wants a return call, needs you to fly to San Francisco this weekend if you have time," she said.

"Do I?" Donnie asked. She knew his schedule better than he did.

"Yeah if you want it."

"What is it?"

"Meet with Pablo Phoenix to talk about ETIS. I told Sam you'd call him on that one. Need you to sign this. Budget increase for collections and distributions," she said, walking quickly to keep up with his long stride.

Donnie signed the papers without reading them. His trust for Shanna was thoughtless. He had hired her right out of high school a couple of years before, making her the youngest, least qualified employee ever to work for the Olivers. She was intelligent for her age, and very sharp, but a lot of the other employees seemed to have a problem getting used to her being there. Even after two years, people would still stare at her when she walked into the break room. Donnie had warned against talking down to her, and that part of it had at least desisted. But as long as her salary remained, nothing would bother her. She made more than a lot of the technicians, and she was untouchable as long as she worked for Donnie. No one could quite pin down what it was that made her so important to Donnie, but he told her things even some of the other executives didn't know.

"One more thing. You know the Discovery crew's here, right?" she said.

Donnie stopped in his doorway. "Yeah. On my way out to meet 'em. Call Sam and tell him no on the ETIS meeting. It's bullshit."

Shanna pushed him into his office and pushed the door closed behind her. She leaned back against the door and sighed. "Tell me why, Donnie."

Donnie grabbed his suit jacket from the back of his chair then stopped and sat on the corner of his desk, pointing at her. "Think about it. I'll tell you what he wants," he started.

"What who wants?" she interrupted.

"Phoenix. He wants to buy space on my ship for his shells. It's ridiculous. We've never even been to Mars and he already wants to bury people there." ETIS was Phoenix's company. Extra-Terrestrial Interment Services offered people a chance to have their mortal remains buried in exotic locations, such as the Moon, or space. So far, he hadn't been able to add any other planets to his brochure.

"You know how much money you could make on that though, right?" Shanna said, raising her hands. "He charges almost thirteen thousand for a lunar burial. This would probably be double that for a shell that weighs eight ounces. Your price tag could be twenty grand per shell!"

Donnie nodded. "Yeah, but it's bullshit. The very thought of carrying people's ashes to Mars disturbs me. Number one, that means we have to take time out of our schedule to dig graves for these shells. Number two, we don't have room on the ship for them." He stood up, waving his hands madly, then pulled his jacket on and brushed the dust off his slacks.

Shanna stood in front of him helping him straighten his jacket. "Well I want you to think about it, Donnie. If you limit this guy to fifty shells, you've made a million dollars, and at only twenty-five pounds of cargo."

Donnie looked up at her and sighed. "It's so…"

"I just want you to think about it. You have 'til Thursday to let me know so I can call him."

"What day is it?" Donnie said, frowning.

"Tuesday. Go get 'em," Shanna said, and opened the door for him. He raised his hands to his sides widening his eyes at her. "Yes, you look fine," she said.

The Discovery crew rolled tape on every authorized area of the warehouse, and interviewed Thaddeus Cloys for almost an hour as he walked them around the storage area explaining things to the camera. Donnie and Shanna sat in chairs at the far end of the warehouse watching him point out almost everything on the shelves and describe how the crane worked.

"He's perfect for the job," Shanna said, pulling a lock of hair behind her ear.

"Yeah. I may have to make him the new spokesman," he said, nodding.

"Spokesperson. We have to work on your PC, Donnie."

"Oh come on. Spokesperson is so fruity sounding. And it takes too long to say."

"But it's PC, Donnie. If you're going to go on television talking about stuff like this, you need to sound correct."

"Well look at Angie. She calls herself the spokesman. Not the spokesperson," Donnie said.

"No she doesn't! Maybe around you she does, but not in public!" Shanna argued.

"I'm telling you she does," Donnie assured. Angie Jackson was the company spokesperson, and had arranged the entire schedule by which the Discovery crew would be shooting. She was now poring over said schedule in the conference room with several Discovery Channel production executives.

"Whatever." Shanna shook her head.

"You know I like women that don't pay any attention to that bullshit. It's all bureaucratic pretentious hogwash."

"Donnie, you own a very large, very visible company. You of all people should be more aware of your politics."

Donnie snorted. "Politics is one thing. But it's taken way too far, and I don't have time to play those middle school games. Guess I'm just old-fashioned," he said, removing a piece of lint from his jacket.

"Well if you ever let me go into space with you, I'll call myself a spaceman. How's that?" she said, looking up at him.

Donnie nodded, pursing his lips. "Yeah, but I need you to stay down here and run things for me."

Shanna made a sour face, for she knew he was serious. If he were gone, it would almost appear that she were second in command behind Samson. It wouldn't be a literal promotion, of course, as she wouldn't actually control anything, but she would definitely speak in Donnie's stead. Even Samson was on board with this; he trusted his brother like his brother trusted Shanna. Samson didn't even keep his own assistant Mary in the same loop as Donnie kept Shanna.

"Oh, I would much rather be in space though. Think of how much more fun it would be to write home about," she said, staring at the high ceiling.

"Write home from space?" he said, smiling.

"No, dummy. Write home from here when I get back."

Donnie nudged her shoulder. "If I took you into space, your parents would kill me. They already think I've stolen their daughter from them."

"You have," she reminded him.

At the company softball game two years before, the Oliver Company was playing against Tempo

Research, where her father was a data analyst. Shanna and her friends were in the bleachers shouting and whistling at the men, even being a little flirtatious. The ballpark was right across the street from the high school, so students were always at the game, and the corporate teams rarely paid them any mind.

Donnie had missed a catch at third base, and Shanna's father had scored because of it. In the dugout between innings, Shanna had rattled the fence behind him and gotten his attention.

"You hire me, I'll play third base for you. He'll be out next time," she said.

"Come again?"

"That's my dad who just scored on your error. You hire me and he'll be out next time," Shanna repeated. She was smiling pleasantly at him, as if she were serious.

"Are you old enough to work?" Donnie asked.

"I just graduated."

"High school?"

"Yep."

"Congratulations. You plan on going to college?"

"I want to go to Rice. Be a math major. Don't think my parents can afford it though," Shanna said, still staring at him. Her eyes never left his. She was very forward and as far from shy as one could be, right out of high school at least.

"You come work for me, they won't have to," Donnie said. After an elegant pause, he added, "*And,* you can tag your dad out."

Shanna had come to apply formally the next day. Donnie gave her a full tour of the complex, asking her irregular questions and testing her about various things unimportant. Without her ever knowing it, she had been hired. They had returned to his office after the tour, and he had leaned against his desk.

"You have any questions? Need something to drink?"

"No. No thank you. Thanks for the tour. I do have some questions, but…" she trailed off.

"Great. I'm sure we'll get to them in due time. I'm kind of pressed now though. I don't want to be late for my massage. I like walking the tour beforehand though, in order to be nice and sweaty for the massage therapist. Can you be here Monday at eight?"

"Um, yeah. I was just wondering…" she trailed off again.

"Oh, yeah, about the salary… Well, I'll come up with something over the weekend, and run it by you Monday. I'm sure you won't be unhappy with it," he said, opening the door.

All she could do was grin and nod. "Okay then. See you Monday." She started out the door, then stopped halfway. "Oh. One more thing."

"Sure," Donnie said.

"What exactly will my position be?"

"You'll be my personal executive assistant. You bring me coffee, you fax my papers, you take my calls and you schedule my meetings. You speak for me when I'm indisposed, you defend me when I'm not around – if that's ever needed – and best of all, you get to ride around in my car with me," he said. "Sound fair?"

"See you Monday, Mister Oliver," she answered.

"One thing, Shanna. Never ever call me Mister Oliver. That's for the commoners. You call me Donnie."

*   *   *

After several hours of filming, the Discovery crew finally packed up and left for the evening. They would be back the next morning around eleven, the production manager had said. It was well after nine p.m., and Donnie was in his office, scanning through a series of research documents he was putting together for the Mars trip. Some of them were strictly procedural, such as how to properly collect, identify, tag, and prepare any items they planned on bringing back to Earth. There were strict guidelines about decontamination and cleansing without ruining the substance, as well as contingency procedures in the case that someone was infected by a Martian virus of some sort. Others were notes on what to bring, and what to do at certain points of the journey.

Shanna knocked twice and opened the heavy door to Donnie's office. As she stepped in, he held a finger up to halt her a moment as he finished reading a sentence, then saved the document. She sat down as he turned to face her.

"What's up? God, woman, why are you still here?" he said, looking at his watch.

"Hey if you work I work, right?" she replied.

"You're crazy. You should be out with your friends," Donnie said.

"So should you."

"I don't have any."

"Well there is that…" After a lengthy pause, she said, "You're first on the cameras tomorrow. They want you in makeup by eleven-thirty,"

"I'm not wearing makeup," he said, shaking his head.

"It's just base so you don't look like a ghost on the camera. Besides, it won't take five minutes to prep you."

"I'm not wearing makeup," he said again. "If I look like a ghost, so be it."

Shanna sighed. "You are so bullheaded. Donnie, you know how white you will look under those high beams?"

Donnie chewed his lip for a moment. "Who's putting the makeup on? You?"

Shanna smirked at him. "If you like, yes."

"Good. If it ain't you, it ain't happening."

She shook her head quickly. "Okay. Why does it matter who puts it on?"

"I don't want anyone to know I'm wearing it. You put it on, it will be our little secret."

"God, what a freak you are." She moved to the corner of his desk, then continued. "Who's gonna be on your crew, Donnie?"

"Shit, I don't know. You tell me," he said, shrugging.

"How would I know?" Shanna said and frowned.

"Well you know what time they start filming me, I figured you would know who all's gonna be there."

"Your Mars crew, Donnie," Shanna said levelly.

"Oh. That crew. Well, let's see. It'll be Jonathan Rodgers, Gary Grant, Andy Duryea, Paul Reznor, Mike Thurman and me." He paused a moment, then said, "Something tells me you knew that."

"Who's Andy?"

"The medical officer." Donnie was fiddling with a pen on his desk.

"No women on board?"

"Andy is a woman. Well, at least in the literal sense of the word." He waited for Shanna to smile. She didn't. "Where are you going with this, Shanna?"

"You know I want to go, don't you?" she said, standing to move around behind his desk with him. She sat on the desk again, this time within touching distance of him.

Donnie stared at her, twirling the pen. When he finally answered, he sighed audibly. "Shanna, I really don't think I can do that."

"Why not?" Her young mind still hadn't grasped the politics she had preached earlier in the day.

"Number one, it'd be a conflict of interest. You're my secretary! Secondly, there are scientists and astronomers that have been working diligently since the birth of this company, hoping to have a seat on that shuttle. I can't just bump them so I can take my assistant."

Shanna didn't answer. She stared at the pen Donnie was twirling, nodding her head slowly. Donnie finally stood up and took her by the shoulders, looking closely into her eyes.

"You're a good girl, Shanna. You know I'd take you if I could. I don't mean to sound demeaning, but you just really aren't qualified."

After a long moment, she pushed him away and stood up herself. "Well don't you need a navigator?"

Donnie smiled. "No, not with the navigation systems installed on the shuttles. These days the computer does everything for you. A burger flipper could fly that ship into space."

"Well I'm a brilliant mathematician," she said, holding up a finger. "So if you change your mind, I'll be ready. Besides, I can ride all the roller coasters without getting nauseous, so I know I can handle the training.”

“Well you’d be in luck there. Though you hardly need any physical training anymore either. With the shuttles built the way they are, all you need is antigravity time training,” he said. After another long pause, he finally concluded, “I’ll keep you in mind.”

“Thank you, Donnie.”

Donnie could see the defeat in her eyes, and felt sorry for her. He remembered being in her shoes before, having older, wiser people tell him he couldn’t do something he so badly wanted to do.

Shanna looked up at him and forced a smile. “I’m gonna get outta here. See you tomorrow,” she said, turning for the door.

“All right. Have a good night, Shanna.”

“Thanks. Oh. I’m gonna take off next Tuesday. It’s my birthday.”

“Oh yeah. Cool. Stop by then and I’ll take you to lunch,” Donnie said. She nodded and left.

Eleven o’clock came quickly to Donnie. He had been up since five getting things in order and trying to find ways to make his schedule accommodate the interview, which would last around two hours. They would cut the parts they needed of him and end up using five or ten minutes at best, but all of it was necessary. He knew it wouldn’t be the only time he was on their cameras either. Being the chief coordinator and astronaut in charge of the Mars Mission, he would be in constant contact with it, as they were sending up a mass of equipment and cameras to film every bit of the experiments and landing.

Discovery Channel was a partial sponsor for the 59-million-kilometer trip to Mars. They were putting up twenty-five percent of the cost in return for having their cameras and equipment brought along. They wanted raw footage of every significant event that took place during the eighteen-month round trip, especially of the experiments on the surface. The Discovery crew would be training someone on the crew of the shuttle to use the cameras and equipment so as not to have to send one of their own people along.

Shanna had made him up an hour ago and he felt a little better about wearing it. But he still wanted to stay in his office until the shoot, so as not to be seen in it. A knock on Donnie's door made him look at his watch. "Damn, I gotta go. The cameras are ready. Okay, I'll call you later," he said and hung up the phone. He opened his office door and stepped into the warehouse where the camera crew was waiting for him. They had him sit in front of a giant stellar map of the Milky Way with bright insets of the solar system and its components. The lights came on and nearly blinded him, and the fun began.

"Okay, first I want you to talk about the distance to Mars, how long it will take, and what you and the crew plan to do in the down time," the interviewer said. "Roll cameras." He counted down with his fingers, and Donnie began to speak.

"At the time we plan to launch, which is February ninth next year, Mars will be at its perihelion, and will be aligned with Sol and Earth. This only happens about every fifteen to seventeen years, so the timing is perfect. At this point, the Earth will be about fifty-nine million kilometers away from Mars," Donnie answered. He was excited to be sharing his information, as he had been loading his head with it for the past several years.

"How many miles is that?"

"Uh… What is it, 35-36 million? Roughly?"

"Say it, please. You won't have my voice on it when it goes to production."

"That's about 35-36 million miles."

The interviewer nodded then continued, "Good. Now move on to the rest of it."

"The trip itself will take about three months. Three months is a long time in space, so we'll be performing various experiments and such during the trip. We'll be on Mars for right around twelve months. We have to wait for the planets to realign for the return trip," Donnie said, adjusting in his seat. The lights were already causing him to sweat. "So fifteen months after leaving Earth, we'll start packing up to come home."

"Do you have enough to keep you busy for an entire year? That's a long time on a foreign planet, I would think," the interviewer said.

"Well, anything you can think-"

"Don't say 'well'. Restart that sentence."

Donnie cleared his throat, a little annoyed. "During our stay, anything you can think of trying, we will be trying. I have a feeling we'll be like kids in a candy store. Aside from our daily exercise routines and playtime, we'll be spending a fair amount of time building our base camp for experiments, and conducting those experiments."

The interviewer had him talk about the specifics of the experiments, what was being taken, and other things generally covering the trip. The specifications of the shuttle would be covered by the Systems Officer in a later meeting, and Donnie would be on camera again later in the day to cover the basics of the cargo and the shuttle's payload. After two hours in the intense heat of the movie lights, the interview was finally over. The lights were switched off and Donnie felt immediate relief as the cool air once again took control of the area.

Shanna was waiting for him with a wet hand towel in hand. "You done good, dude," she said in a hard southern drawl.

Donnie laughed. "Thanks. God, that was hot!"

"Yeah I could tell."

"What'd I miss? Anything important?" Donnie dropped heavily into the chair behind his desk. Shanna sat on the corner of his desk holding a stack of manila folders against her chest.

"Not a thing. I really was impressed, by the way, with the way you handled that. You had all that stuff memorized?"

"Yeah. This trip has been my life for the last three years."

"Well, you sounded very knowledgeable and professional. I'm proud of you, Donnie," she said, smiling.

"Thanks. Glad you liked it." He wiped his forehead with the towel and leaned back in his chair. "So what's in the folders?"

"Ah nothing really. Bunch of cargo matrices and boring shit like that," Shanna said. "But I think something's wrong with the weights and measures tablet. I'm going to have to recheck it."

Donnie nodded, twirling the pen on his desk. "All righty then. Go home. Do it there."

"You don't need me?"

"Nope. Have a night."

Shanna frowned, looking at her watch, and realizing it was just after one o'clock, turned and left.

Brian Bradley, the Systems Manager for the Atlas, was sitting in the pilot's seat running over a series of checklists. He and his team were responsible for the care and maintenance of the shuttle Atlas. There was a Systems Management team for each of the shuttles. They would order new parts and run general tests on them according to the maintenance schedules. All the Systems Management teams reported to Paul Reznor, the Director of Maintenance.

Also being an astronaut, another of Brian's duties was deployment coordinator for the satellites. He and Donnie made all the satellite runs together. He had never been on an extra-orbital mission though, nor had he ever flown aboard the shuttle Atlas. Flipping through a manual, he looked at his watch when Jonathan Rodgers entered the flight deck breathing heavily.

"There you are," Jonathan said. "Hey man, I need some information about the trailer."

"Like what?" Brian set the thick systems manual on the control panel.

"How much of it's been sent up already?"

"Almost all of it has. All but the perishables and water supply. Why do you ask?"

"Well we're going to need to add a whole van worth of shit to it, looks like," Jonathan said, flipping a stack of papers marked "Confidential" on top of the technical manual. "I don't know what the hell happened, but it seems someone forgot half the test equipment."

Brian skimmed through the pages quickly, frowning at the white papers. "I'll be a son of a bitch. All this stuff got left?"

"Every bit of it. It's still sitting in the decon room wrapped in ice," Jonathan said. The decon room was the cold storage room used for decontamination of items before being sent into space. As they didn't want to bring extra-terrestrial viruses and organisms back to Earth, nor did they want to take any of Earth's garbage along with them on a mission to another planet. Everything was kept at a hundred degrees below freezing in decon.

The trailer in question would be docked with the shuttle before leaving for Mars. It was waiting at Alpha – the International Space Station, where it had been assembled and filled little by little over the last few months.

"Have you told Donnie about this yet?" Brian asked. His heart was beating fast already. An oversight this major could be expected to cost someone his job.

"No, no I haven't," Jonathan said, as if it were no big deal. "I really don't think it's a big deal yet. We're still eight months out; I think we can get something out there before then."

Brian was leaning his head on his hand, grabbing large wads of hair. Eyes wide with frustration, he sighed heavily. "How could that have been overlooked?"

"It might not have been. I just noticed the crates in there this morning. I'll talk to Donnie; find out if it was by design. Anyway, what I really came down here for," he said, waving his hands, "I wanted to make sure you got that actuator on order for the EVA arm."

Brian was still rubbing his head. "Oh, for Atlas?" he said. Atlas was the shuttle they would be taking to Mars. "No. No, I haven't had a chance yet. I'll get to it though," he said, standing up to stretch. "Let's go downstairs." They walked down the stepladder and across the hangar to Brian's office. The ceiling was over forty feet high, so one could not see it from the ground – assuming he could even see through the rack lights. Even as high as the ceiling loomed, the floor area of the hangar was much larger than the building was tall. Just looking at the length between the shuttle and Brian's office was intimidating. The shuttle was huge by ship standards, but when sitting in the hangar, the grand scheme seemed to make it shrink, like the NASA Space Shuttle riding piggyback on a 747.

As they approached Brian's office, the two men slowed their pace slightly and Brian noticed Jonathan was out of breath. "You okay?" he said.

"Yeah, I'll make it."

"What was the part number?" Brian said, sitting down behind the computer and logging onto the Lockheed Martin customer website.

"I don't remember it by heart. It's in your e-mail though. If you can get it here by Friday that would be great. I need to start my phase testing," Jonathan said.

"Yeah man, yeah, I'll get on it now."

"Thanks Bri. You be at the luncheon tomorrow?" Jonathan said, stopping on his way out the door.

"I don't know. Still don't know if Heather's working or not. If she's off, we'll be there."

"Cool then. Thanks again," Jonathan said, then turned and left.

Brian turned back to his terminal, opened his e-mail, retrieved the part number and plugged it into the search box on the LM site.

"Seventy-four hundred dollars," he said to himself. He smirked and nodded, then turned to close the door to his office.

The next day, with cameras and crews spread throughout the warehouse, Donnie locked himself in his office for most of the day, trying to avoid the chaotic buzz that clouded the complex. At half past noon, just as he sat down to eat his sack lunch, his phone rang. It was Rodgers. Donnie had been a little irritated at being bugged in the middle of his pastrami sandwich, but maintained his cool when Jonathan told him of the two crates in decon. Jonathan asked Donnie if he had known about them. Donnie hadn't answered, but instead hung up to go check it out himself.

He left the sandwich half-eaten on Saran wrap beside his keyboard, and grabbed a jacket from the hook on the wall. The walk to the decon room was almost perilous with cameras swinging on cranes and bright lights everywhere. Donnie ducked and dodged as many people as he could in an effort to make it to decon and back without being stopped. But almost every group of people he passed had at least one member who would like to stop him for just a moment. He tried to move quickly and efficiently, as if he were on a mission. And he was. But it didn't work. Pipe dream.

He was stopped three times just on the way there.

When he arrived, he pulled the cold steel handle and the door hissed open, spilling its cold breath onto the concrete floor outside the door, icing it over instantaneously. The room was dimly lit, but he had with him a Mag Lite. He didn't have to look long. There in the middle of the floor were two steel pallets, and on top, the two crates. They stood like two forgotten tombs, patiently biding the time with perfect still silence in the deep cold. Donnie walked over to them, his boots scuffing deadly on the frozen concrete, and looked at the manifest tag on each of them. *Sure enough. These damn things got left behind.* He sighed heavily – his breath visible in the frozen air – then turned and walked out of the freezer shaking his head and cursing to himself.

Ten minutes later and back in his squeaky leather chair, Donnie tapped his fingers on the desk, staring at nothing and biting his lip. Donnie leaned back and pushed the intercom button. He called Jonathan and

Brian Bradley to the carpet, along with the loadmaster, Robert Keith.

"I was going to ask you if it had been forgotten, or if it had been left deliberately for a later trip," Jonathan said.

"Can you tell me one logical reason why these two equipment crates would be saved for later? Why wouldn't I send them up with the rest of the equipment?" No one answered his question, so he continued. "We've run three drop-off trips, gentlemen. Three. That's three chances. Why would I want to make four, when there was plenty of room on at least two of the others?"

Again no one said anything. "Okay, well what we have to decide here is who's going to fund the mission to take them up."

"Pardon sir?" Robert said.

"Well I don't want to pay for this trip. You're the loadmaster are you not? These crates were your responsibility," Donnie said, pointing at Robert.

"Yes sir, but I can't…"

"Do you know how much this is going to cost? Do you know how much it costs just to send a shuttle up to dock the ISS?"

"A lot more than I have, sir."

"I know that. This will cost almost two million dollars. And all we're doing is dropping off two crates."

"I'm sorry sir. I really don't know what happened," Robert said, shaking his head.

"Nor do I. But if I'm going to have to pay for this, then I'll be damned if I'm going to let it happen again. I want a report on my desk by the end of the day, summarizing what happened and why those crates are going to cost me two million more dollars. You can drop it off on your way out," Donnie said.

Robert was about to speak, but Donnie put up his hand, shaking his head. The meeting was over, and they all knew it.

Robert and the others stood and exited the room without saying anything further.

Donnie stopped Jonathan before he got out the door.

"Jonathan. Send in the girl."

Shanna closed the door quietly and pulled out a chair in front of Donnie's desk. She laid her leather-bound portfolio in her lap and clicked her pen open. She tucked her hair behind her ears, crossed her legs, and cleared her throat. She was ready.

"Put out a call for a loadmaster. I want at least five years experience, prior military preferred. Duties require precision in measurement of mass and volume. College degree required if no military," Donnie spoke without looking up from his desk.

"Salary?"

"Not yet. Competitive pay, room for growth, booming company, all that bullshit. We need one fast," Donnie said.

"More?"

"Nope. Get the board together. We're going up."

| CHAPTER *three* |

The yard was crawling with cranes and machines loading the shuttle that would carry up the forgotten cargo. The shuttle being used for the three-day mission was the primary satellite shuttle, routinely used for small cargo trips to the ISS and satellite deployments. Even on a short mission, and only to take up two crates, the ship would have to be loaded with food and supplies, water and fuel, emergency kits and rescue pod. With all the supplies, fuel, and man-hours required to make the mission happen, it would cost two million dollars.

The takeoff window was set for one-fifteen p.m. They had eight hours left to load and prep the shuttle for launch. The word 'launch' was a little ambiguous. For one thing, the shuttles employed by the Oliver Company – like many other companies – didn't launch in the conventional sense of the word. These shuttles didn't stand on their engines and shoot up into the sky like Apollo 13, but rather, they took off like conventional aircraft. Depending on weather and traffic windows, the shuttle would then either pull into a slick bow, bringing the nose around to direct vertical, or it would maintain a direct angle and accelerate straight out of the atmosphere on a constant incline. Donnie had launched using both methods, but much preferred the 'straight shot', as he called it, because it was less taxing on the shuttles and the crew. The straight shot launches took less fuel than did the broad arcs, and were easier for most crewmembers to handle. Seen from the side, it would look like the numeral 6, the loop being the Earth and the stem being the flight path.

This is not to say the launches were unimpressive, though. The volume was incredible, making a B-1 or an F-15 takeoff with full afterburner sound like a child's toy rocket. The craft would tear down the five-mile runway, reaching speeds in excess of 800 kilometers per hour before it ever left the ground. Then the pilot would pull back on the yoke, and the bird would streak up into the heavens like a bottle rocket, cracking the sky with a magnificent roar. A ground observer without earplugs would likely remember the event as the last sound he ever heard.

Hence the desert.

On occasion, sonic booms would rock the earth below as the shuttles underwent slight speed changes during takeoff. In concert with the general ripping-the-sky-open, certain restrictions were placed on facility locations. Most private companies with space-ready vehicles were required to be located in the deserts of Nevada and Arizona.

Paul Reznor, the Systems Officer, and Mike Thurman, the Senior Engineer, were already running the preliminary checklists in the flight deck. The systems team that reported to Mike was conducting external tests on the avionics, hydraulics and power plant, by the light of large halogens powered by generators.

Donnie Oliver was leaning against the side of the seat in the flight deck, standing with his arms crossed as he watched them conduct their preflight checks. He had run them hundreds of times himself, but had finally decided to delegate the responsibility.

"All right. Everything looks good," Paul said.

He still hadn't given up control entirely though. He still liked to watch. To be there. Just in case something went wrong. Just in case. He'd many times been called a control freak, to which he typically didn't object.

After a few minutes of watching the tests, he felt a soft tap on his shoulder. He turned to see Shanna standing there holding two cardboard coffee cups. She looked solemnly into his eyes. He stood for a moment, arms crossed, looking between the cups and her face before he finally took one.

"You okay?" he mouthed. He would have to shout to be heard above the noise of the APUs.

She didn't answer.

He looked hard into her eyes again, then keyed the intercom to address the two men on the flight deck. "You're on your own, fellas. I'll be back in a bit." Donnie turned and nodded toward the stepladder. Following Shanna down into the cool dark morning, he looked around at the launch site.

The two crates had been brought out now. They sat on steel pallets, a skin of ice clinging to them like frozen cobwebs. Donnie shook his head in wonder at the load that would short his company such a grand amount of money.

Unconsciously, he had fallen into a stride alongside Shanna, sipping his coffee and blowing off the steam as they headed in the general direction of the machine shop. "You want to tell me why you're up here so early?" he said, thumbing the lid of the coffee cup. Their footsteps sounded dead and fell without echo, suspended in the darkness as they trod across the concrete. It was hard to believe this very concrete would reach temperatures in excess of 130 degrees in the heat of the day, some ten hours away.

"Couldn't sleep all night. Didn't figure you'd make coffee for yourself. You never do," Shanna said. They walked in silence, sipping hot coffee for a few minutes, slowly putting distance behind them.

Donnie looked up at the stars – bright specks of brilliance in the inky black expanse of sky above them. Without the pollution of city light for miles in every direction, every star in the sky was visible, and the light they produced was enough to read by. It looked to Donnie as though God had spilled white glitter on his carpet, covering every possible inch of the universe. He gazed into the distance, breathing deeply in the excitement that he would be going up again soon, and walking on another planet's surface. It gave him a chill every time.

He wouldn't be going up for the forgotten cargo trip today, which was a company precedent. He had been on every shuttle that had left the company grounds since they had started the whole program. In a way he was relieved to be ground-bound on this one. He would get a different perspective of it. He had discussed the possibility of sitting in on the mission control side of it with Julia Callahan at PSS. She had said there would be no problem with it, and he was excited by the prospect. The Oliver Company had in its best interest hired Privatized Spatial Services to head their mission control. PSS employed the most state-of-the-art technology, and the strongest minds. To date, every satellite the Oliver Company had put in orbit had been done so under their assignment. And they had all been flawless missions.

His other alternative was to head the mission control here at the complex. When a mission went up, copies of all the documentation and procedures went to PSS. The originals stayed at home base, where the ground crew would monitor the mission secondarily. PSS took full control of the mission from launch to land, and covered all bases including contingency planning and recovery. But the ground crew at Oliver Base would be monitoring as well, in the cases where there was a need for proprietary information to be transmitted. Delegation of this amount of control to PSS had been an option Donnie had originally been against. The cost of giving up this control seemed a preposterous notion to him. He felt the Oliver Company was better equipped to handle the missions, being more familiar with the equipment, the crew, and the general plan of the mission. In the long run, Samson had convinced Donnie it was the best thing, as PSS was undoubtedly more experienced in mission control, and besides, this way they could listen and learn, and be a backup.

The luxury of having another company handle their missions had become evident on the first mission for Donnie. The stress levels seemed to be more controlled, and in the long run, the advantages had overshadowed the cost. Donnie was impressed with the experience and professionalism PSS had shown during that first mission, and was happy to have them as part of the Oliver team. Even within all this confidence in their newfound partners, Donnie was still content with the kill switch they had had written into the contract of services. If for any reason during a mission the Oliver Company deemed it necessary to reassert their power, it was done by spoken word, and the delegation part of the contract was null and void immediately. They had never had to use it, nor did he think they would ever have to. But it was there. Just in case.

"So why couldn't you sleep?" Donnie finally said as they came to a stop by the chain-link fence that skirted the machine shop. His coffee cup was half empty and growing cold quickly. The desert was extreme in both directions; at night someone could freeze outside, but in daylight be burned badly, at least without sun block. He tossed the cup in the steel garbage can just inside the fence as the passed through the gate.

"I don't want to bother you with it, Donnie."

"Why did you come get me then, Shanna?"

"I brought you coffee, Donnie," she said with a sour exaggeration of a smile.

"I thought we were on a level. You told me when stuff was upsetting you, and I looked at you funny." They had always had a personal attachment that underlay their relationship without interfering.

She sighed. "I've been thinking a lot lately. You know, Brett and I have been talking a lot lately about moving in together," she said, then tossed her own cup in the garbage.

"No, I didn't know that," Donnie said and crossed his arms. He had never heard her mention it, and felt a slight shock as he heard the words. Was that a tinge of jealousy he felt? He liked Brett alright. Donnie had met him several times before, and Shanna spoke of him sometimes, but not much. Brett seemed like a good enough guy; he had his head on right, was going to school, he dressed nice, and didn't treat her like shit. Donnie had never felt jealousy over her before. It never even crossed his mind. She was a subordinate. A friend at most. Sure, he had grown close to her over the years, but not to the point he let her become an object of desire. But here, he felt he had just been stung. Perhaps it was the reality of her relationship with Brett, finally presenting itself before him, as though she had laid it on a cool red tablecloth for him to inspect.

"Well it's not that big a deal I guess. We've talked a little about it. I know my parents wouldn't approve, but…" she trailed off. Donnie thought he saw fear in her eyes.

"But what," he said.

"Well," she shrugged slightly and put her hands in her jacket pockets. "I guess I just wanted to hear what you had to say about it," she said, staring him dead in the eyes. He knew why. He knew she liked to see people's first reactions. He had worked hard at not being shocked by her words specifically to avoid painting his emotions on the wall for her.

Donnie frowned. "Why? What the hell do I know about relationships?"

Shanna smiled pleasantly at him.

"Look. You've been with him for what, a year?" Donnie said and waited for her to nod. "Well that's quite a commitment. It's a big step for any relationship. Suddenly all your shit's his shit too. And all his shit is yours. And if something happens, it's harder to get out."

She nodded silently, still looking him in the eyes. He paused and gazed at her in the darkness. He respected that about her. If she wasn't paying attention to someone talking, they would never have a clue.

"I don't think I'm against it. It's the best way to know if you'll be able to live with him after you marry him, you know?" Donnie said, and Shanna busted out in laughter.

"No, God, I'm not going to marry him!"

Donnie frowned. "Then why the hell are you thinking about moving in with him?"

"He's my boyfriend, Donnie. That doesn't mean I want to marry him!" She said it as if she were now the teacher – the wise one in this situation.

"Well then you're asking the wrong man. I've never carried on a relationship past the point I realized there was no chance of my marrying her," he said, looking at the ground.

"What?" Shanna said, the laugh still evident in her voice. "You wanted to marry everyone you ever dated?"

Donnie stared at her for a moment. A speaker crackled to life somewhere behind them, announcing a phone call for Ms. Henkley on line two. He didn't think he had even heard of a Ms. Henkley. He frowned at that for a moment, then responded to Shanna's hanging question.

"That's not what I said. But the whole reason behind a relationship is to get to know someone. To see if you're compatible for marriage. At least that's the way I was raised. Not that I've had a whole bunch of relationships – I've always been too interested in studies – but the ones I've been in always followed the template my upbringing burned in me.

"If it's made readily obvious that there's no chance I'd ever want to marry the woman I've been seeing, then there's really no point in continuing the relationship. Unless it's just for sex," Donnie said, and looked back up at Shanna in time to see the smile fall from her face. She finally realized he was serious.

"You're serious," she said simply. He nodded. "Relationships are just tryouts for marriage to you."

Donnie shrugged. "Sure."

Slowly, a nod began to creep into Shanna's posture. Donnie didn't know whether it was one of conviction, acceptance, or agreement. Somehow, he guessed it wasn't the latter.

"Well, right now I think I'm too young to be thinking about marriage, Donnie. That's all I'm saying. I'm having fun right now. I'm twenty-one years old. I shouldn't be allowed by law," she said, raising her hands and looking to the sky as she spoke, "to think about marriage at this age." Her eyes came to rest level again, looking at Donnie, a smile of amusement beset on her face.

"Amen to that," Donnie said, and pulled a pack of cigarettes out of his jacket. He pointed the pack at Shanna, who rarely took one. But she did this time. He lit them with his silver Zippo. "Well all I guess I can say is be careful. Make him sign the lease," he offered.

"Why is that?" Shanna pulled on her cigarette.

"So you can leave on a moment's notice. You never know when you might need that out. Just like a good poker player is always counting his outs."

"Poker, Donnie?" she said, frowning.

He shook his head quickly. "Never mind. Just know your outs."

Shanna nodded slowly, studying Donnie's eyes. "Yeah. I guess you're right."

"Damn right. Always make the man sign for stuff, and you'll always have an easy exit. I know this isn't breaking news, Shanna, but you're probably a lot smarter than most guys you're going to run into. So it never hurts to play your smart cards where it counts."

Shanna shook her head, squinting at his words. "I've never heard you talk like this, Donnie! You take stuff like this that seriously?"

Donnie didn't answer, but his expression answered for him.

"Well I see your point. I can still have fun while being safe."

Donnie made a tight smile, trying not to flinch at her harsh words. She had shaved the rough right off them but they still sounded heavy to his mind. He was beginning to recognize his fear as jealousy. It was looking more and more like that was the case. With this realization, he breathed in heavily. The buzz of his cell phone against his hip saved him from having to say anything else.

With the preflights done, the inspection crew sat on steel boxes outside the shuttle watching the sun come up, drinking coffee from aluminum cups like hunters in a concrete wilderness. Mike Thurman tilted his cup up and let the last few drops fall into his open mouth. He looked out over the horizon and lit a cigarette. He held it awkwardly in front of his mouth without smoking it.

"Gonna be a hot one today, boys," Mike said, his voice rough.

"How do you know that?" Brian Bradley said.

"No clouds, friend," Mike said, staring evenly at Brian. Mike had never taken to Brian. Brian had always seemed to be hiding something. Holding something out from the rest of them. At the company barbecues outside the machine shop, they would all drink their beers and have their laughs, grill their steaks. But Brian always seemed detached, as if he were there to spy. Mike had been friendly to him in an effort to at least learn more about him, but all to no avail. Brian was a loner.

As the months turned to years, the separation only grew, and Mike did nothing to hide his dislike for the man. He had tried before. If Brian didn't come around, screw him. Ball's in his court. And Mike wasn't the odd man out. It was as if everyone in the Atlas crew felt the same way, they just weren't outwardly expressive of their dislike for him. They hid it. Mike had never been one to hide his emotions though. *If you hide it, it eats at you. You let it out, it eats at them. Ain't my problem he's an asshole. Let it eat at him.* So Mike let it be almost painfully obvious where he stood. Mike was one of the friendliest men in the company, and almost everyone liked and respected him well. For someone to be on his bad side was a statement of that person's character that was worth looking into.

The technicians who ran avionics and power plant inspections, Tony Valentino and Rick Sanderson, sat staring between the two men, curiousness on their faces. Jason Shepherd and Dennis Masters – the equipment crew – sat on either side of Brian, and the fuel troops – Chris Chitham, Blake Prescott and Tom Noonan – were scattered about the group. Paul Reznor stood leaning against the engine cowling, sipping his coffee. No one tried to ignore the confrontation and mind his own business. It was not uncommon for Mike Thurman to open up and let go on Bradley when he needed it. Mike could work with him just fine, and was dedicated to the mission, but sometimes Bradley needed an ass chewing to set him straight. Mike was the best man for the job.

"Know how to keep a Sun Devil from drowning?" Rick finally said, breaking the silence.

A few of the men chuckled silently. None of them necessarily wanting to be the one to make a joke about Mike's alma mater, but neither wanting to miss out on the punchline.

"You have no couth whatsoever, do you?" Jason said, trying not to laugh.

Blake Prescott buried his face in a hand and shook his head.

"What? He don't give a shit," Rick said, waving his hand toward Mike.

Mike was only showing the slightest hint of a smile, and staring hard at Rick. Blake seemed to be the only one who knew there was more than one type of smile. He knew that sometimes Mike would stare at someone with that smile when that someone was about to get chewed out. Or canned.

Rick grunted, deciding better than to say anything. "Never mind."

"Ah, what a wus," someone said.

"Finish the joke, pussy!" said another.

"Yeah, I want to hear this one," said Mike.

"Ah. Well," Chris said, clearing his throat. He then decided it was time to light a cigarette. "I forgot that um… the punchline." The group broke up with laughter. Chris stood up and walked over to the coffee thermos, patting Mike on the shoulder on the way by. Mike rolled his eyes and shook his head.

After a moment of pensive smoking and coffee intake, a quiet had fallen back over the group. "How's the bird look outside?" Mike asked to no one in particular, but looking at Tony.

"A and P looks fine. This bird's gonna fly," Tony said, leaning back on his elbow on the concrete, fiddling with a piece of safety wire. His jeans were almost completely black with grease and soot from crawling around in the dirtiest parts of the shuttle. His tan work boots were smeared with it as well. He lay back on his side with his legs crossed.

"You know something?" Blake said, leaning forward and resting his elbows on his knees. He was seated on a steel crate. He ran a fuel-stinking hand through his greasy hair. "They could go up with the shuttle on Feb Nine," he said, pointing at the two crates deicing a few yards away.

"What're you talking about?" Mike said, looking in the direction of Blake's point. He finally put the cigarette to his lips and pulled from it. There was no smoking allowed anywhere on the pad, by federal mandate. But they all knew their ships and the limitations of them. They knew the rules, they knew the regulations, but they also knew the playground and how it really worked. It was like the father telling his boy if you drop a cigarette in a puddle of gas it will explode. Until the boy actually tried it, he wouldn't know how full of shit his father had really been.

Blake still stared at the crates, pointing. "Them sumbitches would fit on the Atlas, final load."

Mike stared long at Blake, not saying anything. Then his gaze finally made its way over to the two crates again. He looked back at Blake again and nodded slightly. "Don't you think Donnie would have thought of that? Before agreeing to send a whole mission up for it?" He pulled from his cigarette and rubbed his stubble-covered face. No matter the time of day or the day of the week, he always had stubble. Some thought it was in an effort to make up for what little hair he had left up top. Mike had scars along his jaw line from an old motorcycle injury, and liked to keep them covered with stubble.

"Well probably. I know he's smart enough, but maybe – shit I don't know. But they ain't taking shit up on that ship when they go. All the equipment's already at ISS," Blake said knowingly.

"You know Mike is going up on that crew, right Blake?" Brian said. Mike looked at him through a smiling frown. Brian tried too hard. That was his problem, Mike thought.

"Uh, half the people out here will be on that crew, won't they?" Blake said, looking around the group of men. "Well y'all got room on it don't you?"

Mike nodded and smoked. "Well we know we have the room. We always have that extra space, 'cause we need it for return weight. But in this case I think we have double enough, come to think of it. But I think Donnie wanted the equipment all together, all waiting, all ready for us. Give it time to adjust and settle before we pick it up, you know?" He paused and looked back at the crates again. "I'll run it by him though. See what the old man says about it."

The sun was full on the rise now, a dark red sphere of hazy shimmering heat just above the eastern horizon. The thin layer of frost on the two crates was beginning to drip on the east-facing side, and the ground just around them was dark with wetness. The crates stood looming behind the line of generators and air movers, defying the morning light with their own cold darkness. These crates were not wooden like conventional crates, but steel like safes. Their smooth surfaces were unflawed and unmarked except for a single black arrow on each side pointing toward the heavens for which they were eventually bound.

Mike stood up and crushed his cigarette out, then dropped it in the canvas FOD bag he wore on his belt. Everyone with pad admittance was required to be on constant lookout for Foreign Object Debris, which could cause severe damage to the turbines of the engines if it were sucked up. Even the tiniest piece of safety wire could shell an engine and render hundreds of thousands of dollars in damage.

"Well, is she ready for fuel?" Mike said, turning to look at Blake and his crew again.

Blake nodded, then stood up and headed for the steel fuel doors set in the concrete under each wing of the shuttle.

Donnie stretched his legs and stared out the window of the private jet watching the approaching runway. He was alone on the airplane, save for his pilot. They were flying into Ellington Field, the regional airport in Houston, Texas, where there would be a Town Car awaiting Donnie's arrival. It was almost noon, and looked like it was going to be a beautiful day. At least in Texas it would be. *Poor assholes are gonna bake back home.* Sparse clouds spotted the sky, like wisps of pulled cotton painted purple by the sun. The ground below stretched out like a miniature-scale train set; tiny brown roads with tiny red and blue cars moved by a thousand feet below; tiny cows spotted tiny pastures with tiny trees in them.

He put his cigarette out in the ashtray and moved to the forward compartment to watch the landing through the front window. It was a three-hour flight from the Oliver Company Launch Facility in Dennehotso, Arizona to PSS headquarters in Houston, Texas. He had never met his Mission Manager in person. Julia had been assigned to his account after he and his brother had already toured the facilities and bought the services, some four and a half years previous. He had talked to her on the phone hundreds of times, and had been in constant contact with her during all of his missions, but had never met her face-to-face. He was excited by the prospect, as he had many times found himself wondering what she looked like.

Her voice was like fine-grain sandpaper, and slightly deeper than most women's voices he had heard. Donnie knew she wouldn't look anything like he had imagined. But it wouldn't be for the better. She would be a short, fat woman with thick-rimmed glasses and a double chin. She was sweet as sugar, and her voice was more than just sexy to him, but he knew voices like that only came from women who were as desirable as traffic accidents.

He had told himself many times that it really didn't matter what she looked like – of course it didn't. She was an absolute professional, and was a master at what she did. But now, he was almost disappointed to be finally meeting her – spoiling the mystery. To Donnie, it seemed better to think there was a chance she might not look like he imagined than to meet her and remove all doubt. He shook his head as he looked out the front windows of the private jet, aware of his childish obsession with this charade.

Touchdown was uneventful – it always was in the leer jet – and they had made good time. Donnie wondered if his ride would already be there waiting for him, or if he would be the one who ended up waiting. They taxied to the private hub and parked out in the open of the near empty lot. Just on the edge of his vision, he could see headlights. He wouldn't be waiting long.

As he stepped out of the jet, he was immediately aware of the humidity. It felt like a sauna. It must have rained in the last couple of days, he thought. He jogged down the stairs and walked across the parking lot to the terminal POV lot, where privately owned vehicles were allowed to park. Headlights were still required anywhere on airport property. He saw the black Town Car pull into the parking lot and the back door opened. Donnie braced himself for disappointment as a woman stepped out of the car, so he was almost knocked over by the shock of her appearance when Julia Callahan came bounding across the tarmac to greet him.

She took his breath away.

Donnie was so stunned he was afraid she would see it in his eyes. She would be blind not to. His eyes were wide as rivers.

"Hi Donnie!" she said, quickly walking over to shake his hand. He could only stare in wonder.

"You're Julia?" he said stupidly.

"Yep! That's me!" she said, and shook his limp hand. His normally overpowering handshake had forgotten to show up.

"Are you okay, Mr. Oliver?" she said, tilting her head slightly.

He finally shook his head and blinked. "You were right the first time. Call me Donnie. Yes, I'm fine. I apologize, I've acted like a schoolboy."

"That's okay," she said, laughing easily. He could see the blush in her cheeks though, and regretted having embarrassed her.

"Is it always this humid here?" Donnie said, trying subtly to change the subject.

She made a face and shook her head. "It's the only thing I hate about Houston."

For a moment, they stood smiling at each other, then she finally said, "How was your flight?"

"Oh it was fine. It feels good to age a little slower for a while."

She nodded slyly as they got into the cool car. "Yeah, but you'll pay for it on your way back. So, are you ready to head to the control center?"

"Yeah," he nodded. "Yeah. Let's go see the control center."

The PSS headquarters building was excitingly hi-tech. The walls of the foyer were lined with large stereographs of local and distant space, with brilliant reflections of the Milky Way and Andromeda galaxies, as well as others Donnie didn't readily recognize. The stereographs were mounted on aluminum backboards that stood out several inches from the wall, mounted to it by steel posts an inch thick. They were all interactive, as well. Along the sides, there were insets of particular regions of the galaxies spotlighting important events and stars, with buttons that would play video clips in the center frame when pressed. Donnie thought this would be a magnificent learning experience for students, were they to get the opportunity to tour this facility.

The elevators were dim-lit, almost dark, with high ceilings that looked like star fields. They were backlit panels that shone light through tiny dots bore into the flat steel ceiling, giving the impression you were standing atop a mountain at midnight, billions of stars peeking down at you. It was staggering. Donnie had seen it on his original tour, but had forgotten how fantastic a scene it really was. The whole facility was full of surprises and wonders like these, around every corner. It looked as though the facility had been built with the tourist in mind, like a museum. He wondered how anyone got any work done with so much to look at.

The mission control room was different; it was secluded and concentrated. Not at the expense of technology, though. There were fifteen stations, all with large flat-panel monitors and desktop readout panels. Each station was self-supported and -controlled, and was already manned with a technician.

They were way ahead of the game, preparing for the one-fifteen. Along the wall that all the stations faced were three six-foot projector screens, with data already flowing across them like water running sideways.

One thing Donnie found particularly interesting was the fact that the room lighting wasn't in the ceiling. It took him a moment to realize the lights were recessed into the floor, flush and flat like stickers on the white composite tiles. The lights were softly illuminated, very pleasing to the eye, and produced no glare on anything.

Julia had told him there were five other mission rooms identical to this one. The one they were in now was the one in which all the Oliver Missions had been controlled. The Olivers had only gotten to look into the mission control rooms through ionized windows, and even then very briefly.

"Okay, here's our environmental data on this screen," Julia said, pointing to the first projector screen with an open hand. "Weather conditions, satellite positions, and air traffic."

Donnie stood staring with his arms crossed, nodding his head as he took it all in.

"The next one is shuttle data. Everything from temperature to air pressure, interior and exterior, crew status, and gauge readouts. If you're low on fuel, we'll see it here," Julia said, smiling at him. Donnie smiled back.

"What's the third screen?" he said, nodding toward the final projector screen.

"Oh, that's a duplicate of the first," she said, looking back at the screens. Donnie felt foolish for not having noticed.

"Excellent. I-" he stopped, suddenly looking down at his trouser pocket where his cell phone was vibrating. "Excuse me please," he said.

"Sure!" Julia turned and made her way over to one of the command stations to talk to one of the technicians as Donnie took the call.

"Oliver," he said.

"Donnie, it's Mike. Prescott brought something to my attention earlier that I hadn't considered."

"Yeah, what's that?" Donnie said, staring blankly at the moving data on the first projector screen over his head.

"You know we built the load for Feb Nine planning to have Phoenix's dead people on board." He was referring to the elusive prospect of having shipped two crates full of urn shells, but Donnie had refused to even meet with Pablo Phoenix about it.

"We did? Why the hell would we do that? Who told you to account for that?"

"I don't know, Donnie. Keith said those were his orders. I don't usually double check his work."

Donnie sighed. "You know what the hell we're talking about here, Mike? Those shells are eight ounces apiece. If you carried a hundred of them it would only be fifty pounds. I doubt there would have been two crates worth of them on board. That shit's expensive as all hell."

"Well I had never read the specs on 'em. I just figured we were talking about canisters the size of conventional urns. I guess I'm to blame for this one, boss. Damn, man. I am so sorry," Mike said.

Donnie shook his head, closing his eyes. "Nope. Thanks for calling me about it Mike."

"You got it. I thought it was worth mentioning. Didn't mean to second guess you."

"That's why I hired you Mike. To second guess me. I ain't right all the time. I'm glad you called. One-fifteen's off man."

"What? You're canceling today's mission?"

"Yeah! Why the hell do we want to go up if we can take those crates on the Feb Nine? Call it off, Mike. You just saved me two mil," Donnie said and flipped his phone shut. He looked around the mission control room, suddenly short the weight of the world, and extremely relieved, but at the same time greatly unnerved.

"Ms. Callahan?" he said. She turned to look at him, eyebrows raised. "Mission's off. We're not going up today."

It seemed someone had dropped a silence bomb on the room. Everyone sat staring at Donnie, as his words hung in the air. At first, Julia had smiled, and then it had slowly faded. Then she had smiled again, thinking he was joking. Then her mouth dropped and her eyes widened. She took Donnie by the arm and led him out of the room, into a private conference room across the hall, and never taking her eyes off his. She had a look of mischievous curiosity in her eyes.

As the door clicked closed behind her, she led him to sit on the expensive cherry wood table with the high sheen top. He stood there leaning against it, arms crossed, and a million and one things rushing through his mind. He was excited. He was disappointed. But most of all, he thought he was embarrassed. This really didn't make him look like he had his stuff together. Still, it seemed better to avoid a trip and not spend the money than to go up and take those hundred thousand risks – all for no reason.

"Are you okay, Donnie?" Julia asked, still wide-eyed in wonder.

He bit his bottom lip and nodded, not wanting to look her in the eye. "Yeah. Yeah, I'm fine."

"What's going on?"

"Some shit got- sorry. Some stuff got left off the manifest. We thought we needed to get it up there today. Turns out the manifest for the Feb Nine was-"

"The Feb Nine? That's the big event, right? The Mars trip?"

"Yeah. That manifest was built with an extra couple of crates in mind. Well those extra couple of crates never materialized. They had been counting on a contract with some other company. But I never did it. So we're gonna have plenty of room on the Feb Nine for the forgotten crates that were going up today," Donnie explained.

"I see. Well!" Julia breathed in deeply, then looked at the floor as Donnie looked up at her. "I guess that's good then! Save the trip!"

Donnie nodded thoughtfully. "Look, I'm real sorry for the trouble. I thought…"

"Don't be. Don't worry about it. I wouldn't want to send up a useless mission either," she said in agreement. After a short pause, she said, "Donnie, do you mind if I ask you a question?"

"Not at all."

"What were they counting on sending up? You don't have to tell me," she said carefully.

"No, no, it's not that at all. It's not a big secret. Have you heard of ETIS? That company in California?"

"Yeah. Sure," Julia said, nodding thoughtfully. Her brow was furrowed in concentration as she listened to Donnie.

"Well Phoenix – the C.E.O. out there – wanted to meet with me and discuss the possibility of sending up some of his urn shells. Well I'm supposing that's what he wanted to meet about. But I never took the meeting."

"Ahh… So they made room on the ship thinking you'd agree to it," Julia said.

"Yep. I don't know how they even knew I was supposed to meet with him. Unless…" he trailed off as a thought struck him. He had heard about Phoenix wanting to meet with him from Shanna. Supposedly, Shanna had heard directly from Samson. Had Sam told someone else about it? Mary – his assistant maybe? Had she gone and blabbed? He knew damn well Shanna wouldn't have. There would be nothing in it for her. Somehow, though, the loadmaster had found out about it. Robert Keith. That son of a bitch Donnie had just fired. And he had made room on the Feb Nine for it. What the hell was he thinking? Was he intending to sneak behind Donnie's back and make a private deal with Phoenix? Was he intending to sneak urn shells onto the shuttle and keep the profit? It would be easy enough, Donnie realized. Donnie never checked the manifest. That was the loadmaster's job.

Worst of all, had Keith already done all this? Because now he was long gone. And if he had made a dark room deal with Phoenix, then he had probably already taken payment for it. *I'll be a son of a bitch.* Donnie felt his stomach sink. If Keith had already made a deal, he would now be forced to take the box of shells up. He couldn't just leave them. He couldn't just tell Phoenix *Sorry! I know you thought you were buying Mars tickets, but you paid the wrong man!* He would have to take the boxes, or be short the money. And that was money he had never seen.

Donnie breathed in heavily as another thought crossed his racing mind. If Robert Keith made a deal with Phoenix, he had deliberately left the two crates in decon. He arbitrarily picked two crates he didn't think would be needed and served his own interests by replacing them with urn shell boxes. Those two crates held test equipment that would be needed on the mission. Keith had made a command decision and had left those two crates freezing in decon, thinking no one would notice them – namely, not Donnie. *No way. No one would be that stupid.*

"Are you okay, Donnie?" Julia said, putting her hand on his shoulder.

He snapped back into the present. "Yeah. Sorry. Just wondering what the hell happened."

Julia stared levelly at him with an unwavering gaze. Donnie raised one eyebrow. "Guess you think I'm a nut job, huh?"

"No. Not at all. I do think you need to get back there and find out what's really going on. You look pretty troubled. And an extemporaneous mission is nothing I'd take lightly either," Julia said, and dropped her hand, letting it slide down his arm before it fell to her side. Donnie's spine tingled.

"Yeah. You're right. Thanks for your understanding, Ms. Callahan. I'm sorry again for the mix-up," he said.

"No trouble at all. Call me Julia."

The flight back seemed to take weeks. Donnie sat in the back staring out the window, biting his thumbnail. He contemplated every possible scenario he could think of, but found no comfort settling on any of them. The more he thought of, the more he added to the sandstorm in his head. Not only did he have a thousand different scenarios running around in his head, but now they seemed to be interacting; sharing data, trading information with one another. He saw images of shadows shaking hands and signing silhouette contracts, people whispering as he left their rooms, stuffing dark papers into dark envelopes, draining his company bank account. And his worst fear – the scenario he tried hard to push away, to pull the curtain on – was that Shanna was somehow involved.

He had come to trust her with everything he had over the last two years. She knew his bank account number. She had a copy of his debit card, and his PIN. He had many times sent her out to get money for him, and had never asked for a receipt, or checked his statement. He didn't need to. He paid her well enough that she would not have had to steal from him – or the company – or so he thought. But now he was beginning to wonder.

Donnie reached over and opened the miniature fridge set in the sidewall of the cabin, and pulled out a small bottle of whiskey. Maybe that would wash the shit away – the billion or so thoughts that seemed to be banging their way through his mind with cymbals and bass drums. He sipped and closed his eyes.

The stereo blared, but was barely audible above the roar of machinery and engines in the warehouse. Forklifts squealed around lifting small pallets while the main crane clambered on above. Mike Thurman was leaning against the crane control booth as Thad Cloys put the essentials back on the shelves. "You know what bugs me the most about it though?" Mike said.

"What's that, boss?"

"That little Keith shit is gone. If he was still here we would at least have someone to question. No one else seems to want to talk."

"I know what ya mean. Seems like the birds all scatter when sump' happens, don't it boss?" Cloys said, raising his thin eyebrows. His bald black head was a foot above Mike's when he stood up. In his control chair, they were almost equal.

Mike nodded. "Yup-yup. Well you know the heads are gonna roll when Donnie gets back. Speaking of which, he oughta be back within the hour."

The crane grinded and whined as it lifted another life support crate from its steel pallet. The chains that ran the gears of the crane were the definition of power and strength – like bicycle chains, for God's bike. The hydraulic pistons were big around as small trees and the gigantic yellow crane arm had the strength to lift a building from its foundation. Heavy machinery. Mike loved working around it. It made him feel powerful controlling and working with machines that could crush him without expending a cent of energy. Handshaking with technology that in the wrong hands could commit ruthless unstoppable murder on the man with the controls.

"Guess they are, boss. I don't wanna be around when that happens."

"You're safe, Thad. I think you're the least of his worries," Mike said, slapping Thad on the shoulder. "Well I'm gonna run out to the pad and pick him up."

On the drive back to the warehouse, Donnie didn't say much to Mike. At least not at first. He felt like he needed to be a little guarded with his suspicions. Donnie told him about Julia, the PSS building, and all the generic trivialities, in an effort to sound relaxed. But he had a feeling he wasn't coming off that way. Mike was good at people. He had probably already read Donnie, who was no master at hiding it anyway.

"So you like this girl, huh?" Mike said. Donnie was relieved to be let off so easily. Mike was humoring him.

"Yeah. She's a tart. Know how she's got that kind of- I don't know – husky voice?"

"Yeah. It's a little edgy. I like it myself," Mike said.

"Yeah. Well I figured she'd be a fat husky woman."

"Not the case, huh?" Mike said, looking over at Donnie with a subtle grin.

"Not even close. She's short. About five-five I guess, but she ain't fat. Well not in the waist she ain't. I think you'd be hard pressed to put your arms around her chest though."

Mike laughed aloud. "Oh not I, chief. You wouldn't have to press me hard. So she's top heavy, eh?"

"Oh yeah. She looks good though. They ain't like them oversized balloons. They're just nice and big," Donnie said, making claws facing his chest to indicate size.

"I'll be damned. How's she look in the face though?"

"Oh man, she's got it covered. She's a knockout. She's gorgeous. Literally. She has one of those faces like Monica Potter, boy. Pure and perfect like a doll."

"Wow. That's pretty serious. So she's got the looks and the tits to go with it... There's got to be something wrong with her then," Mike said, holding his hand up.

"Well if there is I ain't found it yet. I walked behind her all the way through the front foyer, and she's got it in the rear too. Perfect body, perfect face, perfect voice... What else is there?"

Mike laughed again. "Well that's all I would need. As long as she can cook."

Donnie joined his laughter, shaking his head. After they had finally gone quiet, he broke through the ice he had been hiding behind. "Well Mike, what the hell we gonna do about this?"

Mike shot him a piercing glance. He knew Donnie wasn't talking about Julia any longer.

"Don't know, chief. I was hoping I could come up with some answers for you. Unfortunately, I have none. And the prime suspect, well you fired him three weeks ago."

Donnie stared quietly out the side window, biting his lip. Then he lit a cigarette and reached over and rolled down the window. He held the pack out to Mike, and shook a cigarette through the opening. Mike took one and lit it.

"I'm at a serious loss here," Donnie finally said after a long pause. "I suspect everyone now. I've had these visions of everyone being in on it."

"Know what you mean, man. You gotta be that way, I guess."

"Well until we get all this sorted out, there ain't nothing going up. But I don't want anyone to suspect anything out of the ordinary. I want the company to run like normal. So don't say anything about any of this to the crew," Donnie said, unnecessarily pointing his cigarette at Mike as he spoke. Donnie snorted then dragged from his cigarette.

"What do you want me to say about the cancellation today? You know they're going to be asking me about it. The whys and whens," Mike said. His elbow was resting on the window frame, his cigarette hovering inches from his mouth.

"Whatever you think is best, Mike. I trust you. You're one of the few people I trust now," Donnie said, looking straight at him. "Get this right, Mike. I don't even trust Shanna right now."

That piercing glance from Mike again. Mike's eyes widened with horror, then disbelief.

Donnie had known Mike Thurman since middle school. They had played football together all through high school, then gone on to college at Arizona State. Mike had gotten married a couple of years before he graduated, and Donnie had been the best man. Donnie had dropped out shortly afterward to pursue military avenues. He had grown bored of school, and was too fascinated with women to maintain any type of scholastic regimen. It had always scared Donnie to see Mike settling down like that. It meant somehow their playing days were over.

Well they had only been over for Mike. So Donnie was left to play the field on his own. It used to be a contest to see who could get the most girls; to see who could pocket the most phone numbers in one night. Mike had even been so vain as to write them all on one piece of paper. He would meet someone, then after all the thrills and woes, he would ask for her number. He would pull out an index card and write the new number and name directly beneath the five or six others he had already gotten that night. In plain view of the girl he was asking. *Cause you know why? Cause fuck 'em, that's why.* That's what Mike would always say.

He always got more numbers than Donnie. He was better looking. Girls always told him he looked like Will Patton; dark eyes and a rugged face. Donnie got his share too, but he didn't look like any movie star. They weren't always the Select or the Prime, but he got his share. Mike had put it to an end when he married Lucy, though.

Nights out with the guys were almost never graced with Mike's presence after he got married, and Donnie and he had seen each other less and less. Then Donnie opened his own company and solved that problem quickly. "You'll come work for me, Mike. Be my lead technician. My senior engineer," Donnie had said. Now they spent ten hours a day together. So what if it turned out Donnie couldn't trust Shanna? She was young anyway. Women will always have something behind the curtain. They'll always have a hidden agenda. Donnie would always have Mike Thurman.

✳   ✳   ✳

Shanna was sitting on Donnie's desk when he came into the office. He had pushed past the camera crews and ducked under moving cranes and fixtures, and was surprised to find her when he pushed his door closed behind him.

"Hey stud. How was your flight?" Shanna said.

Donnie wasn't in the mood for the slang, but let it slide. *It's the way she is. It's in her nature.* "Long. Boring. Seven hours' worth of flight, two hours' worth of wasted time, I'm ready to crash. Should have taken a book with me," Donnie said, dropping his jacket on the hook and moving around behind his desk.

"Well, before you do that, we need to talk, Donnie," Shanna said. He looked up at her sharply. Her eyes said nothing.

"Okay. Wanna walk?" Donnie said. That was their normal method.

Donnie walked with his hands in his pockets, staring at the ground as Shanna took the long way getting to the point. She was good at padding the words that would hurt someone, but Donnie was getting to the point he didn't much care for it anymore. He liked things short, simple and concise. Shanna knew this. But when it was bad medicine, she always sugar-coated it.

He had a pretty good idea he knew what she would be telling him. *Listen, I screwed up and went behind your back and you remember that meeting you never made with Pablo Phoenix, well I kind of, you know?* It would be coming any minute. She would lay it on him like a load of lead. He prepared himself for those words of treason, steeling himself for the admission of betrayal.

"Are you excited about the Feb Nine, Donnie? I mean, I know you are, but are you really psyched?"

"Of course, Shanna. It's big."

"Big? It's going to be the most important event in the history of space exploration! You know it. Discovery Channel knows it. That's why they're sending up millions of dollars' worth of equipment," she said, talking more with her hands than her mouth.

"Yup. So what are we out here talking about it for?"

"Well it's just such a big event, I mean, not only for the company, but for the wor-"

Donnie stopped in his tracks and held his hands up to stop the conversation. "Shanna. Shanna, Shanna, Shanna."

"Yes?" she said, finally coming to a stop and turning to face him.

"You know why the decaying particle never jumped off the needle?"

Shanna frowned hard, pulling her head back. Then she laughed out loud. "What? What the heck are you talking about?"

"It's a question," Donnie said.

"Why did the decaying particle never jump off the needle?"

"Because he never got to the point."

She laughed again, then breathed deeply. "Okay. I'm sorry. I'm just not anxious about disappointing you."

Donnie took her by the shoulders. "Well I'm not anxious about growing old, but I will before you finish telling me what the hell you are talking about if you don't get to the damn point!"

"Okay, okay, okay. I'm going into space with you." There it was. Plain and clear as day, out in the open. And it was the absolute polar opposite of what he had been expecting her to say.

Donnie stood back and looked at her seriously. "Shanna, we already talked about this. I'm sorry, but…"

"Discovery Channel's sending me to run the camera equipment," she said, shaking her hands.

Donnie stood there for a long moment, not saying anything. Then suddenly, "Cool! Why would I be disappointed? This is a dream come true for you. Not what I thought you'd be talking to me about, but that's great, Shanna!"

"You're not upset?" He shook his head. "Holy cow, I thought you'd be mad as hell!"

"Why in God's name would I be mad about something as important to you as that?"

"Well, I…" she trailed off. "I guess I just…" She ran her fingers back through her hair, smiling at the ground.

"Shanna, if they have assigned you the task of manning the – sorry – of *personing* the equipment, then I'm as happy as you are! I can't take you for my own reasons. I can't just bring you because you want to come along. But if you have been given a duty… An assignment as important as this, then by all means, you have achieved!"

"Oh my God! I'm so happy!" she screamed and threw her arms around his neck. "I was so stressed out that you'd be upset with me! I thought you would think I went behind your back or something."

Donnie had his hands raised behind her back, not touching her. He was on unfamiliar territory within her arms. "No, I know you wouldn't do that. There is one thing I'll need you to do though."

She pulled away and stepped back to face him. "Sure, Donnie. Anything."

"You need to make it known that I had nothing to do with the decision. Not the recommendation, the suggestion, or the final call. You need to make it known that you applied of your own accord and they chose you. I don't want people thinking…" He didn't finish. He didn't need to.

"Oh I will, Donnie. I promise I'll let it be known. There is one thing though," she said holding up a slender finger. "One thing I think you should know."

Donnie widened his eyes, putting his hands on his hips.

"I didn't really apply. They kind of just asked me if I would be interested in doing it. I said yes, but I would have to check with you to make sure it was approved and everything."

"Nope. I won't have anything to do with the decision. If you can get on without my help or my command decision, then so be it. But I won't make the final call," Donnie said.

"Well you ultimately have the final call on anything having to do with who goes on your ship, Donnie."

Donnie sighed. "Did they ask anyone else? Was it a lottery?" he said, then continued, "Or were you just the lucky girl?"

"I guess I was the lucky one," she said, returning her gaze to the hard dirt.

"Then I guess you don't really need my approval for it. They chose you. I won't shoot it down, but I don't need to approve anything. Just act like you never said it."

"Said what?"

"That you'd have to check with me."

"Okay. Okay, I can do that," Shanna said, nodding frantically.

"Good. So is there anything else you need to tell me?" He hoped she would say no. She had always been pretty straightforward with him when she had something to disclose. She had never lied to him. Not yet.

"No, not that I can think of. Well I'm glad we didn't have to go up today. That would have been a big waste of money," she said smartly.

"You got that right."

"Find a new star yet?" Julia said. She hung her raincoat on the hook by the door and walked up behind Mark, who was pounding away furiously on the terminal keyboard.

He turned to look at her over his shoulder and smiled. His hair was disheveled and his eyes were bloodshot. He looked as though he had been sitting there for a really long time. It was six in the morning. Julia had been up for less than an hour. And he had been at it all night.

When Mark found a project he liked, he would dedicate himself to it completely. Even when the project was devised by irrational thought, or a whimsy passing joke. Some of his ridiculous notions and trains-of-thought had gotten the best of Julia's sense of humor. But his dedication to bringing whatever it was to conclusion could only stir her admiration for him. He had one time sat down and come up with a statistical foundation for the odds of a plane crashing into his house. He lived ten minutes from an airport, and thus airplanes were always flying directly over his house at one- or two-thousand feet. He had constructed a control set based on the current technology, assuming it remained, and then stretched the project to infinity. Assuming the control set, was it *A: plausible; B: probable or C: inevitable* that a plane would eventually crash into his house?

Julia had laughed so hard she nearly wet herself. When she finally regained control of herself, she had realized he was serious.

He said, "With infinite time, there would be an infinite number of planes flying over my house. At five-minute intervals, would you not think it would someday be inevitable that one would crash into my house?"

"No, because the odds reset every time one flies over. The odds don't increase with each plane that passes, like trying to pull an ace from the deck. There, your chances increase with every discard," Julia had said, still taken by a need to laugh. "But here, every plane has the exact same chance of hitting your house as the last one did. Which is what? A billion to one? Something incoherent like that?"

Mark had then spent some five hours plotting out all the variables and configurations, trying to find a scientific backup for his theory. To this day, Julia was still waiting for said backup. "Your 'inevitable' logic is based on statistics. Well there are no statistics for eternal flights over your house," she said. He had looked at her with a new excitement in his eyes, as if she had challenged him. So he went on his eternal endeavor to find an answer.

Perhaps, she thought fleetingly, he's found that answer now, and he's pulled me out of bed to prove it to me. It wouldn't be unlike Mark to do such a thing. And quickly she came to the decision that if he had woken her for something so trivial, she would pour scalding coffee on him. Or flatten his tires.

"No, no stars. But check this out. Remember that object we found between Mars and here?" He picked up a mug and glanced in it briefly before sipping from it with a sour face. He hadn't even bothered to reheat it.

"Sure. You finally get something out there to look at it?"

"Hang on. This is what we have from Hubble 9." Mark turned and grabbed a sheet from his messy desk, and held it out to Julia. She took it and frowned over it for a moment. It was a black and white photograph of stars. But in the right corner someone had taken a photo pen to it and circled something. It was there plain as day, a blot of stars missing from the photo.

"Wow, that's exciting stuff, Mark."

"Shut up. Don't you see what's happening?"

"Forgive me."

"Look." He turned and brought up another window with coordinates on it and highlighted a particular line on the screen. "Look any different?"

"Different than what, Mark?"

"Than the last time we saw it!" he said, shaking his hands for emphasis.

"Forgive me."

"Well they're different. The chords are different," he said.

"Mark, I don't remember what they were the first time. Will you cut the mysterious suspense novel shit and tell me what's going on?" Julia said. She squeezed his shoulder for effect.

"Okay. Well I just wanted you to see the math first. But now, here we go. Check this out. You ready?" Julia nodded. Yes, she was ready. For whatever the hell it was. "It's moved. Significantly. It's out of Hubble 9's range now. That's why the photo is so boring."

"Okay," she said, nodding slowly. The suspense was killing her. By way of boring her to death, it was killing her.

"It's gotten farther away, Julia! So far in fact," he held up a finger and turned to face the terminal again, "Aha! That in fact, it's moved right into," he clicked on another window and brought up an image of the stars from a different angle, "It's moved right into view of Star Seeker!"

Julia leaned forward and squinted hard at the screen. There in the corner was a tiny object, too small and of such poor resolution that it couldn't be identified.

"No need to squint. We're talking Star Seeker here, babe," Mark said. Julia looked at him with one raised eyebrow. "I can zoom all the way in. And that's precisely what I did."

"Okay." Julia yawned, then rubbed her sleepy eyes.

Mark stood up and took her by the shoulders. "I hope you're ready for this. 'Cause this is some serious shit. You've never seen anything even remotely close to anything like this."

"Show me," Julia said. Somehow she couldn't find enthusiasm. All she could think of was the fact that it was six in the morning and he had called her and told her to "get her ass up here right away". She would check out whatever the hell he thought was so mind-boggling, then go home and get back between her warm sheets and cuddle up with Krueger. Krueger was her eighty-five pound hound.

"All right. Have a seat," he said, rubbing his hands together. He stood behind her and leaned on the chair back. "Brace yourself. This shit is gonna freak your ass out."

"Mark, please."

"Sorry. But I'm excited as hell about this."

As if she couldn't tell. She could read him like a book. In the four years she had known Mark, he had always excited easily. And Julia thought he would surely bust if he didn't show somebody real quickly what the hell he had found out there. So she thought she had better go ahead and look. "Okay, I'm ready, Mark."

"Push F-10," he said.

Julia pushed the F-10 key and the image instantly filled the screen. She yelped and covered her mouth. In this quick movement, her hand knocked over the coffee mug, spilling cold grainy coffee over everything in sight. She stood up, pointing at the screen and staring at the image that had haunted her with instantaneous efficiency. In the back of her consciousness, Julia Callahan was only vaguely aware of Mark's raucous laughter booming in from behind her. Her thinking mind had left the building.

| **CHAPTER** *five* |

Drops of sweat spotted the court as the sun beat mercilessly down on the six men playing ball. Relentlessly, they played on, the jam box blaring Beastie Boys on the sideline. Rap was the only thing worth listening to during the three-on-three matches. Likewise, some thought the only time worth listening to rap was when they were playing ball. Mike, Blake, Donnie, Thad, Tony and Jonathan were on the court beating the hell out of each other, and scoring madly. Full contact basketball. It was the best stress relief and exercise these men ever got.

"You remember that blond – used to work in finance? What was her name?" Jonathan said, standing under his own net. He checked the ball in, then passed to Tony, and took off down the court.

"You talking about Shelly Naff?" Donnie said.

"Yeah, that's her!" Jonathan said, taking a pass back. He traveled a few steps, but no one noticed – or they didn't care. Shoot for three. Miss. "You know I saw her the other day." He ran back the other way. Blake now had the ball.

"Where the hell at?" Mike said. He was the oldest one on the court, save for Donnie, and had a little trouble keeping up with the younger men. He took a pass and immediately passed to Donnie, who shot from the zone and scored.

Jonathan took the ball again. "I was at the deli over there on Walnut. She came struttin' in showin' her shit." He checked the ball. Passed to Thad. Running down the court, he panted, "You know how she wore them tight whites?"

"Oh yeah," Mike said. Thad shot for three and sunk it, nothing but net.

"Good God, how could we forget?" Donnie said, wiping sweat off his brow. "I need a break." Mike dropped the ball under the net as the whole group went for water on the sideline. Thad swooped it up and swished it, then dribbled it off the court.

"Ain't she married now?" Tony said.

"Shit, I don't know. I wasn't really paying attention to her ring finger either." A collective laugh. "She looked good though, boy."

"You know I don't think that woman owns a bra," Thad said, then squirted water on his head and in his mouth.

"Hey that's fine by me," said Tony. Several grunted in agreement.

"So what'd you do? You talk to her?" Blake asked.

"Didn't get a chance. It all happened so fast, you know. Before I realized what was going on, she was leaving. I was mesmerized."

"She has that effect. She wears those tight t-shirts nine sizes too small and just-" Tony said, but was hushed quickly by the others' warnings.

"Woman," Jonathan said furtively.

"Lady alert," Thad said in his deep voice.

Donnie looked up. Shanna was coming up the sidewalk.

"It's your girl, Donnie," someone said.

"Uh oh. Here comes your boss, boss," someone else said. Donnie couldn't tell who said what over the laughter. Nor did he care. It was routine. It seemed like every time he was relaxing with the guys, taking a breather from the stress of the grind, here she came. And they always had something creative to say about it. *Who's in charge here? Hey, is that your daughter, Donnie? The King has entered the room, coming to collect the queen.* It never ended.

Shanna came through the gateway smiling, bright white teeth and dark black shades. She was dressed in a peach tube top and khaki shorts, rope sandals and a straw hat. She looked like she belonged at a beach.

"What the hell is she doing here? It's Saturday, for shit's sake," Donnie said under his breath. Everyone's gaze was fixed on Shanna.

"I dunno boss, but she ain't dressed for work," Thad said. He looked at Donnie, his huge smile stretched full across his face, the basketball pressed between his big black hands. Donnie had to grin.

"Can't you sons of bitches think about anything but tits?" Donnie said, shaking his head.

"No," everyone said in unison.

"How'd you know we were thinking about tits, unless you're thinking about them yourself?" Blake said.

Shanna was close enough to hear now. Donnie supposed she knew they were talking about her, if not for the way they all stared, then simply because there wasn't much talking going on anymore.

"My God," Mike said, turning to face away from Shanna as she got closer. He was rubbing his forehead and shaking his head. Then Donnie noticed why he had said it. It hadn't occurred to him that there was no real practical way to wear a bra with a tube top – save for a strapless one, but it was obvious that wasn't the case. And it was very obvious. She had worked for Donnie just over two years, and he had never once seen her dress in anything but business casual. At the Oliver Company, business casual covered everything from shorts to jeans, sweats to skirts – but not tube tops. And he had never known just what she was hiding. Any mystery she had carried with her was now removed.

"What's up, guys?" she said casually, tilting her head. She made a visor with her hand.

Seeing no one was going to answer, Donnie spoke up. "Takin' a little break. What's up with you?"

"Just thought I'd stop by and watch you guys for a while. You told me I should come check out your game sometime," she said.

Mike laughed out loud and had to cover it up with a cough. Everyone else either turned away or snickered quietly. But they were all thinking the same thing.

Dammit! Donnie thought. He knew he was blushing by now.

"What's so funny?" Shanna said.

"You wanna play, Shanna?" Tony said.

"Well I'm not that good, but I guess I could. If you guys'll take it easy on me."

At least this time they all held their snickers under their breath. But they all smiled. *She has no idea what she's doing.* "Tony's kidding, Shan," Donnie said, looking at Tony. "We're uhh… We're actually through playing for now."

"Oh. I thought you said you were taking a little break."

This time the laughter was loud, and had full participation. All but Donnie, who was shaking his head now. He could feel the red in his cheeks. How the hell did she plan on playing basketball with five other sweaty men, in nothing but a tube top? And rope sandals, no less. "Well I was just…"

"That's okay. I probably shouldn't play in my sandals anyway. Thanks for the invite though, Tony. I'll take you up on it next weekend, for sure."

Mike sighed audibly.

"Can I talk to you for a minute, Donnie?" Shanna said.

"Sure. Be right back, fellas." He stood and stretched, and threw his towel at Tony who spit and swiped at his face as the sweaty towel fell to the bench.

Donnie and Shanna walked off the court through the gateway and started around the side of the fence.

"What's up?" Donnie said.

"What's going on in there?" she said, pointing back at the guys inside the fence.

"You really have to ask?"

Shanna pulled her head back, frowning. "What do you mean?"

"Shanna." Donnie stopped on the concrete path, and turned to face her. Shanna stopped and looked at him curiously. *She really doesn't know.* "Look at yourself. You come down here wearing that in front of a bunch of dirty old men…" he said, waving his hand in the general direction of her breasts, then toward the court.

Shanna looked down at her chest. "What? You can't see anything!"

"Uh huh. Shanna, trust me. You can." Donnie looked her in the eyes, waiting for her to speak. She only stared at him. "Shanna, they bounce when you *walk*. You don't think they would – I don't know – bounce when you played ball?"

"Sorry, Donnie. I didn't mean to embarrass you like that."

"No, you didn't embarrass me," he lied. "Don't sweat it. I'm just trying to save you from embarrassing yourself." He looked at her for a moment, then started walking again. "So what did you come out here for? Really."

"Really, I just thought I would watch for a while. I'm meeting Delilah Danley at two. So I have a little while." She stared at Donnie a moment longer, and then continued. "Listen, I know you've been stressed out the last couple of days. And I don't want to ruin your basketball game. But there's something I have to tell you. I didn't think it could wait."

Donnie frowned at her. "Okay. Lay it on me," he said. Was this the confession he had been waiting for? Was she finally ready to talk? He had made up his mind she had nothing to do with the missing crates, but was easily shifted by such things as 'I need to talk' or 'I have something to tell you'. Until he knew the facts, he could be talked into believing it was anyone.

"I went looking for you yesterday before I left. I remember I told you I needed to leave early, but I wanted to find you and make sure everything was okay." She stared him dead in the eye.

Donnie nodded thoughtfully. He couldn't read her.

"Well I peeked into Paul's office, thinking you might be there."

"Paul Reznor? Why would I be in his office?" Donnie said, crossing his arms.

"That's not the point, Donnie. I looked in like four-hundred offices. But those aren't pertinent to the topic."

"So I wasn't in any of those either?" Donnie said, a smirk crossing his mouth.

Shanna shook her head, sighing. "Well, while I was in there, his phone rang. And my natural instinct made me pick it up."

"You answered Paul's phone?"

"Yeah, it was-"

"Don't tell me who it was, Shanna." Donnie raised and waved his hands. "His calls are none of my business."

"No, I was going to say it wasn't who called that mattered. But the gentleman asked me to take a message for Paul, so I said sure. I started looking for a pen, but couldn't find one."

Donnie lowered his gaze on her. He thought he could see where she was taking this. Paul had been the Director of Maintenance for the Oliver Company for the last ten years. Was she about to pin the blame on him?

"Well I opened his desk drawer and found a pen." She reached into her purse, and said, "But I also found this." It was a business card. Donnie's heart stopped. "I took the message, and just kind of stared into the drawer. It was staring out at me plain as day. I couldn't help but notice it."

Donnie took the business card from her and turned it over in his fingers. His mouth was suddenly dry. He wanted to speak, to say something, but he couldn't think of anything to say. Perhaps there were no words for him to say. He wondered if he would even be able to speak them if there were.

"I'm sorry, Donnie. And maybe it's nothing. But I just thought you should see it," Shanna said.

He still didn't speak. A lump rose in his throat. Before handing the card back to her and walking off silently, he looked at it one more time.

Extra Terrestrial Interment Services
Pablo Phoenix, C.E.O.
301.555.5922

She had ruined his basketball game.

| **CHAPTER** *six* |

unrest

The moonlight shone through the window like a mischievous child, ignoring the rules of the curtains. It was a full desert moon, big and bright like a spotlight, and looked as if it were producing its own light. And that light beamed right into Donnie's room. He wasn't sleeping. Sleeping was a pipe dream at this point. Sleeping was a luxury. Sleeping was a place he doubted he would visit any time in the near future. He lay staring at the ceiling, his sheets and comforter a twisted mess to his right. His arms were crossed behind his head, and his eyes felt heavy as lead, but they wouldn't close. Those gears hadn't been oiled in a long time. He had worn them out with the viscosity of conspiracy theories and unnecessary worry.

If Paul Reznor had betrayed him then he would have to find a new man to head the maintenance teams. It was a big job with a lot of responsibility, but he did it well. There were nine teams – one for each shuttle – and they all were perpetually in motion.

Donnie had originally offered that position to Mike but Mike hadn't even wanted it. Donnie had therefore made Mike his senior engineer, which was a generic but political term for "Donnie's Right-Hand Man". This put Mike in charge of a lot more of the company than he would have been had he accepted the Director of Maintenance position.

Paul was also slotted to be the systems officer on the Feb Nine mission – the most important mission the company had ever conceived. A betrayal of trust would be the end of the road for all that, though. Something as simple as sneaking business through the back door could mean death and burial for the company. Donnie had to remind himself to blink. His eyes were drying out staring at the moonlit ceiling. It was hard to believe that as well as he paid Paul there would be a need to betray the company for money.

Now Shanna, on the other hand… Donnie was close with her. He knew she looked up to him like a big brother, while at the same time being his common sense advisor. She was there to help him with personal decisions as much as she was to answer his phone, to file his papers. Donnie had no short of common sense. His problem was that he didn't slow down enough to stop and realize that the answer to everything was staring up at him – and had been the whole time. Donnie was the type to spend an hour looking for his keys, turning every cushion, moving every paper, only to find he had been holding them. That's why he hired Shanna.

Her interview had been strictly to feel her out. To find out how sharp she was. Donnie believed someone could be sharp without necessarily being smart. While Shanna was no dummy, she was still young and thus cursed with the naivety of a young girl. But she was sharp, and Donnie loved her wit. She could pick out the bad guy in the first fifteen minutes of a movie. She would have the plot figured out before the climax – twists and all. And she would guess the end before the first man died. She certainly had the cleverness to orchestrate a darkroom deal. Had she written it all out, blueprinting every character and every interaction, she certainly could have pulled it off. That was how she worked. Shanna was a math whiz. If it dealt with numbers, or was based on the principle foundation of them, she could definitely be the culprit. And this was all about numbers. The number of zeros before the decimal in someone's bank account.

Donnie feared with her youth, she might be blowing through her fat checks with no regard for future, no thought of saving for retirement. While her checks were moderately ink-heavy, he had no doubt she could blow through one in a single weekend with the help of her young friends. They all thought alike, he knew. He had seen it. A young girl suddenly introduced to wealth had no regard for the value of a dollar. All she knew was she had many of those dollars, and knew it would buy her and all her grab-ass youngster friends a good time at the mall – which she frequented like a necessity. Shanna's friends had become enamored of her when she got the job. Donnie had noticed it from a bench seat on the sideline. Yet she hadn't appeared to notice at all. The sudden change of attitude, the sudden acceptance of her ascendancy. She was suddenly the boss. The Golden Rule, Donnie thought. The one with the gold rules.

Some of those mall trips Shanna had taken her friends on in an effort to purchase happiness had probably worn her pocketbook a little thin, and she needed the cash. Donnie could easily see that happening. She saw the opportunity to make the deal – knowing Donnie would never call Phoenix himself, knowing Donnie would never check the manifest himself – and she hopped on it like a moving sidewalk: both feet at once. Now all Donnie had to do was find the evidence. It would have been easy enough to palm that business card and say it was in Paul's desk. Donnie knew that. He just also knew the ramifications of believing it. Believing Shanna was to disbelieve Paul. Neither seemed appealing. He wasn't particularly close with Paul on a personal level, but having had him around for so long, felt like he could trust him.

And then there was the thought that none of it meant anything. Maybe the business card had come in the mail – or someone had outside contact with Phoenix. Either was as plausible as the other. After all, Phoenix was a salesman.

But that Shanna had thought it treasonous made Donnie a little suspicious of her. Why would an ETIS business card lying in someone's drawer mean anything to her? She had known Donnie didn't want to meet with Phoenix, but she hadn't known why there ended up being room on the Feb Nine. She hadn't known someone had made room for ETIS crates on it. As far as Donnie knew, when he canceled the forgotten crates mission, he and Mike were the only two people who knew about the Atlas manifest calling for the two crates. He and Mike and, of course, Robert Keith. It had been held under wraps strictly for Donnie's investigative satisfaction. There were too many reasons for Donnie to disbelieve Shanna, and to trust Paul.

The ceiling fan swatted lazily at the cool air in the bedroom, like an old man swatting at flies in his lawn. The shadows of the fan blades against the ceiling blinked intermittently as the moon pounded its heavy reflected light through the window. And Donnie's eyes stared idly, connecting the pieces to a million puzzles in his mind. His head was a swim, five senses fighting for control of the thought process, trying to make something out of almost nothing. There was the background noise of the ceiling fan motor, a cyclic whirr that comforted him, and the glass-muted crickets singing their songs of the night, and beyond that, Donnie heard nothing. It was perhaps in this silence, this listening for some voice to step out of the shadows and tell him everything would work itself out, that he finally slipped through the realm of awareness and dropped like a brick on the pallet of sleep, which had so efficiently evaded him for the last six hours.

"Okay, what we're dealing with here is obviously just some miscommunication. I seriously doubt anyone is going behind your back, Donnie." Samson had been pacing and staring at the floor for the last fifteen minutes, and was now leaning back against his magnificent desk. He scratched his chin as he thought and his eyes darted around the room for something to grab.

Donnie leaned his head back in the chair and ran his fingers through his hair. This was not going the way he had planned it. He had hoped he could get his brother to side with him. Out of all the miscreants employed by his company, he had hoped there would be a sure-fire connection. A partner. Truth be told, he had no qualms with any of his employees until this shit started keeping him up at night. "This is just too quirky, Sam. I don't believe it's all a coincidence." Donnie was shaking his hands emphatically as he spoke. "Who the hell else would have called for room on that ship? If you didn't, who did? Why was there space for ETIS's garbage on our manifest?"

Samson traded his pacing fidgety impatience for Donnie's calm and sighed deeply. "I don't know what to say, Donnie," he finally said after a lengthy pause. "I mean, come on! I can't even picture Paul doing something like that. We pay him almost a million dollars a year, don't we? And Shanna? She's not business savvy! She wouldn't have any clue how to get those crates on the shuttle! In fact, if she's guilty, it automatically means more than one person is in on it."

Donnie looked up at Samson through the tops of his eyes. Samson was right. He leaned back and crossed his arms. Both men were silent, and Donnie stared at the three-thousand-dollar rug that held up the desk.

"Smoke?" Samson said, holding out his pack to Donnie. Donnie took one without saying anything, and lit it. Samson then lit his and dropped the pack on the desk.

"Yeah I guess you're right. It would have to be someone who has access to the ships, so that pretty much rules out Shanna. No one else associates with her anyway. Not that closely."

Samson stood staring at Donnie, smoke drifting coolly away from his face. His hands were crossed behind his back as the cigarette dangled from his lips. "Look," Samson said, taking the smoke from his mouth and pointing it at Donnie. "I trust your judgment – you know I do. But you're acting out of character here. I think what you should do is take a few days off. Let things sort themselves out."

Donnie sighed again, then turned his head and pulled hard on his smoke. He stared at the glowing cherry and squinted his eyes hard. "What the hell would I do with a few days off?" Donnie finally said.

"Well you have the MOM out in California next week. Leave a few days early," Samson said, waving his hand in the general direction of California. The Meeting of the Minds was an annual event that lasted almost thirty hours, spread over four days. There, the greatest minds in the nation gathered to discuss the latest advancements in physics and molecular science.

Now there was a thought. He would only be attending the first day of the conference, as he had to speak about the upcoming trip. But to take a few days off in California with Callie Simmons... They could lie on the beach and drink margaritas all day. And he could head back Monday after his speech. Donnie noticed his head was beginning to nod slowly.

"That's a good idea. Is Callie leaving early too?" Donnie finally asked, then smoked.

"She usually does," Samson said. He turned and knocked the ash off his cigarette. "She usually takes a couple weeks vacation around the meeting."

Callie had no real set schedule. As long as she was at the board meetings, she could come and go as she pleased – as could most of the Oliver execs. She carried a satellite phone so she could always be reached for technical questions, and that was about all they really needed her for in most cases. Donnie was nodding again.

It was one week away. Donnie could go home now and pack and they could catch the first flight out tomorrow and start enjoying their time off. Samson looked down at his cigarette, rolling it in his fingers.

"I think it would be good for you. You haven't taken any time off in years, and you never get to see Callie anymore. Go. Have a blast. Get some sun."

"Yeah and burn my ass off," Donnie scoffed. He breathed in deeply and crushed his cigarette out in the ashtray beside his chair. "I think I will go, Sam."

Samson stared at him. "Good. You need the time off. I'm sure things will clear up here before you get back. But for God's sake, don't sweat this thing. And don't waste your time thinking about it when you're out there in LA," Samson said, pointing at him. "We have a full staff of professionals paid to do nothing but worry about shit like that while you're gone."

Donnie smiled and stood. "All right, you sold me. How we getting there?"

"I assume Callie's flying commercial. You'll have to check with her. If not, take the Bingo," Samson said. Bingo is what he called the private jet sitting out behind the facility.

"Nah. I'm not gonna tie it up for a week," Donnie said and opened the door. "Thanks, Sam."

Samson nodded thoughtfully at him, but didn't say anything. Donnie pulled the door closed and snapped his phone open. Within the moment, Callie was picking up the other end. "When you going to Cali?" he said.

"Leaving Friday! You gonna come?"

"Yeah, but we're leaving tomorrow. Can you do it?"

"Yup. Have your driver pick me up," she said.

Donnie slapped his phone shut, then called Shanna. "Get me two tickets to LAX tomorrow. Early as possible," he said quickly, then hung up.

Donnie sat on the aisle flipping through a Discover magazine while Callie stared out the window. She had been drinking the complimentary cocktails ever since the plane took off, and seemed a little tipsy now. She slapped her hand down on Donnie's leg and leaned her head back, staring at him. "We're gonna get tan on the beach, you know that?"

"You're going to get tan on the beach. I will be under an umbrella. I'll burn like a match," Donnie said, looking away from his magazine.

"Well we can buy some sun block. You have to be out in the sun when you go to California. It's like a souvenir!" Callie stated, returning her head to its upright position. It wobbled slightly, and Donnie could see space in her eyes. She wasn't tipsy. She was drunk.

"You know the effects of alcohol at altitude?" Donnie said.

Callie frowned for a moment then grinned wildly at him, and slapped his leg again. "Yup. I love getting drunk six and a half miles above the Earth."

Donnie stared blankly at her, shaking his head.

"I know, I'm crazy," she said, and turned to look out the window again.

"No, that doesn't make you crazy. You know why I think you're crazy?"

"Why is that, Donnie?"

"For ever leaving Royal," Donnie said.

Callie swallowed. After a lengthy pause, she spoke. "Bohr made me a better offer. I was getting sick of the secretive bureaucracy there," she said, looking away once again.

"You always seem so nervous talking about it." Callie didn't answer. "They really put the fear of God in you, didn't they?"

"That was the general idea, yes."

"You miss it at all?"

"Nope," Callie said, and turned up the little plastic cup, washing ice into her mouth and crunching. "I'll tell you what I do miss," she said with a mouth full of slush, "I miss my friend Walter."

"What ever happened to him?" Donnie said.

"He got transferred to Fiji," Callie said with a sigh. "It's like they find out you like someone, and they move you as far away from them as possible."

"Shit, I didn't even know RRC had an office in Fiji," Donnie said.

"Don't think they do," Callie said, screwing up her mouth and shaking her head.

Royal Research had always seemed to Donnie to be hiding something, and not just something small. Something grand and magnificent. They were the dark company that loomed in the shadows, never dispelling their secrets. The company where all its employees left by the back door late at night. And moreover, no one really knew what the company did. Not even the employees. There were many speculations, but none ever really panned out. Most research companies dealt with research; marketing, statistics, surveys and the like. Royal Research, as far as any commoner could tell, had nothing at all to do with research. About the best description anyone could come up with was that Royal was a technology company – broad as that description might be.

Now Donnie had sitting next to him a former Royal employee, and she was still bound by her non-disclosure agreements. Callie still respected and feared Royal, and wasn't about to disclose anything that might bring about the wrath of the dark company, revealing the side of it she had only heard about in whispers in dark bars – far away from the Royal break rooms. That side was the side that dealt with those caught disclosing proprietary knowledge about the company. It was rumored that people disappeared when they knew too much about the company. Just like the horror stories about the government and Area 51 and all the other nonsense conspiracy theorists babbled about. It did seem, however, that if Royal Research Corporation was involved in erasing any talkers, they did it with some authority, because there were never any 'scandals' or investigations looking into the inner workings of the company.

Donnie didn't expect Callie to tell him any of Royal's secrets. In fact, the less she divulged, the more admirable she appeared in light of her working for him now. Her character was revealed in her being true to her own word. He did, however, wish she felt a little better about sharing some of her experiences within the Royal walls. Donnie wanted to hear about what her workdays were like, what the inside of the building looked like, the company meetings – all the interesting details about working there. But every time he brought it up, she shied away, got nervous and uneasy. Callie had obviously not had the best experience with Royal, and preferred not to talk about it at all.

The rest of the flight, Callie seemed ill at ease, and Donnie regretted ever having brought up the company in the first place. He finally leaned his seat back and drifted off to sleep. The flight was about three hours with a stopover in Phoenix. America West didn't have a non-stop flight from Flagstaff to Los Angeles. Coupled with the hour-long flight from Oliver to

Flagstaff, Donnie was already sick of flying and wanted to get to the beach.

They had made reservations at the Regent Beverly Wilshire, having lucked into an opening in a suite only moments after a cancellation. They would be sharing a room, but the bed was big enough for a family of five, so neither had complained. With Callie's sleeping habits, Donnie wasn't sure he would get any of the covers, but was sure he would be too drunk when his head hit, he would never know the difference. Not that he had actually slept with her… but he had seen her asleep before.

When the plane touched down, they were both sleeping, and Callie's head had somehow found its way onto Donnie's shoulder. His eyes popped open as the wheels hit and he turned to look out the window. Palm trees screamed by and he felt the immediate relief of vacation becoming reality, knowing within the hour he would be kicking his feet up bare in the sun as he lounged by the pool.

The pool was too bright to look at directly. Electric light danced sickeningly across the surface in a never-ending array of confusion and chaos. Donnie squinted hard through his dark glasses as he listened to one side of a conversation taking place next to him. Callie had been on the phone since they checked into the hotel. Donnie had always thought of a vacation as a time and place to 'get away from it all', whereas it seemed Callie came here to get in touch.

Donnie lit a cigarette and leaned his head back against the chair. Callie's bikini top lay noncommittally across her chest and Donnie wondered why she wore it at all. *What is the point of leaving it on if you're not going to latch it?* He looked at the soft rise of her tanned belly and the small silver hoop she wore through her navel. He admired the breeze of almost invisible blonde hairs that lined her stomach from her waist to her chest and found himself wanting her again. There had been one other time he had found himself in want of her. He had thrown a party a few weeks before her graduation. Mike had helped Donnie throw the party. The next morning, after everyone had either gone home or passed out on the carpet, the three of them finally dropped into the bed together, having spent every last ounce of energy drinking all night. Mike passed out instantly.

Lying there congratulating each other on a job well done, Donnie had seen in Callie something he had never before noticed. A strange sensation had risen up in him as he looked at her, and he had blinked and swallowed, resolving to look away – to forget about it. He knew Callie wouldn't have him anyway. He had known her several years by that time, and they had become too close of friends. Having never actually considered sleeping with her any more than just a passing thought, Donnie was unsure from where the sudden urge came that told him to roll over and sink his mouth into hers. And as he lay there staring at her open mouth, he breathed in slowly, assuming it must be his inebriation – nothing more. It did seem as though she would have let him kiss her though, and perhaps go further. For she had been staring at him as well. Donnie had never been the kind to take chances, at least not when the outcome was less than certain, so he thanked her for all the help and rolled over to sleep.

Now he lay here smoking and staring at her exposed flesh and found himself in the same predicament. There was nothing unappealing about Callie Simmons. He just respected the fact that she had other ideals about men. Ideals and desires and a whole set of schedules he was unfamiliar with – unfamiliar except that he knew he wasn't on them. What could he do? Now he would be sharing a hotel room with her for the next few nights, and drinking by the pool as she lay with her unconnected top across her breasts. What should he do? She obviously trusted him enough to do that much. They were friends more than business partners, and in Donnie's mind, close enough to have recreational sex, and never feel the taxing sting on their relationship. But he knew she didn't see it that way. As far as Donnie knew, Callie was still a virgin. He couldn't recall her ever having a boyfriend, at least not since he had met her some ten years ago. Callie was a loner by choice. She had dated a few guys, but never let it progress, and – Donnie guessed – always broke it off before sex abounded. And Donnie was a loner by design. He still saw his women. He had a few of them he kept in touch with, but scarcely had time to try and make a commitment work these days.

Rather than having a live-in girlfriend and an extra set of clothes to wash, an extra mouth to feed, and all the other liabilities that come with seeing someone, he celebrated his male desires in short sessions. Once or twice a month, he would invite someone over for drinks and a movie. What woman wouldn't abide? His three-million-dollar home was far too appealing to their greedy money-spending minds. And the women – no matter how far detached – all had the same emotional wiring. He knew it as well as they tried to hide it. They all associated sex in some small way with love and commitment, thus the ardor with which they would visit him was capitalized. By some far off disconnected reasoning, they thought if they loved him enough, he would come around, and – more to the point – share his wealth with them.

They couldn't change Donnie though. No woman could. He loved his work too much. He loved his freedom, and his entertainment system. The twenty-thousand-dollar theater he spent his evenings in had no room for chick-flicks. He took what he wanted from the ladies, and said goodbye at the end of the weekend. Until one of them showed him reason to be different – how a commitment could improve his standard of living somehow – he would never change. He had sex without the overhead.

Callie, he knew, was just the opposite. While she hadn't committed to anyone in the last forever, he knew it wasn't because she was getting what she needed without it. She just didn't have time. He knew she would someday find Mr. Right and settle down with her bunny slippers and a new last name. She wasn't the type to sleep with men just to quell her powerful womanly desires. She had more self-respect than that, and morality to boot. She would find him someday. And whoever that man was, Donnie knew he would have a good woman. Callie was special.

Donnie dropped his cigarette in the ashtray, and hell froze over: Callie hung up the phone.

"I was beginning to think you had come here just to use the phone," Donnie said, and sipped from his beer.

"What do you mean? I brought it with me..." She was frowning at him from behind her dark shades.

"I know, I just… Never mind," he said. *What's the use?*

Callie sat forward and, with the deft fingers of a professional, had the bikini top connected behind her back before it had a chance to fall and reveal anything. Donnie nodded at her expertise. He had been hoping she would let her friendship with him be a pass to excuse her from modesty. They had been friends long enough for her to traipse around topless.

"Let's get in the pool," she said. Callie dropped her hand on Donnie's knee as she spoke.

"It is a little hot, ain't it?" he said. "I'm gonna have to go in before too long, lest I burn like a lobster."

"Donnie. You are in California. You have to enjoy the sun while you're here," Callie said, looking over the tops of her shades at him.

"Same sun we get in A-Z, Cal," he replied.

"Yeah, but here in California, there's this thing called humidity…" Callie made a sarcastic face and stood up, pulling the back of her bikini bottom away from her butt and straightening them. Donnie watched intriguingly. She snapped them in place and dove into the pool with her shades on. Donnie removed his white t-shirt and jumped in after her, with a little less grace. Waves splashed up and soaked the deck where they had been sitting. Callie looked up to make sure her phone was on the chair.

"So what's on our agenda for the weekend?" Donnie said, wetting his hair.

"Well tomorrow, you're taking me shopping on Rodeo, then we'll catch a movie around two, then we can go check out Griffith," Callie said. "After that, whatever you want."

"Whatever I want, eh? I can't wait." He ran his fingers back through his hair and wiped his face with his hands. "Hope you brought your own money, little lady."

Callie looked sharply at him. "What is that supposed to mean?"

"I know how much damn money you can spend in a single shopping expo. Even I can't afford your spending habits."

Callie splashed him in the face. "Ha-ha. And you don't spend money like that? I've seen your Jeep collection."

"Yeah, and I've seen your shoe collection," Donnie said, holding his hands up.

Callie splashed him again, but said nothing. She twisted her mouth and turned away from him. Her shoe collection had gotten so large it was almost uncontrollable. She needed an extra closet built into her room specifically to accommodate the shoes. But she wasn't joking about his Jeep collection either. Donnie owned seven Jeeps, all different styles and colors, for all different purposes. He'd had a ten-car garage built to house them all.

As the afternoon wore on, Donnie's mind began to unwind a little. He slowly let go the thoughts that had plagued him of late. All the conspiracy theories he had secretly entertained began to vanish, and his stress wafted away on the gentle water of the pool in which he relaxed. After the first couple of hours, Callie had warned him of his color, and he had put his t-shirt back on. It was too late though, as he was already badly burned.

The two of them got drunk by the pool and talked half the day away before Callie finally decided she wanted to go out. Seeing he couldn't go out in his current condition, Donnie recommended they both take a nap to freshen up a bit. But drinking heavily all morning then lying down for a nap was bad news. Taking a two-hour nap helped kill some of their sleepiness, but left them haggard and hung over. With their heads pounding and Donnie's skin burning, they resolved to sit on the overstuffed couch of the suite and watch television for the rest of the night.

The next day, Donnie got more 'going out' than he had bargained for. By the end of the day, his feet were about to fall off, and Callie was still ready to go out for drinks. They had spent almost five hours on Rodeo Drive, then they stopped for lunch at the In-N-Out. After lunch, two hours at Griffith Observatory, then several at the mall in Los Angeles, they stopped into the theater to see the new Kevin Spacey thriller. Donnie was ready to sleep for a week straight, and his sunburn wasn't helping the situation.

Thursday and Friday were much the same — running around like headless chickens, spending stupid amounts of money, but having nothing to show for it at the end of the day. All the show was in the bags Callie had stacked in the corner of the hotel room. Donnie had nothing.

On Saturday they rented a Maserati and blew down the PCH at a hundred and sixty miles per hour. Callie screamed and hollered, but the smile never left her face. She had pressed herself back against the seat and gripped the door handle with fierce white knuckles — but she never quit smiling.

Donnie took the Redondo Beach exit and swung up Juanita Drive, overlooking the ocean, to stop in and see an old friend. He introduced Callie to Rocky and his wife, Shariss. He had known Rocky since third grade. The men spent the evening on the balcony staring at the sea with a bucket of Dos Equis and limes between them while the women went to the mall. *Can a woman ever get enough of the malls?* Callie had taken to Shariss rather quickly, which obviously meant they needed to go spend money together.

Sunday, Donnie rested. Finally. He had slept in, savoring the solitude the day left him. He would have the suite to himself all day while Callie was out tearing up the town with her seemingly inextinguishable energy. Donnie couldn't take any more of the shopping and running around. He watched *Western Wagons* reruns for most of the morning, and drank lots of water. After lunch time though, he began to get stir crazy, and decided to spend just a little more time in the lounge chair by the pool. He hadn't planned on spending more than an hour or two in the sun, but after he met the woman, his stay was demanded.

It was Monday that would matter. On Monday, the Meeting of the Minds would kick off. As long as he was ready for his speech at the meeting, who said he couldn't enjoy himself a little more? Today, he could still get away with blowing off a little.

He had been flipping through the last few pages of the morning paper, and was just about ready to head for the darkness of the suite to cool off and get out of the sun. And when he dropped the paper to look at the pool, there she was. Not in the pool, but right there – in the chair next to him. Donnie almost jumped.

"Whoa, hey!" he said.

"Sorry. Didn't mean to startle you," the woman said.

"That's all right." After a brief pause, he said, "Have you been sitting there long?"

"Actually I just sat down. I didn't want to disturb you though. I couldn't help but notice you were white," she said.

Donnie frowned. What the hell did his color have to do with it? Was he the only other white person checked into the hotel? Surely not…

Seeing his confusion, she continued, "I mean, you're white. Like me," she said, touching his leg. It left a white spot that momentarily returned to the pink of his burned skin. "Seems like everyone out here is already dark brown, so I always feel awkward laying out."

"Oh, right. Gotcha," Donnie said, nodding.

"I'm Andrea." She extended her hand.

"Donnie Oliver." He leaned forward and shook it, then rested his elbows on his knees.

"Nice to meet you," Andrea said.

Donnie was instantly attracted to her. His being single for so long almost insured instant attraction to almost anything with breasts. And she was easy on the eyes, being that she was white – not baked like a potato. She had long legs and was thin as a rail, but not bony. Her blond hair was pulled into a neat ponytail that hung just below the strap on her bikini top. The bikini interested Donnie as well, as he was able to see more than ninety percent of her flesh, and there didn't seem to be a flaw on it. She had no cleavage at all. The natural puff of the bikini fabric either hid her breasts completely, or she had none.

And for some other reason entirely – Donnie had no idea why – that also appealed to him. He was reminded of Prissy White from his days in high school, who was a late bloomer. The girls all made fun of her for being flat-chested. "Put your bra on backwards, it'll fit better!" they would mock. Donnie didn't though. He took her to prom.

His conversation with Andrea had strolled along leisurely, mostly chatter. He wasn't particularly fond of the meaningless prattle people generated in order to inconspicuously arrive at the desired conversational destination. He would rather skip it and get to the good stuff. The stuff he knew they both wanted to talk about.

She was simple, which was nice for a change. He didn't have to talk tech to her, or explain to her the advantages of a modular satellite over a conventional fixed-purpose satellite. He didn't have to discuss the latest developments in the space program, or tell her why sending a man to Mars was so important. He had realized quite quickly that even if she had been interested in all that, she might not have understood.

It was almost two hours later that she finally asked him where he was staying. He pointed playfully at the hotel behind him – the very one by whose pool they were sitting. "No, silly. What room." Donnie had known what she was asking, but was too modest to want to tell her.

"The penthouse," he finally said.

"Oooh! A man with class!" she said. "Will you show it to me?"

"Sure. I need to get in out of the sun for a while anyway." Finally. He needed to get her up into his penthouse and get her naked in the shower with him was what he needed. And having her ask to see his suite was a step in the right direction.

As they stepped through the rooms of the penthouse suite, she crossed her arms and stared dumbly at the thousand-dollars-a-night accommodations. The air conditioning was on fairly high, so Donnie reckoned she really did have breasts and was now trying to cover up the only proof he might ever see.

"Wow!" Andrea said. "This is spectacular! What did you say you do?"

Donnie didn't think it really mattered what he said at this point, but he humored her anyway. "I build satellites." She hadn't asked him for specifics earlier, and he wasn't about to make sure she was filled in now.

She walked slowly through the monstrous suite, arms crossed, and jaw hung slack. After she had seen it all, she stopped at the giant bay window overlooking the ocean, and shook her head. "This is incredible."

"It really is nice," Donnie agreed.

He noticed her hand reaching up her back where she unhooked the top part of her bikini. Donnie's heart skipped a beat as she turned around, bare-chested and put her hands on her hips.

"So you wanna fuck?"

Donnie had – only for an instant – been almost humored that it appeared she had removed her top as if to coerce him into lying with her. Not very powerful tools of persuasion when you wear less than an A-cup, he thought. Even still, it hadn't mattered. Small or not, she looked exquisite standing there in nothing but a thong.

Donnie had failed to look at the time before he engaged her, and was later decidedly of the opinion that he couldn't have been blamed for it, as his mind was on other things. He hadn't noticed it was almost five o'clock when they had entered the room. But it wouldn't have mattered anyway, as he also hadn't known what time Callie would be returning. So when she came strolling into the room at half-past five, he was nothing less than horrified.

Callie Simmons was not a sheltered little girl. People unknowing thought of her as a prude, or a goody good. If prude was synonymous with virgin, then prude she was. Otherwise she was far from it. She had been around the block – she just hadn't run any stop signs, so to speak. She had always come home on time, her innocence still close in tow behind her. If sexuality was a precipice, she had peered over to the other side. She had never swung her leg over the crest, but she had seen it. She had seen it all. She had been handled and kissed and tasted, fondled, loved and brought to climax many a time. She had just never been taken. It had only shocked her to walk in and see Donnie in his present state, because she thought he would have been a little more discreet about his sexual endeavor. But discretion, she realized, was not his concern as he was right there in the center of the bed, facing her. He only needed to look up to make eyes with her. Apparently, the bimbo blonde with her legs up over his shoulders hadn't even been aware Callie had entered. She only kept screaming as Donnie rocked her on the thousand-dollar comforter.

Donnie had looked up and met Callie's surprised gaze. He didn't stop what he was doing, but he was clearly shocked as she was. His eyes were wide as windows and his face had gone white – not red with embarrassment. It was as if he didn't expect her to be coming home any moment. He looked like a boy who had just been caught masturbating by his mother. And all she could do was stare in amazement.

After a long moment of their staring at each other, Callie finally moved silently to the restroom. Donnie wondered why she hadn't just let herself back out of the room. How was it going to work when they were finished? Surely, Andrea would need to clean up in the restroom. When Callie emerged, they were still going at it, and Andrea was still unaware. Callie snuck to her suitcase and dug quietly through it. When she turned around she was armed with her digital camera.

What a Bimbo, Callie thought as she left the room smiling. *She never even knew I was in there.* Callie went down to the pool and got herself a margarita from the straw-covered bar. She had changed into her swimsuit and grabbed her large straw hat and shades, and now felt stupid for wearing them, as it was almost six, and the sun was no longer a threat. All that was forgotten as she scrolled through the pictures she had taken, each one appearing on the LCD on the back of the digital camera. She had taken ten blackmailers.

She giggled like a little girl as she stared at the photographs, drinking her margarita. When Donnie and the bimbo finally emerged, Donnie was staring at her with his mouth twisted – sharing her secret. He walked up next to her chair and introduced the bimbo to her.

"Hey Callie, you're here," he said. "Andrea, this is Callie – an associate and old friend of mine."

"Hi Callie," said Andrea, shaking her hand. "Wow, what a small world!"

Callie lost her smile momentarily as she tried to decode that last statement. Did she know this woman? She didn't think so. "How do you mean?" Callie said, trying to be polite.

"Well I just mean – well, what are the odds that we would be staying at the same hotel as you!"

Callie suddenly felt the need to erupt with hard laughter, but held back. "We're here together," she said, nodding slowly, and watched as the smile left the bimbo's face. She was catching on.

"Ahhhh… Okay, then that makes sense!" Andrea said.

"I'm gonna get a drink. You want anything, Andrea?" Donnie said. Perhaps there was a chance to salvage the situation yet.

"Oh, no thanks. I really should be getting on up to my room. I have dinner plans this evening. It was nice to meet you though, Kelly!"

"Callie."

"Sorry. Callie. Have a good night!" Andrea turned to walk off and paused lightly at Donnie's side. She whispered something to him – inaudible to Callie, but Callie imagined she was requesting a call.

"So what do you plan to do with all those pictures?" Donnie asked. He now had a Corona and a lime.

"I dunno." Callie smiled at him mischievously. "Maybe I will put them on the Internet."

"Oh, that'd be nice."

"So guess who I ran into today," she said with a sigh.

Donnie frowned as he looked at her. Who could Callie possibly know here in Beverly Hills? Someone with whom they were mutually acquainted, obviously, but Donnie could think of no one here in the Hills who Callie knew. He shook his head after a moment of deliberation.

"I don't know. Who?"

And Callie's answer made quick work destroying Donnie's plans for the rest of the trip.

Soft music wafted through the air, floating on the smoke of pricey cigars and arrogant discussions of things monetary. Donnie sniffed the wine and nodded. The waiter poured him some of the thick sweet red. Donnie glanced at his watch for the third time in ten minutes. He felt tight in his khakis and Polo shirt. Since he had stepped off the plane, he had been in nothing but shorts and swimming trunks. He had no idea he would be sitting first class in the Belvedere, called to a dress code. It was fortunate he had brought his business casual mock up – by the off chance he and Callie ended up somewhere a little fancy.

Tonight, though, Callie was not here.

He was sitting here alone. Alone, waiting for his company to arrive. Callie had told Donnie all about her encounter, and how the man had requested a meeting with Donnie the next day. Donnie had been forced by good courtesy to accept the offer. And now, here he sat waiting.

He stared out the window at Little Santa Monica Boulevard, watching the crowds as he sipped his wine.

People were laughing and kissing and having fun outside. And Donnie was in here waiting.

Finally, a knock at the table. Donnie turned and rose.

"Hello, Mister Oliver! It's a pleasure to finally meet you. Pablo Phoenix."

Donnie nodded politely. "Well met. Call me Donnie, please."

"Donnie it is then!" said Phoenix. The waiter returned and took his drink order.

"So how are you liking California?" Phoenix asked. He was grinning like a madman. Donnie was uncomfortable with his grin, and the prospect that this cat thought he was hosting Donnie's first trip to California. *How are you liking California? What kind of shit is that? Think I've never been here, asshole?*

"Same as always, a little too nice to go home," Donnie said. He sipped his wine again. As long as Phoenix was picking up the check, Donnie intended to warm his chest with the wine and fill his stomach with the fifty-dollar filet.

"I hear that. It's hard for me to leave home. Gorgeous view, isn't it?" Phoenix said, waving his hand toward the window.

"Very nice," Donnie nodded. *Now you own the place?*

The waiter returned and poured Phoenix a glass of the expensive wine. "Leave the bottle," Phoenix said.

"Very well. Have you gentlemen decided?" the waiter asked.

"I know what I want," Phoenix said a little too excitedly. As Phoenix ordered, Donnie found himself amused by the fact that he could take to some people – Andrea, for instance – so quickly, and then find himself loathing others in no less time. Of course, he had no intention of sleeping with Phoenix, which was probably the deciding factor. He didn't guess he had actually *liked* Andrea. He just liked parts of her. His mind wandered.

"And for you, sir?" asked the waiter.

"I'll have the filet, medium rare," Donnie said absent-mindedly.

"Excellent choice, sir."

"So listen, Don," Phoenix started. Donnie corrected him in his mind. "I wanted to thank you for the opportunity to work together. I thought since you were in town – why not do it in person?" Phoenix said. He spread his hands as if to give the restaurant to Donnie.

Work together? Donnie had suddenly lost his appetite.

Callie sat with her legs crossed, fingering the remote control, and trying to find something worth watching. The late night TV schedule was poor these days. A bag of Cheeto's and a can of Planter's cashews sat on the tray in front of her on the bed. Crumbs littered the tray and the comforter, and she had come close to spilling her Big Red several times. Her satellite phone, which lay in her lap, rang again and she answered with a mouthful of Cheeto's Puffs.

"Lo?" she managed.

"Callie Simmons?"

"Who's this?" she said, wiping her mouth with a paper towel.

"You got three guesses."

"Walter Watson."

"What's up girl?"

"Walter what the heck are you doing?"

"Not much of anything. Check it out though, where are you?"

"Ooooh, Walter, I'm in California on vacation."

"Hmm, wow. Small world, eh? I happen to be enroute to LAX. I'm over the shiny lights of Vegas right now."

"Oh my God, are you serious?" she shouted.

"Yep. Was wondering if you wanted to get together."

"Heck yes I do! How have you been?"

"Hanging in there. What about you? You still work for the Olivers?"

"Yes, and loving it. They make me feel so important here, Walter."

"You are important, Callie. Well I'm trying to get out of this hellhole."

"You still work for Minus?" Callie said.

"Yup. Well, no. Yeah though. I mean, no, I don't work for Minus anymore. He finally got moved to Chicago or something. And I'm back in Dallas, but I don't think it's gonna last long."

"Okay, Walter, you're going to have to tell me all about this Fiji stuff. And how the heck you got back to Dallas, too. God! We have a lot of catching up to do!"

"Yes, we do, friend," said Walter. "Well I should be there within the hour. Maybe we can meet somewhere tomorrow or something. Unless you don't have any plans tonight…"

"No, I'm free tonight! What time will you get there?"

"My plane arrives at eight-twenty nine."

"Ooh, that's fifty minutes. I'll be there."

"You sure you can make it that fast?" Walter said.

"Yeah! We've actually rented two cars, so I can take the cheap one. Donnie got the Maserati."

"You're there with Donnie?" Walter said, his voice betraying a little disappointment.

"Yeah. We're here on business, Walter."

"You said you were on vacation," Walter reminded her.

"Yeah, but it's based around the Meeting of the Minds."

Walter coughed. "Damn. Meeting of the Minds? We do have a lot to catch up on. Okay, well I'll be there in about an hour."

"I'm so excited, Walt!" she said.

"Yeah me too. Excited as a retarded goldfish. It's been like four years hasn't it?"

"Uh huh." She bit into another cheese puff. Walter rattled off his flight information, which she jotted on a business card and they hung up. She shook her fists and smiled and shook her head at the ceiling, excited about seeing her friend again. It had been years. She bounced up and down on the bed, shaking the phone in excitement. This time she spilled her Big Red.

Donnie shook his head quickly. "I'm not sure I follow, Pablo. Work together?"

"Yes, of course!" Phoenix held his glass out to toast. Donnie didn't raise his own. After an uncomfortable silence, Phoenix continued. "Well I'd like to think we've opened a magnificent avenue for revenue, all for almost nil overhead."

Donnie leaned forward, crossing his arms on the table. "I'm not sure I'm with you. What business are you talking about?"

The smile finally slid from Phoenix's face. "You're kidding, right?" he said.

Donnie widened his eyes, shaking his head.

"Am I to assume you're reneging on the contract you signed?"

"What contract are you talking about, Mr. Phoenix?" Donnie said.

"You're kidding me. I can't believe this. I'm being played for a fool," Phoenix said. He looked about the restaurant, as if for a rescue.

"What contract are you talking about?" Donnie asked again. He was a little less patient this time.

"What, do you want to see it? You need to be reminded?" Phoenix said.

"Being that I have never signed a contract with you, yes I will need to see it."

Phoenix had brought it. He opened his black leather portfolio, never taking his eyes off Donnie's. He looked as if he couldn't believe this was happening. Donnie stared back with an expectant expression. He was ready to see this supposed contract that bore his name. Then there it was. Phoenix slid it across the fine surface of the table. Their plates hadn't even arrived yet, and Donnie was ready to knock Phoenix's lights out.

He scanned the front page of the three-page contract. It laid out all the details of an extra-terrestrial burial in fine black print. On the second page was listed the names of those deceased – those whom he would supposedly be burying. The third page was signed. By Donald Aloysius Oliver. His own pen.

"I'll be a mother f-" Donnie trailed off.

"That's your signature, is it not? Do we not have a deal?" Phoenix said. He was fingering the contract to illustrate his ascendancy in this predicament.

"How did you get this?"

"Get what?" Phoenix said, straightening.

"This contract. Did you do it by fax? Email? How'd you get it signed?"

"Well it was VirtuaSign." Phoenix spread his hands, begging for a case.

"This isn't my signature, Pablo," Donnie said. He slapped the contract back down on the table. "I mean, it is, but I didn't sign it. This is a forgery."

Phoenix leaned back in his chair, sighing and looking away. "What the hell happened." He was talking to himself.

"Someone went behind my back and authorized this." Donnie too leaned back as the waiter set down the plates of sizzling meat. Neither of them touched their plates. They stared at the meat, sitting quietly in their own thoughts.

Donnie finally broke the long silence. "Look, I'll be in touch." He backed out of the table and stood up. Phoenix stared at him, hands on the arms of the chair, unspeaking. Donnie didn't want to take the crates up, he knew that much. But with Phoenix already having paid for the service, and presumably having already sent the crates to the Oliver Company, Donnie didn't just want to leave them behind. Not that he gave a shit about Phoenix and his money spent. He did have a guilty feeling about all the poor idiots who had paid Phoenix thousands of dollars to have their loved ones buried on Mars. Obviously, they had received contracts promising their loved ones would truly be sent to Mars on the Oliver Company's mission, and not buried out in the flat lands of Arizona somewhere. Donnie Oliver didn't want to be the one to drop that ball.

He had a feeling that if the crates were already up on the space station, he had be forced into taking them anyway. "I'll call you. I have a little investigating to do, but I'll be in touch. I don't know what kind of deal you worked out, and who you worked it out with, but we'll work something out."

"It's all right there in the contract, Donnie."

Donnie picked up the sheaf of papers and tucked them into his back pocket, where they stuck out like a magazine on a trip to the men's room. He looked around quickly, then leaned in close to Phoenix. "This 'contract' is on hold," he said, pointing his fist at Phoenix. "If you say a fucking word about it, my lawyer will be so far up your ass you won't know whether to shit or make a phone call." And then he walked out of the restaurant.

Callie tucked her hair behind her ears and pushed her shades up her nose a little. She was walking up to the terminal on the moving sidewalk, which she had never quite gotten used to. People were packing into planes and scrambling down the long corridors trying to get to their flights. Why was it, she thought, that people were never in the right place? Someone ought to organize a new system that would put people directly beside the gate at which they needed to board. She reckoned people could save five months of walking when all was said and done, if they could simply park – or be let off – right beside the proper gate.

She could feel the excitement rising in her again, her chest and stomach tingling as she moved closer and closer to the gate at which she would be reunited with Walter. She licked her lips and adjusted her purse strap on her shoulder. Was this a new kind of excitement she felt inside, or was it just that she had not been excited at all in so long that she had forgotten what it felt like? Either way, it was a happiness she had been looking forward to for years.

She arrived at the gate and stepped off the moving sidewalk, glancing about the new throng of people who had just burst out of the taxiway and into the airport. Walter stepped into the terminal from the taxi ramp with his shades on, and looking. She almost didn't recognize him, it had been so long. The last time she had seen him, she had still been with Royal, and that was two companies ago. He didn't look older, just different. It was as if his face had matured in some way. He now had a three-day growth on his beard, and his hair was a little longer, but every bit as wild as it had been before.

Callie screamed as she realized it was him. "Oh my God, Walter!" She took off running through the reception area and threw her arms around him. He picked her up with his free arm, spinning her around much like her father used to do.

"How you doin' babe?"

"Oh my God! You look so good, Walter!"

"Yeah? So do you," he said, pulling away from her to get a better look. "You look hot, Callie Simmons."

"Oh Walter, I've missed you so much! We have to go get drinks!"

"Yeah, well right now I've got to get a smoke. I've been dying in that plane."

"Okay, come on, let's go now. Do you have any luggage checked?"

"Nope. I'll buy whatever I need."

Callie led him by the hand out of the airport, hustling to the nearest entrance. As soon as they got outside, Walter lit up, disregarding the NO SMOKING WITHIN 200 FEET OF ENTRANCE sign, and the bellhop servicing the curb nearby. They blasted across the street, Callie smiling and squealing like a little girl, Walter in tow, smoking and smiling like a high school student who knows he's about to get laid.

Ten minutes later, Callie and Walter sat on high stools at a small round table sipping drinks. Callie's leg swung under the table, occasionally rubbing up against Walter's leg as he filled her in on the last four years. She held the miniature straw between her fingers, sucking sweet Margarita through it, smiling and giggling with delight. She had dropped her sandal on the floor so she could feel Walter's leg with her toes. He reached under the table and grabbed her foot with a strong hand, squeezing it and rubbing his thumb across its delicate top.

"So tell me how much you miss Royal, Callie."

"God, I don't. Not even." Callie sipped from her drink, then carried on, "You know, I used to have dreams about that place. I am so happy to be gone."

"Yeah, I think everyone that works there has dreams about it. Not all of them desirable."

"I kept having them too. Until like two years after I had quit. I'm so happy here at Oliver Company. It's so much better."

"In what ways?" Walter said, leaning onto the table.

"Well, it's even more lax a work schedule than when we worked for Minus at Royal. If you can believe that. I really don't report to anyone but Sam, and that's just the org chart. It's not like he tells me what to do and when to be there."

"So what exactly do you do as the CTO?"

"All of the research. And it's a lot of work. I have my own department, really. It's like anything they want analyzed or researched comes through me. And of course, I have my own projects going. Which is a constant. I'm always coming up with these ideas I want to test out and stuff. To put into reality and see if they work." Callie smiled and sat up straight. "It's like I've been given a license to invent and fabricate all my fantasies, Walter. You would love it there."

"Yeah. Working for you? Hah. You know I can't get away from Royal." Walter pulled long from his beer, then spoke again. "So, Callie… You're not going up on that Mars mission are you?"

"Heck no!" She frowned and slapped his shoulder, then bent over to suck from the straw of her drink. "Why do you ask that?"

"Just checking. Wondering."

"Oh yeah, Walter. You were going to tell me about Fiji."

"Well, Callie, you know I'm not supposed to talk about it."

"No, I don't know that. What do you mean?"

"Come on! How often were you allowed to talk about what you actually worked on at Royal?" He held his hand out to delegate her pause. "You didn't even tell me you were working on that quantum computer. You talk about a sock in the chest."

"Yeah, I know, Walter. Royal is all about confidence. But come on. I'm your bestest friend. You can tell me. Tell me all about Fiji."

"There is no Fiji, Callie. You know that."

"Well, so to speak, yes I do. But I don't know that they haven't set up some rudimentary camp out there to field some agents either." She sipped and popped a chip in her mouth. The salsa was Walter's. "So it's just a figure of speech, eh?"

"Yup." Walter pulled from his beer bottle. "They call it Fiji. Many people have been sent to Fiji. But no one ends up in the same place."

"Soooo… Tell me where you went Walter!"

"Oh, well that's not really important. That's not the interesting part. I was in New York, no big deal. The cool thing was the technology I was working with."

"Like what?"

"It's a new kind of camera, Callie. You will totally dig it. You can take full color pictures in the dark."

Walter pulled his pack of Celtic Classic cigarettes from his shirt pocket and lit one. "It's bad ass, it really is."

Callie frowned. "Why did you have to go to New York to work on that?"

Walter stared at Callie. She couldn't read his expression. But something about him had changed. Something in the last four and a half years had changed, not just in his countenance, but his demeanor. True he was a little more laid back, but something had developed of his ability to withhold things from Callie. That was unheard of in their past lives. Maybe he was getting her back for that quantum computer project she had kept from him. Whatever it was, Callie was suddenly and alarmingly aware that Walter wasn't shooting straight with her. He was holding something back. Maybe it was the project, maybe not. But she knew that New York was a symbol just like Fiji. Walter hadn't any more gone to New York for a project than Callie had gone to Spain to learn German. And she could see it in his eyes.

It was almost midnight when she finally got back to the hotel, and Donnie still wasn't there. She took a shower and got into bed to read as she waited for him. About a half-hour later, Donnie stormed into the room, ready to pack his shit and get the hell out of Dodge.

Callie was sitting on the bed, her knees pulled up, reading a book. When the door swung open, she jumped quite literally off the mattress. Donnie threw his keys and papers onto the dresser by the television and stomped over to the mini-bar to twist the top off a stress reliever.

He was half-shouting and waving his hands erratically, spilling beer on the carpet, expecting Callie to know what the hell he was talking about. It wasn't until he finally looked over at her that he realized she had no clue what was going on. Not only was she in the dark, but her face was white as if she had seen a ghost. Donnie stopped mid-sentence, and stared at her. She sat there staring wide-eyed at him, her hand on her heart.

"What. You okay?"

"Yes. You scared the ever-loving shit out of me," Callie said.

"Oh. Shit. Sorry, Cal." Donnie took a sip of his beer. "Well if you wouldn't read them damn horror novels you wouldn't set yourself up for it."

Callie looked confusedly at the cover of her book before returning her gaze to Donnie. "Donnie, it's Melville."

"What's that about?" he said, unbuttoning his shirt.

"Herman Melville. Moby Dick, Donnie."

"Ha-ha-ha, whatever," Donnie said. He pulled from his beer again.

Callie held up the book for him to see the cover. Clearly, she was not amused. "You wanna tell me what you're running around yelling about?"

Donnie dropped his arms to his sides. "What? Didn't I tell you what was going on?"

"What, with Phoenix?"

"Yeah. No. Well, yeah. Look. Just look at this," Donnie said. He threw the sheaf of papers at Callie, who caught it ungracefully, and dropped her book, at the same time knocking over her glass of ice water on the bedside table.

"What's this?" Donnie said, standing beside the bed and pointing at the red stain on the comforter.

"Oh that. Yeah, it's Big Red. I'll probably have to pay for that."

Donnie snorted. "Yeah?"

She finally got settled again and looked at the papers. "So? What's this for?"

"It's a contract, Callie."

Callie nodded sardonically, closing her eyes. "I know, Donnie. What's it for?"

"Well you know what Phoenix does, right?"

"Of course. He sends dead people into space. Makes quite a good bit of money doing it so I've heard," Callie said, nodding.

"Yeah. Anyway, that's beside the point. The point is that that's a contract for sending two crates of those dead people into space on my ship."

"All right! Way to go, Donnie!" Callie yelped, standing up on the bed. She quickly adjusted her panties and tugged on her shirt tale.

Donnie stared at her. "Callie, that's not my signature on the back."

Callie turned to the last page and lost her smile as she looked at it. "Okay, dammit, get to the point, Donnie. You've made me feel dumb as that bimbo you were nailing earlier. Congratulations, I have no idea what's going on."

"Callie, you're not dumb. You're-"

"Thank you. So tell me what the heck is going on then. I'm tired of this guessing game."

"Sorry, Callie. I'm not going to be able to make the meeting Monday. I have to go back and find out who signed my name on that contract."

Callie gulped. She decided to hold off telling Donnie about her surprise meeting with Walter.

"They know."

"They know what?"

"They know the contract was forged. I don't think it's safe here."

"Don't sweat it. And don't you move a muscle. If you go running off, they'll know it was you."

"Okay, so what's the plan then?"

"Well, don't they still suspect the load master?"

"How the hell should I know?"

"Because we pay you to know!" the voice rose.

"Okay, okay. Sorry. I'll get back to you. Give me a day to snoop around."

The other end disconnected without another word. There would have to be some nonchalant asking around, finding out who knew what, and what they thought of that load master who had been shit-canned. As long as he was still the prime suspect, everything else could be pinned on him.

Jason Shepherd was supposed to be waiting at the airport to pick Donnie up. The dry heat of the Arizona desert was immediately recognizable as Donnie stepped out of the front doors of the airport. Callie was close in tow behind Donnie, and they looked like they had been on vacation. Callie wore a long wrinkly skirt and a light sleeveless blouse that tied above her navel. Donnie was dressed in his khakis and a crisp white Polo shirt, his shades drawn against the sun. Callie had tried to talk him into staying at least for his speech at the Meeting, but he had refused, saying he wouldn't be able to concentrate on anything until he resolved this issue.

Initially she had been disappointed to learn that their trip would be cut short, being that as old friends they almost never got to spend any time together anymore. But seeing it as a business emergency, she decided they would put it off together and go some other time. At least she had gotten to go shopping, and they had been there for most of a week.

Now, as they stood out in front of the terminal, Donnie looked slowly across the busy pickup lanes, trying to spot their ride. Shepherd had said he would be there. Donnie could not see him. Callie looked about casually.

"Who's coming to get us?" she asked.

"Shepherd. Should be here by now," Donnie said. He looked at his watch, then reached for his satellite phone, and pulled the antenna out with his teeth. Just then, a small Nissan pickup pulled up in front of them in the passenger pickup lane.

"Who's Shepherd?"

"Jason Shepherd. He's an A&P guy – one of Mike's boys."

"Ahh."

Donnie looked up as Jason honked. He held his hands out to his sides, then pushed END on his sat-phone. "How does he expect us all to fit in that?" Donnie said, pointing his antenna at the compact truck.

Callie didn't answer. She knew Donnie was about to be in one of his rather severe moods, having just made the four-hour flight, only to arrive to a poorly planned pickup. She knew to keep quiet; as long as she was silent, he would stay mad at someone else.

Donnie walked over to the truck and opened the door to talk to Jason. "You expect Callie to ride in the back?" he said.

"No sir. I-I didn't know she was…"

"Go home. I'll find another ride," Donnie shut the door and turned away.

Then Jason did something that bought him serious points with Donnie. He opened the driver's side door and got out.

"Mr. Oliver!" he said over the top of the truck. "It's nice and cool in the truck. Why don't you two go ahead and drive back, then you can send someone back for me later."

Donnie had stopped in his tracks, and turned to look at Jason Shepherd over his shoulder for a moment – considering.

"Go ahead, sir. I can get back some other way."

Donnie turned back to Callie, then picked up the suitcases, loading them in the small bed. He walked around the front of the truck, and got in the driver's side as Callie boarded herself in the passenger seat. "All right, I'll send someone to pick you up."

Donnie pushed his office door closed and sat behind his desk as Shanna dropped into the chair across from him. He slid the note punch in front of him and thumbed through the messages Shanna had taken for him. After spending several minutes looking at the notes, he finally turned his monitor on and leaned back in his chair. He was finally ready to talk.

"Anything important?"

"Nope. Not really. Mike needs to see you whenever you get a chance, but it's not urgent. Want some coffee?" Shanna said, crossing her legs.

"Yeah. Sounds good. How's Discovery?"

"Still busy. They're not here today, said they would be back next Monday for phase two – whatever that means." Shanna poured coffee into his thick mug and dumped a large load of sugar in after it. Setting the mug in front of him, she rounded the desk and returned to her seat. "How was your trip?"

"It was good, Shanna. It really was. I enjoyed myself thoroughly."

"That's good. Sad to hear you had to come back early," Shanna said. She pulled her hair back and worked on her ponytail.

"Yeah I bet you are. Things get shitty?"

"No, not at all. So tell me, Donnie: did you find you some hot little California girls?"

Donnie looked up at her, a serious look on his face. "Now what makes you think I'd be doing that?"

"Because you went with Callie Simmons."

Donnie frowned hard. "I'm not sure I catch your logic."

"Well, I just mean… Well, I don't know what I mean. But I just-"

"Spit it out, King," Donnie said, still staring at her.

"I don't know. Just wondering if you had fun, that's all," Shanna said. She was blushing now.

"Uh huh. Yeah, I made arrangements. How was your week?"

Shanna took a deep breath. "It was hell, Donnie." Donnie looked at her in silence. She continued, "I told Brett about me going up on the Feb Nine."

"Really?" Donnie said, widening his eyes.

"Yep. He's not happy about it. In fact, he's trying to hold me back."

"Boy, he's a clingy one, ain't he?" Donnie said with a grin.

"Yeah, I guess so. He's acting like a protective father about this."

"Well that's not so bad, Shanna. That's a good thing – he cares about you," Donnie said. He sipped his scalding coffee, then made a face of approval.

Shanna rolled her eyes. "Yeah, I know, but who in their right mind would turn down a trip into space? I know he wouldn't. But he's trying to limit me."

"Well I'm sorry to hear that. Makes it hard to live with someone when they try to change your mind about shit, don't it?" Donnie said. He leaned back and clasped his hands behind his head.

"I moved out, Donnie."

Donnie's smile instantly washed from his face. Now he felt like a fool. "Aw, shit, Shanna. I'm sorry."

"It's okay, Donnie, I'm a big girl. Just thought you should know."

"Well yeah, I should know," he said. He moved around to the front of the desk and leaned against it, crossing his arms. "You need help finding another place?"

Shanna looked at the floor. She was messing with her fingernails, not making eye contact with him. This was a first for her.

"Shanna?" Donnie said. She looked up at him. "Where are you staying?"

Shanna jerked her head toward the small couch in the corner of the office. Donnie looked over at it, seeing the pillow and the ruffled blanket on it. There was a tote bag on the floor just in front of it, overstuffed and bursting at the seams.

"Ah, hell, Shanna. Let's go find you a place. You can't stay here," he said.

"Why not? I don't have much stuff. I have a few other bags up in the attic, but this is pretty much it. I'm a simple girl."

"You can't stay here, Shanna. This is my office."

Shanna looked at him again, a flash of pain in her eyes.

"Well you have too much to do to be helping me find another place to live, Donnie. I can make do. I'll be out by Saturday," she said. "If I can just have through the rest of this week to look, I bet I can find a place and be moved in by Saturday."

Donnie looked at her for a long moment before speaking. He finally broke the silence. "Okay, Shanna. You'll stay with me through the end of the week. If you find a place before that, great. If not, no big deal. Take a few days off 'til you find something."

He thought he saw a spark of excitement in her eyes as he said she could stay with him. He hoped he wasn't passing the wrong message. And it would look real bad if anyone from the company found out she was staying with him. Then suddenly there would be hushed conversations about their sexuality – not to mention a sudden explanation for her being a crew member on the Feb Nine.

"Donnie knows about the contract."
"How did that happen?"
"He flew out to California and ran into Phoenix."
"Okay, well you plant the contract then."
"What's that going to do?"
"It will get your ass off the hook."
"What about Keith?"
"You don't have to worry about him."

The rain was blasting heavily against the windshield as Mike and Donnie made their way across town. It was well after dark, and the rest of the sane world had already turned into their homes for the night. It was a treacherous drive, but they figured now was the best time to do it. They had a little business to take care of with Robert Keith. And now would be the least likely time for him to expect their arrival. Donnie doubted Keith even considered a visit from the two of them, as he had long ago been forgotten. But to play it safe, they had waited until now – after eleven, and while it was raining angry hell in town.

Mike pushed in the lighter and pulled the pack of Hangman's Hardcut Cigarettes from his shirt pocket. He tapped the edge of the pack and pulled a smoke out, then lit it with the glowing coils of the lighter. The smell of fresh smoke filled the interior of the Jeep. "You know what I think?" he said. Without waiting for a response, he continued. "I think that little trickster is up to no good all around. I'm bettin he's got a lot more going on than just some behind-the-scenes scam."

Donnie looked over at Mike and snorted. "Like what?"

"Well I bet he's working something big over on whoever he's working for now. And I bet he hit us a lot harder than we think. It'll be months before his little evidences start surfacing, but I'll bet they do," Mike said, pointing at the steering wheel with the cigarette between his fingers.

"Yeah, I've thought about that. If it was him, we'll be finding little traces of his ass for years."

"You're damned right." Mike leaned back in his seat and pulled heavily from the smoke. "I'd just like to have some undeniable proof he was involved. I'd like to see his ass burned."

Donnie nodded. He leaned forward and slowed way down. "Is this it?" he said, squinting at a road sign.

"Yeah, Jeter Road. That's it."

Donnie turned onto the dark road and pushed the car into third gear. At the end of the street ahead, they could see the apartment complex looming in the darkness. There was very little light coming from the parking lot, and through the rain it looked almost ghostly. As they drew nearer, Donnie grabbed his cigarettes off the dash and lit one himself. He was a little nervous about a confrontation, but was determined to see it through. A quick smoke would ease his nerves a little bit. The money had shown up on the contract. Someone had taken delivery of Phoenix's package, and had received the money. Unless this was all some bullshit contract thrown together by Phoenix – which Donnie didn't believe, after all, he had seen his own signature at the bottom of it – then it would be a wasted effort. But at least they would get some closure on suspicions, even if he didn't say much. Donnie knew Mike was a pretty good judge of character, and was likely to be able to see through any bullshit façade Keith might have erected for the occasion – however spur-of-the-moment it might be.

The Jeep rumbled up to the first entrance of the complex, and Donnie turned in, slowing to read the numbers on the buildings. Building I was visible on his right. They were looking for building XVIII, and room 1806. Donnie thought it odd that they used a Roman numeral system, seeing as how most people couldn't read numbers that way intelligibly. He made his way through the complex, barely slowing for the speed bumps, and passed the central mailbox pavilion, which presumably stood in the direct middle of the apartment lot. The rain eased up a little for the first time in several hours, and Donnie pulled into a space just outside the building they needed. They sat idling for a few moments as Donnie finished his smoke.

"You wanna do the talking?" Mike said.

Donnie shrugged. "I don't care. If you think of something you need to say, feel free to speak your mind. I don't really have an agenda."

"You think he might fess up to anything?"

"Dunno. I hope. But I'm betting we'll see it in his eyes, regardless."

Mike nodded. Donnie killed the car and rolled down the window. A rush of cold wet air blew in to meet them. After a long silence filled with smoke, Donnie finally spoke again. "Hey Mike, I need to talk to you about something."

Mike looked over at Donnie, but said nothing. He nodded slowly.

"Shanna just broke up with her boyfriend, and moved out."

Mike raised his hand to stop the conversation. "Donnie, I really don't think you need to tell me this."

"Why not? It's not what you think, Mike."

"Isn't it?" Mike turned and looked out the window, then took a long meaningful drag. "How long have we known each other, Donnie?"

"Fifteen years? Twenty? I don't know. I just…"

"Donnie, you know what everyone already thinks of you two."

Donnie tried to cut in, but Mike raised his hand again. "You know I've never asked you if you were fucking her, and I never will. I don't want to know. It's none of my business, and-"

"Mike, I'm not sleeping with her."

Again, Mike raised his hand. "Fine, Donnie. If you say that's how it is, fine. But I don't want to know anything. And until you ask me for my opinion on your situation, I'm not going to talk about it."

"That's why I brought it up, man." Donnie blew smoke out the window and rested his hand atop the steering wheel, staring at the streetlights.

"Are you asking me what I think?" Mike said.

"Dammit, Mike, you know you can speak freely. Talk to me."

Mike pulled from his smoke, then after a long pause, finally spoke. "I think you either need to fire that girl, or put her in another part of the company. Your job is all politics, Donnie. If anyone finds out she's staying with you, you'll never recover from-"

"She's on the Feb Nine." A silence ensued. Its thickness could have been cut with a knife.

Mike sighed and dropped his cigarette out the window. "She's on the Feb Nine."

"She's on the Feb Nine," Donnie repeated.

"What, you need someone to file your papers on board? Take your phone calls?"

Donnie laughed out loud. "I didn't put her there, Mike. In fact I told her I couldn't take her when she asked."

Mike just stared at Donnie, waiting for more.

"She made a deal with Discovery. They're training her to run the cameras."

Mike nodded, pursing his lips, and breathed in deeply. But he said nothing.

Donnie spent the next fifteen minutes justifying Shanna's presence on the Feb Nine. Fighting this inner battle about Shanna was taking its toll on Donnie, as he really didn't know why he was defending her at all. There was nothing to hide. But why he liked her so much, he couldn't begin to guess. Why it was so refreshing to have her on board was a mystery to him, as well as to everyone else. If it were sexual, then – regardless of how unethical – it would at least be understandable. If they were sleeping together, it would answer all the questions, and somehow absolve him from the mystery of his attraction to her. He knew he loved her for her mind. That was no secret. She was brilliant in her own way, though young and sometimes naïve. She was simple, and common sense prospered in the environment of simplicity. That was desperately what Donnie needed.

That, and Shanna was perhaps the only person who wasn't afraid to tell him when he was out of his mind. "You need to sit your ass down and listen to me, Donnie," she had said on more than one occasion. She flat-out commanded him to listen to her, and to do this, that or the other thing sometimes. People who happened to be present during one of these outbursts would often look perplexed and mistaken, as if they'd had it all wrong the whole time about who was boss of whom. But Donnie always listened, as he did when almost anyone bossed him into doing something. This is provided that someone actually had the balls to try it – which no one ever did, but Shanna. He was always willing to listen to reason, when reason was ready to speak. And more often than not, it spoke through Shanna's lips.

It was Friday night. The week had sailed by like a stiff breeze, leaving no memories and no rewards. Shanna had been off all week, and Donnie had hardly seen her. He had meant to check in with her and ask about her progress in finding a new place. He knew it wouldn't be difficult, but he had seen her suitcase in the hallway when he had come home from work this evening. Did that mean she was leaving? Left? Gone? If so, then he had made it through without anyone knowing she had stayed in his house for the week. At least he still had that secret. If Mike knew about that, it would seriously weaken Donnie's stance on this whole business.

Explaining his feelings about her necessity to anyone else seemed futile to Donnie. He couldn't well explain why he needed her, but knew he desperately did nonetheless. Two or three days without her made all evidence of that readily available. He would miss meetings and luncheons, forget appointments, and just all together look like someone totally disoriented with reality. She kept his bearings greased for him, and he didn't know what he would do without her. Secretaries were a dime a dozen, but Shannas were hard to come by.

"Well let's make our move before I get old and change my mind," Mike finally said.

"You think I'm stupid, don't you?"

"Wh- Shit, no, Donnie! I think you're… Yeah. I think you're stupid. This is political suicide. But hey, you're the boss," Mike said. He opened his door and stepped out into the wet night, tugging up on his belt loops.

Donnie got out and crunched his own cigarette out, then shut the door quietly with his hip, immediately realizing his mistake when he touched his jeans. They were wet now, and smeared with grime from the dirty car. One of those nights.

They walked across the parking lot, glistening like a sea of stars. The smell of the fresh rain mingled with the smell of dirt and parking lot oil. The overall smell wasn't an unpleasant one, and Donnie found himself taking deep breaths of it. It hadn't rained in centuries, it seemed. They walked across the grass, soaking the edges of their boots and the cuffs of their trousers as they made their way to the stairway on the end of the building.

The apartments were old, and looked in need of some refurbishments. The stairs were wooden, and creaked loudly as they ascended, boots clopping like horse hooves. Donnie grabbed the handrail and almost lost his balance as he realized it was more rickety than the staircase itself. Atop the first staircase, the walkway went around the edge of the building and disappeared into the darkness, where it formed a hallway between the sets of rooms. The doors faced each other across the hallway, rather than facing the outside of the building, giving the whole complex the eerie feel of an old abandoned barracks. No doors were visible from the outside, only windows running along the outside of the walls – one, two, and three stories high.

The hallway was so dark they couldn't see the numbers, and Mike finally had to draw his SureFire flashlight to make sure they weren't about to run into a wall – or a boogeyman, for that matter. Either the lights had burned out long ago, or the whole electrical system was faulty and shorted out. Each was as likely as the other, Donnie figured. The whole of the place smelled rancid, like animal, and he suspected there were a few raccoons that had taken up permanent residence in these hallways.

Mike gestured with a tilt of his head, and Donnie caught up, then looked at the number placard by the door. This was it. If anyone was inside, he was asleep. Robert Keith, it was evident, was no party animal. It wasn't even midnight yet, and the sound of TVs and radios were not present. Donnie nodded at Mike, who knocked sharply on the thin wooden door. The echo resounded throughout the hallway like they had used gavels. Mike frowned and put his fingertips against the top of the door and pushed slightly against it. The door pushed back away from the jamb where his hand was, but didn't open. It was thin and cheap, like cardboard. Donnie smirked, realizing if they needed to kick it in, all it would take was a generous push, and it would break away from the knob like a twig.

No one answered.

Donnie crossed his arms and nodded at the door again, and Mike knocked. Mike shook his head and furled his mouth. "That sumbitch knows we're here now. He ain't gonna answer."

Donnie tried the knob. It turned slightly. It was locked, but the lock was cheap, so that when it made a partial turn, it was enough to do the trick. The door pushed open with the sound of paint being broken, as if the door hadn't been opened in several months. And as soon as it pushed away from the jamb, the two of them threw their arms over their mouths and noses.

"Oh my God," Donnie said through the cloth on his shirt. Mike's face was full of disbelief and disgust. The smell was sweet and pungent like decay, and strong enough to make them both retch. Mike reached in and flipped the switch just inside the door. Nothing happened. He then pulled the SureFire from the Velcro holster perpetually hung on his belt, and clicked it on.

Donnie pushed the door open farther and stepped back so Mike could take the lead. As they stepped into the darkness, it was evident the air conditioner hadn't been on in days, and the clocks on the microwave and the VCR didn't shine. There was no power here. It was silent as a tomb, and it became quickly obvious that's exactly what it was indeed. Mike led the way down the hallway off the main living area of the small apartment, Donnie following closely behind. He shone the light over the walls and floors as they made their way to the bedroom, where the door was closed. Mike turned the knob and pushed the door open, and they were greeted with an even stronger version of the pungent odor.

As soon as Donnie saw the body, he had to turn and cough into his elbow, holding back a hard gag. He was quickly assaulted by the full force of the odor as his arm came away from his face. He gagged again, and almost choked, then stumbled through the door and down the hallway trying to get back into the fresh air of the outside. Mike stayed behind in the room as Donnie moved like a drunk through the dark cluttered apartment. He tripped over several unseen items, and banged into the walls several times, all the while holding one hand out in front of him to guide the way, and the other over his mouth. The darkness was complete though, and he quickly realized he was already disoriented to the point he couldn't make his way out. He fell and found himself on the Linoleum of the kitchen floor, and reached out to find the cabinets. His hands touched something soft and wet, horrible and evil feeling and he yelled out in terror as his mind raced to shock.

"Donnie!" Mike was shouting, running through the small apartment in search of him.

Donnie called out something incoherent, but the sound was enough to guide Mike to him in the darkness, like a beacon. As Mike bent and helped Donnie up off the floor, they both got a look at the floor where Donnie's hands had been. "Christ," Donnie said. "Get me out of here, Mike."

Donnie was leaning against the squad car, arms crossed, and smoking a cigarette. Mike had his hands in his pockets and was lingering nearby, talking to one of the officers. They had been out here answering questions for what seemed like hours, and – as Donnie saw it – were really none ahead for it. It had come up that Robert Keith had been fired, so seemingly there was reason for Donnie to have killed him. Mike had tried to explain the reasoning in this to Donnie, but it wasn't sticking. "If I wanted him dead, I'd have killed him. Not fired him," Donnie had said. Donnie had then gone on to mention how easy it would have been for him to have an on-the-job accident, what with all the equipment and machinery, but Mike had cut him off with a throat-slashing motion.

"Can we have just a minute please?" Mike said, and dragged Donnie off to the side for a private discussion. "Don't say shit like that, Don."

"I'm trying to illustrate that-"

"I know what you're doing. But now if it ever happens… If someone ever dies on the job, you're the prime suspect."

Donnie stared at the ground and sighed. "You're right. I'm so stupid sometimes."

"Don't say another word to them until Robin gets here," Mike said. "If this is the line of questioning they're going to follow, then we don't speak without our lawyer."

"Good point." Now here he stood, waiting on Robin to get out of bed and make her way out here. She rarely stayed up past nine, and was hard to wake – certainly past two, anyway. After several smokes and some mindless chatter, Robin finally arrived and stepped out of her Mercedes with a breeze of professionalism and control of the situation.

"Mr. Oliver, come please," she said. Donnie dropped his cigarette and made his way to the back of Robin's car.

"What have you told them?"

"Nothing. I don't know anything."

"But you've been talking to them for the last three hours, right?"

"Well, yeah."

"What have you told them?"

"Well, I told them I fired him," Donnie said. "Then I said 'if I wanted him dead I'd have killed him, not fired him'."

Robin stared at Donnie blankly for a moment. "You're serious. You said you would have killed him?"

Donnie nodded, raising his eyebrows.

"Next time, don't say a word until I'm here with you, okay?"

"Well nothing I've said is admissible without you anyway, right?"

"Why would you say that?" Robin said. She was frowning.

"Well, I just thought that was the case. I haven't been arrested."

"This is politics, Donnie. They've done an informal interrogation here. It's trickery. The informality is a ploy to get you to talk. Everything you said is admissible, and I guarantee they will use it."

Donnie stared at her for a moment, then closed his eyes.

"Donnie, I need to know something right now." Robin raised Donnie's chin to look him in the eyes. "Did you do it?"

"No! Of course not!"

"Then don't worry about it. I'll handle it from here."

Donnie watched Robin as she rounded the Mercedes and approached the small group of officers assembled in front of the squad car. Mike came round the back and put his hand on Donnie's shoulder. "Don't sweat it, bro. She's good. That's why you hired her."

Robin stepped up to the officers and pulled her hair behind her ears. "Is my client under arrest?"

The lead cop looked at the others, baffled. He finally shrugged. "No, I guess not. If we need him, we'll call."

"Very good. We'll be on our way then."

"Uh, ma'am," one of the officers said as she was walking away. "I'm sorry, I didn't catch your name."

"That's okay," Robin said smiling.

The three of them – Mike, Robin and Donnie – met in the break room of the office to discuss further what they had said to the police. The meeting took an hour, and Donnie chain-smoked and drank three root beers. When they finished, Robin stood up and straightened her slacks.

"Now I have to go home and shower so I don't smell like I've been at a bar all night."

Donnie smirked. "Sorry. I smoke when I'm nervous."

Robin looked at him through the tops of her eyes for a moment. "Who are you fooling, Donnie?"

"Thanks, Robin. Sorry to get you out of bed. Tell Buster we said howdy."

"Don't worry about it, Donnie. That's why you pay me so damn much." She slung her purse over her shoulder and ran her hair back behind her ear. "You guys stay out of trouble, okay?"

"I'll keep an eye on him," Mike assured. Robin blew them a kiss as she left the building.

Mike leaned forward on the table and grabbed his smokes, then lit one as he pointed at Donnie. "You need her."

"You're damn right I do. I need all you people. I tell you, I don't what I would do without you all."

"She's so wicked, ain't she?" Mike said, leaning back and pointing with his thumb.

Donnie nodded. "Yeah, she's incredible."

After a few moments of silent smoking, Mike finally spoke again. "So tell me about Shanna."

"What do you want to know?"

"I want to know what everyone that works here is dying to know. What everyone asks me when you're not around, thinking I have some inkling of a clue."

"What's that?"

"Why her."

Donnie leaned back, shaking his head. "Everyone asks you about that?"

"Yup. Always. No one knows why you keep her around. They all assume it's for sex, and of course I dispel it because I know you. But I really don't know either."

"Mike, you know I'm not sleeping with her."

"No, I don't know why you keep her around."

"Well it's no big mystery. If any of you guys would have a conversation with her, you would understand. She's sharp as a whip, Mike. She knows shit that no one else thinks of."

"Donnie, she's hasn't even finished college."

Donnie stood up and made his way to the fridge. "Oh, don't start that shit with me, Mike. That's horseshit. You know as well as I do you don't get smart at college. You refine a skill you already possess. And I don't think a course in the world could give her an ounce more of common sense." He pulled a fresh root beer out. "Want one?" Mike nodded, Donnie tossed him one. "That's what she's got. She's got more of that than anyone else I interviewed for the position."

"But how does that mean experience? How does that mean she's qualified?"

"She acts as my common sense when I don't have any. Shit, look at me tonight. If you hadn't been there, I'd have got myself convicted on the spot."

"Your point. But she's so young," Mike emphasized with his hands.

"Yeah, but she's wise beyond her years. Mike," Donnie took a seat again, "you know I'm not stupid. Grant me that, at least." Mike nodded. "I knew it when I interviewed her. She's brilliant. Sometimes it's just the little shit I can't see 'cause my glasses are fogged. But most of the time it's just plain brilliance."

"Well she sure is something else to look at, I'll give you that."

"You don't think that's why I hired her."

"No, I don't. I know you better than to think you're that shallow. But I also know you're a man. And I know that having a foxy young girl living with you might just tempt you beyond your ability to resist."

"Pssshh. Don't even start, Mike. I've got plenty."

"Well if you say so, then cool. I'm just watching your back for you, Donnie."

"Well I'm not stupid. If something happens and I end up boinkin' her, I'll get rid of her."

"Get rid of her?" he said, pointing an imaginary gun to his head.

Donnie laughed.

Mike shook his head and stood up. "Well I better get home 'fore Lucy calls the cops on me."

"Night, Mike. And thanks for bailing my ass out tonight."

Mike turned and pointed at Donnie. "I'm glad I didn't have to bail you out tonight. You should be thanking Robin Banks."

Lights flickered within the house. Through the fogged glass of the front hall window, Donnie could tell the television was still on. As he made his way up the walkway he flicked his cigarette into the grass and pulled out his keys. He got to the front porch and stood next to the window, using the light to find the right one. *Nice of you to leave the porch light on for me.* Donnie rarely used the back garage door these days. Ever since he'd had the ten-car garage put in, he had come in through the front. He looked through the window, trying to make out shapes. Was Shanna still awake, or had she fallen asleep watching MTV? This was going to be an interesting week.

Finding the right key on his overstuffed key ring, he threw the lock and let himself into the cool air of the house. In fact, it was overly cool. It felt like about sixty degrees. He slung his keys onto the entry hall table and crept into the living room, being careful not to wake her if she had passed out. As he crossed the living room to turn off the television, he glanced back at the couch and the ruffled blankets to check on

Shanna. She wasn't there. The light in the kitchen was on though, so he headed that direction. The kitchen was empty as well. *What the hell?* As he went down the hall, he flicked on the light to have a look at the thermostat. He kicked it up to a more reasonable cool, then turned the light back off and finished the hallway. Shanna was surely in the restroom. But the light was off. *What the hell? Did she leave?* That was probably it. She's out with her friends. It's only three-thirty, after all. What the hell was he thinking? She'll probably be out 'til five o'clock.

Donnie pulled his clothes off and chunked them in the hamper inside his closet, then hopped in the shower to wash the day off. He didn't see Shanna walk into the bathroom and lean against the counter. Thus when he stepped out of the shower, instead of covering himself, he nearly had a heart attack.

"Holy God, you scared the shit out of me!"

"I'm sorry, Donnie, I thought you saw me."

"You wanna hand me that towel?" he said, pointing at the towel against which she was leaning. He caught her taking a peek as she reached back to grab it for him. "What exactly is it you're doing in here?" he said. He took the towel and began to dry his hair, completely immodest. She had already seen him now anyway. Not much point in trying to hide it now, he thought.

"Well I thought you might want to talk for a while before you hit the hay."

"Can't you see I'm naked?"

"I can see you're about as modest as you are white, Donnie. If I actually thought you cared, I would have knocked first."

Donnie stood staring at her. She was right. But there were certain points he had against her argument. There were a few people with whom he was modest, and whom he felt should never see him naked. Besides his mother, his secretary was one.

"Don't you think this is a conflict of interest, Shan?"

Shanna frowned for a second, then without an ounce of hesitation, whipped her shirt off. Barebreasted, clad in nothing but panties, she now stood there with her hands on the counter beside her. Her hair was pulled back in a ponytail, and she looked as though not only were she completely comfortable like this, but that she belonged like this. It was a perfectly natural and routine thing for her to be naked in front of her boss. And the first thing that cracked into Donnie's thought process was how quickly she would break his resolve. At this pace, he would be on her before they left the bathroom.

Donnie tried not to look. It wasn't working though. "Shanna? What are you doing?"

"You want me to put it back on?"

Now there's a question. *A beautiful young woman just waltzed in here and whipped her shirt off. Her tits are pointing at me like I've done something wrong. Do I want her to put her shirt back on?* Donnie sighed. "Yes, Shanna. I think you should."

"Well, I'm sorry, I thought you would be more comfortable with your nakedness if I joined you in it."

"Shanna, you just said you knew I didn't give a shit. You know I'm not modest."

"Well there you go! Then why should I be?"

"Shanna, I am modest with you. You walked in here without my knowing it. You can't blame me for being naked in my own bathroom." Donnie finished drying and wrapped the towel around his waist. Partly because that's where it went, but also to help hide his growing interest in Shanna's sudden state of toplessness.

"Why are you modest with me? Why am I any different than one of the boys?"

"Shanna, you work for me."

"Not any more. I just quit."

Donnie's white face got whiter. His mouth dropped open, and his eyes widened like saucers. "What? You're kidding me! You're going to terminate your employment so you can stand here naked with me?"

"If that's what it takes, yes."

"Oh my God. You seriously need to rethink your priorities, Shanna." Donnie exited the bathroom and sat down on the edge of the bed, facing the wall. He needed to think about his position on this. He knew he wouldn't ever sleep with her. But that was because she was his subordinate. He had never actually considered it, because that was all she ever was to him. But if she was going to quit, that would be a different story. Wouldn't it? He was rising quickly just thinking about it.

He sensed her come into the room, and stand at the foot of the bed. Then she spoke. "Donnie why are you afraid of me?"

"I'm not afraid of you Shanna. You're a little girl. You work for me. I know your parents."

"None of that matters." She rounded the bed and came to stand in front of him. "I'm old enough to make my own decisions. Do you not think I'm attractive?" She stepped closer to him gently and put her hands on his shoulders. Her chest was some twelve inches from his head, but he was not looking up. He was staring at the floor between his feet, breathing deeply.

"That's not it, Shanna. I think you're-"

She put her hand under his chin and tilted his face up. The light from the bathroom cast an evil shadow across her chest, and Donnie found himself mesmerized with the subtle hang of her breasts. And before he could finish his sentence, she was smothering him with the warm softness of them. They were larger than he had expected, and they surrounded his face. He instinctively turned his face to take in their fullness, their pleasure. And she just stood there. Her hands still on his shoulders, her legs perfect stakes between his knees, and her breasts in his face.

Donnie's heart raced like a stallion in the final lap. He closed his eyes and tried to block out the thoughts that wanted to barricade his progress. Her body was perfect. She had thick soft thighs, and wide hips that looked as though she spent hours on the treadmill. She had no cellulite on her body. Her breasts were the perfect size. They would be more than enough to hold onto while she straddled him. Her back was without a mark, smooth as a baby's cheeks. She was a poster advertisement for great sex. She would be perfect.

But she wouldn't be his executive assistant when he woke in the morning.

How hard would it be to find someone else? Someone who could tell him when he was running late for a meeting. Someone who could get into his head and tell him what he was thinking, and when he was wrong. Someone who was not *afraid* to tell him he was wrong, just because she worked for him. Someone who could keep him in line and out of trouble. His hands had slid up the backs of her legs, and now caressed the flesh of her rear. There would be nothing but absolute bliss, were he to sleep with her.

But she was his executive assistant.

He had many times dreamt of her, but his dreams were not of his own will. He couldn't control whom he dreamed about any more than he could control the winds or the rain. He had never consciously entertained any thoughts of sexuality with her. He had always maintained his professionalism with her, and to the point of looking away when she bent over. He had tried to be the perfect boss. Yet here she stood with her tits in his face, and he was kissing them. With his eyes closed.

"Nope. You'll be at work as usual Monday." He stood up and kissed her on the cheek, then went into the bathroom and tossed her shirt out at her before closing the door.

When Donnie came out of the bathroom wrapped in his towel, Shanna was lying on her stomach on the bed with her chin on her hands. Her feet were up in the air, and she was flipping through a magazine. This time though, she had her clothes on like a good girl. She was still sans the pants, but at least she had on underwear and a t-shirt.

"So you wanna tell me about your night? What did you guys go do?"

"Little nosey aren't you Shanna? You're just bold as all hell tonight!"

"So shoot me. I'm just wondering what kept you boys out so late tonight. I didn't think Mike still had it in him to be out this late anymore. Guys' night out or not."

"Well we didn't go out for fun. We had some business to take care of. I can't really tell you anything though. It's confidential."

"So was he there then?"

"Come again?" Donnie said, turning on her. He was digging in his dresser for some boxers and a shirt.

"I said 'was he there'. Bobby Keith. That's who you went to see, right?"

"Now how do you know that, Shanna?" He dropped his hands at his sides. Had she found out about the contract? He hadn't mentioned it to anyone but Mike and Callie. And Callie wouldn't associate with Shanna to begin with. Callie was polite in her evasions, but it was obvious she didn't take much to Shanna. So unless Mike had something going with Shanna…

"Donnie, you pay me to know things. Relax, I'm not going to tell anyone. I'm just wondering how it went."

Mike sure had been interested in what Donnie had going with Shanna earlier in the evening. Was his interest in their affairs due to jealousy? The feeling of intrusion on something? Surely Donnie would know if his best friend were poking his secretary. Besides, Mike wouldn't do that. "It didn't go well, Shanna. But I want you to tell me how you knew that."

"It only makes sense, Donnie. Are you going to trust me or am I going to have to tell you every little detail of how I come across things?"

Donnie stared at her for a moment. She had a way. Her way of avoiding the question by invoking the element of trust was starting to get at Donnie's nerves.

She was right though. He should trust her. *She knows things because I want her to. She knows things because that's what I hired her to do. She's just doing her job. She's – like she said – not going to tell anyone. She won't disclose anything dangerous. She's always been good at keeping the private things private.* He finally sighed and moved on.

"It went bad, Shanna. He was dead."

"He *was* dead?"

"Is."

"Oh my God! What happened?" Shanna sat up straight on the bed. Donnie couldn't help but notice the bounce of her breasts beneath the fabric of the shirt, and he doubted he would last the weekend with her if she didn't find a place and get the the hell out of the house.

He sighed again, trying to look away before she caught him, but failed. "I don't know what happened. But he was dead."

"You mean… You guys didn't kill him, right?"

"No. He was already dead. Dammit! Why the hell do people keep asking me that? You're the second person to ask me that tonight. My own employees! You should know me better than to think I'm a killer, Shanna!"

"Donnie, calm down. I don't think you are a killer. It just sounded like something happened while you were there. You didn't say he was already dead."

"Yes I did. I said, 'he was dead'. He'd been dead for a couple of weeks or so, I guess. I almost lost it when I walked in and smelled him."

"So what happened?" Shanna said, folding her hands in her lap.

"I told you I don't know what happened. He was just-"

"No. After you saw him."

"Well, I had to get out of the room quick. It was bad. And I fell in the kitchen or something. I don't remember. But there was a dog in there… Shanna it was bad. I can't…" Donnie turned his head and leaned back against the dresser. He felt his gorge rising, and had to think of something else quickly.

"That's okay. You don't have to talk about it."

"Thank you," he said with an overly fake smile.

"So what are you going to do?"

"I don't know. It doesn't really matter I guess. I'm not losing any money by taking up the crates at this point, so I just-"

"Crates? You mean the ones from Phoenix's company?"

Shit. He had slipped. She already knew more than she should. With him feeding her bits of the puzzle, he was effectively letting go his suspicions of her. If she brought it up, or he found something she was hiding, he could catch her on it. But if he was giving her the clues, it would be useless. If she was the suspect, he would never find out. Anything could easily be passed off as *"Hey, you told me that, Donnie!"*

"No. The two that got left behind," he said, trying to cover his tracks. Shanna nodded slowly, a look of perplexity painting her features. He doubted it had worked, and so took the easy alternative. "I really need to get to bed, Shanna. You gonna sleep in here?" he said. Shanna's eyes brightened.

"Sure."

"Fine. See you in the morning." He grabbed his pillow and walked out to the living room to crash on the couch.

| **CHAPTER** *eleven* |

Saturday morning, Donnie awakened to the smell and sound of bacon cooking. It had been a long time indeed since he had been awakened by cooking breakfast. He squinted and shielded his eyes against the sun that streamed through the window in the kitchen. Who the hell was cooking bacon? It didn't take him long to remember Shanna was company in his house. And as he recalled her being his guest, the memory of her standing nearly naked against him in the bedroom last night snapped into his mind. His heart skipped a beat as he remembered it. Politics, it seemed, had recently become his worst enemy. God, was it already Saturday? What had happened to the week?

He sat up and turned, dropping his feet onto the carpet, running his hand through his messy hair. He picked up his phone off the coffee table to see what time it was – the glare from the light in the kitchen was too much to read the clock on the mantle – and frowned when it started buzzing in his hand.

"Hello?"

"You're not up yet. You know you should be up, Donnie. In fact, you should be ready, and – well, in fact, well on your way to picking me up."

"What have I forgotten?"

Mike sighed on the other end of the conversation. "It's us against them, man. We gotta get moving!"

Donnie frowned, then scratched his forehead. It was too early for this shit. His heart was racing now. He had missed an important appointment. But wait… Wouldn't Shanna have reminded him if he had an appointment on Saturday morning? She would have, unless… Unless she didn't know about it. Or unless it was a basketball game.

"You there?"

"Yes, I'm here. Are you talking about a damn basketball game Mike?"

"Hello? Yes! It's us against fuel today, what the hell is wrong with you?"

"Oh my God!" Donnie said, standing up. Shanna heard him from the kitchen, and came around the corner to check on him.

"Donnie, are you okay?" she said.

"You got me all worried and shit about a basketball game?" he whined. Shanna turned and disappeared back into the kitchen.

"You're startin' to worry me man. You okay?"

"Yeah. I thought I had missed an important appointment or something. Don't do that shit to me Mike!"

Donnie snapped the phone closed and slid it back onto the table, then made his way down the hall to get ready for the day.

Shanna pulled out of the driveway. She hung up her cell phone and let it drop onto her lap, grabbing the wheel just in time to swerve, narrowly missing the chain-driven iron gate. She had an egg sandwich in one hand, squished against the steering wheel, and was shifting gears with the other. She had fed Donnie, thinking he would love her for it. She was under the impression he never had breakfast cooked for him. In truth, he rarely did. But she thought it would make a bigger impression on him than it did. Like maybe he would actually thank her or something. After the rejection he had handed her last night, she would be happy with a simple thank you. He had read the newspaper through breakfast though, and set his dishes in the sink, speaking only about the basketball game he was about to go play. He didn't say word one about how great the breakfast was. *That's the last time I cook for his ass. F him.*

She stopped at the end of the drive and turned onto the main road when her phone rang again. She laid the egg sandwich on the passenger seat (it was leather) and picked the phone up, looking at the screen to see who was calling her. There was no name – just a number she didn't recognize. Though why she ever looked to see who was calling was beyond even her. She always answered it, no matter the caller. She hit the send button to accept the call, and looked up just in time to see a telephone pole kiss her bumper. It ran down the entire length of the right side of the car, knocking off the side mirror and several layers of paint before she corrected and got back onto the paved part.

"Wow. Hello?"

"Hey Julia, how's it going?"

"Julia? I'm sorry. Who is this?"

"Burt. This is Julia, right?"

"No, you have the wrong number."

"Oh, shit. Sorry." Click.

Shanna dropped the phone on her lap again and cursed herself. *I banged up my car for a wrong number? For Burt? F Burt!* Now she would have to be without her car for a week while it was repaired. She could drop it off Monday, but today, she was dedicated to finding an apartment. Had Donnie conceded to his desires the night previous, she might have found herself staying there for longer than just the weekend. Alas, he had been the good boss he always had been. But what the hell, it was worth a shot. She had to try, lest they never discover their true feelings for one another. *Life is about being bold in the right places! Being right at the right time.* And watching the Goddamn road. Shanna had wrecked her car thrice. None of them had been anything more than fender-benders. Nothing that would take the car out of commission, just small stuff that tore up a little paint and plastic. This was the fourth time she would have to take it in for repairs because of stupid people calling at the wrong time.

She came to a stop at the intersection of Broadway (Donnie's street) and Throckmorton Parkway. A thought struck her while she sat at the intersection: the Grand Venetian stood just three blocks down Throckmorton on the right. The most luxurious apartments in the city, albeit the most compact for the money. She could get an apartment at the Grand Venetian and live less than five minutes from her beloved boss. She turned right and pulled into the parking lot in front of the leasing office and she laughed as the old adage ran through her head, from a first person perspective: *If I lived here, I would already be home.*

Monday was uncomfortable, for nearly all parties involved. It was the Feb Nine staging meeting, and everyone was supposed to be at his best. At least everyone was supposed to appear to be at his or her best. Being an exciting time for the company, the management were always looking for the team players. Not being excited was the best way to stick out like a sore thumb, and company meetings were the best place to be spotted. The staging meeting was to cover any last requests and details about the Feb Nine mission to Mars. Barring any unforeseen obstacles, it would be the last meeting about the mission before it happened.

Donnie was uncomfortable for obvious reasons. He was a little ashamed for having had Shanna even stay a single night at his house, and was hopeful that no one would discover that was where she had been. Having her put her tits in his face didn't help. It made him feel guilty. On top of this was the visit he and Mike had paid to Robert Keith. Seeing his body in that condition made Donnie's stomach sour, and every time he thought about it, he felt nauseous. On their way into the building that morning, Donnie and Mike had been stopped by Jonathan Rodgers, that he might inquire how the visit went. He was the only one who had known about their intention, as Mike had thought it best to at least let someone know where they were.

Donnie had stopped and held his breath, and was clearly about to be sick thinking about it. Mike had come to his rescue and answered for him, putting his hand in front of Donnie's stomach as if to hold him back. "Uh, he was dead, Jonathan. It's not good. He's been in there for almost a month."

"What? Dead? What the hell happened?" Jonathan asked.

"We don't know. He had a dog in there with him. The dog – well, he hadn't been fed for some weeks, so he – look, can we talk about this later?"

"What? The dog started eating--"

"Jonathan! Later."

Donnie's face had gone white, and Mike had been afraid he was going to get sick. Mike had pulled him into the men's room and gotten him some water. Now here he sat in the meeting feeling sour all over. He had almost had an affair with his assistant, and he had seen one of his former employees in a gruesome state all in the span of a few hours. His stomach was doing rolls.

Shanna was her usual self, but seemed to be fidgeting more than normal, constantly doodling and darting her eyes around the room. She was sitting beside Donnie, as per the usual seating arrangement, accommodating departmental authority, and she was making him nervous and sick with every scrawl of her ballpoint pen. She had found an apartment – incidentally, the first one she had walked into Saturday – and had moved in by late Saturday afternoon. She was now a tenant of the Grand Venetian.

Mike was leaning back, slouched in the high-back leather chair, hands crossed on his stomach, and staring at the table. He seemed to be off in another world, as were most of the employees in the room. It seemed the spirit of the Oliver Company had been transported to another place, and the empty shells of its people were present here in this meeting – absent of mind and care.

Callie Simmons leaned her head on her hand, staring at the tablet on which she was writing. She clearly didn't want to be there any more than the rest of them did. Something was on her mind, and it was probably evident through the passage of her pen onto that tablet. Her meeting with Walter had been grand. She had enjoyed the couple of hours they got to spend together, but at that moment she had realized he had lied to her, Callie's heart had sunk. She knew it was business – it was the nature of the game. Especially when one works for Royal Research Corporation. Having worked there herself, she knew firsthand that most of what she was involved in was secret. And now, being an ex-employee, Walter could not technically put the same confidence in her. Technically. But they were best friends. She felt strangely betrayed and let down by the fact that he had maintained his loyalty to the company and the promise he had made to them, over her. Disappointed, she had been less than her chirpy self for the remainder of the evening with him. She thought he had noticed her disappointment, but he had not said anything about it, which made her feel even worse. It was like they were both playing a game of Let's Not Say Anything About the Red X on Callie's Forehead. He wouldn't even acknowledge that he had hurt her feelings, yet he knew he had hurt them, and knew all he needed to do to mend the situation was to apologize. "Sorry, but I just can't tell you, Cal." That would have been fine. It was like he wanted to one-up her on knowing something, and felt good about doing it.

Callie realized she was probably taking it a little far, but felt no better for it. And when they called her name in the meeting she didn't even hear it. Donnie looked up and noticed her attached to the notepad, startled when they called her again and she came to. He sighed, knowing something must truly be wrong if Callie Simmons was down about something. She was always happy and bouncy in the presence of others. It was so seldom otherwise that it was closer to being never. And Donnie thought of her in this instant like a weather rock: if she's scared, there's something to run from; if she's sad, there's something to cry about; if she's not here, there's somewhere else to be. And what could be more important than the Feb Nine staging meeting?

Even Samson seemed a little quieter than usual. He looked at the people when they spoke, but didn't smile or nod his head or laugh, or display any emotions at all. It was as if he was there because he had to be, and for no other reason, and he had left his mind in his office down the hall.

With the Feb Nine mission still several months out, there was still time to reconfigure details that needed attention. There would be plenty of time to prepare, and indeed, most of the preparation was done. The entire cargo package was assembled and waiting on the launch deck at Alpha – the International Space Station. All the crew needed to do was take off as usual in the Atlas, dock with the trailer, and pull out headed for the Red Planet. Nothing needed be done now but the paperwork and the fueling.

Or so they thought. It was after the staging meeting that Donnie and Shanna took a stroll through the administrative offices of the complex. They stopped into a break room so Donnie could get some coffee. He filled a Styrofoam cup with dark liquid and put it to his nose. "Good God, that shit stinks," he cried.

Shanna laughed out loud. A phone started ringing somewhere down the hall.

Donnie sniffed at the coffee again, then splashed it out in the sink. "You need to come over here and teach these people how to make a pot of java, Shan." The phone continued to ring. It was the annoying sound of a cell phone playing bad MIDI music.

"Yeah, well that's probably been sitting there all day."

"That means not enough pe- what the hell, will someone please shut that damn phone off?" Donnie said. He threw his foam cup in the sink and took off down the hall. The ringing got louder as he approached an office. Shanna was following closely behind him, chattering on about the coffee and people's drinking habits.

Upon entering the office, he swung around the desk and found a fat leather business bag, stuffed to the gills with papers and junk. Donnie plunged his hand down into the side pocket and pulled out the squawking cell phone. The rubber protective case around the phone pulled with it a sheaf of papers. Donnie held the off button as he rolled his eyes at Shanna.

"Some people need…" but he trailed off as he looked back down at the papers. It was the contract from ETIS. Donnie quickly looked up at the name placard affixed to the oak door. It read PAUL REZNOR in big bold letters.

*   *   *

"Who else we got?" Donnie said. His hands formed a steeple beneath his chin. He was staring at the screen saver on his monitor. Mike sat in the chair across the desk from him, and Shanna sat next to Mike, taking notes.

Mike rubbed his forehead and sighed. "Well, we could get Brian Bradley."

Donnie snorted. "I don't think I could stand to be around him for that long. He's a short-trip guy."

Mike nodded approvingly. "Yeah, there will be some relaxation time, now that you've cleared that quagmire you've been wading in for the last few months."

Shanna smiled. "Are you finally a little more comfortable with the company, Donnie?"

Donnie looked at her seriously. "You know, Shanna, you had me worried for a while. But yes, I think everything is kosher now." He leaned back and put his hands behind his head. "It just really, really hurts to lose someone like Paul."

"He's been here ten years," Mike said. "I guess any of the systems guys would be all right." He was rubbing the stubble on his chin.

"Who all is there?" Shanna said. She clicked her pen open in preparation.

"Well let's see, there's Felix Cheng, Randy Nowack…" Mike said.

"Brandy LaMerre," Donnie added.

"Nah, she ain't been here long enough."

Donnie shrugged. "Chris Taylor, Bill Tremonti," he said, pulling back fingers as he listed them. Shanna was writing them all down. "Hank McManus…"

"Miles Harrington, Charlie Kennedy…" Mike added.

"Who are we missing? That's eight, right?" Shanna said.

"Yeah, plus Bradley equals nine," said Donnie.

Shanna jotted his name down, then crossed through it. "Okay, so Brian Bradley is out, Brandy is out. Who else? You've got Felix, Randy, Chris, Bill, Hank, Miles and Charlie."

Mike and Donnie met eyes. Then simultaneously, they both said, "Charlie Kennedy."

Donnie nodded. Shanna circled his name. "Yeah, that will work, let's call him in here." Donnie said.

"We'll need to be thinking about a promotion now to fill Paul's shoes too," Mike added.

Donnie nodded again. "You sure you don't wanna do it?"

"No, I'll take my fucking from the wife, thank you."

With five months left, and Charlie Kennedy on the roster for Feb Nine, everything was in place. At least Donnie was beginning to feel like it was. And so it was that the next five months were absolutely uneventful. Donnie and Mike had found the crates with ETIS stenciled on the sides of them, and had sent them back to Pablo Phoenix. Donnie had spared Paul Reznor the record by not getting the police involved, but had required that he resign immediately and with full confidence that there was nothing else on the ship. While Paul had never openly admitted to the deal with Phoenix, he came to agree on the arrangement fairly quickly. He would at least still have his pension plan.

The suspicions of treason and dishonesty had finally begun to fade for Donnie, and he was regaining a positive outlook for the company and the mission. Everything was lining up the way it was supposed to. Until the final physicals that came on January 16. It was a sudden surprise to Kennedy to learn that he had stomach cancer. And Donnie was back to the drawing board to find his replacement. After a quick meeting with Mike, they had both agreed that Brian Bradley was the man for the job. He had been with the company a long time, and had been on many satellite deployment missions with Donnie.

The meeting between Brian and Donnie had been brief and heated. With just a few weeks before launch, Donnie wasn't up for a bunch of negotiating. It was time to lay down the law and get someone's ass on that shuttle. But Brian seemed fidgety and shifty, and was constantly looking about the room, as if for a means of escape. Donnie had asked him if he was okay, and he had nodded. But Donnie doubted the truth in that nod. Donnie stood up and closed the door, then sat on the desk just in front of Brian.

"Donnie, I don't think I can do it. I mean – it's still a few weeks away, but I just don't think it's in me."

"What do you mean not in you? What the hell do you want me to do? You're out last hope! We have to have a systems officer on board!"

Brian was shaking his head. "I know. I'm sorry. I just – I've been thinking about my family lately, and – well, I just don't think I can do it."

"What, are you scared?"

"Yeah, I guess."

"Dammit, Brian, don't do this to me. Not now. I mean, hell – if anyone knows how safe that ship is, it would be you! You're the one that keeps her tip-top!"

Brian looked up at Donnie, then looked away quickly.

"Right?"

"Yeah. You're right," Brian said. He was still looking away.

"Brian, you have to be on that ship. I can't do it without you. And it's too late for me to find someone else. We've gone through two others already. And you have tenure."

"I just don't-"

"Brian, I need you," Donnie said. He put his hand on Brian's shoulder. "I need you. You're the man." Brian looked up at Donnie again and sighed. And before he had a chance to answer, Donnie ended the meeting. "So go out there and pump yourself up. Do whatever it is you need to do to be ready. You want to take a week off?"

Brian sighed, then nodded slowly. "Yeah, I guess that would be okay."

"Good. I'll get it done. You get on out of here. Be back in a week. That leaves you a week and..." Donnie leaned back and turned to look at the calendar on his desk. "Well almost a week and a half before quarantine. That's plenty of time for finals, right?"

"Yeah. That should be plenty."

"All right. Enjoy your time off. Go be with your family."

Brian sighed again. "Okay, Donnie. I have some stuff I need to get wrapped up before I leave, but I'll leave after that."

"Whatever you need," Donnie said, clapping his hands together. he had won. he had talked Brian into joining the mission. He hoped. Now if he just didn't back out last minute, everything might work out. Brian stood and made his way to the door, then opened it.

"All right, I'll see you in a week." Then he left Donnie's office. That was at a quarter to ten a.m. Brian Bradley didn't leave the office until after midnight that day.

"They want me on the shuttle."

"Well that's a given."

"I thought my work was done here. I didn't think I needed to be on the mission."

"That's not a question. You will be on that trip. End of discussion."

"But I thought the point was to dis-"

"The point is to do what it takes to get the job done. You're covered."

Sigh. "Thanks for the support."

"Don't mention it."

| CHAPTER *twelve* |

It was raining – it had been for the last ten hours straight – and it showed no signs of relenting. The wind was blowing hard and furious, and it was colder than it had been in several years. For late January, it almost seemed appropriate, but was rare nonetheless in Arizona. The Dennehotso weather station had missed this one entirely. The forecast at the beginning of the week had called for clear skies for the next two weeks. Having them miss a rainstorm like this put Donnie's heart in his stomach. He was getting critically close to the day of importance, and needed things to be going a little more right than they seemed to be going. His faith in the weather was slipping, as was his grip on the positive attitude he had possessed for so long about the Feb Nine mission. They were exactly two weeks out now, and he was of the opinion that things should be lining up like a well oiled machine by now. He could hear the gears of the mission turning, and they were most definitely squeaking.

The long phone conversations with Julia Callahan had become more and more frequent as the critical day approached. He was constantly asking her opinions on things, and pinging ideas off of her. She had always been happy to comply, saying she was intrigued by the thinking behind some of his ideas. They discussed things that were too far out even for science fiction books, wildly imaginative, yet somehow practical. Donnie and Julia ran on the same wavelength, and seemed to be able to complete each other's sentences – read each other's minds.

Donnie found these long conversations put his mind at ease about the trip. Callie had told him he might be trying to slip off of reality a bit to avoid some of the stresses of the mission. he had blown it off, but was now of a mind to give it more and more consideration. If nothing else, it had at least primed his brain and gotten him thinking of new and different things. And it made for excellent conversation between the two space freaks.

One night, Donnie got drunk on whiskey and called Julia as part of what was becoming a nightly routine. Only he hit the wrong speed dial button, so it wasn't Julia who had answered. Being two o'clock in the morning wasn't a problem for Julia, as she and Donnie were both night owls. Callie adored her precious sleep, and though it took Donnie a few moments to realize it wasn't Julia he was talking to that night, he had noticed how thick her voice had sounded with slumber.

The next morning, he walked into his living room and saw the two whiskey bottles standing on his coffee table. One was empty, and the other was halfway there. Before that night previous, he had never had more than a couple of shots in one sitting, and now he had drained an entire bottle in less than twelve hours.

At half past one, Donnie called Callie on her mobile phone. He felt stupid and childish having called her in the middle of the night, babbling like a drunken fool. She answered on the first ring. "Hey, it's Donnie. I wanna take you to lunch."

"Okay, sounds good. I'm actually in my car. I was just about to pull out of the driveway to go get something to eat."

"Excellent," Donnie said.

"You want me to meet you somewhere?"

"No, just wait there, I'll pick you up."

Donnie grabbed his shades and hit the garage. He picked the most assembled Wrangler and opened the overhead door behind it.

Callie was standing on her driveway under an umbrella when Donnie pulled up ten minutes later. She was on the phone with someone. She climbed in and shook the umbrella, then slammed the door. When she leaned over to hug him, her already dangerously short dress hiked way up, showing him a lot more Callie-thigh than he had expected to see. She had a couple of the best legs he had ever seen. Donnie shook his head blinking, then watched as she fumbled with a stretch hair-tie with her free hand. He reached over and held her phone for her so she could tie her hair back into a tight ponytail. When she finished, she took the phone back from him and gave him a thumbs up to signal her ready. And off they went.

El Queso Grande – Callie's favorite Mexican restaurant – was packed. There was a fifteen-minute wait for a table, but neither of them minded, especially

Callie, who would give her sight for one of their home-cooked Mexican dishes. As they waiting on the wooden bench, Donnie leaned back and lit a cigarette. "So what's with the dress, Cal?"

"What do you mean? Do you not like it?"

"Love it. Just not used to seeing you in stuff that short."

"Yeah, it takes a lot of courage for me to wear it. I have two others that are about this short. I almost never wear any of them. I just felt daring today, I guess."

"Well you look really nice."

"Thank you, Donnie," she said and smiled.

"I wanted to say sorry for calling you in my drunken stupor last night. I don't know what the hell got into me. I guess the stress of the mission is starting to break me."

"Maybe you shouldn't go, Donnie."

"Ha!" Donnie coughed on his smoke. "No, not a chance. No way. I'm going. I'll be okay as soon as we leave the planet. It's just the nervousness of the takeoff, I guess. Since this is the most important mission in the history of – well, of ever."

Callie nodded, looking around at the other patrons. Quite a few of them were staring at her, or – more specifically – her legs. She pulled the hem of her dress down as far as she could, and put her purse on her lap. The two huge wooden doors that led inside blew open and a family of sixteen came out laughing and shouting. Callie stared bemusedly at the loud family, then turned back to Donnie.

"Well it's no big deal. I'm just glad you weren't calling me to bail you out of jail."

"Ha. No, I don't think that will happen again." He took a long drag from his smoke. "I think I've finally outgrown that whole drinking and driving gig."

Callie made a face that said 'oh-my-god' and dug in her purse for a mint. "I'm extremely glad you've kicked that one." She tilted her head and looked at him almost squinting. "You know what I'm wondering now, though?"

Donnie looked up, then shook his head slowly.

"What are you gonna do about that?" she said, pointing at his cigarette.

Donnie looked back down at the smoldering cigarette, then shook his head.

"It's a little late to start a smoking cessation class now, I guess," Callie said. "How long have you been smoking, Donnie?"

"Hell I don't know. Fifteen years? Something like that."

"Oliver, party of two," the intercom rattled. They stood up and walked into the cool restaurant, leaving the rain and wind outside, along with their previous conversation. That was the last anyone spoke of the smoking. It was true, Donnie would have to quit smoking before they left for Mars. He imagined he would be buying a whole case of nicotine patches, as most of his crew were smokers. There wasn't much other choice, he realized. It dawned on him again how important Callie and Shanna really were to him. They were always thinking where he wasn't. Callie had rescued him more times than he could count, and Shanna had saved him from stupidity on more than one occasion. He shook his head as they walked into the restaurant and followed the hostess to their table. As they sat down, he had a sudden precognitive vision of everyone onboard the shuttle halfway to Mars, and bearing down to blows because everyone was stressed out over not being able to smoke for the last month.

During the lunch, they spoke a lot, covering a lot of ground they hadn't covered in quite a long time. He missed the time he used to get to spend with Callie, and found himself wanting the lunch date to stretch well into dinner and beyond, just so they could catch up.

Was he perhaps a little jealous of Walter now? He wondered as he stared at her, watching her eat her enchiladas. Her big brown eyes darted from her plate to Donnie, to the people at the bar, and he had to take a deep breath to keep from saying something stupid. He had to remind himself that if it were going to happen with Callie, it would have happened many years ago.

The other side of the argument nagged him as well, though. He was running out of time before the mission. If anything were going to happen with anyone, he would have to get on the ball pretty quickly. There were two weeks left until February ninth, but only one with which he could do anything. For the last seven days the Atlas crew would be in quarantine, separated from society by steel walls. There were booths much like those in prisons where loved ones could come visit, but they would be speaking through telephones and looking through two-inch thick glass. Quarantine was hard time, and it was effectively just like the first week of the trip. They would begin on Earth what was inevitable in space: complete and total confinement.

Chewing the sizzling beef of his fajitas, Donnie finally realized his only problem with women. He was always only too late. He waited too long, and they always became friends with him, smothering any chance for romance – at least by their own rules of engagement. Donnie Oliver was always just a little too late.

| CHAPTER *thirteen* |
loading

The concrete floors of the warehouse were perilous to anyone not on the same schedule as the traffic they accommodated. It was like the roundabout in a Paris intersection: people coming from every which way, heading every other which way in complete chaos – but none of them hitting each other – like they were on tracks and timetables. It was a constant roar with all the shouting and footfalls and machinery and radios crackling and telephones ringing. The ambient temperature – despite the twelve industrial-sized A/C units running full time – was almost ninety degrees. Ties were loosened, as well as a few blouses – though no one seemed to care, or even to notice for that matter. Cell phones were chirping and people would stop in mid-step to push it tightly to one ear while covering the other with a hand full of papers or a clipboard. Small meetings were taking place all about, their members standing about in rough circles holding coffee cups and laughing, shouting back and forth, smoking cigarettes and pointing at certain other groups in the warehouse – each one with its own important mission. A long red carpet had been laid out, stretching from the Feb Nine rack on the west wall to the Mission Staging area to the east of the shuttle, which sat perched on its gear in the middle of all the chaos. The carpet marked the direction to the proper rack, as it was easy to get turned around amidst all the hubbub. The shuttle itself was on a rotating platform that accommodated different directions of entry for different equipment, saving the crane from having to move all about the warehouse. In this manner, the crane could quickly and efficiently load equipment into the open bay of the shuttle without having to maneuver between crowds and work its way around other equipment and crates. The path the crane followed was gated off with short steel rails painted yellow, and as long as everyone stayed out of that path, they would be safe. Thaddeus Cloys sat in the control console, swiftly moving the crane back and forth loading the shuttle with supplies and perishables from the backs of flatbed trailers parked in the north bays. Thad had his headset on for communicating with the load crew, but wore a headset over the top of that small earphone that blasted his music as he worked. He could be seen in the small control box bobbing his head to the beat of his music.

The shutters in the roof of the warehouse were louvered; at the moment they were vertical, allowing the hot air to escape into the cool desert morning beyond the warehouse roof. In one corner of the room, a welding crew was prepping the hitch assembly that would pull the trailer behind the shuttle. The trailer was already completely loaded and waiting for the shuttle at the Alpha Space Station. Upon docking with ISS, the shuttle crew would remove the hitch assembly from the bay and connect it to the back of the ship, as well as to the front of the trailer. With no drag or gravity, the weight of the trailer was meaningless, and using the antimatter drive, there would be very little difference in speed. Motorized dollies and carts wheeled about the warehouse under the control of contract workers brought in specifically to load the shuttle. Announcements were sporadically made over the warehouse intercom, and at the appropriate times for specific groups and individuals, they'd look up and listen. Each message began with a color code. If a message began with 'Orange Team', the load masters would take note of the message, and so on.

Standing on the floor, one couldn't see past the people in his immediate vicinity, and everything looked hopelessly out of control. But from the platforms around the upper office deck, it was a different kind of madness. It was a beautifully chaotic scene, if one actually had time to stop a while and watch. Everything and everyone was moving quickly and loudly, shouting commands and passing off papers and small boxes of equipment to others they passed. But it all happened with such precision – such machined perfection – that it was hard to believe it wasn't rehearsed. In a way, of course, it was. But each mission was completely different and unique and apart from every other mission. Each one was a stepping-stone and a learning experience for the next. The experience shone through in the fluid movements of the collective group on the floor below. Donnie stood with his hands on the rail looking down at the beautiful madness twenty feet below. He loved the way they all came together and worked so well under such great pressure. Mike Thurman stood beside him, one hand in his pocket, the other gripping a tin cup of coffee.

"My, my," he said, taking a sip of the steaming brew.

"You ready for this shit, Mike?"

Mike looked at Donnie with smiling brown eyes. "You're damn right, I am!"

"Great Greece, we're going to Mars!" Donnie said, grabbing Mike by one shoulder. "Can you believe this shit?"

Mike shook his head. "Not yet. I won't really believe it 'til I'm looking back at Earth through the back window."

"There is no back window, Mike. You'll have to use the side mirrors." They both broke out in easy laughter.

As Donnie and Mike were making their way down the grated metal stairs, Shanna came rushing up with a hand full of documents, waving like a madwoman. "Donnie, quick-quick-quick, I need you to sign this stuff real quick!"

They both stopped and waited as she ran up the last fifteen or so stairs to meet them. Mike turned away, rubbing his forehead. Donnie stared thoughtfully.

"What the hell is it?" Donnie said.

She now came to rest, panting on the step right below Mike and him.

"Some of them are release forms for the AccuWeather equipment, and the rest is insurance shit." Donnie winced at her use of the word. It was rare. "Quickly, please! AccuWeather is here right now, and they're about to leave."

Donnie looked up across the warehouse and spotted the group. They were the ones in jackets and ties. "Uh huh," he said, staring at them. "Those dicks had four months to get that shit to me, and they wait 'til the week before launch." He turned around and walked back up the stairs, never taking his eyes off the suits. Likewise, they were looking back at him, talking and smiling as if they didn't notice he was staring a hole through them collectively. "Bring it in here," he said, pushing open an office door.

He stopped short in the doorway, noticing the office was occupied. Liz Grammatica was on the phone, but looked up and waved him in quietly. Donnie and Shanna squeezed into the office while Mike waited outside. Donnie sat across the desk from Liz, scooting up and dropping the papers onto it. He made a writing gesture in the air, and Liz handed him a pen.

Fifteen minutes later, the documents were all signed and they quietly made exodus from Liz's office. Donnie would later recall that little signing session, and wonder why the hell he didn't read any of what he signed. He had made bad habits over the last couple of years. His implicit trust for Shanna had caused him to stop reading what she told him he was signing. And being in Liz's office while she was on the phone had prevented him from speaking out loud to Shanna in inquiry. He was rude enough to barge into someone's office and steal her desk and pen while she was on a potentially confidential phone call. But he was polite enough not to talk while doing it.

As they made their way down the stairs, Donnie found himself sweating. "Whew." He wiped his forehead with his sleeve. "You tell your parents bye, Shanna?"

"What do you think?" she said, making a sour face over her shoulder at Donnie.

"Well I would like to think you did. I know it's been a while since you talked to them."

Shanna turned around on the stair on which she had suddenly come to a stop. "Did you call your parents, Donnie?"

He smirked at her. "What do you think?"

"All right kids, looks like we got just enough time for some round ball 'fore it starts getting hot out there. You up for it?"

Donnie turned to look at Mike. "You're serious."

"Damn right I'm serious! We're leaving for another *planet* in two weeks! I may never get to shoot hoop again!"

Shanna was frowning. "Round ball? You guys actually call it *round* ball? Like there's any other kind of ball?"

"Well sure! What if it's got no air in it? Guess it would be a flat ball then, wouldn't it?" Mike smiled.

Donnie added, "And, uh – a football's nowhere *near* round!" He grinned.

Shanna didn't grin back. "You guys are retarded." She turned and walked off, disappearing quickly into the crowd.

Mike looked at Donnie. Donnie shrugged. "Think we can sneak the boys out for a quick match?" said Mike.

Donnie nodded. "I think we can manage. Get someone to fill the crane for Thad."

| **CHAPTER** *fourteen* |

outbound

At seven o'clock tomorrow morning, the scheduled quarantine lockdown would begin. It was coming up on seven p.m. and everyone was still partying, and still drinking. They would enjoy and make up for in their last night what they would be missing in their last week on Earth – and indeed, for the next eighteen months. Donnie's house was rocking, and had been since all essential personnel had been cleared to leave at three that afternoon. The loaders and systems guys had stayed on, having still had several large pieces of equipment to load, and several more tests to run. Presumably, they were done by now, but there was no way to tell without calling and checking up, which no one at the party wanted to do. It had been planned as long as the trip itself had, and everyone who was anyone was there. Even Samson Oliver had missed his bedtime to party up with his brother before seeing him off. The AnyVite Shanna had prepared boasted in large red letters "OUTBOUND PARTY – ALL OLIVERIANS BE THERE!" It wasn't necessary to note the location, as everyone automatically knew it would be Donnie's house. He was the only one with a sport court and an Olympic-sized swimming pool. He had given Shanna charge of arranging the party, and with the help of her friend Delilah, she had spent almost ten thousand dollars preparing for it.

Fifteen kegs were present, mostly Shiner Bock and Pirate Flag, and five of them were already floated. Donnie had also told Shanna to make sure there was plenty of Corona. She had brought in ten cases of it. Nearly three hundred people had shown up for the party – and that didn't include the staff they had hired to cater and serve drinks, and the DJ. Donnie had a state-of-the-art entertainment system in his living room, which played through speakers in every room in the house. Each room had a slide-switch embedded just beside the light switch which controlled the volume for that room's speakers, and could turn them off. That stereo was on, and the 300-CD changer was set to random. The DJ handled the backyard around the pool where he spun everything from dance to jazz – but nothing slow. He was given that specific order. "We're leaving for preflight lockdown tomorrow morning. I don't want any sad shit played to slow us down. Oh, and positively no Bette Midler. I don't need that to be the last music I hear on Earth."

Elrod's Barbecue handled the catering. There were three long tables set up by the pool filled with barbecue and potato salad and bread and beans. They had been full only an hour ago, but were now beginning to wear thin. Everyone had torn it up, then come back for seconds and thirds. The food was good, the beer was cold and the music was loud. The air was cool, but nice, and the pool water was pleasant. During the summers, Donnie kept it refrigerated to somewhere in the mid-eighties. The trees that outlined the backyard, which was about three acres in size not counting the sport court, formed a substantial sound barrier, as well as a fence. The loud music might have been an issue if the neighbors weren't at the party, which they all were. Shanna had even gone so far as to hire five ladies to look after any and all children who somehow ended up at the party. Most of them were in the den in the front of the house, where they had 350 square feet to crawl around and plenty of television to watch. She had asked Delilah stop by the video trading store and pick up every Disney title she could find on DVD. A large cardboard box now sat in the front room, filled with just about every title.

The large banner stretched across the back patio overhang read "ONE GIANT LEAP FOR MAN" and below that, "BEST WISHES ATLAS CREW!" Beneath it stood a podium, upon which sat an open guest book. Delilah had been directing traffic to it all night, and was pretty sure she had gotten everyone to sign. The front of the green leather-bound volume was engraved with silver words that read

ATLAS to MARS
February 9, 2015
The Oliver Company

-

Outbound Party Guests

That alone had cost three hundred dollars. Shanna considered the little things to be the most important when it came to big stuff like Mars trips. "Every angle must be covered!" she had told Donnie when she was bragging about how great the party was going to be. A professional photographer was walking around snapping pictures of the crowd and couples all night, for an exclusive album to be labeled in much the same way as the guest book. Everything was covered – from the food to the fresh towels to the valet service, and beyond. There was even a shuttle that would pick up the out-of-towners from the Marriott (of which Donnie had rented the entire ninth floor) and take them back when they were ready to leave. He wanted everyone to be there, but didn't want anyone to have to resort to driving away drunk.

The sun was setting behind the mountains, and the globe lights around the pool had clicked on just a few minutes before. As Donnie stood on the deck looking out over the pool, he smiled and nodded to himself. It was an exquisite success. Steam and laughter rose from the pool as a group of probably very inebriated people played water volleyball. There was a lot of scoring going on. He put his cigarette to his lips.

"Really great party, man," Mike said as he walked up to join Donnie.

Donnie nodded. "Looks like it all worked out."

Mike handed Donnie a fresh bottle of Corona, then pulled a smoke from his shirt pocket. "Not real, man. Just not real."

"What's that?"

"Leaving the planet in one week. It's just so far out."

"I hear you, brother. That's been kicking my ass for the last several hours too. Well, the last several months really. But here we are now, seven days out, and I'm just – well, I'm floored."

Mike nodded his agreement. "How about a toast?" He raised his bottle, and Donnie raised his to meet it. "To lifelong friends, and getting all the way the hell off the planet with 'em."

"Hear, hear." They clinked and drinked.

And like clockwork, Shanna came swishing up in her bikini, dripping like a wet dog, and dragging some other girl behind her. "I've been looking for you guys all over the place!"

"Looks like you've been looking in the pool," Mike said, taking a drag from his cigarette.

"Donnie," Shanna said, ignoring Mike's comment, "I want to introduce you to my friend. This is Delilah. Delilah, this is Donnie."

"Ah, you're the young lady that helped Shanna arrange the party, aren't you?"

"That's me. Glad to finally meet you, Donnie."

"The pleasure is mine. This is Mike Thurman, my senior engineer, and go-to-guy."

"Yes, I've met Mike," she said, but shook his hand anyway.

Donnie had to keep talking in order to keep his jaw from dropping too noticeably. He hoped it didn't shine through in his words. "So what do you do, Delilah?"

"I work in retail, actually."

"Actually?" Donnie said.

"Actually, Mike, can I talk to you for a moment?" Shanna butted in, then looped her arm through Mike's elbow, effectively removing all audience from Donnie and his new love. Mike bowed out and gave Donnie a small salute.

"What kind of retail?"

"I sell cameras."

Donnie nodded. "That's pretty cool." He took a drag of his cigarette, then washed it back with a long pull from his bottle. "You know why we're throwing this party don't you?"

Delilah laughed heartily. "Yes. Shanna has told me all about it. I helped her plan it, remember?"

"Yeah, that's right." He paused for a moment, looking out over the pool, then said, "I was just-"

"Hoping to find someone to score with before you left for Mars?"

Donnie's heart nearly stopped in his chest. Had it been that obvious? He didn't think so. "Well that wouldn't be such a bad bon voyage," he said and shrugged.

"Huh." She looked him up and down for a time, seemingly amused by his inebriation and his loneliness. Here he was – the richest man in the state – with his house full of three-hundred people or better, and no one to sleep with. He must look like a fool standing out here alone, he realized. If he had been smart, he would have invited Julia Callahan up from Houston to hang out with him. No one knew her from Eve. She could pass as his "girlfriend from out of town" with little or no suspicion. At least he could have gone downtown and picked someone up so he didn't look so idiotic standing out here by the pool by himself, hitting on Delilah.

After a long moment, she finally spoke again, the smile having left her face. "Well, Donnie, I'm not going to sleep with you. But I can keep you company, so you don't feel so alone. How's that sound?" She pushed her fist against his shoulder softly.

He nodded. "Yeah. That would be great." He had only ever seen Delilah once, and didn't remember it well. So maybe it was okay after all – no one else would recognize her. Maybe they would all think she was here for Donnie, and everything would be dandy. Vanity, he realized, was something that lately seemed to be getting the best of him.

She looped her arm through his elbow, and they walked around the pool toward the row of kegs. "So tell me about you," she said. Donnie responded, and loosened up a little. He felt at ease talking to her. She was just what he needed right now, mentally: someone to take his mind off the stress of the coming week. After she refilled at the keg, they made their way back through the pool area, then over to the pavilion out away from the crowd. There were chairs on the wooden deck of the pavilion that faced the back of his property. From the pavilion, one could look out and see nothing but nature. Skirting the pavilion was a deck, also filled with reclining chairs. Donnie and Delilah each found a seat in one of these chairs and talked for two hours before they realized any time had passed at all. Donnie had felt a turning somehow – like this woman was more than just someone to sleep with. Maybe it was just the alcohol, he thought, but he liked the feeling. She was intelligent and funny, and didn't seem to take any shit from anyone; very independent. He liked that a lot – the type of woman he could turn loose with the credit card and the keys, and not have to worry about her for a few hours during the hockey game. The kind of woman who wouldn't get all clingy if he wanted to have a night out with the guys.

Delilah was almost six feet tall, standing just a couple of inches short of Donnie, and thick. Donnie had noticed when she first walked up how her stretchy shirt ended just below her midriff, exposing a roundish belly and a little above the hips. She wasn't frumpy at all, just thick. Her arms and legs were thick as well, and it looked as though she used to run, but didn't anymore. She had glossy jet-black hair that fell just around her shoulders in sort of a choppy cut, and pale blue eyes that pierced Donnie's skin when she looked at him. He found that the more he looked at her, the happier he was to be alone tonight. Now, as it bore down on time to lockdown, he realized he had less than ten hours to make this girl stick around and wait for him. Every time he looked at her, he realized more and more that she was exactly what he loved in a woman physically.

They finally got up and made their way back to where the rest of the crowd was beginning to thin out a bit. On their way around the pool, he looked up at the stars. *Why couldn't I have met her two months ago?* He almost lost his balance as he realized he was looking at Mars. Delilah steadied him, keeping him from falling in the pool. As he looked back down, he was startled to see Brian Bradley standing just a couple of feet in front of him, looking particularly nervous.

"Hey man, what's up?" Donnie said.

"Hi Donnie. Good party you've got going on here."

"Yeah, man, I'm glad you could make it out." They stood there for an uncomfortable moment, then Donnie remembered the girl wrapped round his waist. "Oh. Shit, I'm sorry. Brian, meet Delilah, my…" he almost said something stupid.

"Girlfriend. Hello, Brian," she said.

Brian nodded politely at her, seemingly unimpressed with Donnie's good fortune. Her comment had fazed Donnie though. His heart had once again almost stopped beating when that word escaped from her lips. What he had thought would take two months had taken only a few hours. Unless, he realized, this was just part of her scheme to make sure he didn't feel alone. He didn't know how far she intended to take it, and whether or not that included playing the part of his girlfriend. Either way, she was hanging all over him, and that wasn't half-bad, considering after tomorrow he wouldn't be seeing any women aside from Shanna and Andy for the next eighteen months or so. Shanna was hot, but that was restricted airspace. Andy, on the other hand… Andy was free for the taking, but she was a little homely in Donnie's eyes. If he had to resort to lying with Andy, he had more problems than just not being able to find someone to lie with.

"Is everything okay?" Donnie asked Brian.

"Yeah. Just a little nervous, you know. I kind of…"

"Brian? What's wrong?" Donnie put his hand on Brian's shoulder. "You gonna make it, man?"

"I think so. I th-" he stopped again, then suddenly turned pale as powder. "I…" Without further warning, he blew a throat-full of hot vomit all over Donnie and Delilah as they stood there beside the pool.

Donnie was immediately shouting and cursing as the odor of it filled his nostrils, attacking his sense of smell like ants on a lump of chocolate. Delilah raised her arms slightly and wiped the mass of it off her cheek, but remained totally calm and cool throughout the entire ordeal.

"Are you okay?" she said, taking Brian by the shoulders and leading him to a lounge chair. "Here, you should lie back here. Let me go get you some water." A small crowd had begun to gather, and a few muffled laughs could be heard from the direction of the pool, accompanying the whispers that floated above the water. As she turned, someone else took the initiative.

"I'll get it." That someone trotted off in search of a cup of water among tables of beer and liquor. It was like searching for a nickel in a large jar of quarters.

"You gonna be okay? Here, lie back," Delilah said. She guided him back onto the chair, putting her hand on his forehead. Brian was dazed and unresponsive. He hadn't even realized he had thrown up on her, yet here she was taking care of him.

Donnie had wandered off in the direction of the spigot. He cranked the hose on and started washing himself down. The horrific smell stuck like glue, in spite of the cold water in which he was dousing himself. A separate crowd had gathered around him at that point, and someone ran in to fetch him some fresh clothes. *It isn't a party*, he thought, *until someone yarks on the pavement.*

The party went on until nearly three o'clock, when the final head hit the carpet. A large pallet had been assembled in front of the television, where all the women lay sleeping. The men were all scattered about the room on the couches, and most were snoring. They had killed the lights and put in "Mission to Mars" on DVD. By the time everyone had been settled in for a couple of hours, they started realizing they were a little drowsier than they had accounted for. And so it was that everyone who had stayed and watched the movie had just stayed the night.

Donnie and Delilah had parked themselves across the living room on the love seat, huddled in close to each other, laughing and talking throughout the entire movie. What with the intensity of the speaker system and the theatrical setup of such, they hadn't disturbed the movie-watchers in the least. They had told each other stories and filled each other in on all the important get-to-know-you details they could think of – all in an effort to fight back the sleep that threatened to consume them where they sat. The conversation hadn't worn thin; they hadn't run out of things to talk about. But the vigor with which they wanted to learn about each other far exceeded the energy left to propel them into decent conversation. They were too tired to think straight and only holding off the inevitable. Neither Donnie nor Delilah wanted the night to end. Donnie was ready to call off the mission just to have more time to spend with her. The thought had crossed his mind in more than just a serious manner on several occasions throughout the evening, and when he realized he had four hours until quarantine, that desire to call it off was stronger than thirst to a dying man in the desert.

Donnie's eyelids finally became too heavy to keep open, and he knew he would pass out shortly. He leaned up and kissed Delilah on the cheek. She looked up at him, then pulled him back down for a real kiss. She planted her lips full on his and kissed him long and hard. She then whispered in his ear, "I'll be right here when you get back."

"Right here? On this couch?"

"This very one," she played. They kissed again. "You have to have something to look forward to coming home to, don't you?"

He knew the next seven days in confinement would be worse than the eighteen months in mission. Being able to see her through a thick window but not being able to touch her hand, or hear her voice without the fog of a phone would be harder to handle than just not seeing her at all. And the urge to break all boundaries and just have his way with her was suddenly pouring in on him through the thick kisses she kept giving him.

He finally put his hands under her arms and pulled her up even with him, and she turned to face him in the confinement of the small seat. With her hands wrapped round his face, she began kissing him more passionately, and his hand found its way to her belly. Shortly, she moved it to her breasts, and then reached back and released her bra for him. Donnie pulled a blanket from the back of the chair and beneath it they hid their excursions. They found each other in a series of small explorations and spent the next hour entwined in each other's fondling hands.

It became obvious to Donnie that she had been transformed in much the same way he had, and she'd had to reevaluate her level of commitment to him. He was excited by the thought of her being here when he returned a year and a half later, but wondered if he would survive that long. They played until they could no longer physically restrain the sleep that threatened at their door. Her independent, free-spirited nature made her glow with resplendence. If she had been trying not to fall for Donnie, she had failed miserably. By the time their eyes fell shut, Delilah had fallen head-over-heels in like with him.

All was quiet. The only sound came from the massive amounts of grasshoppers that had gathered to watch the parade. They would click and scratch as they bounced about the pavement like table tennis balls set on mousetraps. It was like the plague of locusts all over again. Everywhere someone stepped, he would crunch five to ten of them. There were no clouds in the sky, and a shimmering queasy sun was rising above the hills in the distant east. There was an eerie feeling about the complex. Not only by the silence, but the apprehension. Everyone was nervous or anxious in his own way. Not only was this the biggest mission in the history of humankind, but it also seemed the most frightening. Everything was perfectly prepared. But how fitting is it to say prepared, when the mission is to a planet on which no one has ever before set foot? It was like packing bags in preparation for a trip into a black hole. What to pack?

Everything had long since been loaded in either the shuttle's cargo bay, or on the trailer that awaited them at Alpha. There was nothing left to do but wait now. It was six a.m. and still just dark enough to require headlights. They had spent the last week in quarantine, and finally came to board the shuttle an hour ago. The confinement of quarantine had been taxing on everyone, but they had made it. The crew of seven souls had all emerged healthy and ready for flight. And the blast of fresh air they experienced when they hopped off the shuttle bus was almost overwhelming. It was undeniably exquisite.

Several vehicles sat at the edges of the runway, engines cut off and headlights aiming in different random directions, like flashlights tossed into a cellar. It was a cool morning, but dry. The weather was absolutely perfect for a nice flight off the planet. The runway had been walked and checked for FOD (foreign object debris) to ensure nothing would get sucked into the massive intakes of the shuttle. The fuel carts had been backed away and put inside the concrete barrier of the flight line – the barrier that separated the work from the play. On the flight line, maintenance took place. But out here in the desolate stretches of concrete they called the launchway, freedom was found. The license to leave the planet's surface – if only for a little while. This was where you came to put the force of flight into action.

Fire bottles lined the edge of the runway, yellow and lusterless with cracking black rubber hoses – worn from nonuse. An emergency rescue truck stood idling at the far end of the launchway, its lights flashing in silent morose. Its crew stood outside the truck, arms crossed; smoking; observing. Women stood in the open hangar just over two hundred yards from where the shuttle Atlas waited on the launchway. Most were grim with the reluctance of letting go. Sending their husbands and sons and brothers on a mission was one thing, but this was for a year and a half. Some stood with arms crossed, biting their nails, others wringing their hands, and others stood still, hands on the shoulders of their children. But all were silent.

A group of maintenance men sat atop the wing of another shuttle, watching silently. The police cars parked just inside the barrier were empty. The cops who drove them leaned against the hoods, staring in detached silence. The Dennehotso news crew was present, but they weren't allowed anywhere close to the launchway. Their vans stood idling outside the chain-link fence that surrounded the restricted areas of the complex – namely, the flight line, taxiways, hangars and launchway. They had zoom lenses on their cameras. They stood outside the vans, poised and waiting for the big event. Silent.

The shuttle Atlas stood eerily silent in the middle of it all, a powerhouse waiting for ignition. The very definition of potential energy. After nearly an hour of silence, the APUs (auxiliary power units) finally kicked on, and the countdown to greatness began. The only thing left standing between the shuttle Atlas and the Red Planet for which they were eventually bound was time and space. And it didn't seem like much of either.

Inside the shuttle, Shanna was readying the camera equipment in its steel, flight-worthy cases. She had done her walk through of the cabin, filming everyone – each in his own world, strapped in tightly and somber. The hum of the APUs was barely audible inside the cabin. Hot air hissed from the undersized vents along the ceiling. Those vents were much like those on airplanes, she thought. In a few moments, it would be cool, and laden with the scent of recycling pipe. Shanna herself was trembling as she tried to get comfortable. She was to remain strapped in until they achieved orbit. Once in orbit, she would be free to film a little more. The steel camera cases strapped into the coveys with tension belts held six cameras. All of these were digital and wireless, and sent their signals to a centralized data box that was strapped into the cargo area beneath the seats on the starboard side of the shuttle. This alleviated the need for tapes or memory cards, as the data box collected all video and stored it on solid-state memory modules. It could hold up to ten terabytes of video feed, which would more than accommodate the eighteen-month mission.

The blastoff would commence in fifteen minutes or so, she knew. From there, it would take about twenty-five minutes to reach orbit, then four hours beyond that until they reached the ISS. It would take eight hours to get the trailer ready and connected to the shuttle. The humongous gas jets behind the shuttle would be removed and refitted with antimatter accelerators. These accelerators would extend around and behind the 100-foot trailer and connect to the proton propulsion chamber. This chamber is where the antimatter would come in contact with its counterpart and be transformed into energy. In this chamber there would be three-hundred-thousand explosions per second, and the energy from these explosions would blast them across the void between Earth and Mars.

Like magic.

Shanna had read over the navigation charts and the flight plans, not knowing how to translate them into useable data for the most part, but getting a general idea of what was going on. Donnie had told her about the navigation systems on the Atlas: there was no need for a human navigator, as you just plugged in the proper coordinates and let the computers chart the course. It was humans, however, who prepared the charts before the coordinates ever went into the onboard navigation computers. The navigation charts were on thick white grid paper with blue ink that mapped out the constellations and planets in relation to the direction they were traveling. She had memorized everything she could get her hands on in an effort to attain some sort of knowledge on a mission where she didn't really belong – and indeed didn't know anything.

The math made perfect sense to her, though she had never taken an astronomy course. Math was, after all, math. If it had to do with numbers, Shanna could break it down and understand it. And the math involved in putting a ship on a foreign planet was incredibly complex. An object traveling at 17,000 kilometers per hour, leaving a celestial body that is in orbit around a distant star, while that body is spinning – and heading for another planet that is in orbit around the same star, and spinning. It was enough to make her head spin. But she realized the importance of the navigation charts. It was a wonder that the planet would be where it was supposed to be when they reached the rendezvous on the maps. If one little equation had been wrong in the planning, they could arrive at Mars, only to find Mars wasn't there yet.

As the systems began clicking on one by one, she could feel the air finally getting cooler, and wondered just how cool it would get in the cabin. She leaned her head back against the seat and breathed in deeply. She was quickly being overcome by the overbearing sensation that she was actually seated in a shuttle that would take her to another planet. Until now it just hadn't seemed real to her. Here she was sitting in a state-of-the-art antimatter-propelled shuttle, about to embark on the most important step mankind had ever taken, and she wasn't even twenty-three years old yet. The thought made her shiver. She reached up and twisted the air nozzle so it wouldn't blow directly on her. There were no windows near her in the cabin. She had the sudden sensation that she was trapped in a 200-ton coffin with no escape, and the belts across her abdomen seemed to tighten. Shanna found it hard to breathe, and was almost overcome by sudden claustrophobia. She finally had to close her eyes and take deep breaths again. She would not freak out. She would not chicken out and ask to be let off the shuttle. She would stick this out come hell or high water. It took every ounce of strength and willpower she could muster just to stay in her seat, strapped in like a child in a papoose waiting for surgery.

In the flight deck, Donnie and Mike were running over the final preflight checklists. Julia Callahan at PSS was on the radio talking them through the specifics. Donnie glanced at the mission clock embedded in the console. It read six minutes, and was counting down.

"Avionics?"

"Check."

There were over two hundred items on the pre-flight checklists that had to be covered, all of which could be checked in less than ten minutes. Everything had cleared so far, as usual. If something were awry, it would have thrown an alarm long ago. The lists were generally used to make sure all the switches were in the right positions.

"Hydraulics?"

"Check."

Donnie looked over at Mike, who smirked at him and raised the sleeve of his shirt to show off his nicotine patch. Donnie smiled and shook his head. The week they had spent in isolation had been rough enough. But now, being out and unbound by quarantine, he felt that need all over again. This would be tougher than he thought.

"Flaps?"

"Check."

"Slats?"

"Check."

His stomach was knotted, and his breathing was shallow. He always had a little nervousness before a liftoff, but this was uncommonly unsettling. It would clear, he told himself, as soon as they were docked up with Alpha, and everything was working on schedule. He could see the group of people standing under the eave of the warehouse, where he had told Delilah to be so that he could see her. Of course she was too far away to see, but knowing she was there was good enough for him.

"Okay, Atlas, switch to prime power. Start the engines."

"Roger that, Houston," Mike said. He powered up the engines and killed the APUs. The ship rocked forward slightly. It was a feeling of raw potential energy waiting to be unleashed. They would be taking off heading west down the runway, then bank over upside-down toward the east, to use the Earth's rotation as a speed boost. Once they reached 28,000 kilometers per hour, they would change course to rendezvous with Alpha, which would take place somewhere over Russia. The space station would lead the chase for a few hours, in which time they would orbit the Earth twice. And at that speed, they would orbit the Earth almost 19 times a day.

Donnie swallowed. His throat was dry and burning. He was aware of Mike moving and talking beside him, but couldn't quite hear what he was saying. Somehow, Donnie felt detached and disturbed. It was as if he was watching a video of someone else's life inside the shuttle's flight deck, and he had no real control of it. He looked over at Mike and shook his head quickly, trying to wake up – as he knew it must be the sleep deprivation causing him this uncomfortable sensation. Mike looked at him inquisitively.

"You okay?"

"Yeah man. I'm just tired as hell," Donnie said.

Mike grinned widely. "Yeah, you were up all night talking to that girlie, weren't you?" He had spent the night in the visitor's area, talking through the thick glass.

Julia's voice beamed in over the headset, "Girlie? What girlie? Donnie, did you get a girlfriend I don't know about?"

Donnie shook his head and sighed. "No, Julia. You're the only one for me. He doesn't know what he's talking about."

"Oh, okay. Just checking, Donnie."

"Nope. Nothing to worry about, dear."

"Good. So what's her name?"

"Delilah."

"Okay, we're up to full power here, Ms. Callahan."

"Thank you, Mike. Standby."

Donnie watched as the power station indicators intermittently lit up with a green glow. These bars represented the potential energy of the entire powerhouse. Once they launched, these indicators would suffer slightly.

"Atlas, standby for linkup," Julia Callahan said over the headset.

"Roger that, standing by." Once she called ready, Donnie would toggle the linkup switch, which opened the port for data download.

"Atlas, ready on linkup."

"Roger that. Going now, Houston." Donnie toggled the switch, which began to blink rapidly like the traffic light on a network hub. Each blink of the LED light represented a packet of data being transmitted or received. After sixty seconds, it stopped blinking.

"Atlas, drop linkup."

"Roger that," Donnie said. And then, "Dropped."

"Okay, boys, that's it," Julia said. "All systems go. Is your crew ready, Atlas?"

"Yes'm. We're ready and waiting," Mike said after looking at Donnie. They stuck their fists out and knocked them together.

It was time. The moment they had been awaiting for many years had finally arrived.

"Very well, then. I'd like to wish you gentlemen the best of luck and Godspeed."

"Thank you, Julia," said Donnie.

"Donnie, can you bring me back some Mars rocks or something?"

Donnie grinned. "I'll see what I can do, Houston. We're pretty much maxed on payload."

Julia laughed. "All right. Atlas, standby for countdown."

Donnie's stomach tensed again, and he began to tingle from his neck to his fingertips. It was real. It was here. His lifelong dream was finally beginning to materialize into a reality. All checks had been paid, all balances settled, all dues absolved. He was leaving Earth with nothing but official equipment and a prayer in his mind for safe return. His throne was a very expensive, electronic shuttle seat, upon which he controlled the galaxy. Shortly he would be stepping out of it and setting foot in the history books beside Neil Armstrong and Christopher Columbus. His blood raced through his veins and his heart beat wildly in his chest.

"Atlas, prepare for takeoff."

"Roger that, Houston, preparing for takeoff." Donnie breathed in deeply then nodded at Mike. Mike did the honors, engaging the engines and locking down on the ground brakes. He pushed the throttles forward until they stopped at the tops of the slides. They clicked into place and the engines roared into life. The shuttle rocked in its place like an angry hornet. The sound was deafening inside the cabin. Everything shuddered and rocked, and it was hard to look at any of the gauges or instrumentation as it was bouncing around like an old pickup on a lane full of potholes. Once they broke free of Earth's atmosphere, it would be quiet and still, as there was no atmosphere to mediate the sound, and no gravity to have to fight.

The green bars on the powerhouse thrust indicators climbed steadily to the top, achieving maximum energy. Donnie turned to Mike and shouted, for that was the only way to communicate at full augmentation of the engines. "This is it, man!"

Mike laughed out loud, thrilled to be where he was at that moment. "Yee haw!" he shouted. "Like a fuckin' roller coaster!" Donnie felt the same way. They had ridden it many times before, but it never lost its excitement, and the anticipation hung in the air like smoke in a bar. The green bars reached the top of the kinetic status indicators, and a bell sounded somewhere in the cockpit. They only heard rumors of it through the headset, where it was amplified – but not loud enough to defeat the roar of the massive engines pushing hundreds of thousands of pounds of thrust out into the cool February morning.

"Houston, we have maximum power. Ready for takeoff."

"Roger that, Atlas. Standby for clearance."

After a brief pause Julia's voice came back over the headset and announced the words that put them in the business of visiting other planets: "Atlas you are clear for takeoff in five... Four... Three... Two... One... Takeoff!"

Mike pulled the ground brake release, and the hydraulic actuators slammed the brakes into their ready position. The ship bolted forward sharply and shot off down the launchway, immediately exceeding 100 kilometers per hour. Donnie's head against the headrest of the seat, he fought to keep control of his hands, which could easily follow the soft steer of the front gear if allowed. They shook, but maintained. He kept his heading, bearing down hard on the rudder pedals. The end of the launchway appeared on the horizon and raced up to meet them at over four hundred kilometers per hour.

Donnie pulled back on the yoke and immediately the shaking of the shuttle was reduced to nominal trembling. The gear left the pavement and Mike pulled the retract lever, sending them folding up under the wings. The shuttle made a long arc, following the inside of a U-shape in the sky. Within minutes, the ground became the sky as they headed back toward the east, tearing through the sky like the saw of a destructive god. Shortly, they would break through the thermosphere and into the exosphere where everything was quiet and distant from the planet it surrounded.

The climb felt more like falling now, as they peeled away from the Earth inverted in flight. The sky became rapidly darker, and the pressure in the cabin became greater. Static played over the headset as they bore through massive amounts of friction in their speed. Julia's voice finally became apparent, and Donnie had to ask her to repeat what she had said.

"Shut down engines, Atlas. Do you copy?"

"Roger that, Houston. And wilco on the engines." He pulled the thrust levers back to the bottom of the slides, and clicked them into the off position. Then suddenly it was over. Everything was silent. They were now on borrowed power. The Earth's gravity and Newtonian physics would take over from here. They sailed through the darkness with Earth directly above them, wrapping their traveled path behind them like a fine line of spider's silk. Atlas was now in orbit.

"Atlas, jettison external fuel tanks."

"Roger that, jettisoning externals." Donnie looked over at Mike, who nodded and pulled the pylon release handle. Simultaneously, both empty tanks dropped off and the pylons disconnected. They would float aimlessly for several minutes as they drifted back into the pull of Earth's gravity, whereupon they would burn up in her atmosphere.

The Earth in all its glory spun silently beneath them, visible through their upper windshield as a peaceful blue-green globe – serene and silent in the night sky, nestled among the stars like a god. Donnie closed his eyes and thanked God they had made orbit.

| **CHAPTER** *sixteen* |

orbit

Julia Callahan smiled as Mark Bragg leaned over the terminal shaking his head. His eyes were full of wonder. He sighed a deep relief as he looked at her. There was something special about a takeoff where the destination was insanely far away. The moon was minor. The space station was cookies – a walk in the park. Mars was a fantasy – the Hollywood of the solar system, and it felt good to be a part of the mission control.

The red airplane-shaped icon danced across the screen, rapidly moving away from the space station. If Atlas were to turn around in mid-flight, they would run right into it, in a collision worth every bit of 55,000 kilometers per hour. The idea was to circle the globe in its pursuit and sneak up behind it nice and easy.

Mark shook his head again, then spoke. "Wow," was all he said.

"Pretty intense, isn't it?"

"Like nothing in the world."

"Were you trying to be punny?"

"Actually, no. It sort of just came out that way."

Julia smirked and nodded at him. Then she sighed and stepped away from the terminal to make her rounds. Now that Atlas was in orbit, she could take it easy for a while. She would have nothing to do with the docking of Atlas with Alpha, the Space Station. That would be done completely by visuals. It wasn't a precise procedure anyway, and would only take a few moments to accomplish. Her next task on this job would be to help them set their course for Mars, and then – barring any unforeseen situations – get them ready to come back when it was time. PSS still maintained contact with the Atlas throughout the entire trip, though through most of it there wasn't much they could do.

She walked around the floor, peeking at everyone's monitor and asking each technician if everything was showing the desired readings. As she neared the end of the row, Beth Sullivan, her communications officer, stopped her and removed her headset.

"Ms. Callahan, the families are present at the complex."

"Okay. After they've docked we'll try to get some talk time in there."

Beth nodded and turned back to her console. After the refit of Atlas was complete, and they were ready to leave ISS for Mars, there would be a one-hour period in which the crew of the shuttle could communicate with family members. These people would gather in a room somewhere – simply to be ready and available – and they would take turns speaking to their loved one on the shuttle. Beth would patch the phone call through to the shuttle. As it stood, there was no way to communicate with anyone on that ship except through Beth. If someone had a message they needed to get to a crew member, Beth would be his point of contact. This protected the crew and kept interference to a minimum.

Julia finished her rounds and made her way back to her desk. She leaned on her elbows on the desk, staring at the navigational map laid out under the plastic cover. Their path would be almost straight as an arrow, with a curl at either end where they left and entered orbits around the respective planets. They would be leaving Earth on a counter-clockwise orbit and entering Martian orbit the same way. In this way, they would use the Martian axis to slow them down before landing. These dispositions were based on the nav-charts, which showed the solar system as a flat group viewed from above, as per Earth's North Pole.

She traced the outline of the flight path on the hard plastic map protector with a red map pencil, circling Mars several times before dropping her pencil in the cup and looking up at the display screens again. Mark was standing there with his arms crossed watching her though, blocking her view of the screen.

"You gonna make it Julia?"

She smiled and stretched. "Yeah. I'm just excited for them. And I feel so useless sitting down here watching."

"You need to be up there on that shuttle with them. Is that what you want?"

"No way, Joe. My butt stays terrestrial. That's all there is to it."

"Ah, come on! You wouldn't go to Mars if they asked you to?"

Julia looked up at him with skeptical eyes and a screwed up mouth. "Mark. Not a chance. Why do you think I'm an astronomer, and not an astronaut?"

"Ah, man, I just don't understand that. How you can love space so much, but not want to go into it…"

"I kind of have this fear of leaving my home planet. I don't know what it is. But I'm happy right here on good old Earth soil," she said, pounding the arm of her high-back leather chair repeatedly.

"Fair enough. Well I'm going to smoke. Wanna come?" Mark offered.

"Sure." Julia stood up and stretched again, then clipped her cell phone on her jeans pocket. "Why not."

It wasn't for lack of effort; Donnie had tried with everything he had to stay awake. It just hadn't worked out like that. Within twenty minutes of reaching orbit, he slipped into oblivion. After a thirty-minute nap, Mike woke him up.

Donnie shook and sat up quickly in his seat, looking out the window at near-empty blackness. "What's up?" Mike's hand was on his shoulder.

"Wake up, man, we're there!"

"We're where?"

"Mars! You slept for three months."

"I was out that long?" Donnie said, rubbing his eyes.

"Thirty minutes. I figured a half-hour or so would do you good. You feel better?"

"No. But it felt like a month."

"Well you can sleep for a month once we get this shit taken care of. But you'll have to lock yourself back in the cabin for that. I don't think I'd stay sane if I had to listen to your snoring ass for a month."

Donnie smiled and unbuckled himself from the captain's chair. "How we doing?"

"Right on course, boss," Mike said, slicing his hand through the air toward the windshield.

"Good. I'm gonna make my rounds." Donnie ducked through the doorway and into the cabin where most of the crew sat staring at him. "Y'all doing okay?"

Everyone nodded, some smiled a little. Brian Bradley was wide-eyed with fear and nervousness, his face white with it. Donnie looked hard at him for a moment, then raised his eyebrows and gave him a thumbs-up. *You okay?*

Brian nodded slowly, gripping the ends of his armrests with fists of steel. Shanna was staring at Donnie when he looked her way, and smiled wanly, as if to show him her courage. He knew it took a lot of courage for a young girl to leave the planet. He was impressed with her tenacity of seeing this thing through.

"Well, you're all free to move about the cabin." A few buckles clinked open, and the crew began getting up, letting the absence of gravity take them where it would. Donnie pushed his way over to where Shanna was sitting, and pulled himself into the seat next to her. He buckled himself in, so as not to have to fight the weightlessness.

"You doing okay, Shan?"

She nodded, smiling at him.

"What do you think of zero gravity?"

She breathed in deeply before speaking. "I'm scared shitless, Donnie. I don't…" she trailed off and covered her mouth as tears formed quickly in her eyes. She tried to blink them away and smile, but it didn't work. Before she could say anything else, they were drifting away from her face as perfect little spheres of saltwater. Donnie reached up and flicked one, watching it explode into tiny pinpricks of mist that scattered in every direction. He smiled and put his arm around her, pulling her in as close as the seats would allow.

"It's okay, Shanna. You'll get used to it. The worst of it is over with. The next thing we have to worry about is landing, and that's three months from now."

Shanna nodded, wiping her eyes. She was feebly attempting to stop the flow of tears, which was obviously not ready to be stopped. Her body shook with silent sobs. "I just don't know what the heck I was thinking," she managed through a wet voice.

"I'm proud of you Shan. You've got guts. It takes a lot of guts to blast out of the atmosphere. And that's the hardest part."

"That's not what I'm worried about. I'm claustrophobic out here. There's no windows. And even if there were, I don't think it would help, 'cause there's nothing to see but stars zooming by."

Donnie smiled. "I know what you mean. It's actually not even that exciting, Shanna. If you look out the window once we're on the way to Mars, you'll be utterly disappointed. There's billions of stars to see, but they ain't moving."

She frowned at him.

"Even if you were traveling at twice the speed of light, they wouldn't appear to be moving. They don't zoom by you like a Windows screensaver. Space travel is pretty boring, by way of motion. It looks like you're sitting absolutely still in the middle of the galaxy."

Shanna laughed a little, continuing to wipe her eyes. "Well that's no fun."

"You're right. But I know how you get claustrophobic. I did too, my first few trips. You get used to it in a couple of days, and it'll never even cross your mind after that."

"I think it's the thought that even if I wanted to, there would be no way I could just walk off and go see my family. Or drive my car. Or go to the mall," she said.

"Ahh, the ever-important mall. Now we see the truth. Shanna misses the mall."

"You're damn right I do," she said, laughing through her tears. "It's kind of scary knowing there's nowhere to go. No one to call home to."

Donnie nodded. "Just think of the reward though. You'll be one of the first people ever to set foot on another planet. And I'm sure you can talk Andy into letting you get off first. You'll be the first woman to set foot on another planet."

Shanna's eyes widened and she looked up at Donnie. "For real?"

He nodded, biting his lip. "I'll talk to her for you. She doesn't really get excited by much, so I'm sure it's not a thing."

"That would be awesome. Oh my God. I'm just a young girl, too. Can you imagine what my friends would say?"

"You'll be famous," Donnie said, unbuckling himself from the seat.

Shanna put her hand on his leg as he got up, stopping him. "Thanks Donnie."

"For what?"

"For everything. Thanks for letting me be an astronaut."

Donnie grinned wildly. "It's cool, ain't it?"

Shanna nodded. "Thanks for being strong when I was – well, when I was being stupid."

"I don't think you were being stupid, Shanna. You have to follow what your heart tells you is right. It's just sometimes not the right time."

She nodded again, closing her eyes. Donnie could see she was fighting back the tears again, and they leaked from her eyelashes. She patted his leg and wiped them. "Just thank you."

He squeezed her shoulder and made his way to the rest of the crew, checking on them one by one.

"How long 'til they dock?" Mark said, flicking the ash off the end of his cigarette.

Julia looked at her watch. "Just over three hours now."

"So can I ask you a question, Julia?"

"You just did, Mark. How many more shall I allow?"

"A personal one," he said, grinning.

"Sure."

"How old are you really?"

Julia grunted, shocked he would actually dare to ask her that. "No, Mark! You know I'm not going to answer that!"

"Ah, why not? It's not really that big a deal. And I'm betting you aren't as old as you say you are."

"How is that? I haven't said how old I am."

"You said you're older than twenty-five."

She raised her hands. "Mark, we are not having this discussion. I've told you I'm older than twenty-five, so be happy you know that much."

"Yeah, I'm just not sure I believe it."

"Well your disbelief is a compliment to my vanity," she said, crossing her arms. "I do, however, plan to keep my age a mystery. My boss doesn't know how old I am, so there's no reason for my subordinates to know."

Mark shook his head, screwing up his mouth. "Still say you're not a day over twenty-five," Mark said under his breath, taking the last drag from his cigarette.

Once back inside, Julia's attention immediately locked onto the middle display screen, where a red alert was flashing in the corner. "Systems, what's my alert?"

"Uh, we have strange ballast, ma'am."

"Okay, can you clear it for me?"

"Yes'm," the systems tech replied. Shortly, the alert disappeared.

Julia sighed relief and found her seat. Strange ballast just meant the shuttle was cruising at an angle greater than 41 degrees. This wasn't terribly out of the ordinary, and would probably be corrected soon, as the crew of the shuttle became aware of it. Seeing an alert of any kind appear on the screen was frightening though.

Mark was once again over her shoulder. "You okay, Julia?"

"Yes, I'm fine. I just like to see my mission through with no alerts. Alerts cause heart attacks," she said.

Donnie, while making his way back into the flight deck, felt the bird tilt sickeningly forward, then right itself. He swung into his seat and looked over at Mike, who had his hands on the yoke. "Easy there, partner. What's going on?"

Mike shook his head. "It's the damn ballast, man. This damn bird wants to fly nose-up."

"What are you telling me, Mike?"

Mike finally looked over at Donnie. "Take the yoke."

Donnie put his hands on the control and Mike let go. Immediately he could feel the drag, as the shuttle tilted toward the sky again. The yoke wanted to push toward his lap instead of holding steady in the middle. "What the hell's going on? There's no gravity!"

Mike nodded slowly, his eyes wide, and sighed.

"So we're going to porpoise all the way to Mars?" Donnie said.

"Looks like it. Unless we brought a spare AP."

Donnie keyed the mic, which would blast his voice over the speakers in the cabin. "Brian, can you come to the flight deck, please?"

After a few moments, Brian appeared in the doorway, his hands on the handholds beside it. "What's up, guys?"

"Did you bring parts?"

"Of course I brought parts. What do you need?"

"Did you bring a spare AP?"

"Psssh. You're kidding, right?"

Donnie's face was stern and serious. "Does it look like I'm kidding?"

Brian's face straightened. "Donnie, we don't even keep spare autopilots in stock. I brought components; I might be able to fix one, but I didn't bring a whole nother AP."

Donnie said nothing, but stared at Brian for a moment.

Mike finally stepped in and spoke on Donnie's behalf. "Brian, look at the attitude." He let go of the yoke and the nose immediately rocketed up, bringing the Earth into full view in the windshield. Brian had to grab the handholds again, and nearly fell forward from the imaginary sensation of falling. Flying inverted around the globe made it look as if you were about to plunge back into the atmosphere.

"If we don't fix this AP, we're going to porpoise all the way to Mars."

"Porpoise? Why do you say that? Is it trying to correct itself?"

"No. But I won't let her fly like that. I'll correct it. And that makes us porpoise," Mike said.

Donnie finally stood up. "Dammit. I can't believe this. We've been spaceborne for an hour and we already got shit messing up." He pushed past Brian into the cabin, shaking his head.

Brian came forward and took his seat. "We can't let it do this, Bradley," Mike said. "Once we hit Alpha, you need to get that shit fixed."

Brian nodded, taking a deep breath. "I don't understand though. What effect does that have on flight if there's no drag?"

"The ship will be doing backflips the entire time. It's ridiculous."

"But it doesn't slow us down."

"Get smart, Jack. If you ain't holding onto something, the ship will do flips around you." Mike leaned in real close to Brian and stuck his finger out. "If we have to cancel this trip on hold for an autopilot, it's gonna be a red dawn for you." He unbuckled and pushed up, and headed for the cabin. Before he passed through the doorway, he turned on Brian again. "Hold the yoke. Keep us at fifteen cruise."

Brian nodded quickly, then took the yoke.

Mike met Donnie in the galley, where he was hanging against the wall with one hand, a tin of coffee in the other. He looked up as Mike approached, shaking his head. The tin could be open by pressing against it with your lips. When the slot opened, whatever liquid was inside was free to escape. Liquid came out in perfect spheres this way, and though it was awkward to swallow, it was easy to manage, and even easier to clean up. It was impossible to spill anything, as whatever it was would just float up into the nothingness to be easily collected again.

Mike took the tin from Donnie's hand and sipped some himself. He grabbed onto a steel handhold and let his legs float up behind him. "Bad autopilot. Could have figured."

Donnie snorted. "He took a week off, Mike. I'm sure when he got back, he knew about it. He just didn't have time to do anything about it."

"I can't believe this shit."

"Think he can fix it?" Donnie said, taking the tin back from Mike.

"I told him once we hit Alpha, that's his number one priority."

Donnie sighed again. "Dammit, Mike. Why'd we stay up so late last night?"

"Speak for yourself, friend. I got plenty of sleep. If you hadn't been chatty Cathy with that broad all night, you'd be doing as well as me."

"Man that was rough. All week I've been staring at her through that barrier, wanting to badly just to touch her. I think that made it worse." Donnie took a sip from the tin. "She got more beautiful every day too. She's a looker, ain't she?"

Mike nodded, smiling. "She really is. What's her name again?"

"Delilah. Delilah Danley."

"You're a lucky man, Donnie. She's a keeper."

Shanna finally gathered herself up enough to move around the cabin a little with a still-shot camera. Most of the crew were willing to smile for the shots, some didn't. But she clicked away with no less spirit, trying to capture some of the essence of the first few hours of the mission, before it escaped. Once they had docked with the Space Station, she would be required to capture as much as possible on film with the digital video camera. Live action shots were what appealed to the public. And she had three months of flight to catch plenty of action just on the way to the Red Planet.

They would spend twelve months on Mars, then begin their journey back home. Weights and balances had been accounted for so precisely as to include the Martian rocks and other objects they would be bringing home, as well as the objects and equipment they would be leaving on the surface. They would be leaving an American flag for one, along with several small monitoring devices, and a wind-proof shed that would house plant life and waterborne experiments. This is assuming they could get anything to grow in the first place.

Shanna slid up into the flight deck to find Brian Bradley looking a little lost behind the controls. He flinched as he looked up and saw her.

"You scared the hell out of me."

"Sorry about that. Where're Donnie and Mike?" she said.

He shrugged.

"Smile for me, Bri Bri," she said, trying to entice him into a smile rather than have him force one. It didn't work.

"Please don't call me Bri Bri. And I'd prefer you not take my picture, Shanna."

Shanna dropped her arms in front of her, losing her own smile. "Sorry. Well I have to take photographs. That's my job. So whether or not you want to look good in them, that's up to you. But I have to take them."

"You don't have to take any of me."

"Are you going to be this difficult for the whole trip?" Shanna said.

Brian rounded quickly on her, pointing an accusing finger. "Don't you talk down to me, Shanna," he whispered loudly. "Let's get one thing straight right now. I don't like you. I never have liked you, and I never will. Your lollygagging little girl ass doesn't belong on this mission, and I'll only tolerate you because I have to. But that doesn't mean I have to like it. You'd do best to steer the hell out of my way."

Shanna stood there speechless, her mouth gaping open in disbelief. She almost started to speak, then Brian cut her off.

"If you don't stay the hell out of my way, I'll make this entire trip miserable for you. This ain't the mall, Shanna. And you'd do well to remember that."

Shanna swallowed, trying once again to hold the tears back, and turned around to make exodus as quickly as possible. She didn't need the humiliation of breaking down and sobbing in front of the rest of the crew. It was bad enough she had already made a fool of herself in front of Donnie.

Thirty seconds later, Mike and Donnie were flying back through the doorway and into the flight deck. Donnie was fuming before his eyes ever even met Brian's. "What the hell is going on in here?"

"Ah, nothing, Donnie. I just told her to-"

"Why the hell are we pitching? I thought I told you to man the yoke," Mike said.

"Oh shoot. I'm so sorry, it totally slipped my mind." Brian turned quickly back to the controls and pushed the nose back down.

"What in hell are you doing here? How the hell does it slip your mind to steer a shuttle?" Mike shouted. "Get up. Get out of that seat." Brian quickly got out of the captain's chair and Mike slipped past him and buckled into it. "Why don't you get back there in the cabin where you belong? I don't want to see your ass up here again." Brian turned and paddled his way out of the flight deck, a look of relief evident about him.

Donnie settled into the first officer's chair and looked over at Mike, a smirk set on his ruddy face. "Little rough on him weren't you?"

Mike grunted. "First three hours and I already almost hit the guy."

"Need a smoke, do you?"

"Do I ever."

Two hours passed uneventfully while Mike and Donnie went over the docking procedures. When Donnie slapped the technical manual closed, he closed it in the control console beside him and looked out at the emptiness ahead of them. Several hundred kilometers in front of them, he saw something shining like a star.

"Aha! There she is," Donnie said, pointing.

Mike breathed in deeply. "Good God, it's about time. What's it about an hour away?"

"At least. Man, I couldn't be happier to see it though."

Mike nodded. Their current speed was some five hundred kilometers per hour faster than the speed at which the Space Station was orbiting the Earth. Within the next couple of hours they would close that gap and decelerate, drifting softly and silently into the docking bay like a whisper.

Julia Callahan stood staring at the display screens, twirling her hair on her finger and biting her lip. Everything looked good, but she couldn't find a settling, somehow. Somehow she felt she should be doing something – as if something should be wrong, but wasn't. Or something was wrong but she just wasn't catching it. This uneasiness wasn't typical Julia behavior.

Lisa, a station operator, approached her, putting a hand on her shoulder. "You okay?"

Julia nodded. "Just have a funny feeling, you know? Can't really pin it."

Lisa raised her eyebrows.

"I'm sure it's nothing," Julia said.

"How long 'til dock?"

"Twenty-five minutes."

Brian Bradley sat staring at his hands folded in his lap. He was shaking and pale. Andy had asked him repeatedly over the last hour if he was okay and frequently suggested he needed to lie down and rest. He wouldn't have it though. He fidgeted, chewing on his fingernails and nervously looking from side to side – his eyes never settling on anything for longer than it took to look away.

The intercom beeped and Donnie's voice rang out through the crew cabin. "Okay, everybody. It's time to get excited. We dock Alpha in twenty minutes! Those not in their seats at that time might well become close friends with the bulkhead directly in front of them. And I'd like to direct your attention to the view out the starboard side of th- … oh, wait. You don't have any windows back there. I'm so sorry."

Most of the crew laughed at this. Brian Bradley sucked in a deep breath, as if the comment had only reminded him of his fears, and then closed his eyes, wiping sweat off his forehead.

| CHAPTER *seventeen* |
docking

Without a sound – and no one around to hear it had there been a sound – the shuttle Atlas glided smoothly into the docking holds of the International Space Station. Two long guide beams ran the length of the docking bay, and between these beams the shuttle's fuselage would slide to a halt. The beams could be slid closer together or farther apart, depending on the type of shuttle. Once it came to a halt, the beams would run alongside the fuselage, just atop the wings, and the shuttle would be locked into place by electromagnetic force.

The ship sailed silently into the outermost reach of the guide beams and began its slow trek toward lockdown. From the cabin, Donnie adjusted the yoke with tiny movements and clear precision, and the nose of the dock run – painted with yellow and black concentric circles – inched closer and closer. His headset squawked and Julia Callahan's voice filled his ears.

"Houston to Atlas: you've still got fire."

Donnie frowned and looked at Mike, who was frowning right back at him. "Uh, negative, Houston, we've been in glide and deceleration for the last few hours, over."

"Roger that Atlas, I suspected you were following procedure. We must have an instrument mismatch. I'm reading a five-percent propulsion. Request resynch."

"Houston, could we do this a little later? I am about to dock here…"

"Negative on that, Atlas. Abort docking procedure until an instrument resynch is effected."

Donnie looked at Mike again, his mouth agape. "Houston, are you serious? You're telling me not to dock here? I'm ninety seconds out!"

Mike looked at Donnie, then cut in on the conversation. "Houston, this is Thurman; we're already committed here. You're effectively telling us to fire reverse within the confines of the structure."

"Standby, Atlas." There was a pause on the radio, wherein Donnie and Mike sat tensely, holding their breath. Nervousness was thick, and neither one of them seemed ready to handle it. Nervousness was rare in the flight deck.

"Roger that, Atlas. If we can't resynch before your dock, you will need to fire reverse thrusters. We cannot allow an unsynchronized system to dock with Alpha. If you dock before synchronization with us, we will lose you."

Donnie frowned again and shook his head. "Unbelievable," he said before keying the mike. "Aren't you synched with Alpha though? Isn't it six of one, half dozen the other?"

"Negative Atlas. Abort dock procedure."

"Dammit!" Donnie pounded his fist on the console, then keyed the mike again. "Why the hell didn't you tell us we were flying a dead bird two hours ago? It's too late!"

"Atlas, come again."

The nose of the craft was fifty meters from the end of the docking run. He knew as soon as the craft hit home it would start a resynch pattern with the space station's computer system. There were four simple aluminum strips on the upper nose, just below the windscreen, each about nine inches long. When the craft stopped, those four strips would come to rest against four similar strips on the contact panel of the communications probe, which protruded from the top of the nose bumper.

The top of the wings now hit the bottoms of the docking beams, and the ship lurched, sending Donnie sprawling for a handhold. He found his seat quickly and flipped on the intercom. As the shuttle approached the end of the run, it bumped a few more times against the padded arms of the dock, like a log ride at a water park being brought back into the station. The nose of the ship was twenty meters from the end of the dock run, and the communications probe glistened in the light of the sun, which was just coming up over Earth's horizon behind them.

Donnie leaned back and stared at the incoming dock, then spoke into the mike, his voice resounding once again through the interior of the shuttle. "Ladies and gentlemen, we've been asked to abort docking until our computer systems have been resynchronized with Houston's. This shouldn't take more than about twenty minutes, but it puts us off schedule, so go ahead and start prepping what you can to get the trailer attached. We'll go ahead and do a space walk to knock off the thruster cones, and that should get us back on schedule."

Donnie looked over at Mike and shook his head again. "Push us back, Mike."

"Roger that," Mike said, then re-engaged his headset. "Aborting dock, Houston." He then fired the over-wing thrusters and pushed the shuttle back away from the beams of the docking run, and into free space.

While the computers were re-synchronizing, Donnie stared out the side of the windscreen in an effort to see the EVA arm extending from the cargo bay. All he could see was the tip end of it though, so he settled back into the captain's chair. He was beginning to feel the effects of having stayed up all night. That triggered a memory of Delilah, which triggered an altogether different set of emotions. Excitement pulsed through his veins at the thought of her, and once again he wished the mission weren't eighteen months long. If he could go back now, he would do it. He briefly considered the ridiculousness of aborting a lifelong dream and something so grand for something as simple as a week-old puppy love.

Outside the spacecraft, Mike Thurman pushed himself to the back, with only a flex cord and an oxygen line connecting him with the Atlas. The thruster cones would take about fifteen minutes to remove, whereupon they would float away, finding their own orbit until they ultimately dropped away and into the great ocean below.

Shanna had made her way to the back of the crew compartment and was looking through a small porthole window that saw into the cargo bay, where the broad arced doors stood open. The EVA arm was craned up and out of the bay, and from the end of it dangled the twisted braid of hose and cord that kept Mike Thurman alive and resident. She couldn't see him any longer, as he had disappeared behind the ship and was now presumably already at work removing the giant cones.

Brian Bradley had finally gotten the courage up to leave his seat, and now found Shanna at the back bulkhead. "Can you see anything good out there, Shanna?"

She turned quickly around to meet him. "No. He's already out of sight." She regarded Brian distantly, and pushed away from the bulkhead. "You're not going to get sick on me are you? You don't look so hot."

Brian sighed. "No, I'm not going to get sick. I feel fine, I'm just a little nervous."

Shanna frowned. "Nervous? Why? You've been in space before. This is my first time, and I'm not all that nervous."

"I have my reasons," Brian said, and turned around, exiting the rear compartment.

Shanna frowned again, and shook her head. *What a freak.* She returned her gaze to the magnificent view out the bulkhead window.

Mike slipped the casing off the final bolt and whirred the bolt out of socket with a power tool tethered to his belt. With the bolt in a canvas bag, he keyed his radio and spoke with Donnie, who awaited him in the flight deck. "Atlas deck, this is EVA. We are clear for cone release."

"Roger that, EVA. Ejecting cones now."

A motor spun up and the insides of the cone couplings spun a quarter-turn counter-clockwise, and they were free of the ship. Mike had his hands on the edges of the cones, and as soon as they were free, he pulled them back and away from the shuttle, sending them flailing out into space behind him like lost ballet dancers.

"Objective complete. Returning to ship."

"Roger that, EVA."

Mike pulled his tether and yanked himself back around the edge of the shuttle, smiling at the formalities of radio conversation. Everything spoken into the headsets was recorded by the ship's computer, and had the potential to be rebroadcast. Everything had to be formal, short of announcements made over the general intercom.

When Mike was safely back inside the cargo bay, the doors were cranked silently closed, and the airlock was allowed to open. He pressurized inside the airlock, then took off his EVA suit and entered the rear cabin to find Shanna there waiting for him. She was smiling pleasantly.

"You have a good spacewalk?"

Mike smiled back and pushed through the rear cabin and back up to the flight deck. "Good to go," he said to Donnie. They buckled themselves back in and prepared for the docking procedure that should have taken place over a half-hour ago. "Computers resunk?"

"Resunk?" Donnie said, frowning awkwardly.

"Past-tense of sink. Sunk." Mike smiled and Donnie finally caught on.

"Yeah. They're sunk. I just hope we're not sunk, Mike."

"Ladies and gentlemen, this is your captain speaking. Please return your seatbacks to their upright position, and extinguish all cigarettes. We are now enroute to Alpha. For real this time. Lock yourselves in, and we'll dock here in about ten minutes."

Under-wing thrusters kicked on and shot jets of pure nitrogen into the nothingness. The shuttle crept slowly back toward the space station. After several minutes, the tops of the wings hit the beams of the welcome dock, then settled on a flat path to the end of the run. Shortly afterward, the nose met the end of the run and stopped the ship with a sharp jolt much like walking into a wall without slowing.

Immediately, electromagnetic rotors kicked on within the docking run, locking the shuttle into place. The comm-probe married with the patch panel on the shuttle, and synchronization began. The Atlas had finally made dock with Alpha.

Donnie pushed his way down the entrance tunnel to Alpha's main operations quarters while the maintenance crew readied the trailer, and Brian Bradley began removing the autopilot. The tunnel was lined with fluorescent lights that seemed to flicker when he wasn't looking directly at them. He suddenly had a screaming headache he very much suspected had come from his lack of sleep the night before. His reassuring comfort was that they were now in the realm of indistinguishable daily passage. There were no nights or days in space, and – aside from their daily exercises and experiments to be conducted on the way to Mars – there was no reason Donnie couldn't sleep for twelve-hour spans.

After fumbling his way dizzily into the terminal room, he logged into the docking log terminal and signed in the equipment they were to drop off for use in the Alpha test facilities. There were two cargo boxes full of equipment he would be responsible for getting unloaded while the rest of the crew was at work on the propulsion system. He completed the log and made the necessary changes to the weights and balances matrix, then made his way back to the dock to operate the cargo crane and remove the crates.

Donnie pushed open the airlock door and made his way into the depressurization chamber, then out into the vast empty wilderness of space, just above the nose of the shuttle. He favored this very spot on the space station, as it faced away from Earth and put ninety percent of Alpha behind and below him. From this point, he was surrounded on all sides by nothing but the backdrop of flickering stars, so far, yet so seemingly close. It was easy to imagine floating in space with no aid around him anywhere, and no connection to anything terrestrial. He could be lost in space with no hope of rescue, no chance of return. And it was comfortably spooky.

| CHAPTER *eighteen* |

enroute

The mass antimatter storage trap, commonly called the MAST, consisted of two anti-polar magnetic penning chambers hardwired to the blast chamber in the rear of the shuttle. From these two steel-encased chambers – each about the size of a small safe – particles were extracted and sent to the blast chamber along copper tubes. The blast chamber is where the fusion took place. This is where the particles of antimatter met their negatives and annihilated each other, releasing disproportionately large amounts of energy, and all this happened three-hundred-thousand times per second, propelling the ship with silent force.

Each of the penning chambers contained about ten kilograms of antimatter particles, which was more than enough to last the fifteen-month trip, if fired on schedule. Once the ship was up to speed, there was no need to fire the engines, as the shuttle would remain in motion by force of natural physics. Only minor adjustments to the attitude of the shuttle were needed during most of the journey, and those were made with sharp blasts of nitrogen from small jets strategically located around the shuttle.

The converter cone (which directed the energetic blasts into useable force) and the fusion chamber had been installed with no hitches, and shuttle Atlas was now ready to depart for Mars. As the crew settled into their seats and buckled down, nervousness was once again present in the Atlas. But this time it was an expectant energy that seemed electric with hope and excitement. They were finally about to point their ship at a foreign planet and blast off to meet it.

Donnie and Mike checked in with Houston again and said goodbye, knowing they wouldn't be able to see Earth again for quite some time once they left. It would disappear away and behind them, curling on its orbit, long out of sight and on its way to the other side of the sun. Donnie felt the excitement in his stomach as he tightened his harness and looked at Mike.

"We got four minutes. Anything we're forgetting?" he said.

Mike looked out the front windscreen, then back at Donnie. "Well we could swing by and pick up the girls," he said, shrugging.

Donnie nodded and looked back at the Earth again, hovering so closely above them. "Yeah, that would be nice. It's gonna get a little lonely out here with just Shanna and Andy."

Mike scratched his neck and made a point of trying to act like he hadn't heard that part about Andy. "Check it out," he said, pointing out the windscreen. A lightning storm was visible over a small piece of the Atlantic. Small was relative though; they knew it was hundreds of miles wide.

Donnie drew in a deep breath, then looked at the mission clock, steadily counting down the remaining seconds until they were cleared from Alpha. They would have to wait until they reached the dark side of the planet, putting them on a path straight to Mars. They had made good time on the repairs and refits. The clock read thirty seconds.

Mike nodded and pulled back on the dock release handle. A loud clang sounded somewhere behind them, and the Atlas began rising away from the space station. With a few minor adjustments from the nitrogen jets, they were pointing straight into their destiny. At ten seconds he pulled back on the antimatter thrust levers. The air felt crisp and dry in the flight deck all of a sudden. Donnie clicked off the approach lights. They looked at each other again, shook hands, and let her wail. Within five seconds, the Atlas was tearing through the galaxy at close to twenty-thousand kilometers per hour, and still accelerating.

Donnie unbuckled himself shortly after achieving cruise speed, and now yanked the rope handles attached to the walls, pulling himself back into the cabin to speak with his crew.

"Congratulations, ladies and gentlemen. We are officially on our way to the Red Planet. The engines have been shut off; we are drifting at a comfortable twenty eight thousand kilometers per hour, and are eighty-eight days away from being the first humans in history to visit another planet. It's okay to get excited now. We're finally on our way and nothing can stop us from achieving and attaining celebrity."

"Woo hoo!" Mike yelled from behind Donnie, raising his hand as if to toast with a glass of champagne. Other cheers erupted from some of the crewmembers and some even got out of their seats to hug and clap each other's backs. Brian Bradley, however, remained almost motionless, staring at the wall beside his seat. He was pale and sickly looking. Donnie shot Andy a piercing glance and twitched his head back to get her attention. She made her way over to him and they excused themselves into a different compartment.

"What the hell is wrong with him?" Donnie said, pointing back toward the cabin.

Andy raised her hands and closed her eyes. "Slow down, Donnie. He's extremely nervous. He's got…"

"Nervous? What the hell does he have to be nervous about? He's been on ten missions with me!"

Andy reached back and grabbed a handle by the doorway to keep herself from banging into the ceiling. "Not to Mars he hasn't, Donnie. You have to take it easy with him."

Donnie took a deep breath. "I am. I have been. That's why I'm talking to you instead of him."

"Good. Keep doing that. And tell Mike to do the same thing. I know how much they grate on each other," Andy said.

"Yeah. Matter, antimatter."

Andy smiled. "And you tell Mike he can't speak to Brian from now on but by Andy proxy. Brian doesn't need the stress right now."

"Oh come on!" Donnie said and waved his hand at her. "You're talking like he's a child or something. We're all nervous here, Andy. This is ridiculous."

"Donnie, calm down!" Andy said, grabbing him by the shoulders. "You're forgetting how taxing something like this can be on someone's psyche!" She grabbed the handle again with one hand. "You hired me to take care of your crew, did you not?"

Donnie nodded reluctantly. He liked the element of control, and felt it was slipping from his grasp.

"Well you can either let me do my job, or turn this ship around and take me home."

Donnie laughed out loud. "Okay. Do your job. But you know I'm worried about him aside from just being pissed off at him. You know if he dies we have to deal with him."

Andy was taken aback by his extreme example. "Donnie, he's not going to die. He's just a little in shock. He'll be fine. He'll adapt."

"Okay. I'll take your word for it. I need him to be well. He's my systems guy."

Andy patted Donnie on the shoulder and smiled, then turned and made her way back to where the rest of the crew was celebrating.

The crew worked a twelve-hour day, performing experiments during most of the shift, and checking their own parts of the ship as schedules dictated. Gary Grant oversaw these experiments; Jonathan Rodgers controlled the EVA and its functional capacities;

Shanna King kept the video and camera equipment, and logged everything captured therein; Brian Bradley kept a close eye on the general systems of the shuttle; Mike Thurman watched over the entire project and maintained the computers; Donnie flew the bird and commanded the schedule, which he pronounced "shed-jewel" just to be funny, and Andy Duryea kept an eye on all the people.

When the twelve-hour shifts were spent – or the respective schedule was met (whichever came first) – the crew had nothing but downtime. And with no dawns or dusks to mark the passage of time, sleep schedules were loose and irregular at best. After three weeks of it, everyone started to fall gently into the routine and become comfortable with the new way of life, and the culture shock faded gracefully.

Exercise routines were rigorous and fierce – as the body would lose up to eighty percent of its bone mass in a six-month stint with no gravity. The shuttle had a small section that rotated, which generated a centrifugal force equivalent to one and a half Gs. Each of the crewmembers was required to spend at least three hours a day exercising within the simulated gravity.

The seats in the rest area formed a rough circle where the crew could sit and chat during the downtime. Several of the crew were gathered there now. It was the twenty-fourth day of the mission, and the crew had settled comfortably into the rhythm of space flight. They had been sharing anecdotes for the last hour or so when Donnie came into the room and caught the tail end of one of Gary's.

"So I'm lagging a little behind because I had to tie my shoe. Both women are already past the swing set on the way back to the car, so I jog a little to catch back up. Now keep in mind, I was fresh out of the Navy, and in great shape. But my dexterity was still a little behind schedule.

"Well, I decided I'd be cute and jump *through* one of the swings."

Several laughed at this, seeing where the story was going. The lights flickered momentarily, and Shanna looked up nervously. She looked as if she were about to speak when Donnie quelled her fears. "Don't worry. Electromagnetic field. Probably from the solar flares. It's harmless."

"So anyway, where was I?" Gary said.

Jonathan reminded him, "You jumped through the swing."

"Yeah, so I think I'm in pretty good with these girls – I might get laid tonight, you know, the usual thoughts a guy has at that age."

"At any age, Gary," Andy said. More laughter. "That's not something you men appear to grow out of at all."

"Well they both liked me and it was looking good, and I was confident and excited. I guess a little too excited, because I decided to jump through that swing. My foot caught it and I went face down in the hard-packed dirt. It wasn't like some slow arc toward the ground where I had time to throw out my hands or anything. It was rapid. And I ate dirt. Literally."

After the roaring laughter died down a little, Andy caught her breath enough to speak. "So did they see you or what?"

"No, they didn't. I think they heard the sound though, because one of them turned around to see what was going on, and there I was laying on the ground, wiping dirt off my face. She saw the swing still swinging, looking up and down between it and me, and put two and two together. And I could see it click in her eyes. I saw it dawn on her, and she just freakin' lost it. They laughed at me 'til they were crying."

The whole crew was laughing now, and Shanna and Andy were wiping tears from their eyes. "I'm crying now, and I wasn't even there!" Andy said.

"So I guess you didn't get laid that night," Shanna said.

Gary shook his head. "Nope. Didn't happen."

"Oh man, you handled it wrong. I got laid *because* of stuff like that," Mike said. "I slipped in a puddle at the mall one time when I was about sixteen, walking toward a group of girls sitting by a fountain. I didn't even see the 'wet floor' sign, and my feet went right up in front of me. I landed hard on my ass.

"But I'd been walking toward those girls with the intention of picking at least one of them up, so I carried on. I got up and brushed myself off and walked right up to them. They were laughing so hard they had milk coming out their noses, but I approached them anyway. I said, 'So I guess I just ruined any chance I might have had with you ladies, didn't I?' They kept laughing, but one of them said no, and patted the seat beside her. She was telling me to sit down. I got her number and everything. We went out that night and I had her in the sack by the weekend."

"Mister Smooth," Shanna said, smiling broadly.

"Well, you just have a way with women, man. I've never been that keen," said Gary.

Andy said, "I think some women just like goofy guys though too. Which is probably why Lucy married you." The crew laughed again.

After the party had broken up, several went to sleep shift, and Shanna stopped Donnie in the main hall.

"Donnie, will you explain to me what that freakish light show was?" she said.

He frowned for a moment, and then remembered the flicker of the lights a few minutes before. "Oh, that. There are clouds that hang out in the vacuum of space that hold nothing but electromagnetic energy. We sometimes run through them. Usually you don't even notice because the clouds are so small, and we travel so fast. But sometimes they're large enough to actually interfere with our systems."

"Isn't that bad though?" she said, more curious than worried.

"Nah," he said, shaking his head. "The only system it interferes with is the lighting, and that's only because it's basic electricity. Sometimes the clouds are so large that the lights flicker for a minute or two. And a lot of this may be caused by the solar flares. They're worse than they've been in about a hundred years. We may see a lot more flickers before this thing is over with."

"Okay. Well it scared me a little."

Donnie looked her up and down. "So, have you been shooting some good video?"

Shanna shrugged. "Sure. I guess. It's all pretty much the same stuff as always. I'm ready to get outside the shuttle and get some pictures of it. And of course to film stuff on Mars. That will make it all worthwhile."

Donnie nodded again. "You say you're ready to do a spacewalk? Are you sure about that?"

"Oh yeah, absolutely," she said.

"Well I'll see what I can do next time there's a reason to go out."

Shanna's eyes widened. "Really? Oh my God!"

"You excited?"

"Hell yes I'm excited, Donnie! You'd really let me do that? I don't have to have any training or anything?"

"Pfft. No. You just tether yourself to the ship and jump out."

"Oh my God, that would be so bad ass," she affirmed.

Donnie assured Shanna he would find her when it was time, and made his way back to the flight deck to check things out. Brian Bradley had repaired the autopilot at dock, and they had experienced no other problems with any of the systems since. Time seemed to have slowed though, as the minutes stretched into hours, the hours into days. Days in the void. The trading of anecdotes became a favored pastime, as did simple games that brought the crew together and took their collective mind off the vast expanses of time they had to fill. The powerhouse pushing them across the empty distance – along with most of the other systems onboard the shuttle – was taken for granted by everyone but the systems officer. And it seemed he was paying more attention to it than even necessary. But all found their own ways of dealing with the downtime. And there was a lot of downtime with which to be dealt.

Shanna's time came more quickly than she had expected. A week after she had spoken to Donnie about the EVA, he came to her in the communal room where she was studying up on some of the specifics of the foreign planet. She had strapped herself into the seat and had a laptop snapped to the chair arms so she could read easily.

Donnie pulled himself into the room by way of the handles bolted into the tunnel wall. "Shanna. Get ready."

She looked up, a little confused. "What? Ready for what?"

"I'm kicking you out of the ship."

"Really? Oh my God, I'm so excited!" she nearly screamed, and unbuckled herself. Donnie talked her through all the hazards and precautions, and then enlisted Andy to assist in helping Shanna suit up. It took at least two people to connect and check all the fittings, then run pressure checks to make sure there were no leaks in the nylon fabric.

Almost an hour later, she looked like a marshmallow man in the unisex suit, which was twice her size to begin with. Donnie connected the lifeline – the tether cable that would keep her from floating away coupled with the oxygen hose – and pushed her into the airlock chamber with Mike, who would be joining her on her first spacewalk. Together, they were to inspect the fusion chamber and make sure everything was in place. Of course it would be, but

Donnie had to create inspections like that – necessary as they really were – to kill the time.

Shanna had taken the video camera out with her to get some good footage of the shuttle and the outside view of the Milky Way, but was so excited about being outside the ship that she almost completely forgot she had it with her. Most of the footage was spinning dizzy and vague, as she was moving about so much. There were a few good seconds' worth of video that could be used, and Donnie was able to show her what she had done so that she would be better suited for the next time she went out. He promised her she would get another chance, and told her how to make the most of it when she went.

Shanna was keeping a journal of her daily activities in addition to the professional video and photography journal she was in charge of. She would write letters to her mother and father telling them of her experiences and how exciting it was to be in space. She had Andy take some pictures of her doing various things around the shuttle, which she would eventually have printed and placed in a photo album. The whole thing was almost overwhelmingly exciting for Shanna, but one would never tell by looking at her. Her organizational skills coupled with her massive amounts of pre-trip planning made her look like a seasoned professional.

By the time the sixth week rolled around, she had filled two leather-bound journals with letters, notes, comments and feelings. She had even written a poem to capture the essence of her feelings.

Several of the crew asked for copies of the poem, and all were impressed, but Shanna apologetically told them that one was for her. She said she would write them all another one some other time. And some of the crew who had perhaps previously thought of her as just a dumb bimbo started to develop a little respect for her.

It was the forty-fifth day of the mission. Mike was checking the course and the flight deck computers and gauging the readings against the Expected Readings Charts when he received a radio transmission from Houston. Shortly after departure from Alpha, the radios had been switched to the Bell-Binary system, which used a text message interface as opposed to the vocal transmissions. The farther from Earth the shuttle got, the longer it would take to transmit and receive radio dialog, even using photon-optic technology. Even at light speed, radio transmissions would take minutes to send one way. The Bell-Binary system was instantaneous communication.

The shuttle's radio base station monitored E-particles, whose other halves existed in the base station of Houston's radio. The E-particles were binary in disposition, thus if one switched positions, its other half – no matter where it was in the universe – would follow suit instantaneously. The Einstein-Boseman theory suggested that these particles were connected through a deeper reality. Within the proprietary nature of these particles, communications between the two units was exclusive – not to mention private – by default.

Mike looked up when the terminal beeped at him. A message was blinking on the screen:

```
HOUSTON;pss-704/jCallahan@ >
INCOMING, GENERAL
```

The header told Mike the sender's information in detail, which was unnecessary on ships using privatized space traffic control centers. Ships that were equipped with public radios had multiple channels, much like a CB so the traffic control facilities could pass the shuttle to another facility. In these cases, the header was important. But on this private ship, the radio had only been programmed with the single private channel to Privatized Spatial Services, Inc. Thus on this radio, the header was actually a redundant security accessory to something that happened intrinsically between the twin radio partners.

After accepting the message, the header would drop off, and the rest of the incoming messages would be prefaced with HOUSTON only. The pss-704 was the company and its federal office ID number, then the user, which was Julia Callahan. The GENERAL stamp meant that the message was not addressed to anyone specific.

Mike accepted the message, and replied.

```
ATLAS: This is Mike. Hello Houston

HOUSTON: Hi Mike. Is Mr. Oliver
available?
```

ATLAS: He's running some
diagnostics, but I'm sure I can get
him up here if it's urgent

HOUSTON: Roger that Atlas. Ms.
Simmons is here and needs a private
chat with Mr. Oliver.

Mike frowned at her sudden transformation to formal radio communiqué, then replied.

ATLAS: Okay, I'll get him up here
pronto, Houston. Stand by

He turned to the PA and keyed the internal microphone. "Mr. Oliver, please report to the cockpit."

Within a couple of minutes, Donnie came floating through the flight deck gangway looking a little perplexed. "Hey, Mike. What's up?"

Mike shook the transmitter from side to side. "It's Houston. They say Callie needs a private chat with you. Says it's important."

Donnie frowned as he took the seat from Mike and strapped himself in. "Callie is there? In Houston?"

Mike nodded. Donnie turned to the keyboard.

ATLAS: houston this is oliver

HOUSTON: Mr. Oliver, Ms. Simmons is
here and says she has an urgent
message for you. Are you alone?

ATLAS: yeah

Donnie turned to Mike and said, "Mike, gimme just a minute, will you?" Mike nodded and backed out of the flight deck and slid the door shut.

HOUSTON: Okay, I'm putting her on now. Thank you Mr. Oliver.

Donnie had a sudden chill, as if in precognitive subconscious awareness. If Callie had flown to Houston just to speak with him, it was more than just a little urgent. She rarely even communicated with him on a mission when it was important. For her to be calling, someone must have died.

HOUSTON: This is Callie. Is this Donnie?

ATLAS: hey hey! caliente! how you doing girl

HOUSTON: Fine, Donnie. I've got something really weird on my hands here.

Donnie's immediate instinct was to think something was wrong with the company, as if it wouldn't survive without him being there. He knew better though. There was Samson, who really did run the company, Callie, who could easily run it, and several others who had it in their best interest to run it right if things went south.

ATLAS: well tell me about it, cal

HOUSTON: We received a shipment
from Lockheed three days ago.

ATLAS: thats great callie

He knew it was more important than her just receiving a shipment – even if it wasn't what she had ordered. She wasn't the type to report things unnecessarily. He was just excited about her getting to the point.

HOUSTON: This shipment was a
truckload. Literally. There were an
itemized two hundred and nine parts
in that shipment. They had all been
ordered at the same time, but some
had to be put on backorder. They
were all shipped together though,
at the purchaser's request.

Donnie thought about this for a few seconds, and – discovering he could make nothing of it – he replied.

ATLAS: callie im not following

HOUSTON: Donnie, these parts were
all ordered for Atlas.

ATLAS: we don't need em! were
almost there!

Donnie felt the relief of some of the anxiety he had been harboring since the conversation began. His extreme exaggeration of their progress was supposed to be a joke, but Callie didn't respond to it. It had been forty-five days, and they were about halfway to Mars.

```
HOUSTON: Well, anyway, these parts
are all here. I had to sign for
them. And I thought it odd they'd
come in after the shuttle left.
They got here about three days ago.

ATLAS: well you said they were on
backorder callie
```

He still wasn't catching her drift, and badly wanted her to get to the point.

```
HOUSTON: Six weeks is a long time
for backorder. And that's a lot of
parts.

ATLAS: callie im still not with
you. we restock common parts all
the time

HOUSTON: Well, that's a lot of
parts at once, and it totaled over
three million dollars. If they've
not been used, that's a lot to be
'restocking'. Do you usually order
that many parts at once just to
restock?
```

ATLAS: no i dont. our parts orderer usually does the ordering callie. i dont keep up with how many parts we order at a time so i dont know if thats unusual or not. if it really bothers you though figure it out and get back to me okay

HOUSTON: That was precisely my intention. I need full authority from you to investigate this though. I need access to people's computers and files - everything.

ATLAS: granted. i think your overreacting about this callie but do what you need.

HOUSTON: Will do. Thanks Donnie. Talk to you soon.

| **CHAPTER** *twenty* |

insecurity

"What was that about?" Mike asked after Donnie had emerged from the flight deck.

Donnie shook his head and furled his mouth, dismissively. "Nothing. Bradley restocked a bunch of parts and Callie's freakin' out over the cost."

"That's unlike her to come calling over something so trivial," Mike said.

"Yeah, well it was over three-million dollars though, so it worried her a little. Usually she doesn't have to deal with deliveries."

"So you cool her off?" Mike said, and nudged Donnie toward the galley.

"I told her to check it out. Hey, you know what?"

Mike pointed toward the galley. "Go. That way. I'm hungry." Donnie started moving again. "What? What's up?"

"Those two forgotten crates got put on here, didn't they?"

Mike snorted. "I sure as hell hope so."

"Well I just don't remember seeing them get loaded."

"There's a thousand crates you didn't *see* get loaded though, Donnie. I'm sure it's like leaving the coffee maker on or closing the garage door. You think about it later, 'cause you can't remember doing it, but it's so routine it doesn't take any thought. I'm sure they're here. That new loadmaster is pretty thorough."

"Yeah I'm sure. I wanna see them though."

Donnie opened the airlock that led into the cargo bay and turned on the cargo lights. They blinked eerily to life, illuminating the cold darkness and casting long shadows against the curved walls. There were hundreds of crates on the flat side, all strapped in and bound tight against the steel walls of the shuttle. He looked over at Mike and shook his head. If they were to find the two mysterious crates, it would be miraculous.

"You know," Donnie said, stopping and turning to Mike.

"Yes?" Mike said, pressing Donnie to continue.

"It would be so easy to sneak shit onto the shuttle. That many people running around the hangar, this many crates back here."

"Yeah I've often thought about that. For as secure as the area is, the process sure doesn't seem very tight."

Mike pushed over to a large lockdown area on the far side of the bay. They both grabbed one end of the web strap that held all the crates and boxes in place, and unlocked it, pulling it away from the wall. Several of the crates moved a little, but most were locked in by secondary chains and cables. In the center of the lock area was a large steel green box that was unfamiliar to Donnie.

"What's that?" he said, pointing at it.

Mike shrugged. "That's not test equipment is it?"

"Not that I've seen," Donnie replied. Mike pushed forward, floating over to the center of the area, directly above the crate. He reached down beside it, searching for a chain or a strap that would set it free. But finding none, he moved to the other side of it. Grabbing the edge of the crate, he pulled himself across.

"Good God!" he shouted, retracting his hand immediately.

"What? What's wrong?" Donnie said, alarmed.

"What the hell is in that thing? It's cold as hell!" His hand was very red from the contact, and looked as though some of his skin had been left on the crate.

Donnie frowned, looking back and forth between the crate and Mike's hand. "Cold? That's strange."

Mike looked up at him. "Dude, it's like licking a frozen flagpole. My skin's gone!" They both looked at the corner of the crate where he had touched. Indeed, there was frosty skin stuck to the edge. Mike grabbed hold of the edge of another crate next to it and pulled himself down to have a closer look, this time without touching the cold one.

"Donnie, you'll want to see this."

"What? What is it?"

"This thing's covered with frost."

Papers lay sprawled all over the living room floor, and Callie sat Indian-style in the middle of it all, a fat potter's mug of cooling coffee in one hand and her wrecked hair in the other. She had not gone to sleep the night previous, after confirmation of her worst fears, and was running low on the six hours of sleep she'd had the night before last. She had flown home from Houston and made a pot of coffee, turned on her radio and plopped down on the carpet to figure it all out. It was four o'clock in the morning and she felt she had gotten no further than when she had started nearly twelve hours ago. She was exhausted and hurting, sitting in her panties and a t-shirt in the middle of the floor. Her back and head had turned to pain factories, and she was in danger of passing out and forgetting where she had left off.

The papers ranged from invoices to purchase orders, from packing lists to personal notes – all from the office of Brian Bradley. But she could see nothing wrong with any of it. There was nothing incriminating in what she was looking at. And yet she knew there was something amiss. Something sinister loomed beneath the surface of the shining white papers at which she was staring, and had been staring at for the last half century of waking. She picked up a sheaf of the papers closest to her right knee and fanned them in her hand, crumpling the bottoms as she squeezed and sighed. Useless. She had wasted all this time, when all he had done was order some parts. Granted there were over three-million dollars' worth of parts sitting in the receiving dock back at work, that's all they were. Parts.

She drew her weak bloodshot eyes over the papers in her hand for the thousandth time, hoping something would jump out at her. If something didn't jump out at her this time around, there was nothing else she could do. She was out of options, and ready to climb into bed for a week. Nothing special appeared on the paper though. Not until her eyes reached the bottom of it. She read the same three words five or six times before she realized what she was reading. It was like listening to the radio while reading a novel – she found herself rereading a sentence ten times before she realized she wasn't really paying attention to what she was reading. Then the three words magically transformed into a meaningful phrase that sent chills up her bare white legs. The bottom of the sheet read:

CANARY – CUSTOMER COPY

She sat up straight, her eyes opening wide, and scanned the room again, looking at all the papers lying on her floor. They were all white, and they were all the same twenty-pound stock. Thick white paper. Not thin, colorful carbon paper, the kind typically used for invoices. These were either copies or contrivances.

"Holy cow," she said aloud. She began rapidly gathering up as much of the paper as she could reach without getting up, and fanned through it. Every sheet was the same weight and color, and most of it contained the same typeface. *So if he was creating his own invoices, what did he do with the real ones?* That was the question. He had probably either burned them or run them through the shredder. She doubted he was stupid enough to keep them at all – much less somewhere in his office – which she had access to. Even still, if he had been stupid enough to use the same fonts and paper stock to make his fakes, she might just be surprised yet.

She pushed herself up with popping elbows and dashed to her bedroom to throw on some sweat pants and a beanie cap. Callie grabbed her keys from the small dish by the door and reached for the doorknob and stopped abruptly. She realized she wasn't even wearing a bra, and on a brisk night like tonight it would be rather obvious. Especially if she spent any longer than a few minutes in Bradley's office. The crews would be showing up for work in the next couple of hours. She ran back and threw on a bra, then headed out the door, barely even turning around to throw the deadbolt.

Shanna lay strapped partially into her bed, reading one of the paperbacks she had brought along, killing some of the long hours she had to herself. Her room light was off, but she had a small reading lamp on behind her head. She looked up as Gary came floating through her open door.

"Hey, girl. How can you read in the dark?" he said, flipping the light switch by the door. A screaming siren blasted into the cold air, ten decibels and wailing with intensity like a sonic staring-at-the-sun. Shanna threw her hands over her ears, her heart skipping several beats, then banging in her chest like a damaged drum. The color immediately washed from Gary's face as well, and – despite their being in zero-gravity, he visibly jumped hard.

"What the hell?" she said, pushing hard away from the bed and toward the gangway. "Move! Move, move, move!" she shouted, pushing Gary out of the way.

The triangular lights in the corridor were blinking in rhythm with the wailing siren, a sickening array of noise and lightning. Quickly, Donnie came rocketing by, grabbing the handles on the wall, thrusting himself down the corridor. Mike was right on his heels. Mike looked at Shanna on his way by – fear evident in his eyes. She shot off down the hallway after them, eager to see what was going on. Donnie stopped and turned toward her, knowing she would be in pursuit.

"Shut that damn door. And get up to the cockpit. I need someone up there."

Shanna's heart sank. She was immediately angered with being shut out. As she turned to head back, a wide-eyed Gary appeared in the hallway behind her. She thought quickly, and – turning to see if Donnie was still visible – made a command decision, and delegated.

"Go! Get up to the cockpit and monitor the internal! And close that door!"

Gary nodded quickly and pulled the door closed behind him. Shanna bolted back down the hallway in the direction she had been headed, pursuing the captain of the ship. They came flying through the common area where Andy was scared stiff, her back against the far wall, holding onto the handles beside her with white knuckles and a determination unmatched.

Down the far corridor, Shanna finally caught sight of Mike's boot again, and pulled with everything she had to catch up. As she made the twenty-degree bend in the corridor, Jonathan Rodgers came barreling out of a side door and slammed into her, knocking her back against the opposing wall.

"Oh my God, I'm sorry, Shanna! Are you all right?" he screamed over the blasting alarm.

She nodded quickly, squinting against the pain she felt in her ribs, and pressed on, suppressing the exquisite desire she suddenly had to cry out. Tears stung her eyes. But she moved on. And as she passed through the next gangway, she smelled smoke. There was mass confusion – everyone was yelling at once, and the screaming alarms were blotting out most of the words. She couldn't make out anything they were yelling above the pain she felt in her ribs and head. But she could see the smoke, and was beginning to recognize the smell of it.

Shanna drifted into the cargo pressure chamber, and everything began to make sense. Brian Bradley was being held against the back wall by an angry

Donnie, and a crushed cigarette floated lazily a few feet in front of him.

"Where the hell did you get it?" Donnie shouted.

Brian shook his head quickly. Donnie shoved him harder against the wall, and Brian looked like he might black out. Shanna felt she could empathize, as she very much felt like blacking out right now, herself.

"Where did you get it? Did you smuggle a pack of cigarettes onto my shuttle?" Donnie yelled.

Brian finally began to speak, but his words were almost inaudible over the alarm. He was pointing furiously at the door that led out of the pressurization chamber and into the cargo bay itself. And Shanna finally became aware of why she couldn't hear Brian. Donnie's hand was wrapped tightly around his throat, and Brian's face was turning blue.

Hot blood pumped through her head, clouding her vision. She could almost see the blood. She pushed forward, but Mike turned and put a hand firmly on her chest, holding her back with barely a struggle. She had no momentum, and there was nothing to give her traction. She was too far from a wall to push, and Mike had hold of a handle.

"Donnie stop it – you're choking him!" Shanna screamed.

Donnie turned to look at her, and – through his red rage – almost seemed to smile at her. Then his attitude changed quickly, regaining its previous force and direction. "Shanna, I thought I told you to get your ass in the cockpit."

She still struggled against Mike's hand, keeping her at bay, and flailed madly around in the dead air. "Donnie, you're killing him! Stop it!"

"Get the fuck in the cockpit, Shanna! That's an order! And get that damn alarm shut off!"

"Donnie don't!" she screamed, now in tears. She didn't like Brian Bradley, but she didn't want to see him die at Donnie's angry hand. "Donnie please!" she said, bawling now. He wasn't letting up. Brian had stopped resisting now, too weak to raise his hands against the attack. Donnie turned and made a slight head gesture at Mike, and Mike quickly responded by turning and pushing Shanna out the gangway through which she had come.

| CHAPTER *twenty-two* |

The office lights flickered as she threw the switch. It was cold and dead in here being unoccupied for the last seven weeks. Callie began looking for clues around the room. The ceiling tiles were a potential, as was the safe that stood at the end of Bradley's desk. It would probably take her an hour to find the code for the safe lock though, and she had nothing to stand on to check in the ceiling tiles. She had already raided the filing cabinet and all his desk drawers, and had spent hours on his computer looking for files. But something told her she was staring right at the answer.

On impulse, she opened the bottom drawer of the file cabinet again and tried to remove it. It slid all the way out, leaving a two-inch gap between the back wall of the drawer and the opening. If she had a flashlight, she could peer down into the gap and see if he had stashed anything down there. She stood up, hands on her hips, and looked around the office. Or she could just lift the cabinet and look under the edge. She squinted and pursed her lips at this new perspective, then pushed on the top of the cabinet's side, away from the desk. It took some rocking, but it went over rather easily and slammed down onto the concrete floor with a forceful bang that reverberated throughout the adjoining hangar with an intensity that could easily have rivaled a grenade blast. The sudden explosion of sound startled Callie, even as she had been armed with the expectation of its arrival.

She had to stand still for a moment and let the scare float away before she moved again. She knelt and looked at the dusty brown outline on the floor where once stood the file cabinet. And in the middle, a stack of papers an inch thick wrapped with a rubber band stood untouched. Bingo. She swooped them up and thumbed through them quickly, confirming her suspicions. As she was about to bound over the cabinet and out the door, she paused and looked back at the computer. It was still humming under the desk. *I better shut that back off.*

She set the sheaf of papers on the desk and sat down behind the terminal. When she moved the mouse, the screen flicked back on and began brightening. And then a thought struck her. If he had been making fake invoices to print out and file, and they all looked the same, then he was probably using a template. She clicked start and a menu popped up. She moved the mouse up the menu and highlighted *Recent Documents*, which opened a long list of documents. In that list there were several picture files mixed in with the rest of the files. *This could be interesting...*

Callie double-clicked one of the pictures, a faint smile painting her face as she realized she was being bad. She had never before been so nosey as to dig around on someone else's hard drive looking for dirt.

But she had just found it. And the smile slid right off
her face.

"So how long have you been smoking?" Donnie
said. They were crowded into a storage area near the
rear of the shuttle. It had been an hour since the alarms
went off. Everyone was beginning to cool off a little.
The boxes stacked along the back wall were tied in
with wrapping plastic, which had been sliced neatly
down the middle. Donnie had opened the box Brian
Bradley had pointed out to him, revealing several
cartons of Ranch Hand, Deluxe Cut Cigarettes.

"I've smoked for a lot longer than I've worked for
you," Bradley said, suddenly adopting an attitude with
which Donnie had not previously been familiar. "I just
don't do it in front of people."

"Yeah, but you do it on my ship."

"Donnie, it's been rough. I've been taking this real
hard, it's…"

"Taking what real hard? You act like you're some
neophyte space traveler! You've been here many
times, asshole!"

Gary held on in the doorway, making sure Donnie
didn't kill the guy. He'd had to pull Donnie off of
Bradley earlier. It had gotten to look like Donnie
indeed was going to choke Brian to death. Gary had

finally stepped in and yanked Donnie back to his senses. "Easy, Donnie."

Donnie looked back at Gary over his shoulder, then returned his focus to Brian. "You know how fast that shit eats up our oxygen? And you brought multiple cartons? What, did you think we wouldn't find out?"

Brian was shaking his head. "Donnie, look. I'm sorry man, but I've been nicking out, and I couldn't take it anymore."

"Yeah, that's why you don't bring that shit on board! If it ain't there, you can't succumb to the temptation. You don't think I want one? Or Mike? Hell, almost all of us are smokers!" Donnie said. "You smoke, don't you Gary?" He looked back at Gary, who shook his head thoughtfully. Donnie stared at him for a moment. "Here. Get rid of these," Donnie said, shoving the three cartons of cigarettes across the room to him.

"What do you want me to do with 'em?" Gary said, catching them all.

"Open hatch. Put them out. Don't think we'll get stopped for littering out here."

"Man, that's a waste of good smokes, Donnie," Brian said.

"You damn right it is. Is that all of them?"

Brian nodded. Donnie stuck his hand back in the open box and dug around for any evidence of more cartons. He pulled another carton free and slapped Brian across the face with it. "What do you think Mike?"

"You know, Donnie… I don't think you really want to hear what I think."

"What the hell are you talking about? What makes you say that? Of course I want to hear. That's why I asked you."

Mike sighed. "I think we could all use one. What's one smoke going to hurt?"

"What, are you crazy?" Donnie said.

"You know Donnie, I think he's right," Jonathan said. "I don't really need one, but I sure wouldn't mind the novelty of smoking one out here among the stars."

Donnie turned to look at everyone in the room. They all stared back at him, expressionless. It was his call. He breathed in deeply, then looked back at Brian. "Who all's in?"

The four men were crammed into the depressurization chamber, where at least the smoke wouldn't set off any alarms. Four cigarettes glowed in the low light as they clung to the walls with shaky hands. The nicotine was affecting them differently out here than it did on Earth.

"You know, I'm not certain," Mike said, looking at the cherry on his smoke, "but I think this may be the best damn cigarette I've ever smoked."

"You can say that again," marveled Jonathan.

Brian and Donnie simply nodded. There were two large windows in the room: one that looked out into the cargo bay, and another back into the ship, toward the rear. On impulse, Donnie turned toward the door and pushed the intercom button. "Gary, you in there?"

A moment later, his reply crackled through the set. "Yeah. I'm here. What's up?"

"Open the bay doors."

"Roger that."

Time seemed to stand still as the four of them hung there among the smoke, waiting expectantly. And after several long moments, the cargo bay doors jolted to life, and began sliding back into the frame, opening a narrow slice of stars that grew to fill the width of the entire bay. When the doors were full open, the view was complete. The four of them stared out at trillions of stars, smoking cigarettes.

And none of them said a word.

Callie had found her second wind and was still going at it for several more hours before she finally had all the pieces together. She stacked all her papers and snapped rubber bands on them, then dropped them into her portfolio. She had been typing up a document with all her points and theories on it, and a series of notes on where she had found what in the documents she had taken from Bradley's office. She was ready to present her case.

It was almost ten o'clock in the morning and the sun was banging hard on the living room floor of her apartment. Her eyes were red and burning, her hair was oily and messy – pulled into a sloppy ponytail, and she was beginning to take on a slight odor that she only caught a slight hint of every once in a while. She had been up for almost two days straight, and felt so exhausted, she was beginning to have hallucinations.

She stood up and leaned back, popping her back loudly, then made her way into the kitchen for a glass of orange juice.

Callie thought a steaming hot shower would wake her a little, but it only made her long for the bed even more. But now wasn't the time for sleeping. She now had vital information she needed to get to Donnie. And that meant she would have to fly back to Houston, just to communicate the information to him. She got dressed and locked the door, got in her car, and drove to work to take the private plane to Ellington Field in Houston. She was thirty minutes outside of Houston when she realized she had walked out of her apartment without the portfolio. Now she would have to wing it.

| **CHAPTER** *twenty-three* |

Donnie stared out the windscreen, relaxing, and on the threshold of dazing when the screen beside him blinked and a loud beep rang out. He shook his head, blinking, and turned to look at the monitor. A message awaited acceptance.

```
HOUSTON;pss-704/jCallahan@ >
INCOMING, GENERAL
```

He accepted the message and replied.

```
ATLAS: hello jcallahan its donnie

HOUSTON: Yes, I can tell when it's
you, Donnie. Don't type much do
you?

ATLAS: hell no not unless i have
to. i have a secretary for that
```

HOUSTON: Nice. Donnie, Ms. Simmons
is here again, and needs to speak
with you. Are you alone?

ATLAS: yes put her on

HOUSTON: Okay, here she is…

There was a brief pause before another message
appeared.

HOUSTON: Donnie, it's Callie.

ATLAS: whats up cal

HOUSTON: I've learned w9i####
####### ########

ATLAS: come again houston your all
jumbled

##USTO##
####################********

Donnie slapped the side of the monitor hard.

ATLAS: callie i cant read anything
your typing

#$$$$$$ $$$$$$
$########################### ####k##

Donnie started pounding the keys on the terminal
keyboard, but to no avail. The jumble didn't clear up.

"What the hell?" he said aloud. He slapped the monitor again, and reset it. At that moment, Mike came through the gangway.

"Hey DO, what's up?"

"Can you fix this thing? I'm trying to talk to Callie but it's all jumbled," Donnie said, slapping the monitor again.

"Hey, hey! Cut it with the disciplinary maintenance! That ain't gonna fix nothing." Mike came to the terminal and looked at the monitor.

"Well, it was working fine for a minute, then it started mucking up," Donnie said, unbuckling and pushing himself out of the way.

Mike buckled himself into the seat and looked closer at the monitor. "Oooh, shit. I don't think this is something I can fix, man. Only her text is getting scrambled. It's something either in the transmission or the descrambler."

"Shit. How the hell did that happen? This thing runs on subatoms. How do you screw something like that up?"

Mike shook his head, and another message popped up onto the screen, scrambled just like the others. "Damn. I don't know, but I'll try to recover the messages she sent."

Donnie frowned. "What do you mean?"

"Well all transmissions are recorded by the main computer. So everything she sent should be logged. If I can find the files, I might be able to open them manually."

"All right, you do that. You know this shit's important for Callie to fly out to Houston."

Mike nodded. He knew anything coming from Callie would be important – Callie was important.

Everything she said was like gold to most of them. Donnie left the cockpit, pulling the door closed behind him.

Back in the common area, Donnie ran into Gary Grant talking with Jonathan. It had been a while since he had checked in on them, and he wanted to see how the experiments were going. He hoped they were having better luck than he was having with the communications.

"What's up, Donnie?" Jonathan said.

Donnie sighed. "Comm is down. Got a message from Callie and it came in all jumbled."

"Damn, what happened?" Gary said.

"I have no idea. Mike's working on it now though. That's some serious shit if our radio goes out."

"Yeah, no doubt," Jonathan agreed.

"So how're the experiments coming?" Donnie said, trying to forget about the comm terminal. Maybe if he ignored the problem it would go away.

"As expected," Gary answered. "We're messing with the springs right now. Man, that Shanna is a sharp girl, Donnie."

Donnie snorted. "Why do you think she works for me?"

Gary looked at Jonathan, and slowly back to Donnie. He was smirking.

"Don't answer that," Donnie said, sighing. He realized his mistake in asking 'why do you think'. He shook his head. "So why is she so sharp?"

"Well she thinks she's found a way to trap the energy from a spring without losing it. I think she's working on the math right now. It's progressive though, and looks to be going well in the no-gravity," Gary said.

Donnie nodded appreciatively and looked at Jonathan, who was staring at him. "What the hell you looking at?"

"Give me a hint," Jonathan said, raising his chin. Donnie shook his head.

The intercom dinged, and Mike's voice sounded throughout the cabin. "Donnie, I need you in the cockpit."

"Guess he's fixed the comm terminal."

"Yeah, I'm wondering what Callie wanted. She flew down to tell you something, huh?" Jonathan said.

Donnie nodded. "Yeah. I had her checking on some stuff for me. No biggie."

Jonathan looked at Gary again, slightly amused. Donnie left the room and made his way back to the cockpit. He didn't see their exchanged glances. They knew as well as he did that anytime Callie made contact, something was on fire.

"What's up, Mike? You get it figured out?"

"Well, no. Not yet. I started checking out the systems though, trying to pinpoint it. And I came across something rather interesting," Mike said, turning to another terminal that was beeping at him. He hit a few keys and the beeping stopped.

"Interesting?" Donnie said, strapping himself into the captain's chair.

"Yeah. Check it out."

Mike pointed at the digital indicators on the terminal screen. "These are the expected readings." He then flipped a switch and the screen blinked over to monitor another terminal. Several terminals shared the same LCD in an effort to save space. Critical systems had their own gauges and monitors, but ancillary systems often herded ten to a monitor.

"And these are actual status indicators."

Donnie noticed the difference immediately. They were low on antimatter. It wasn't yet critical, but it was enough to have another look, and definitely worth keeping an eye on. "Have we been burning the whole time?" he asked, referring to the imaginary burning of the engines that produced no flame at all.

Mike shook his head, looking back at Donnie. "It may be a bad sensor. Off-scale low."

Donnie harrumphed. "Off-scale low. From a digital sensor."

"Especially from a digital sensor. That's the whole problem with the world today. We put way too much faith in computers to do our bidding," Mike said, shaking his head.

"Yeah, but this isn't the world. We're halfway to Mars and we have nothing else to rely on. Get that checked out," Donnie said.

"Already on it, boss."

Callie stood up from the terminal and straightened her skirt, then turned to address Julia, who was hovering nearby. "Something has happened, Ms. Callahan."

"Julia. What is it?"

"Well, their messages started getting jumbled. I don't know if he received my messages or not. He stopped responding entirely after a couple of messages. Either he quit receiving them, or just stopped replying. Maybe his side was jumbled too."

"That's bad. Something's wrong with the Bell-binary. That is our only way of contacting them," Julia said.

Callie chewed her lip, shaking her head. "I think they may be in grave danger, Julia. I'm beginning to get worried."

Julia nodded and put her hand on Callie's shoulder. "Those guys have been through a bunch of missions together. I'm sure they'll get it figured out."

Callie smirked. "Yeah, I guess. It's just a little worrisome when systems start going out."

"You're telling me," Julia agreed.

Mike pulled himself into the rear of the shuttle and opened the hatch that accessed the engine room. This is where the fuel pipes came in from the outside (where they connected to external fuel tanks) and ran into the engines. When the antimatter drives were in use, these pipes were closed off and the compartment was used for storage of the antimatter, and its delivery to the fusion chamber. The two antimatter traps sat coldly against the tight starboard wall, behind and beneath the pipes and fittings, and almost inaccessible to humans. Mike pulled himself through the gangway headfirst and on his back, so he could slide himself up under the pipes and wire bundles. There were no house lights in this compartment, but Mike had already lit his SureFire, and now held it in his teeth as he pulled himself into place. It was tight to the point of being uncomfortable, and it took someone with no fear of enclosed spaces to access the traps. With his chest and arms lodged up behind the pipes, his legs still protruded from the door of the compartment, twisted at such an angle that quick escape was impossible. It took almost fifteen minutes to get in and out without scraping himself to shreds. The traps were easily accessible from the outside of the shuttle, through the exterior access hatch.

Once he had finally wiggled himself into position, he pulled the light from his mouth and sighed heavily. He was not claustrophobic, but could easily imagine the sensations of those who were. After a few moments of catching his breath and allowing himself to cool off, he was ready to check the levels of the traps, which would take all of about a minute and a half. Thirty minutes of movement for such a short data collection seemed ridiculous, but – he remembered – as long as the gauges were functioning properly, no one would ever need to come back here to take the physical readings. And no one ever counted on gauges going out.

Mike pointed the flashlight at the digital readout panel on the side of the first trap. It was cracked and splintered, black characters flickering and fading in and out like a punctured digital watch. "Son of a bitch," he said aloud. There would be no way to tell how much antimatter was still left in that trap. The logical loophole this left him in reminded him of the Schroedinger's Cat experiment. Even if he had the capability of seeing the elementary particles, opening the trap to count them would annihilate them, which would void the entire project.

He moved his light over to the display on the other trap and pushed the level button. It read:

.0250 % of capacity – 250 Megaparticles Remaining

If this was an accurate reading, then it not only conflicted with the reading they were receiving in the flight deck, but it meant they were losing antimatter without even burning it. Mike pulled a pencil and notepad out of his belt pouch and quickly scribbled down some numbers on it. The readout in the cockpit would naturally be adding the product of the two traps together, and displaying total volume. It wouldn't display individual trap readings, as they were designed to deplete equally. It wasn't out of the realm of possibility that this wasn't happening though. The cockpit had said they had sixty percent of the product left. If that was accurate, it would mean the first trap had only twenty-five percent left, and they were burning at unequal depletion rates. Alternatively, it could imply that they had lost that much antimatter just in the time it took Mike to get to the back and take a manual reading.

He scratched a line on the paper and drew a figure. He caught his breath sharply when he recognized the numbers he had just written. If the digital readout on the side of the second trap was accurate, and if his assumption that the first was at the same amount then they were in dire straits. His assumption was that the machines contained equal product. And 500 megaparticles wasn't enough to blast off from Mars and get them home.

| CHAPTER *twenty-four* |

Donnie stared patiently at Mike as he explained what he had seen in the engine compartment. He was fidgeting and chewing his lip, waiting for the bad news he knew Mike was about to lay on him.

"So one of two things has happened here. One, the cockpit gauge has failed – or two, the dispenser has failed."

"How is that?" Donnie said, squinting.

"Because the gauge on trap one is busted. Trap two says it's got less than a quarter percent in it. They are supposed to deplete equally. Right?"

"Right," Donnie said, nodding. He was beginning to do the equivalent of pacing in zero gravity – pushing back and forth between the walls of the rest cabin.

"Well if they are depleting equally then trap one has less than a quarter percent in it too. The cockpit gauge puts us at sixty percent. So either they're depleting equally and the gauge is way wrong, or the gauge is right and trap one is still almost full."

"And you're sure we can't get an accurate reading from trap one?" Donnie said.

Mike breathed in deeply before answering. "Yes. Unless you know of a way to fix the display panel. That thing's split like a log."

Donnie stopped suddenly and looked at Mike. "I don't suppose we keep spares on board do we?"

Mike shook his head sadly. "I really doubt it. I don't think they even supply extras. Hell, I don't know if they even make them anymore."

Donnie frowned. "What? I thought we invented this technology? Who's 'they'?"

"We invented the Pluraler. Not the penning traps."

"And you're saying we can't get indicators anymore?"

"Not like the ones we have. I think they're using full-color screens now on the new models."

"And those aren't backwards compatible with our systems," Donnie said.

"I doubt it. I don't know." Mike shook his head and his hands simultaneously. "Look, Donnie, none of that shit matters. We don't have one on board anyway. So we're stuck with the choice of either believing the cockpit gauge, or believing the dispenser is working correctly."

Donnie shook his head. "Dammit!" He began his space pacing again. "So we're stuck out here. Is that what you're saying?"

Mike waved his hands. "No, no, no. No. If the gauge is wrong, and trap one is full, we have enough to follow through as planned. But that's a leap of faith. Blind faith. We can't find out how much we have in trap one. But if the cockpit indicator is right, we can make it back."

Donnie stopped and rubbed his face with his hands. "Make it back?"

"Yup. If we turn around now."

"So the mission's off either way."

"Well you tell me, Donnie. You want to take the chance that this could be a one-way trip? We can damn sure land on Mars. We can do everything we wanted to do. But if that trap is empty as the second one – which I believe it is – we can't go home. And when we run out of oxygen – that's it. We'd have to wait for someone else to come pick up our projects an-"

"Okay, okay – shut the hell up," Donnie said. He closed his eyes and shook his head. "I'm sorry, Mike. You know I don't mean that. I can't…" he trailed off and let a long silence ensue before he spoke again. "I can't believe this is happening."

Mike said nothing, just nodded slowly, agreeing.

Donnie sighed heavily, then turned back to Mike and spoke quietly, levelly. "So what do we do?"

"I don't know, Donnie. I'm not inclined to believe the cockpit indicator. I trust that the dispenser is more reliable than the gauge. So if I had to make a command guess, I'd say we're out of antimatter." Mike shrugged his shoulders.

Donnie yelled, "Son of a bitch!"

Mike closed his eyes and leaned his head back. "You make the call, boss. I'm behind you."

"What call is there to make, Mike?" Donnie said loudly.

"Whether or not you want to make the landing and take our chances, or-"

"Take our chances? There is no 'chances'! If we land we're stuck there! What 'chances' do you think we have? You think we might uncover a fuel tank on the surface? Find some way to mine antimatter? If we land, we ditch. There's no way back."

"Well, again – that's assuming the traps are equal. Even still, it's an option. The life's work we achieve by-" Mike was cut off yet again.

"Forget it, Mike! Even if I were willing to go along with that preposterous notion, you know Goddamn well we couldn't get the rest of the crew on board! Brian Bradley didn't even want to come! Shanna? No effing way!" He shook his head, his face showing disappointment. He looked like he had expected more from Mike – though Mike couldn't think of what more he could have done. He was only laying out the options – where they stood.

"Andy? Jonathan, Gary? They have families for shit's sake! If it were you and me, it'd be different," Donnie said.

"Okay, Donnie," Mike said, raising his hands defensively. "I was just throwing it out there."

"Well don't! We need to start thinking realistically, Mike."

"Fine. Tell me what to do, Donnie."

"Get the crew together. We have to make the announcement now."

The group filled the chairs in the common area, where they all sat with tense expressions on their faces. Donnie had taken up the position by the door, grabbing the handholds by the gangway, and Mike hovered closely beside him for moral support. This was a tough announcement to have to make, he knew.

Donnie looked over the expectant faces again, then cleared his throat. "Okay, here it is, plain and simple, no additives or preservatives. We don't have enough fuel to make it home if we proceed as planned." He paused for a moment, then continued, "If we turn around now – or anytime before we've used any more of the antimatter – we can make it home, but the current predicament cuts Mars completely out of our mission picture."

"What the hell happened?" Jonathan said, his eyes wide with curiosity.

Donnie looked directly at him and answered slowly, shaking his head. "We don't know. We shouldn't have been burning fuel since the big push away from Alpha. But that is a possible explanation. Otherwise the only answer I can come up with is premature decomposition of the particles.

"The gauge in the flight deck says we have sixty percent left. Which is more than enough to finish the mission. But the gauges on the traps disagree with that. So either they're not depleting equally or the gauge is wrong. And indeed, they shouldn't be depleting at all. We should be coasting."

Mike looked at Donnie, then took over. "Here's the other thing. If we were to continue on blind faith that trap one really is full – and the cockpit gauge is right – then we'd still have to account for decomposition over the next twelve to fifteen months.

If we've only got 250 left in the trap we can read, we know we've lost quite a bit inexplicably. We can only assume we will continue to lose more as we continue," Mike said.

Donnie took a deep breath again. "Any questions?"

Shanna raised her hand, then spoke, "I'm sorry, Donnie, let me make sure I understand what you just said… You said the machines should be depleting equally, right? How do we know that's happening? I mean, couldn't the first trap be clogged up or something?"

"Well clog isn't the right word. These are subatomic particles. But yes, in theory trap one could be malfunctioning, which would cause it not to dispense and deplete properly. In which case we might not be able to get it to start working anyway."

Gary Grant, who had been quietly frowning to himself until now, finally spoke. "So the mission's off then? Is that what you're saying?"

Donnie nodded. "Well the democratic thing to do would be to take a vote, but I am assuming none of you are interested in a one-way trip." He looked around at the faces in front of him, and judging by his assessment, he was right. The ashen-white color most of them had suddenly taken on told him they were heading home. At least so they thought.

In all the time Donnie had spent studying astronomy and the physics therein, he had never really been exposed to the full scale of how big it really was out there. The short distance from Earth to the moon seemed big enough before, as Donnie had never been farther out than that. But now, being exposed to the mean distances he was facing, he was beginning to get an idea how insipidly large it really was. Or maybe it was just that they were so small.

They had passed the halfway point of the trip and everyone had been getting excited about the big event. Then it had been ripped away by the malfunctioning system that measured their antimatter volume. So full of disappointment, they were heading home – not ready to be excited about the return trip yet. With nothing to look forward to, everyone was beginning to get bored. And boredom in deep space, as they found, is much different than boredom on home planet. Boredom at home can be remedied by going for a walk, or driving up to the batting cages, or heading out to the theater. There was no reason to be bored on

Earth. But this was different. They had all run out of everything to do, and all the recreational entertainment was getting old quickly. They were all sick of the limited supply of CDs in their collective repertoire – not to mention everyone's erratically different tastes in music.

Donnie was strapped into the captain's chair rubbing his temples and Mike hovered nearby, contemplating what had gone wrong. "The thing that scares me worst is that it's probably still depleting; I bet if I went back there right now, we'd already see a difference. That scares me."

Donnie looked around at him and nodded. "Yup. I know. And it's been…" he trailed off as there was a knock at the cockpit door. Mike turned and opened it, and Shanna pulled herself into the flight deck. Donnie looked around again to see who it was, then returned his gaze to the darkness outside the windscreen. Shanna came up to take a seat in the First Officer's chair. Strapping herself in, she looked up through the windscreen and frowned thoughtfully.

"What's up, Shanna?" Donnie said, looking over at her.

"Nothing. So where's Mars from here?"

"From here?"

"Yeah? Shouldn't we be able to see it by now?" Shanna said.

"Well, no. One, we're only halfway there. Two, it's going to meet us at the destination. Where we're headed, Mars isn't there yet."

Shanna smiled an embarrassed smirk. "Yup. Orbit. Gotcha. So what's that star?" she said, pointing at a particularly bright one in the left windscreen.

Donnie sighed, looking over at the familiar star. Familiar because he had seen a lot of it lately. "I don't really know. It's not moved though. It's been in about that same spot for the last few weeks."

"Hmm." Shanna nodded very slightly.

"So what's up, Shan? You doing okay?" Donnie said, getting her back to topic.

"Oh yeah. I was just wondering what we're going to do. Since we can't really go to Mars now, and all."

Donnie stared blankly at her for a long moment before answering. "Well, we're going to turn around. But it's the hardest thing I've ever had to do. It's like finding out your dog's got rabies. You know you've gotta put him down, but you just can't make yourself take him in to do it."

Shanna nodded slowly in acceptance of this. "But there's no other way? You're sure of that? We have to go home now?"

Donnie stared expectantly at her for a moment. "Well, yeah. My assessment is that everyone does want to go to Mars, but ultimately would like to end up back on Earth."

Shanna nodded again, looking away. "I'd do it," she finally said, returning her gaze to Donnie.

"I'm sorry, Shanna. You'd do what?" Donnie said.

"I'd go to Mars now."

"Knowing full well that we wouldn't be able to come home? Even if we wanted to?"

She nodded again, then took a deep breath. "Yeah. The product is well worth the cost. Besides, you never know. There just may be a way to make it work there."

Donnie squinted hard at her. "What are you saying, Shanna?"

"Well, technically, we'll never run out of oxygen as long as we're running these converters, right?" she said, looking back and forth between Mike and Donnie. Mike looked at Donnie, unable to meet her gaze.

Donnie shrugged. "Well, yeah, but it eventually gets too thick with nitrogen, and we have to replace the filters. We only have a limited supply of those, Shanna. The end is the same in any situation. We all die of asphyxiation on a foreign planet."

All was silent for a long while. Then Shanna finally spoke, "Well we can't take a vote? I mean – I know you two would rather go ahead with the mission, and there…"

"Wait, wait, wait," Donnie said, waving his hands. "How do you propose to know that?"

"Well, I just know you. I know you would rather go on with it and face the consequences as opposed to trashing everything you've come so far with," she said quietly.

"Well supposing that's true, that makes three of us. There are seven on the crew, Shanna," Mike said finally.

She looked up at him, then back at Donnie. "Well, that's what I was going to say. There may be more people on board willing to go through with it than you think."

Donnie smirked at her naïve persistence. "Shanna, even if this were a 'majority rules' vote, it wouldn't be moral. Human rights overcomes popular vote in all cases. If there were only one who wanted to go home, we can't propose to force him along just because the other six vote to do so."

"Well, I would think," she said, pointing at him, "that that's part of the risk involved with being on this crew. It's something we all knew when we signed up for the role. It's part of the duty."

Donnie sighed. "What you are referring to is different. Right now we still have a choice to save ourselves. It's in our best interest to return to Earth and regroup. We can always come back."

Shanna threw up her hands. "Bullshit! Whatever. This is bullshit. What a waste!" she shouted, and blew out of the cockpit, trying to slam the door.

Donnie harrumphed. "I didn't think we'd get any fight about going home. Son of a bitch!"

Mike nodded slowly. "Yup. Figure she'd be happy."

Donnie sighed long, then said, "Go ahead and set the course change. I guess we head home."

Shanna had star charts spread on the corkboard in her sleeping quarters. She had snapped the clear plastic cover down over the top of it all, and was marking calculations in a red fine-tip dry-erase marker. She had done it several times, and everything looked normal. But the view her computer terminal was showing her was different than what she had seen out the windscreen.

She rotated the cube of space she was working with on the terminal, trying to find something that came close to matching the picture in her photographic memory. Deep space was pretty bland in the way of distinguishing marks, but there were a few. And she had seen just enough to be suspicious. Her first suspicion was that they had simply changed course slightly, and were bending around to the right to make a quicker meeting with Mars. This would obviously require them to accelerate though, as at the expected velocity, they would get there after Mars had already passed. She quickly dumped this notion though, in light of the fact that they had only been traveling for coming up on fifty days. Everything would still look relatively similar to that which she expected.

The star she had seen is what had piqued her curiosity though. For a star to be visible in their windscreen for several weeks without moving, meant they were headed toward it for one. But it also meant that star was not moving – which could mean they were following it in its orbit. Even still, it would seem they would catch up with it at some point. The only other thing it could be was a very far away star whose local light was old. Stars in very remote space could appear to be stationary.

Perspective had a lot to do with the view out the windscreen. It was like driving down a road, where the trees right beside the road flew past in a blur, while the mountains in the distance seemed to be standing still. So it was the same in space, though the parallax was a lot less distinct. Things were so much farther apart that it took many weeks sometimes to show movement between them. It seemed to Shanna that three weeks was long enough to see some movement, though. She made a note to herself to try and sneak in the question surreptitiously to someone who actually had the experience of knowledge.

She also made it a personal project to find out exactly which star that was, as it would force her to use math she had never encountered, and it would kill a lot of down time.

There was a knock on the gangway, and Shanna turned to see Gary Grant hovering there, smiling like a schoolboy. "What's up Gary?" she said, unbuckling herself from her desk to stretch.

"You feel like helping me with some more of my zero-G experiments?" he said.

"You want *me* to help you?"

Gary's face fell. This wasn't a question he had expected to be asked. "Yeah. Sure, why not? You helped with the springs and all."

"I'm sorry Gary, I really don't have time. I'm working really hard on these star charts, and I have to get this done today."

"Today, tomorrow – it's all the same out here," he said, smiling.

"Really, Gary. I can't. I'm sorry."

The smile left his face again. "Oh. Star charts? What the hell are you doing with star charts anyway?"

"Well, I'm just doing some research. Uh, Donnie – er, wanted me to outline some – uh – to, um – well…"

"Shanna," Gary said suddenly. She looked up at him a little frightened. "Spit it out!" The smile jumped back onto his face, full feature.

She sighed relief. "Well, he's teaching me how to read these things, and – well, I think I can save us some gas."

Gary squinted his eyes and raised his chin, looking suspiciously at her. "You can't tell me, can you?"

Shanna smiled wanly and shrugged, shaking her head. Gary finally got the point and carried on, politely excusing himself from her room. And she dug back into her star charts.

Mike pulled the yoke slightly and knocked the ship out of auto-navigation mode. The yoke settled again, and AUTO light blinked off. He thumbed the nitrogen jets and blasted the front end around to make the 180-degree turn to start heading home. The stars outside started whooshing across the windscreen to the right. The digital heading gauge still read the same course heading though. Mike frowned and let go of the nitro jets. The ship finally came to rest with a new heading. But the gauge didn't correct itself. He thought maybe it would take a moment to adjust, but it didn't. It didn't respond at all. And it was supposed to be real-time reading. Under normal circumstances, there would be no lag or delay at all. It was like an analog gauge in that respect. Digital gauges were supposed to be more precise though.

"Uh, Donnie, we've got a problem."

Donnie lowered his magazine and looked over at Mike. "What? What is it?"

"I just blasted a 180. I think. But the heading gauge didn't respond. It didn't register any movement."

Donnie leaned in closer and looked at the gauge. It read:

$$59 \text{ V} - 203 \text{ H} - 17 \text{ A}$$

"Did you reset it?" Donnie said, referring to the digital reset button on the gauge.

Mike nodded and pressed the button several more times for effect.

"Shit. So we have another part out?" Donnie said.

"Looks like it."

"What's that make now? Autopilot, AM traps, communications? What the hell is next?"

Mike sighed loudly. "I don't know, but I'm starting to feel a little sick about this."

Donnie shook his head. "You and me both. Well, I guess we get out the star charts."

Mike looked up at him. "Shanna's got 'em in her room I think. I'll call her up here."

"What the hell's she doing with 'em?" Donnie said, frowning at the thought.

"Hell, I don't know. But I saw them on the nav board in her room last night," Mike said, then shrugged.

Donnie was about to speak, then stopped. Then he started again, "What the hell is she doing with them in her room?"

Mike shrugged.

"Get her up here."

Mike leaned forward and keyed the intercom. "Shanna, to the flight deck. Bring the charts with you."

| CHAPTER *twenty-six* |

Shanna pushed the cockpit door open and slid inside, pushing it closed behind her. She had the charts folded up under one arm. She looked silently between the faces of the two men, then spoke quietly, "So you guys noticed too?"

Donnie hesitated a moment. "Noticed what, Shanna?"

"We're off course."

Donnie started. "What makes you think we're off course?"

"Does this look like familiar territory to you?" Shanna said, waving a hand in the direction of space outside the windscreen. No one answered, so she continued, "I'd go so far as to say we're not even in the solar system anymore."

"Now how the hell did you know that?" Donnie said a little too loudly.

"Well, that star I asked you about before didn't look familiar. So I started trying to find out what it was," Shanna said.

Donnie frowned hard, then shook his head. "Wait a minute. You asked me about that star earlier. Mike, you said you saw those charts in her room last night. What the hell were you doing with them before, Shanna?"

Shanna swallowed softly and broke her gaze with Donnie for the second time in history. Donnie shook his head and looked at Mike, then back at Shanna. "Am I missing something here?"

"I'm sorry, Donnie. I've had them for a few days now because I had suspicions. That star I saw earlier only strengthened my theory."

"Let me get this straight. You have had a suspicion that we were off course for the last several days. And you didn't say something when you first thought of it?" Donnie said. He was trying to maintain patience, but it was wearing thin.

"Hell no!" she said in angry defense. "I knew you guys wouldn't listen to me. I've never even been in space. That's why I had the damn charts! So I could fix a firm argument before I approached you about it! I didn't even know if it was right. I just wanted to check it out and be sure." She looked on the verge of tears, and Donnie felt the battling emotions in his stomach more than his head. He wanted to comfort her – the scared, confused girl who stood before him. But he also wanted to hit her for the anger that was now building up inside him. If they were truly off course, then that meant Donnie wasn't in control. And on his ship, he got angry when he lost control.

Donnie shook his head. "Shanna, we rely on these machines to do our navigating for us. We only ever carry the star charts with us as a rudimentary precaution. We don't know the heavens by heart. No one does. No one can! If one of those computers takes a shit, we're screwed! We'd have no idea."

"Well, I thought I could study those charts hard enough and make some sense of them. And I couldn't. I couldn't find a pattern that accommodated that star. Not on the charts, or in the computer."

Donnie chortled. "You propose to have memorized the patterns of the stars you saw earlier?"

Shanna's face got real serious. "Yes. I have a photographic memory, Donnie."

Donnie laughed out loud. "Oh, Shanna, you never fail to amuse me. There are a hundred trillion stars visible just from here. Only a few have any noticeable characteristics. Those are the ones we chart from."

Shanna didn't respond. She maintained her stern look at Donnie, obviously very angry at him, but willing herself not to react.

"So we don't know how long we've been off course, and we don't know where we are headed," Donnie said. "But you knew all along." He laughed again. It felt good for him to laugh at their predicament, but inside he knew it was a defense mechanism.

And Shanna could no longer hold back. "Well I seem to remember you saying 'these ships don't need navigators. A *monkey* could fly this ship into space.'"

Donnie almost choked as the insult settled on him. And he couldn't say a word about it. He felt his face flood with anger, burning his head between his ears. He stuttered stupidly, stammering short syllables at her, trying to organize a coherent retort. Then he finally resolved to do what he did best. He commanded her. "Just go back to your room, Shanna."

"Oh, now you're going to send me to my room? Donnie, you need to grow the fuck up. You're such a child."

Donnie had unbuckled himself, and now shot up out of the chair, rocketing toward Shanna with enormous momentum. Mike was up and between them, though, and they collided a foot in front of Shanna, slamming into the wall.

"Slow down, Donnie. I can't let you do that."

"You don't have a choice, asshole!" Donnie yelled.

Mike maintained his cool. "Donnie, you need to cool off." Mike had Donnie by the wrists, and was acting as a barrier between him and Shanna.

"You better let go of me before I…"

"Before you what?" Mike shouted. He pushed Donnie backward and away from the two of them. "You need to cool the hell down, Donnie. Think about what you're doing here!"

Donnie gave up the fight, but maintained his hard stare at Shanna. Shanna stood sobbing in the corner as Mike tried to comfort her. Donnie turned to look out the windscreen, where there was nothing but empty space and tiny speckles of light presumably millions of light years away. A wash of stellar glitter poured indiscriminately across the inky black bowl of the cosmos. There were no recognizable characteristics in the vicinity of the windscreen – nothing welcoming or inviting – and he found himself longing for home.

He sighed and pushed past Mike toward the gangway and pulled the door closed behind him. As he pushed out into the common area, he saw that everyone was gathered, and watching him intently. He looked around at their faces, wondering what they were seeing on his face. He knew he didn't wear his emotions well. They could probably read his anger and dismay like a front page headline.

Then he heard it. "Don't worry about it, Shan. He'll cool down and everything'll be all right."

It was Mike's voice coming through the intercom speaker set in the ceiling. Donnie looked up at it suddenly – curiously – as if to see the source of the voice. The intercom was still keyed. As if just one more malfunctioning part to add to the ever-growing list, the internal intercom had remained keyed since Mike last used it – presumably throughout their entire conversation. And everyone had heard it.

| CHAPTER *twenty-seven* |
lost scrolls

Twelve days had passed since the divergence, and all had taken on some semblance of normalcy once again. Emotions were masked, and mostly forgotten so as to carry on about their duties – primary of which was getting home. Mike had done everything to the computer he could think of – short of reprogramming it – and was finding more and more systems out of operation. Simply put, systems were dropping off like flies.

Donnie had gotten very little sleep in the last week and a half, and what little he did get was riddled with nightmares and visions he couldn't shake in waking. Something kept telling him they were lost and stranded. He knew that wasn't the case, as they couldn't ever really be 'lost' within the solar system. Eventually they would come across the orbit of one of the planets. It seemed inevitable. And when that happened, their computers would alert them of it. That was assuming the systems that recognized the orbits even caught it. He was assuming a lot lately.

They had long since turned the ship around and were heading 180 degrees opposite that which they had been traveling, putting the bright star Shanna had seen directly behind them. "When the compass fails, instinct prevails," she had so wisely said. Donnie had even begun to dig out the star charts and start to familiarize himself with them again. He had dug through every chart he could get his hands on seeking some sort of order among the chaos of stars, but was beginning to realize the degree to which someone could actually be lost. The charts were all made with the assumption that the user knew the general vicinity of his location. Otherwise, the random scatter of white dots on the inky blue paper only stood to confuse him even more. Star charts were great for mapping from point A to point B. But they were almost meaningless when you didn't know where point A was.

Twice he had found a pattern he remembered and recognized, only to check his view out the windscreen and find extra stars, or uncommon patches of speckled irrationality. His hope was wearing thin, and his patience was nonexistent. Mike had to keep talking him down, bringing him back to reality, but it never worked. Donnie grew farther and farther from the crew and himself all together. He was slowly but surely losing his very sanity in the midst of the stellar loneliness. He wished more and more every day to be at home with Delilah, but felt farther from her with each passing moment. She was the only thing he felt he had to hold on to, but knew the grip with which he held her was slipping fast.

Donnie spent great lots of time in his quarters alone, either sleeping or buried in the meaningless charts, calling on every source of strength he could find just to keep from losing the will to live. It was a dark season for Donnie, and he couldn't readily pinpoint what had gone wrong. The terrible domino effect had started with something vague, something hazy, somewhere foggy. He pondered what it was that had gotten them stuck and stranded. What had he done so wrong? What had he ignored? What had he done that he shouldn't have? Or maybe it wasn't he at all. Maybe it was someone else. Donnie couldn't bring himself to accept that. Not as the captain of the ship. He had to take full responsibility for everything that happened, and that had happened, that had gotten them here. He couldn't accept that anyone else could have a hand in it. Not until Mike knocked on his chamber door that night.

The corridors were dimly lit in order to save their waning power, and all seemed ghostly and quiet – like a living room on Christmas Eve night. Donnie followed Mike to the flight deck, not saying anything, but eyes wide with excitement and fright. He had no idea what lay in store for him when they got there. Mike's whispering words still echoed in his memory. "You need to take a look at this."

The flight deck was empty. The red lights were on, and the machines – the few that were still useful – were ticking away in the quiet darkness, doing – or not doing – their jobs. And on the main console monitor, a glaring white window stood open, painted with black text more beautiful than anything Donnie believed he had ever seen. They were the words of Callie in their last text communication. The lost scrolls. The answers to all Donnie's questions.

HOUSTON: Okay, here she is…

HOUSTON: Donnie, it's Callie.

ATLAS: whats up cal

HOUSTON: I've learned all about
your parts problem.

ATLAS: come again houston your all
jumbled

HOUSTON: I said I've learned all
about your parts problem. I know
why all those parts showed up here
the other day.

Donnie's heart beat madly in his chest as he read
the words – ghostlike on the monitor – ancient and
cold as if carved on a tomb wall.

ATLAS: callie i cant read anything
your typing

HOUSTON: Donnie your words are
coming back jumbled. Can you read
me?

HOUSTON: Donnie, are you there?

HOUSTON: Donnie, I'm not receiving
anything from you now. I think
we've lost connection. I hope
you're getting this. I'll go ahead
and tell you everything I was going

to say just in case you can read it
- or decipher it later.

Donnie looked up at Mike, who was hovering over his shoulder. Mike was grinning like an excited schoolboy, proud of his discovery. Donnie had to smile back.

"Holy shit, Mike! Thank God she kept typing."

Mike nodded. "Keep reading. It gets better."

HOUSTON: Okay, here goes. I took
the liberty of researching the
ma##ive order, and found out some
pretty spooky stuff. All the parts
we received that day were reorders.
Everything we received were parts
that had al#$dy been replaced on
the Atlas within the #ast few
years.

HOUSTON: The only problem is, all
the copies of the invoices we have
from those original orders are
frauds. So I did some deep digging
into Brian's files and his computer
and found the original orders.
Everything he had ordered to go on
the Atlas within the last few
years, he's been ordering from a
place called Hunter Machinery Corp.
#ut of Chicago. They sell cheap
airliner and shuttle parts.

On a whim, Donnie quickly dismounted the captain's chair and swung over to the guidance system terminal, ripping the front panel off the console. He peeled the plastic protective membrane off the components and ran his fingers down the lubricated steel of the computer housing inside. Along the bottom he felt resistance, and turned to Mike, making a hand motion toward Mike's SureFire flashlight. Mike handed him the flashlight and Donnie clicked it on.

On the bottom of the guidance computer was the manufacturer's inscription. It read:

H.M.C.
Chicago, IL USA

Donnie looked back up at Mike, shaking his head. "That son of a bitch replaced all our good shit with this Hunter shit!"

"That's why it's all going bad. No wonder."

"How would it all just go bad though? What in hell makes all this shit just start going bad?" Donnie said, pulling himself back over to the captain's chair.

"Electromagnetic field. Any number of things, really. Solar flares."

"Yeah, but that wouldn't kill all the systems, would it?"

"Well yeah, if the parts aren't space-hardened. That's why Lockheed parts are so attractive. And expensive. All their shit is space-hardened, so this type of thing won't happen," Mike said, pulling himself down into his own chair.

"Have we even hit an EM field though?"

"Yeah, we hit a pretty big one a few weeks ago. I guess right when the shit started going bad.

Remember, we were all in the common area and the lights dimmed out?"

"Son of a bitch. I do remember that, 'cause I was explaining what it was to Shanna." Donnie bit his lip, staring out the windscreen for a long moment. "So we fried all our parts and didn't even know it. I bet it was those solar flares."

"Very likely. They were strong in the forecast."

"I'll be damned," Donnie said, rubbing his forehead.

"Keep reading, Donnie. You're gonna lose your bricks," Mike said, nodding toward the terminal where Callie's words still awaited him.

```
HOUSTON: But wait, it g3ts worse!
The difference between the price at
Hunter and the price at Lockheed
Martin was significant. And - as
you've no doubt already guessed -
he was funneling that difference
into a personal profit. But here's
the weird part: the %%ofits were
all routed to a numbered account at
a bank in London.
```

```
HOUSTON: It took some serious
hacking, but I still have a few
friends from back home, and we
traced that account. You ready for
this? I hope you're sitting down
(ha ha). That account is registered
to Corporate Client Servic#s in
Boston. That's a subsidiary of
Royal Research's financial facet.
That's where most of the Royal
```

employees bank. The total amount
skimmed over the last five years -
for he was scamming from other
shuttles as well - came out to
almost th&rty million do##ars.

Donnie took a deep breath. "That son of a bitch. Thirty million? I ought to kill him." He looked back at Mike again. "What the hell did he think he was doing?"

Mike shook his head slowly.

"I guess if I killed him he couldn't pay it back."

"He can't pay it back anyway, DO," Mike said.

Donnie stared at him for a moment. "Yeah. But I want his ass to serve time. Hard time." He shook his head and turned back to the monitor.

HOUSTON: Well the parts he ordered
came out of our account, and no
doubt they were for Atlas because
he was scared to make mission on a
bird he had outfitted with cheap
equipment. And the L#ndon account
was empty as well. The last draft
from that account was for almost
the entire amount, and it was
payable to Brad Benjamin in June of
last year.

Donnie's face screwed up, and he looked up at Mike. "Brad Benjamin? Who the hell is that?"

Mike shook his head. Donnie, that's Brian. The double B gives it away. He's using a fake name to scam the money."

"I wonder if Royal knows anything about all this," Donnie said, looking back at Mike.

Mike stared hard at Donnie and nodded. "Are you thinking what I'm thinking?"

"I think so."

"They bought that satellite with our own money."

"That's what I'm thinking."

Donnie started to get up – to go confront Brian Bradley, but Mike stopped him. "There's more. Keep reading." Donnie frowned and turned back to the monitor. "Scroll down a ways."

```
HOUSTON: I hope you can do
something with this, Donnie. And
mostly, I hope you're not stuck out
there with faulty parts. Please
keep trying to contact me. I'm
worried sick about you all.

HOUSTON: Oh, and one more thing. I
hate to throw gas on a fire, but
Brian is also guilty of
intellectual property theft. I
found a whole bunch of files on his
computer that clearly don't belong
to him. I found stuff from Samson's
computer, stuff from yours - all
stuff he shouldn't even be seeing.
But the thing that set it off and
made me start poking around was the
pictures I found on his hard drive.
Remember that blond bimbo you had
sex with in Beverly Hills? Yeah, I
had forgotten about her too.
```

Donnie shook his head as it hung in shame. "Dear God, can it get any worse?" he said. He looked up at Mike and sighed.

"What blond bimbo is she talking about?" Mike said curiously.

"Oh some piece I picked up by the pool at the Regent. We talked for a while, then she followed me up to my room. She said she wanted to see what the penthouse looked like. So I showed her."

"So how does this involve Callie?" Mike said, frowning. He was still smiling though, as he could tell where it was going.

"I was nailing this chick to the bed and Callie walked in on us. I'd forgotten she was supposed to be coming home." He laughed as he continued. "So she dug into her suitcase and came out with her camera. And the blond never knew it."

"That's effin' hilarious," Mike said. "I wonder how the hell Bradley ended up with them."

"Well I guess Callie couldn't resist looking at them at work. I wonder how he had access to everyone else's stuff though. That cock needs to learn to mind his own business."

"Go get him, Donnie."

| CHAPTER *twenty-eight* |

tea time

The door slammed full open so fast one of the hinges cracked, and Mike thought momentarily that Donnie's force had defied the absence of gravity. Before the wind could settle from his entrance, Donnie was across the room and slamming Brian Bradley against the far wall. Brian's face was devoid of all color, and his eyes were wide like an angry horse. He had already almost been killed by Donnie once on this trip, and probably thought he would finish the job this time. Donnie had seemed crazy enough lately.

"Why'd you want off this ship so badly?" Donnie said.

"I was nervous. I really was sick, Donnie, dammit! Chill out, all right?" Brian tried pushing Donnie away, but failed.

"Sick, huh? Is that why you ordered a truckload of parts for Atlas the night before you left for vacation?"

Brian gulped. "I don't know what you're talking about."

Donnie slammed him up against the wall again, getting a fresh grip. "The hell you don't. You've been

busted, asshole. We found it all. The fake invoices –
the London bank account – everything.”

“Brian, I’d start talking if I were you. I think it’d
be easy enough to fabricate an accident out here and
leave you floating,” Mike said. He moved into the
room and pushed the door closed behind him. It took
some finagling with the broken hinge, but it closed.
Brian, meanwhile, looked back and forth between
Donnie and Mike. Sensing that neither of them was his
ally, he decided not to say anything.

“You wouldn’t do that, Donnie. Even if I die out
here, you have a responsibility to bring back every
body that you left with.”

“Not if you fall into a black hole, asshole. Start
talking,” Donnie commanded.

Brian shook his head. “Look, I don’t know what
you’re talking about. Somebody probably planted a
bunch of evidence to make me look bad or
something.”

Donnie scoffed. “Every part that’s gone bad on
this ship is one you’ve replaced in the last few years.
Parts you’ve ordered from Jack’s Backyard Shuttle
Parts. And now you’re the reason we have to go
home! You’re the reason we’re taking the long way
home! You do know we’re not really sure we’re
heading in the right direction, don’t you?”

Brian gulped again. “No. I didn’t know that. We’re
lost?”

Donnie finally let go of Brian, and eased off a bit.
He licked his teeth and nodded.

“How do you get lost in the solar system?” Brian
said, smiling. It wasn’t even a real smile.

“By installing shitty parts in your guidance
system!” Donnie yelled.

It was clear to Donnie that Brian finally recognized the weight of the situation, because he took a deep breath and started thinking. "Okay, what can we do? We don't have spare parts on board, do we?"

"You tell me! You're supposed to be in charge of that!" Donnie said, spreading his arms.

Mike chimed in, saying, "No, Brian. All your spare parts are sitting in the receiving dock at the plant."

Brian suddenly looked ultimately disappointed, realizing his plan had been an utter failure.

"Couldn't get them all here in time could you?" Donnie said.

"Really, Brian, what were you thinking? You thought you could get all the parts in and put them all on the shuttle before we left?" Mike said. He was beginning to rummage through Brian's personal effects.

Brian nodded silently. "Really, Donnie. I'm so sorry. I didn't think..."

Donnie hit him. Hard.

The whole of the crew, short the injured, was gathered in the common area, and Donnie was preparing to fill them in on what was going on. Faces were expectant and anxious, but mostly anxious to get there. Just to get somewhere and be done with the traveling was what weighed most heavily on everyone's emotions. They had been traveling for almost seventy five days. Had everything gone to plan, they would have been thirteen days outside of setting foot on the Red Planet. As it lay, Donnie would now have to tell them there was the chance they might not set foot on any planet ever again. And with the way their odds had played out thus far, it was a pretty damn good chance.

"Look, I don't want to be making this announcement again, but it's my duty."

There was a collective gasp as everyone realized this was more bad news.

Mike and I have just performed a manual check of our fuel supply, and we are out. One-hundred percent gone. We have nothing left at all. Now it would be bad enough that we drifted out here until we eventually ran into the orbit path of Earth. But that's not going to happen. Several weeks ago, many of you may remember we passed through an electromagnetic field – probably caused by the solar flares. I made the mistake of telling Shanna not to worry because it was harmless. Well, they normally are. But you normally have the proper parts on your shuttle too.

"Over the last few years, as the necessity has arisen to replace components on the Atlas, our systems officer has been replacing them with parts he got from the lowest bidder. What this means to you and me is that we have parts on this ship that are not spaceworthy. And now we're all seeing the consequences.

"Now. Before I go on, I'm going to issue a blanket threat here – and this is for all of you. Anyone who decides to take this out on Bradley in any way will be dealt with swiftly and severely. Stay away from him, and he will remain confined in med hold for the remainder of our mission – however long that is to be."

Donnie looked around, checking the faces of his crewmembers. Satisfied they were all taking him seriously, he continued.

"As I said, it would be bad enough having to drift out here – out of gas – until we crossed Earth's orbit. But we won't cross it. Over the last several weeks, I have buried myself in those star charts, as you have all no doubt noticed. Well, it finally paid off this morning when I happened upon a match. The likelihood of finding a pattern of stars that matches your view out the windscreen is nine billion trillion to one. On a good day. Well, I accidentally – and maybe by the grace of God – stumbled onto one, knowing full well I was about a million miles out of sector."

Donnie turned to the whiteboard mounted on one of the walls, and uncapped a marker. He drew a large circle in the middle, and a straight line through it.

"To an outside observer, on our solar plane, the solar system is relatively flat. All the orbits are lined up on a flat plane. Well, except for Neptune, I think it is, that's like twelve degrees off. But essentially, they're flat."

"Hey, Donnie, can you cut the astronomy lesson and get to the point? We all know this shit," Jonathan said, irritation piercing his voice.

"Okay, well the point is that you will eventually run into the orbit of one of the planets if you are following that plane of orbit. But when our systems went out seven weeks ago, something jarred our course of flight. We didn't make a left turn, so to speak, but an up turn. We left that plane of orbit."

Donnie now drew a line perpendicular to the original. He capped the marker and checked everyone's face again. No one seemed to want to speak just then.

"In a nutshell, we went up from the orbital plane, and basically left the solar system all together. Well, a few weeks after that happened, we realized we were low on antimatter, and that's when we made the announcement that we'd be heading home. So we did what we thought was a 180.

"Now the best we can figure is that at that point in time, our guidance systems – basically our space compass – was already malfunctioning. It was still giving us a reading, but it wasn't accurate. So before it crapped out all the way, it still appeared to be working. Well, we didn't make a 180. What it ended up being was more like a 20."

He turned back to address the board again.

"Here you have us going up and wrong. Then we thought we turned around, but actually went like this." He drew a line angling up and away from the orbital plane of the solar system, and the perpendicular line.

"Everyone still with me?"

Shanna raised her hand at this point. "I have a question."

"Go ahead, Shanna," Donnie said, pulling the marker cap off and replacing it repeatedly. His feet were latched to the floor to keep him resident. The floor in most areas of the shuttle was lined with triangular grates, and the boots they wore had a small triangular plug on the front bottom of them. When one wanted to stand somewhere, he pushed the triangle down into the grating and twisted the boot, effectively locking himself in.

"So if we went up and away, then out and away even more – how far off course are we actually?"

"Well I'm getting to that."

"Answer the question, Donnie!" Jonathan said.

Donnie stared at him long and hard, biting his tongue. He tried to keep in mind that he was the commander of this ship, and was to maintain discipline even when everyone else went off the deep end. Jonathan was angry and scared – they all were – and had the right to be.

"About forty million kilometers."

Another collective gasp and sigh passed through the crowd.

"That's two thirds of the way to Mars from Earth!" Gary Grant shouted.

"I know. When we finally realized we were lost, and tried to do something about it, we figured we could just turn directly around – using a bright star we had been seeing for a few weeks in the windscreen. Well, we tried that, and – once again, still thinking we were on the orbital plane – ended up getting even more off course. What we didn't know was that the bright star we were chasing was moving in concert with our course evasion. It has its own orbit, but we weren't seeing it, because we were outside the sun's gravitational command, and thus orbiting the entire solar system on a clock only God can understand."

Jonathan – normally a mild-mannered man – shot up out of his chair and slammed into Donnie, swinging fists and screaming insults at him. "You stupid son of a bitch! You got us lost in space, you stupid son of a bitch!"

Donnie and he were crumpled against the ceiling of the common area, Donnie just trying to cover his face from the incoming blows. But they were persistent.

"All you had to do was fly in a straight line and you screwed it up – you stupid asshole!" Jonathan shouted, still pounding Donnie from every angle he could find.

Mike finally arrived and grabbed Jonathan around the neck, pulling him back and away. With no gravity, leverage was a myth, and motion was slow going. It took a few seconds for Donnie to right himself and for Mike to steady Jonathan against the wall of the cabin. But he couldn't stop his shouting.

"You stupid asshole! How can you bring us all out here unprepared? How could you not know we were lost!"

"I'm sorry, Jonathan," Donnie said, and surprised even himself. He felt suddenly large for shouldering the blame that was so obviously not his own. But simultaneously he felt truly dreadful for their predicament, and Jonathan's outrage.

Shanna was up now, and rocketing toward Jonathan against the wall, where Mike still had him in a half-nelson. "You're the stupid ass, Rodgers! You know damn well this wasn't Donnie's fault. It's Bradley's fault for ordering those mucked up parts! You ought to be mad at him!" She was in Jonathan's face shaking her fist and spitting on him, and all Donnie could do was watch with detached amazement as his crew slowly lost their calm.

Andy arose and began trying to pull the screaming Shanna away from Rodgers, and Mike was yelling from behind to keep Rodgers from lashing out at

Shanna, which he was trying with the might of two men to do. Donnie noticed he still had the marker in his hand and was staring dumbly at all this, unable even to speak anymore.

"We need to be figuring out how to fix this and work together to get home! Not to attack the only person that can get us there, you stupid dick!" Shanna was screaming and wailing. Andy had a pretty good handle on Shanna, considering Andy was only a little over five feet. The word firecracker came to Donnie's mind.

Meanwhile, Jonathan Rodgers was still pulling against his human restraint, and finally resorted to biting Mike's arm. Mike was grimacing, and now very angry, as perfect spheres of shimmering blood wafted away from his bare forearm, floating lazily toward the light. But he still had a half-hold on Rodgers, who was now getting away pretty quickly. And just when Mike's arm came back and grabbed Rodgers by the other arm, Rodgers put his foot back between Mike's legs and pushed himself off against the wall. Before Donnie could register what was happening, Rodgers was out and away from Mike, and clobbering Shanna with his fists.

Shanna's screams filled the cabin, mingling with the blood of Mike's wounded arm. Andy was closing her eyes and trying to back away from the physical outbreak, completely unready for Rodgers's attack. Her hold on Shanna was now worthless as she cowered in an effort to avoid being hit herself. And quickly Rodgers had Shanna against the wall opposing Mike, and was rearing his fist back to put an end to Shanna. But it didn't happen.

A bigger hand closed in around Jonathan's throat and commanded him backward with the force of a two-hundred-pound will. Gary Grant stared him dead in the eye as the fight changed rings and Jonathan got the breath knocked out of him against the ceiling. His eyes seemed likely to bulge out of his skull.

"We don't hit women," Gary said with the calm force of a quiet sea. And amidst Shanna's sobbing in one corner and Andy trying to tend to her, Gary's control of the now fetal Rodgers, and the echoes of a thousand belligerent cries on the air, it was over. Donnie stared at Mike, who returned his stare evenly.

Mike shook his head.

| CHAPTER *twenty-nine* |

It had been decided that they would point the shuttle toward Earth and blast as much nitrogen as they could in an effort to at least get them on their way. But at that velocity, it would take ten years to get home. No one could live that long on the resources they had. At least when they arrived, someone could deal with them – and all the equipment and bodies would be available to whomever cared to have them back. Donnie had done his job in that he had at least filled in the rest of the crew with what their situation was, and how unlikely it was that they would ever get home alive. Unfortunately, they had not handled it the way he had hoped they would. People under such tremendous pressure as they were though, were not likely to behave conventionally. These were truly unconventional circumstances.

Donnie had gone back into his reclusive mode after lining the ship up for Earth, spending almost all his time in his quarters. He only came out for bio breaks and breakfast anymore. There wasn't much point in spending time in the flight deck, he reasoned, as it was just a room full of useless machinery and false hopes. Millions of dollars worth of systems and instruments, and none of them could do a thing to get them out of this quandary.

He spent less and less time wondering what it was he had done so wrong, and more time letting himself hang the blame where it belonged. He hadn't confronted Brian Bradley again since their last interaction, when Donnie had punched him and broken his jaw. For one, Donnie knew seeing him again would set off his emotions, and Donnie would probably hit Brian again. But in a way, he felt he owed Brian his peace. They were all going to die out here away from everything they knew as home, so everyone deserved the chance to come to terms with his reckonings. And no doubt Brian was punishing himself for his mistakes.

When the eighty-eighth day rolled around, a new level of depression enveloped Donnie. Had everything gone as planned, today would have been their day of arrival. Seeing how badly things had messed up, and how far they had actually ended up off course made Donnie sick at his stomach every time he thought about it. He longed for the surface of that elusive red planet now more than he had when they knew they would make it there. He had spent the last ten years of his life planning and preparing to make the big trip, planning the very steps he would take off the ladder and onto the surface. He had spent hours and days just pondering what he would say, journaling everything – thoughts, scraps of ideas and phrases that sounded newsworthy. The story itself would be front-page-worthy, so he would have to sound ready for it. And now that day would never come – short of a miracle.

Mike Thurman had taken it differently. He now spent all of his productive time in the flight deck, reworking the systems, resetting and reconfiguring them in an effort to feel useful in the very least. He couldn't consciously just sit back and watch their incoming demise in the front row without doing everything he could possibly think of to hinder its progress. The steady cadence with which it marched was discouraging, yet slow and maddening. Watching it come at them headlong from millions of kilometers away, it teased them with its slow, steady persistence.

He had become obsessed with putting himself in the commander's chair, thinking – at least on a subconscious level – that that somehow put him in command; it somehow gave him control of the dead-end mission. Perhaps his being there could reverse the inevitable and bring about a different outcome.

Mike's behavior had, in a way, made him reclusive as well, seeing as how he almost never left the flight deck. He would sit and stare out the windscreen, daydreaming of ways to get them out of this mess. Hoping against hope he would spot something that would trigger an idea – an illusion that would conjure a thought – and it did from time to time. He would have brilliant ideas, but not the resources to turn them into realities. Or he would think he had the materials, but not the tools to fabricate a fit. It all seemed so tantalizingly accessible, but mechanically impossible nonetheless. And during one of these sittings of his, staring at the desolate wilderness of the Milky Way, something popped into view at the far left side of the windscreen. Mike was just at the point where he was about to doze off when it registered in his mind. It was a star – and wouldn't have attracted his attention but that it was brighter than those around it. It couldn't go any farther to the left without leaving his field of vision, behind the view of the windscreen.

It caught his eye momentarily, and he held its gaze for a few seconds before he realized the strangeness of its behavior. For it to be suddenly appearing in the windscreen meant one of two things. Either it was moving, or they were turning.

"Son of a bitch!" Mike said, leaning forward to look at the instrument panels. Immediately, his mind went two different directions. He knew the instruments and gauges would be useless; if they were turning or changing course at all, the gauges certainly wouldn't let them know – the gauges had gotten them into this whole predicament to begin with, what with not telling them when they were adjusting. But also, he thought maybe they would say something, because they thought the ship was in need of adjustment to keep going straight.

Nothing showed on any of the instrument panels, and their heading still remained the same according to the gauges. Of course, he realized, it would have to be at least a degree worth of turning for the gauges to even display it – as they didn't break it down any further than one-degree increments. The turn must have been too slight, he finally conceded, and leaned back. But even – he realized – a turn of such minimal measurements this far from Earth, would send them tens of thousands of miles off target in the long run. Mike sighed. And the star crept up ever so slightly, a little more visible in the windscreen – a little farther forward.

What the hell? He leaned forward again and looked hard at it. It seemed to be blinking or changing somehow, its light unsteady and wavering in even its color. And as he watched it, it slid forward a little more in the windscreen. *Okay, so it is moving.* He squinted and wiped his tired, straining eyes to have a better look, just as another thought hit him. *Oh shit! It's an asteroid!*

Mike dove down into the storage bin beneath the navigation panel and yanked the door open, searching for the binoculars. His heart was beating wildly, and he could feel the nervous excitement building in his stomach already. He said aloud, "This thing's going to blow right by in front of us, and I'll have a front row seat!" His hands grabbed the cold metal of the binoculars and he pulled himself back up into the chair, buckling himself in with one hand as he steadied the lenses in front of his eyes with the other.

It took him a moment to find the asteroid, but when he did, a smile crept across his face. *This is intense.* "Oh man, this is so wild," he said. Suddenly, he was groping for the intercom and throwing switches – every one but the right one – trying to get the PA to come on.

"Donnie, come to the cockpit immediately, please," he said, once he found the handset.

Donnie's eyes popped open and his heart skipped a beat. Had he just heard his name? He had been dozing off, and was just starting to interact with his thoughts, dreaming before the sleep washed him away completely. He turned to look at the clock inset in his wall, where it said the day and month, time, and temperature. He had been reading at some point, and started feeling his eyelids become heavy. Now he was wide awake, and his paperback floated spread eagle over by the gangway.

He unbuckled himself from the bed and swung around to retrieve it when the intercom rang out. "Donnie, I need you in the cockpit now, please." That was what he had heard. Mike was calling him. He grabbed the book and whirled it toward the small locker beside the bed, then pulled the door open.

The hallways were dark and lonely feeling as he made his way to the cockpit. The comfortable hum of machinery that usually went unnoticed was now noticed only in its absence. They had shut down many of the major systems that were now unnecessary in the slow return. He wondered somewhere subconsciously how much longer they had, and how quickly they would run out of fresh oxygen.

He pushed open the cockpit door to find Mike hovering just beside the windscreen, his feet dangling beside the chair. His eyes were glued to the binoculars, and he was steadying himself with one hand to the bulkhead.

Donnie shut the door behind him and looked around about the flight deck. It all seemed so foreign and different now. He wondered how long it had been since he had even been in here. He didn't really even feel like he belonged in here anymore. Moving up to the first officer's chair, he looked out the windscreen to see what was so fascinating to Mike that he felt he needed to get Donnie up here.

"What is it, Mike?"

Mike started and turned around, pale as powder. "Oh my God, Donnie. You're not going to believe this shit. Take a look."

Donnie frowned at Mike as he took the binoculars. "Mike, are you okay? You're looking a little pale." Donnie moved forward and put the lenses to his eyes.

"No, I don't think I am okay."

"Well, what is it? What am I looking for here?" Donnie said, scanning the area outside the windscreen and finding nothing.

"That bright star over there. Check it out," Mike said quietly.

Donnie removed the cups from his eyes to find the star in question, then aimed at it and focused. He leaned his head forward to get closer, nearly bumping the glass with the far end of the tool. It took him a moment to get it focused, and he kept losing the star. *What the hell?* He leaned back and looked again with his naked eyes, aimed, and returned the cups to his sockets. And that time he saw it.

Donnie came sprawling back away from the windscreen as the binoculars hit the glass, chipping a small chunk out of the inner layer. His back hit the wall effectively stopping him and knocking his breath out simultaneously. "Where in God's name did that come from?"

Julia pulled her hair casually back behind her ear as she paced behind Mark's desk. He was twirling a pen on the desk's surface, waiting for the image to refresh on his screen. It was rather loud in the empty office, and was beginning to rake on Julia's nerves a bit.

"Will you desist? For God's sake, Mark!"

"Sorry."

"Now. Tell me again why this is taking so long to refresh?"

"Because, the damn thing's moved so far out of range now, we barely have control over it! You told me to keep an eye on that mother, and I have. But it's been a game of chase ever since I spotted it."

Julia was now pulling her own hair. "I don't get it though. How the hell are they coming so close to it? What are the odds? Isn't that like impossible?"

Mark only nodded, still staring at the refreshing image from Hubble 9 on his console monitor.

"I mean – you discovered that thing what, like a year ago?" she said, continuing her pacing.

"Nine months."

"Nine months?" Julia said.

"Give or take. Look, your pacing is effing killing me now, will you sit the hell down?"

Julia stopped and stared at Mark, a look of ferocious energy ready to be unleashed. Her breathing got heavier in a flash. And then she sat.

"Thank you."

"So you found it nine months ago, and then Atlas takes off – which has nothing to do with it – and gets lost. And now they're heading right for it. So did they *know* it was there all along?"

Mark twisted his mouth. "No. Now you're being ridiculous, Julia."

"How is it ridiculous? Look! If they don't know about it, they will when they slam into it! What are the odds of this being a coincidence?" Julia said.

Mark turned to face her, a look of utter seriousness in his eyes. "Julia. You agree that neither of us has seen anything like this, right? Ever."

She nodded. "Yeah!"

"Well, we can't begin to understand its behavior then. It must have been waiting for them out between here and Mars, and when it saw they were off course, it started following them. Observing them."

"Oh, so you mean to say you think there's intelligent life on that ship?"

"God, you're just now getting this?" Mark said, and stood up. It was his turn to pace now. "Julia, ships don't just appear in space. We don't just send empty shuttles out to hang around between planets. Someone piloted that son of a bitch out there. And someone is piloting it now. Someone or something."

Julia sat up straight, suddenly feeling a hard shiver crawl up her spine. Her arms covered in gooseflesh, which she tried to rub away. She shivered verbally. "Oh my God, this is giving me the creeps."

Mark nodded slowly, wide-eyed at her. "That's why I've been watching it!"

Julia looked at the screen, where the image was now nearly complete. She grabbed the pen and started twirling it on the desk. "Now I wish I would have told them about it before they left."

| **CHAPTER** *thirty* |

proximity

Tears formed in Donnie's eyes as he looked at the approaching craft. It wasn't an emotional experience, it just scared him to tears, like telling of a true encounter with a ghost. The shivers up his spine were constant, and he kept wanting to turn around and run, but had nowhere to go. The foreign ship was now close enough to see and make out with the naked eye, and it was very obviously coming toward them. The thought that its precise movements brought it ever closer made Donnie shake even harder. That meant it was manned.

There wasn't much doubt that any spacecraft they would run into in deep space would be manned, but there had been much doubt they would run into anything unnatural at all. There had in fact been so much doubt as to have made Donnie think before there was no such thing. Everything he believed in told him they were the only creatures in the universe. And now, seeing this alien craft pilot its way slowly and methodically toward them made his stomach weak. He felt nauseous with fear and perplexity. What to do?

What to say? Their shuttle certainly had not been outfitted with laser beams or space missiles. He could only hope this would be an affable encounter. And there was little doubt now there would be an encounter.

Mike hovered in the corner, surveying the situation with speechless amazement. His eyes were locked hard on the incoming vessel, a look of mindless curiosity painting his face. He held to the wall with one hand, but the rest of him floated free.

"I-I absolutely can't believe this. Am I dreaming?" Donnie said, finally breaking the thick silence.

"Not unless I am too. Should we call the rest of the crew?"

Donnie didn't answer right away. He didn't know how to answer. On one hand he wanted to tell them because they did have a right to know something was about to happen. Whether that something was big or meaningful was yet to be seen. They had a right to know, and perhaps a need to know in case something happened to Donnie and Mike and left them incapacitated. But on the other hand, he didn't want the crew to overreact or do something stupid either. And then there was the part of him that wanted this to remain his and Mike's secret. That was, of course, assuming that nothing *did* happen, and they were the only ones who ended up seeing it.

"I don't know," Donnie finally answered. "What do you think?"

"Let's give it a minute. See if anything happens."

Donnie nodded. That was a perfectly acceptable response as far as he was concerned. Maybe the other ship would just get close enough to have a look, then dart off into the great unknown. And if that were to happen, Donnie would be glad to have harbored the secret of its passing.

His mind filled with all the times he had heard of people being abducted by UFOs, probed by aliens, and taken to other dimensions. And he had laughed at them. Not only did it sound preposterous to him that any alien – intelligent or not – would want something to do with humans, but the great lengths people went to just to make their stories sound more believable turned him off too. And now here he was facing something potentially capable of making him the subject of their laughter, were he ever to share the experience. Poetic justice, as it were, would be served, he thought.

"I wonder if we should be doing anything," Mike said, not taking his eyes off the other ship.

"Yeah, me too. This is unsettling as hell."

The ship was within a thousand meters now, and closing in slowly. It seemed to have no definitive aerodynamic shape, like Earthly conveyances. Of course, any ship used outside of all gravitational influence wouldn't need a streamlined physique anyway. A perfect cube would be no less effective in space, where there was no wind or gravity to slow it down. This one did seem to have a front end to it, but beyond that, there was no evidence it was built with anything in mind but space.

"Is it going to attack us?" Donnie said.

"I think if that were the case, it would have done so already. Maybe it's approaching this slowly because they're afraid of the same thing," Mike said, and made Donnie feel instantly better about having asked such a silly question.

"Yeah, I can see how they would think that of this ship."

Mike looked over at him to catch the sarcasm in Donnie's eyes. Mike grinned. "This is pretty intense, yeah?"

Donnie smiled back. "Hell yeah." They both looked back at the ship, and suddenly it stopped dead in its tracks.

"Wow," Mike said.

"What?"

"You see how it just stopped?"

"Yeah," Donnie said, looking back at Mike again. He was beginning to feel a little worried again. "What's that mean?"

"I don't know. I just think that's pretty impressive technology to be able to stop so efficiently."

"Space brakes."

They both laughed out loud. It helped cut the tension a little. The ship now turned slowly on its vertical axis (which was almost horizontal to Atlas's) revealing the port side of the ship. Another common conception among neophyte space enthusiasts is the one that all ships meet 'top up', sharing the same vertical orientation. With no set 'ups' in space, the likelihood of any two ships coming into contact with each other and sharing the same up would be almost as unlikely as their meeting in the first place.

On the port side of the ship, a previously unseen door opened, leaving a large black square on the side of the ship, the inside hidden in perfect shadow. Donnie's stomach tensed, and he heard Mike's breathing grow shallow. They waited in nervous anticipation for something – anything to happen. A buzzer rang out in the ceiling, and Donnie's heart stopped.

"Oh my God. Mike, open the door."

Mike turned and pulled the door open. Shanna waited just outside. "What's up guys?" she said.

Donnie looked seriously at her, then returned his gaze to the foreigner outside the windscreen. He heard the door shut to his left.

"What, are y'all not talking t…" Shanna gasped. "Oh my God. What the hell is that?"

"We don't know yet, Shanna," Mike said.

"Oh my God. Oh my God, oh my God." Donnie heard her fumbling with something, then an electric whirr made him turn to look at her. She had her camera aimed diligently out the window, and was now digitally filming history in the making.

"Good thinking," Donnie said.

"Holy shit this is incredible," she said seriously. There was a long silence in which they all watched, waiting for something to either shoot out of the black opening at them, or something to start sucking them in like the ever famous 'tractor beams' of late eighties sci-fi films.

"This is too much. Have you guys always known about this stuff?" Shanna said, still staring at the tiny version of the ship portrayed on her Sony digital camera's small monitor screen.

Donnie looked at her again. "Know about what stuff?"

"Aliens! UFOs! Is this the first one you've ever seen?"

Donnie shook his head. He felt a little disappointed that she had said that, and quickly realized his reservations about people who used those words. The prejudice he so strongly harbored for those who talked all that UFO nonsense was in sudden need of a reevaluation.

"I think so, Shanna," Mike said. His voice was soft and quiet, and Donnie thought Mike probably didn't want to show too much emotion, which was no doubt in great abundance right now.

Something appeared in the middle of the black spot on the side of the strange ship. It was a miniscule white-grey speck, and barely visible. If one looked right at it, it would be lost in the pupil of the eye. To really believe it was there, it had to be viewed almost peripherally.

For several minutes it wasn't evident what was really going on. They could see the spot changing or moving, but couldn't tell how, or if it was getting closer. The ship was still too far away to make out details of great quality. Their initial estimate was that the ship was about a thousand meters away when it stopped, but the radar wouldn't confirm that estimate. The radar didn't appear to even be registering the visitor, and the radar was one of the systems that was still operational.

Shanna used the digital zoom on the video camera, and tried to get in real close to the spot hanging free in the middle of the large black portal of the other ship. Even the zoom wasn't enough though, as the spot still looked like a spot – just a little bit bigger one. Donnie retrieved the binoculars and had the same experience, and the digital readout on the bottom right side of the view plate measured almost six kilometers away. If that were the case, then they had not only underestimated the ship's distance, they had also severely underestimated its size. If that ship was six times the distance away that they had thought, it was gargantuan.

In deep space there are no mile markers, or stationary objects by which to judge the distance of another object, so it was assumed they would be a little off in their estimation, but five kilometers was almost unacceptably extreme.

"Well if they're going to blast us with their alien missile, I wish they would hurry up and get it over with. This anticipation is killing me," Donnie said, breaking the silence. That silence had grown so thick it felt as though they were bathing in it, and the tension in the air was evident in not only the looks of their faces, but the sweat on Donnie's and Mike's foreheads.

"I don't know, they don't really look hostile," Mike said. "I mean I've seen alien warships, and they don't look like that."

Everyone laughed at that. And then it moved. The small white speck began to move forward noticeably, and the black square it had come out of began closing. Within a few seconds, the bay had closed completely, and the ship started moving. They had, of course, been moving the entire time, but matching Atlas's velocity had made it appear absolutely motionless. Relative physics was the only thing more disconcerting than zero gravity in space.

The ship's movement was at first somewhat sluggish, but after about a minute, something changed intensely, and the ship lurched rapidly and blew out of their range of vision within a couple of seconds. And the small white speck was growing larger. The light from Sol, over a hundred and forty-million kilometers away, was glinting off the small object and making it appear stellar. And suddenly, Donnie had a thought.

"That ship looked like a bright star before it came closer. Was that the bright star we had been chasing for all those weeks?"

Shanna knew immediately what he was talking about. Mike frowned at the question. "What do you mean, 'chasing a star'?"

"The bright star in our windscreen. The one that remained visible for a few weeks. You used it as a guide when we turned around," Donnie reminded him.

Mike nodded quickly. "Now that you mention it, yes. It did look like it could have been the same one." He rubbed his arms quickly and shivered visibly. "That would mean this bitch has been following us for quite some time."

Donnie nodded slowly. "I bet that's it."

"Whoa, guys. This is some freaky shit," Shanna said. She was staring at her camera screen, still focused on the tiny speck.

"Did you get that ship taking off?" Mike said.

"Yeah. I got it."

Mike looked at Donnie seriously. "Good. I have a feeling we're going to need all the proof we can get when we start telling this story."

Donnie nodded. "You're damn right. If we live to tell about it, that is."

"So what's this little dude doing? He's still coming closer," Mike said. He took the binoculars and tried to focus in on the speck of light.

"I don't know, but I'm not nearly as afraid of him as I am the big one."

"What, you think this is a ship too?" Mike said, looking back at Donnie.

"Shit, I don't know. I just meant it's not as big as the ship, whatever it is."

"That doesn't make much sense though, that the big one would run off and leave it, if it were another ship," Shanna added.

"Which would make it more likely still that this is a missile or something. They left a bomb and scattered the hell out of here," Donnie said.

Mike didn't say anything. He just looked out the windscreen, chewing his lip.

"Right? What are you thinking? Tell me I'm wrong, please…"

"You're right. That would make sense. But I don't buy it. Why would they want to destroy us?"

"You guys are freaking me out. You think we're going to die out here?" Shanna said, finally looking away from the camera.

"How the hell would we know? We've never encountered anything like this before," Mike said.

"You asked me yesterday, I would have told you there was no such thing as aliens."

"Well you sure are taking this well," she said.

"What the hell you want me to do? We can't run! I can't jump up and down with no gees under my feet!" Donnie said, raising his voice for show.

"Oh my God, it is a ship!" Shanna said suddenly, staring again at the view screen on the camera. "I zoomed all the way in and…"

Donnie and Mike were pushing to get behind her already. And there on the 2x3 LCD screen was a perfectly strange, but absolutely real ship – unlike any they had ever seen before, yet immediately recognizable as a space conveyance. And it was coming right at them.

"Get Bradley up here."

Mike keyed the handset. "Brian Bradley report to the flight deck please."

After a moment, the intercom beeped. Mike keyed the handset. "Go ahead."

"Mike, he's in med hold, confined. Remember? Donnie's orders."

"Get him up here, Andy. Donnie's orders."

In three minutes, Brian Bradley was pushing through the gangway and into the crowded flight deck. White gauze wrapped round his head, covering his bottom jaw, and an Ace bandage covered part of that. He was silent as he entered.

"What is that?" Donnie said, pointing at the makeshift cast.

Brian looked at Donnie from the corner of his eyes. "She didn't have a head brace, or she would have wired my jaw shut."

Donnie raised his head in understanding. "Sorry about that."

"What did you call me up here for? I would like to return to my holding cell and sulk some more."

Mike looked levelly at Donnie, wondering what this was all about. Usually Donnie would consult Mike before bringing Bradley – or anyone else in trouble – to the carpet. It wasn't procedural, but rather Donnie's trust and respect for Mike's opinion.

"I'd like to show you something," Donnie said, looking at Mike now, "but not yet. I'll show you in a minute. For now I want to ask you some questions."

Bradley looked back and forth between Mike and Donnie, ignoring Shanna completely. Bradley was clearly at a loss as much as everyone but Donnie. "Okay."

"How deep does your relationship with Royal Research Corp really run?"

"Well…" Brian started.

"And I want you to answer honestly, because the way in which I will deal with you on Earth depends strictly on your answers here. If you answer honestly, and are forthcoming, you'll be fired when we get home. If you lie to me, or try and skate your way out of this in any way, you'll be prosecuted and sent to prison. And fired." Donnie stared levelly at him for a moment, then repeated. "So I'll ask you again. How deep does your relationship with Royal really run?"

Brian sighed deeply, looking at the floor of the flight deck. There were no answers there, and he hesitated. "Look, Donnie. I really don't know what you think I do. They didn't tell me anything but what to do. I don't know why I did anything or what it was for."

"But you did receive a paycheck from them." Donnie stole a glance out the windscreen, thinking of it as checking the clock. His assumption was that the other ship had been monitoring them for more than two months now, had been able to determine that Atlas wasn't going anywhere (at least not fast), and had thereby decided to send a care package to take care of them once and for all. The ship would be arriving within the next half hour or so carrying a cargo bay full of alien explosive, and that would be the end of it all. His thirst for answers now only thrived on the desire to leave no dead questions when all was said and done.

"Yes. They paid me to spy on Oliver Company."

"You slimy piece of shit. I can't believe your gall."

Brian didn't meet Donnie's gaze. He held his spot on the floor and continued to sigh at all the right spots. His irritation for Donnie was his only want.

"How much have you told them? How long have you been working for them?"

"I haven't told as much as you think. They were only interested in certain things. Five years or so."

Donnie sighed now, checked the window, and continued. "Certain things. Like what?"

"Space travel. Satellite technology," Brian said.

"Oh! You didn't tell them much! You stupid cock! That's everything we are!"

"No, no – they were only interested in knowing things about the technology we used in our missions. And the ST-95s. Not the whole company vision, or whatever."

Donnie shook his head. "I can't believe you! Listen to yourself! That's everything. *Every thing!* To hell with the company vision! You can get that off our web site! You told them proprietary information about our technology! I ought to have you killed!" he said.

He wasn't yelling yet, but felt like he was. The energy he expended in holding back his temper was greater than his normal tantrum produced.

Mike finally felt the need to speak. "So that's why they bought that satellite after all. They wanted to steal our technology."

"Oh, please," Bradley said, looking up at him. "They're so much further advanced than we are they could have built that piece of shit back in the eighties."

"Oh yeah? Then why'd they buy a vanilla from us, asshole?" Donnie said.

"I don't know. Like I said, they never told me what they were doing with stuff."

"But you sent them all the specs for it and everything."

Bradley nodded, staring at the floor again.

Donnie looked out the windscreen again, and noticed the speck of a spaceship was no longer such a speck. It was getting quite close now, and seemed to be growing larger by the minute. He was surprised Bradley hadn't seen it on his own yet. He sighed deeply and pondered over this for a few long moments. And then he surprised everyone in the room with his next question.

"Who killed Robert Keith?"

Bradley looked up sharply at Donnie. "What?"

"You heard me. Who killed him?"

"How the hell should I know? I didn't even know he was killed!"

Mike smirked at this. "You didn't know he was dead? Is that what you're saying?"

"No. That's not what I said. I said I didn't know he was killed. Of course I knew he was dead, dickhead."

"Watch your mouth, asshole. You know I don't like you. And I'm not as friendly as Donnie when I get mad."

Shanna stared on in amazement at this confrontation between three grown men. She had thought all this was behind them now. And without their knowing it, she had been filming from the hip, having never shut off the recording device.

"Oh, so it's okay for you to call me an asshole, but I can't call you a dickhead?"

"No!" Donnie and Mike said in chorus. Then Donnie continued, "Your privileges went right the hell out the door when I found out you were working for the other side."

"The other side. Shhsh."

"Who killed Robert Keith?" Donnie said again.

"I told you, I don't know! You want me to say it was Royal? It probably was! But I don't know, and I don't know why!" Bradley said, and looked up. Donnie knew immediately that he had seen it, because Bradley had flinched. But the dawn of surprise and fear that Donnie had expected to see on Bradley's face had completely failed to materialize, and Donnie's stomach sank with realization.

"You're excused," Donnie said. Brian Bradley stole one more glance out the windscreen, then pushed himself out the door, closing it behind him.

"What the hell was that all about?" Mike asked quickly, with a fierce look at Donnie.

"It's not alien, Mike."

"Come again?"

"The ship. It's not alien," Donnie said, waving toward the stranger in the windscreen. "He saw it. And he wasn't even surprised."

Mike stood still for a moment, hovering in his place. "You mean he recognized it?"

Donnie smirked. "Mike, he didn't just recognize it. He's been waiting for it."

As the cargo bay doors opened, Brian Bradley drifted out away from the shuttle Atlas, tethered by his lifeline. He was outfitted with a jet pack, which had hand controls and a series of nitrogen jets which would right his position and propel him where he needed to go. At the speed in which the other ship was approaching, Bradley estimated he would meet it somewhere around 300 meters from Atlas.

Mike and Donnie watched from the EVA control room, which had an observation window that looked out into the bay – and beyond, if the doors were open. The whole crew had been told what was going on, and to prepare for anything, but maintain total silence unless otherwise was absolutely necessary. Tensions were high, but there was a bit of excitement in the air that made everyone feel a little less threatened.

Mike had asked Donnie what the hell his plans were, as it had seemed that Donnie hadn't been keeping him very much in the loop lately. Donnie had answered patiently and quietly, having pulled him aside into the galley.

"He's been expecting that ship for probably weeks, Mike. He knew it was coming."

"So it's a Royal bird."

"Unless Bradley owns his own company, you're damn right it is."

"This is screwed up. I thought it was too much a coincidence that we would just happen to bump into another ship out here in the middle of nowhere," Mike said, shaking his head.

Now here at the window, Shanna piped up with her assessment of the situation. "I can't believe you're letting him go to the other ship."

"And why is that?" Donnie said with a sigh of impatience. "He probably summoned the damn thing. Why shouldn't he be the one to greet it?"

"What if he takes off in it?" she said smartly.

Donnie tried to hold back a laugh. "Shanna you worry too much. That's pretty unlikely. I know you two don't like each other, but he's still human. I think he cares about the welfare of his teammates."

"That's the problem," Mike mumbled to Donnie, "I think the men on that ship are his teammates. Not the men on this ship."

"Good point. Well he's going to contact us when he's in over there and we'll start sending essentials and people shortly thereafter." He grabbed Shanna by the shoulder, rubbing it through her thick suit. "You should be excited, Shanna! This is a rescue mission!"

The other ship was still incoming, but its rate of progress seemed to have slowed a little. Mike had reckoned that was just a trick of the imagination, for the other ship had halved its distance in the last twenty minutes or so, and doubled in size. What had originally looked like a miniscule speck of a space pod had turned out to be a ship almost as large as the Atlas itself.

The rest of the crew were scattered about the rear of the shuttle, looking out whatever windows they could get their faces close to. Most of the windows that far back in the ship were no larger than a dinner plate.

Brian Bradley was still moving out, about halfway to what it looked like would be the rendezvous point. The ship was incoming with only a slightly greater speed than Bradley was moving, and Bradley only had another hundred fifty meters or so to go. The microphone inside Bradley's helmet was voice-activated, so anything he spoke, they would hear in EVA control.

"How you doing, EVA?" Mike said. He was buckled into one of the motorized chairs overlooking the control panel.

"Moving right along. It's a nice night to be outside."

"Yeah, we saw no rain in the forecast," Donnie said, rolling his eyes at Mike. "You might want to start banging light in their windows. Make sure they see you coming."

"Roger that," Bradley answered. Another hundred meters of lifeline remained on the reel. He had seventy-five of that allocated.

Mike turned to Donnie and shook his head. "Dude's got balls, man. I don't know if I'd be out where he is right now."

Donnie chortled. "Yeah, whatever. You know as well as I do you'd be the first one out the door if I'd asked for volunteers."

Mike shook his head again. "I don't know, man. Thus far it's all been speculation that that's a Royal craft." Mike shrugged, letting the silence finish his sentence.

Donnie smiled. "You want so badly to believe, don't you?"

"I don't know. I just – well, yeah I guess. I'm a little disappointed. I mean when you get lost in space, leave the solar system by accident, make a wrong corrective adjustment, then you run into another ship… You'd like to think it's alien."

"Yeah. Maybe. At any rate, I would like to be out there where he is right now. And by all rights I should be," Donnie said, looking back out the window.

"Nah. Delegation is a leader's primary function. If you die, we have no one to run the ship."

"Ship runs itself," Donnie said, pointing at Mike.

"Not this ship, it doesn't."

Donnie threw up his hands. He had forgotten about all the bad systems – the whole reason Brian Bradley was out walking the plank.

"Uh, guys – is this ship going to stop when I get to it, or just plow right through me?" Bradley said over the radio.

"Stand by, EVA, let me call and ask them."

"You're such an asshole, Donnie," Bradley whined.

"Hey! Maintain radio discipline, EVA," Mike said quickly.

Donnie looked over at him and smirked. "EVA, by my calculations here, you have about twenty meters to find out."

Mike keyed the radio again and said, "Did you try flashing your light at them?"

"Yeah. They didn't seem to respond."

That twenty meters came quickly. And without any warning, the ship just stopped. Right on target, three meters from Bradley, and at perfect midpoint rendezvous. Donnie's pulse raced as he watched. There was the big picture window, where Bradley was almost too far away to see, and a small monitor above the window, which showed everything he saw by a camera inside his helmet visor.

"Well they know I'm here…"

Donnie and Mike just watched. At this point there wasn't much they could do. They certainly couldn't advise him on how to handle it, or interact with it in any way. No one on board the Atlas had any idea how the strange ship was laid out, or where the portals might be.

Bradley went around the starboard side, looking either to be met by someone coming out, or for an opening in which to be welcomed. His breathing was now coming over the radio, which meant it was heavy enough to register and trigger the voice activation.

"Calm down Bradley, you're doing fine," Donnie said.

Mike looked over at him, shaking his head. He made a gesture with his left hand, indicating "balls".

"There's nothing on this side of the ship. It's a little dark over here, but – wait…"

Donnie's heart jumped in his chest as he thought something was happening. His eyes widened, and he noticed a similar reaction in Mike's sudden concentration level.

"No, there's nothing here."

Donnie let out a deep breath. Bradley carried on, dropping under the bottom of the ship to reach the port side, which – relative to Atlas's orientation – was up. The port side of the foreign ship was the dark side, as the sun was at the aft end, and closer to the starboard. From Atlas's point of view, the sun was at one o'clock, and the ship was coming at them from about two-thirty.

Bradley reached the other side of the ship and started moving toward the aft when he suddenly ran out of line. Donnie could feel the lifeline reach the end of its length as it tugged on Atlas, which spoke of the velocity Bradley had achieved with his nitro-jets.

Donnie keyed the intercom. "Shanna are you recording this?"

"Every bit," she replied, the echo of a large room behind her. Donnie reckoned she must be across the room from the intercom outlet.

"I'd like to get closer though, because it's kind of small on the screen."

Donnie let go of the listen button, and without thinking twice, pushed the talk button again. His impulsive nature had a tendency to get the best of him when he was excited. "Don your space suit. Gary can help you get it on."

"Are you serious? You'll let me go out there?"

"Sure. We need footage," Donnie replied.

Mike was staring wide-eyed at him. "You're still concerned about video?"

"Why not? They're already here. We're saved, right?"

"Okay, I've found a door," came Bradley's voice.

"Wait. What the hell – we're moving. Mike why are we moving?" Donnie said.

"Shit, I don't know… Stand by. You want to call him off?" Mike said, scrambling to look at the gauges.

The Atlas had suddenly begun to spin clockwise very slowly, and now was losing sight of the other ship as it sailed around twelve o'clock low.

"Stand by, EVA. We're moving."

"Wh-… C-ch-av-… itors…"

"Repeat EVA, you're breaking up all of a sudden!" Donnie said, now gripping the station handle with a hard fist. His knuckles were turning white, and he didn't even notice. "Shit! Why – Mike, get the hell up to the cockpit and stop our movement!"

The intercom rang. Donnie pushed the talk button. "What is it?" he shouted.

"Uh, Donnie, you know why we're moving, don't you?" It was Jonathan's voice.

"No, I don't. But I want it stopped!"

"His tether hit the end of its run, and he was at full blast. He pulled us out of station."

"Is that possible?" Donnie said to Mike, turning to address him. But Mike had already left the room. He keyed the talk button again. "Is that possible?"

"Absolutely. We were barely moving. For him to even get away from us at that angle, he had to exceed our velocity two times over. He hit the end of the tether, which has a safety spring built in, and…"

Donnie cut him off. "All right, all right. Find out why the hell I can't hear him anymore." He keyed the radio again. "Bradley come in. Can you hear me?" There was nothing but soft static. The other ship was now completely out of sight, and Bradley was on the far side of it.

The door slid open and Andy came charging in. "What's going on? Is he okay out there?"

Donnie threw up his hands. "I don't know! I've lost sight and sound!"

Andy covered her mouth, her eyes wide and white. "Oh my God."

"Where is everybody? Where is everybody?" Donnie said, turning to look around the empty EVA control room.

"I don't know! Why are you yelling at me?"

"I figured everyone would want to be in here!" Then to the intercoms, "Can someone please tell me why we're still moving? And where the hell everyone is all the sudden?"

"Gary and Shanna are in the press chamber prepping her for EVA," Andy said, pointing down at the pressurization chamber, visible out the large window.

Donnie could just see movement inside the small portal window in the pressure door. "That's not everybody. Where's Jonathan?"

Andy shrugged. "I don't know, I haven't seen him."

"Talk to me, Mike!" Donnie said, keying the intercom again.

"Donnie, nothing's showing movement up here. I'm trying to correct the spin, but I think we're out of nitrogen or something."

"Dammit!" Donnie said, throwing the radio handset he had been holding at the picture window. It bounced off with a loud bang, and Andy jumped in her clothes. He turned and left the EVA room, feeling anger and fear at once. He was losing control of everything now, and he had a man outside the ship. There was about to be another body outside the ship. He needed to fix something fast.

"Go down and get Shanna out of the press chamber," Donnie said to Andy. She didn't move though, and before he could react, the pressurization chamber door blew open, a cloud of white oxygen being sucked out into space where it disappeared instantly. And then Shanna was floating out away from the ship, on her way toward the back of the shuttle.

Donnie grabbed the handset and keyed it. "Shanna, get your ass back in this ship! Until we establish station, all personnel are grounded!" He then looked up at the intercom and back down at his handset. It was cracked and splintered where it had hit the window a few minutes before. "Son of a bitch!" he shouted, turning to storm out of the EVA control room.

"Someone get on the radio and get her ass back here!" he shouted, but the only one near enough to hear him was Andy. He pulled himself down the hallway toward the press chamber.

"Wait! Donnie!" Andy shouted. Donnie turned and pulled himself back into the EVA control room, and immediately saw what she had screamed about. A lifeline blew past the window, squirming like a high pressure snake with no head.

"Oh my God." Donnie felt his face physically go white. His hair tingled, and his spine rocked with chills. "We've lost Bradley."

In a fevered panic, he shot off back down the corridor in search of some sense of control. He reached the pressurization anteroom and found Gary Grant at the control panel, closing the outside door.

"Gary, get her back in here! What the hell do you think you're doing?"

"What do you mean?" Gary said. Donnie had obviously startled him as he came in shouting.

"I mean, get her ass back here! Bradley's gone and she took off back behind the ship! Where the hell was she going, and why?"

Gary turned to look out the window, but couldn't see anything from this area. "She was going to film Brian's rendezvous. What do you mean he's gone?"

"Get her back here," Donnie said. "If she runs behind that antimatter drive it'll turn her to dust."

"I thought we were empty though!" he said, already pulling the handle that would reel her back in.

"Get her on the radio. Even when we're out, there'll still be intermittent blasts of energy as the penning traps lose hold."

Gary's hands were trembling as he fumbled with the controls, trying to regain radio contact with her. All he was getting was static, and Donnie could tell he was already shaken. Donnie's hope dwindled more with every second that passed – realizing the weight of the situation.

The reel squeaked and vibrated against the hull as it drew in the lifeline. Within half a minute, the plug came sailing around the edge of the bay. And Donnie hung his head.

| **CHAPTER** *thirty-two* |

rescue mission

What remained of the crew was gathered in the common area, and Donnie was restlessly moving about, wishing for gravity if only so he could pace. Jonathan sat squeezing a piece of the lifeline he had retrieved and snipped the end off of for examination. Gary and Mike stood against the wall next to the door, feet locked to the floor, and Andy sat hugging herself nervously on the floor by their feet.

"I want everyone to stay calm. We can do nothing but bad by panicking. I'm sorry for our loss, but we have to stick together – now more than ever – if we want to pull out of this." He looked at the solemn and sour faces of his crew and drew in a deep breath, trying to push Shanna from his memory.

"We know we lost Shanna. Brian, we don't know. What'd you find out about the hose?" Donnie said, pointing at Jonathan Rodgers.

Jonathan held up the piece of hose and looked at it. "It looks like it was stretched and broken, like it had been caught against something and yanked."

"What the hell could he have gotten caught on?" Donnie said.

"That's what I've been pondering," Mike said. "And all I can think of is that he got in somehow."

Donnie nodded thoughtfully.

"That is a possibility I considered as well, seeing that there was nothing on the port side of the vessel that looked like a potential snag point," Jonathan said. Mike looked at him and nodded, then looked at Donnie again.

"Okay so that leaves us in the same place. Let's assume he's on that ship. We don't know where that ship is. Our radar doesn't see it – not that it has registered anything properly in the last month – and we can't get visual on it. So it's either eclipsed by Atlas, or gone."

"Yes, but I'd also suggest that if he were outside of that ship, his radio might still be operational. We've not been able to get hold of him," Jonathan said. Mike agreed with this.

"Well either way, we got a man outside the ship and we need to find out where he is, and get him back," Donnie said.

"Are you suggesting we spacewalk to collect a cadaver?" Jonathan asked.

"Wouldn't you like to think we'd do the same for you?" Mike snapped.

"I'm absolutely suggesting it. In fact, I'm commanding it. We don't know he's dead anyway."

Jonathan laughed and looked away.

"What's so funny, Rodgers?" Donnie said.

"You don't think he's dead? We have his lifeline. He's got no oxygen, and a hole in his suit." Jonathan held up the piece of hose he had snipped off the end of the lifeline.

"If he made it inside that ship, he's got plenty of oxygen," Donnie said.

Jonathan unbuckled himself and pushed up to retrieve his liquipack. "This is ludicrous! That's an alien spacecraft out there, and you assume they breathe the same air as we do?"

Donnie snorted. "You're still stuck on the fantasy that we've encountered an alien craft."

"Well I don't see a big Royal logo painted on the side of it."

Donnie shook his head at this. Mike scoffed, "Yeah well you don't exactly see Oliver painted on the side of Atlas either, do you?"

Jonathan shook his head and rolled his eyes.

"So here's the arrangement. Mike, you and Mr. Rodgers over here, put your suits on and go EVA. Each of you take a radio. I want a status on the other ship. See if you can find it. And keep an eye out for Bradley. If he's still out there we need to bring him in."

Mike and Jonathan had blasted out the cargo bay on nitrogen jets and swung around the port side of the ship in search of the strange craft. Gary Grant had tethered himself to a bulkhead in the cargo bay and walked out as far as he could, still maintaining line-of-sight with the EVA control room for radio contact. In this way he could see the two cosmonauts and get them back in if he needed.

Andy and Donnie looked on from the EVA control room, albeit without much control at all. Donnie was so anxious for something – anything – to happen that he barely noticed the hunger pangs that would have nearly crippled him otherwise. But upon the nervousness that had his stomach in knots he felt he would get sick if he ate anything at all. He would have to tough this one out. Andy sat buckled into the chair, eyes wide and chewing on her knuckles. Her apparent nervousness did nothing to ease Donnie's.

To have come so close to an apparent rescue, literally within meters of another ship, only to lose it in proximity seemed a travesty. The nervousness in his stomach was wild and burning. The 'not-knowing' part of not knowing where that other ship had gone was eating him away from the inside.

The sun – seemingly ten trillion miles away, and a tiny insignificant speck of light – looked longingly on the project at hand, halfway across the galaxy. Donnie found his eyes wandering toward it occasionally, missing it like a lost child. All those summers he spent cursing it for burning his fair skin now returned to his mind with bitter mockery as he longed for the day when he could just lie out in the backyard and just let it burn him silly. Even being destined to death from skin cancer beat rotting out in space because everything went wrong on a mission that was doomed from the minute it left Earth. And sometimes Donnie thought that was even too late. He had the feeling this mission had been doomed from conception.

There in the shallow distance, the other ship held steady, looming like a threat in the emptiness of space. Mike and Jonathan were only feet from it. Mike brought forth his suction rod and snapped it in place, anchoring himself against the side of the foreign ship, his feet pushing enough to provide a balance like he was hanging from the side of a mountain. He was near a hatch that looked to be roughly of human size, and thought if Bradley had gone in this ship anywhere on this side of it, then this portal had to be the one. His eyes scanned the starboard side again, from front to back, in awe and wonder at the sheer size of it. He spoke toward the microphone in his helmet, relaying the message through Gary and back to Donnie on the Atlas.

"Well, I guess I've found the door. I think it's the only one on the starboard side. If he came in this sumbitch, it had to be through this door."

After a short delay, he heard Donnie responding through dead-sounding air. "Roger that. Is there any sort of handle or anything?"

"Negative on that. I guess I should – I don't know. What should I do? Should I knock?" Mike said. He never imagined he would be in such a predicament so far from his home planet – wondering whether to knock on the door of an alien craft. If this ship wasn't from Earth, he guessed he didn't make a very good Earthly ambassador.

"Yeah I guess, Mike. Sounds as good as anything else I can think of," Donnie said.

"Now wait. What else can you think of Donnie?"

"Well, nothing at the moment."

Mike shook his head. "Okay. I'm knocking. I guess I should prepare for the worst. Just in case this…"

"Hey!" Donnie cut him off through power of base radio. "You were the one who said this didn't look like a hostile alien ship. Maintain your confidence!"

"Roger that. I'm knocking now." Mike reared back and slammed the side of his fist on the door three times, hard as he could. It at first took him aback that there was no sound, but he could feel the vibration against his feet. The door felt like solid steel, and Mike guessed that was probably precisely what it was. He wondered if there had been any sound at all on the inside. Nervousness and anxiety sank into his stomach as he prepared for the answering – if there were to be any.

After a long period of uncertainty, Mike sighed and turned back to see Gary hanging just over the edge of visibility back at Atlas.

"Uh, Donnie, nothing is happening."

"Figures. How much line you have left?"

"About two meters of play I think. I can't do anything with that," Mike said.

Jonathan hung quietly beside him, running his hand along the sleek skin of the craft. They were out of options. If knocking didn't permit them entry, they had nothing else they could do.

Donnie checked the EVA clock, and realized Mike and Jonathan had already been gone for half an hour. He had hoped they would already be on the other ship by now, or on their way back with Bradley in tow. But there was still no sign of Brian Bradley. Donnie was beginning to lose control of his anger. He was losing control of his fear, and he was losing control of his control. "What the hell's going on in that ship?"

Andy looked at him solemnly. She was obviously as clueless as he was, but his desire for someone to know the answers forced him to ignore reason entirely. "We've lost two of our crew to that damn ship. It's a lucky thing I don't have missiles on this shuttle, or I would blow that son of a bitch out of the sky!" he shouted, waving his arms madly in cadence with his words.

"Calm down, Donnie. You're going to give yourself a stroke," Andy said calmly. She was trying to maintain cool for both of them – a cool control she really didn't have enough of herself.

Donnie looked at Andy questioningly. She was right. He knew he would blow a gasket if he didn't slow down. All the stress of the last three months had been building up, and now it was unbearably strong. He wondered what it would take to get rid of all the stress. What would have to happen to relieve it? Would they only have to be rescued? Would making it back to Earth calm him at this point? After everything that had gone wrong, and how many people had had a hand in getting them stuck in space, he doubted the potential for any kind of healing anymore.

Being stuck alive and free to move about on a worthless ship, millions of miles from nowhere, seemed an incessant mockery – almost hellish. It was like being locked in the closet while the parade marched by outside.

"How the hell am I supposed to calm down when I've lost two people in the last hour?" he finally said.

"Donnie, you're assuming you know Bradley's welfare. You can't possibly know if he's alive or dead out there. If he made it onto that other ship though, he's probably fine."

"Yeah, but his hose got cut! He's gotta be dead!" Donnie said, grasping for anything at this point.

"Donnie, you're contradicting your own arguments now. You're starting to sound like Jonathan."

"Andy, you're…"

"Enough Donnie!" she shouted with an authority Donnie had never witnessed. He hadn't previously known she had it in her to yell like that. And it worked. He was silent. He didn't think he could speak had he something to say.

"You are supposed to exert control and leadership over your crew, Donnie. And you've shown me nothing but fear and negativity for the last day and a half!"

Donnie stared dumbly at her, wondering if that was accurate. He didn't doubt it – he had felt nothing but negative for the last month. If it were only starting to show now, he was surprised he had maintained that long. He needed to take charge of his emotions again, and take back command of his ship. He needed to do something drastic.

He turned and spoke on impulse. "All right. Get your suit on. We're going out."

Mike grabbed Jonathan and nodded toward Atlas. "Let's head back. There's nothing here for us." Jonathan nodded and released himself from the side of the ship. Together they pushed off toward Atlas. Gary saw their intentions and started tugging on the lifelines in assistance. None of them noticed the foreign ship's movement as it turned twenty degrees farther down from the direction it was pointed. It's aft end was now pointed directly at the Atlas.

Donnie was staring at the radio when it went off. There was a loud screeching wail, and then hard static for at least ten seconds before a voice came on. And it was perfectly recognizable. It was human, and it was speaking English. It was Brian Bradley. And Donnie's heart skipped several beats in a row. He was suddenly more relieved than he could have ever imagined upon receiving any news regarding Bradley.

"Atlas, this is Tiamat, come in – over."

"Tiamat? Where the hell did you get that?" Donnie said – skipping the *'is-that-you'*s and the *'glad-to-hear-you're-alive-afterall'*s. He was relieved, but immediately disgusted with Bradley's cocky arrogance in thinking he could name the new ship whatever he wanted.

"Well I didn't name it, Donnie. And Tiamat was in Roman mythology, the mother of all that exists."

"Uh, that's great, Bradley. So you want to tell me what the plan is?" Donnie said, doing nothing to hide his disdain for the situation.

"The plan?" Bradley chuckled. "What plan, Donnie? There is no plan. Well, at least not one that involves you and your crew."

Donnie looked about the room for Andy. He then remembered he had just finished packing her into her suit and sent her out into the cargo bay to prepare for spacewalk. He returned his gaze to the window, and saw that Gary had come back and was helping her don a nitrogen jetpack. Jonathan was also on his way back to detach from the lifeline and make the transition to nitrogen.

Donnie keyed the mike. "So let me get this straight. You come in here and fuck up my ship so we can't get anywhere, then hitch a ride out. And we can't come."

"Well, that certainly seems to be the case. Listen, Donnie, this is nothing personal. They just really didn't want you making Mars."

Donnie was instantly so furious he could literally see the blood pumping into his eyes. His vision would blur and jolt downward with every swift beat of his heart. He slammed his fist against the control console, cracking and imploding the monitor just in front of his hand. "Bradley, you better get your shit in order. I'm coming over there, and you'd better be back in line when I get there."

"Ooooh, Donnie. Such foul language! Maintain radio discipline, please. I noticed your boys Mike and Jonathan couldn't figure out how to get in. What makes you think you can?"

Donnie was steaming. He noticed he was squeezing the handset with everything he had. He had tried cutting in with power of base, but it didn't work against the other ship's radio. "What the hell are you doing over there, Bradley? What makes you think you're going anywhere?"

"Well, Donnie, it's not so much that I think I'm going anywhere, as that I know I am. What about you? Where do you think you're going?"

In his rage, Donnie looked out the small portal through the press room and saw Andy, now equipped with nitrogen, hovering close to Gary in the cargo bay.

He keyed the radio and shouted into the handset, "What the hell is going on out there?" A few of them turned to look at him.

Gary responded first. "We're getting ready to head over there, boss."

"Who the hell told you to do that?"

"I thought that was the plan, Donnie. This ship is dead. That's a rescue ship, right?" Gary said.

What the hell? Donnie thought, then realized, Jonathan had probably been talking shit. "Uh, that's a negative. All Atlas crew report back to the pressurization chamber immediately. That ship is leaving without us."

No one appeared to be responding to his command though.

He keyed the mike and shouted into the radio at all who would listen, "Everyone get back here now! Report back to Atlas immediately!" Andy turned and glanced up at him from her position low in the cargo bay, thirty meters from him. She squinted as if she couldn't see through the glass. It occurred to Donnie that she might not even be able to hear him over the radio until she was completely hooked up.

"What the hell is going on? Get back here now! Gary – come back. Andy, you stay right there!"

"What's the matter, Oliver? You losing control of your crew?" Brian Bradley mocked from the other ship. "What, you think the power of persuasion isn't effective? They see the truth here, Oliver. They can stay there and listen to you and die, or come to my ship and make it home."

Donnie opened the press chamber door and pulled himself across to the far wall as fast as he could, cranking his head trying to see the other ship. He still couldn't see it. Gary Grant was staring at something though from his position on the edge of the cargo bay. "Tell me what you see, Gary!"

Gary looked back at him through the portal. "Well the door is open on the other ship. They're going to let us on." And Donnie finally got it. Bradley was trying to lure them across, only to leave them stranded between the ships.

Donnie took a series of deep breaths, and tried to recover. His head was spinning dizzy now, and he felt as though he might pass out. "Brian, I beg you – don't do what you're doing. Get them to bring that ship closer so we can load our supplies and food into it."

"Well, we have plenty of supplies here. But thanks for thinking of us. Anyway, I'm sure you'll be needing what remains of the oxygen and food over there," Bradley said. "Take care, Donnie." And then he heard the sound of the radio losing power. It was as if someone had pulled the fuse. He looked at the base station and saw that the red LED was no longer illuminated. *One more thing goes wrong.*

Donnie threw the radio handset against the window, where it ricocheted harmlessly, and pushed back for the gangway, just outside the pressure chamber. He might still make it if he hurried, he thought. His hands were trembling with adrenaline, and now the pains in his hungry stomach – no matter how futile their fight – were becoming almost intolerable. He wouldn't stop, but he knew if he didn't eat soon, he would surely pass out. The last suit remained in its container, strapped against the wall just outside the pressure chamber. He fumbled with it, trying to pull it on while his legs and arms shook like leaves in the wind. It was a two-man job putting a space suit on, but his ship was empty.

Donnie got the suit up over his shoulders, but couldn't zip and strap it on its back, and was now sweating profusely from the hard work of jamming himself into it. He knew he would be useless once he got out that door if the suit wasn't properly fastened. But he also knew he didn't have a choice. He grabbed the helmet and pulled it over his head, snapping the rubber collar against his neck and hooking the rim of it to the suit. He would be able to get oxygen, but his suit wouldn't be pressurized.

His vision was starting to blur as sweat rolled off his brow and into his eyes. Thoughts of his livelihood, and this one last chance at return swept recklessly through his mind, a pitiful mockery of his ignorance. Why hadn't he seen this sooner? This mutiny had been in order since he brought Brian Bradley aboard. Donnie had truly brought it upon himself. His hope was that they could all somehow actually make it onto the other ship and reason with its crew.

Donnie spun, and on impulse slammed his back against the wall, scrambling for foothold on the grated floor. He pulled himself down, trying to get something on the wall to catch the hook of the zipper on his suit. If he could just get it zipped, it would maintain some pressure. It wouldn't last as long as having it strapped and tightened and checked, but it would do. It would at least get him across the chasm of space that separated him from rescue. The zipper had a small hoop of fabric stretch cord on it. He pulled himself down the wall several times, and finally realized it wasn't going to work. He would have to find a hook or something… He turned and looked around the press chamber. The door handle would work.

Donnie pushed over to the door and maneuvered himself to where his back was against the recessed handle of the airlock door. He pushed and twisted, cursing his failed efforts, and sweating in his helmet like his feet were on fire. And finally it caught. He pulled himself down to the floor and felt the suit tighten around him as it zipped. He had done it!

He quickly reached back and grabbed an oxygen bottle, and hooked the hoses up to his suit and helmet. He turned the knob on the oxygen and felt immediate relief as the cool air poured into his fogging helmet. And with that, he slammed the depressurize button and the chamber locked down. Within a minute, he would be out in the cargo bay and on his way to the other ship.

The door slid open and he felt himself being sucked into the bay. Donnie frowned as he tried to get hold on something. If all the pressure and air had been vacuumed from the chamber, there would be no demand for equalization on the outside. Something had gone wrong with the pressurization chamber, and now Donnie was paying for it. He shot across the bay and slammed into the far wall, and bounced back, heading for open space before he could even get his bearing. As he whipped past some hoses he reached out and snagged a handful, quickly slowing his ascent into the void outside. But it wasn't enough. He was still moving, and the equipment connected to the hoses was now coming with him. After a few meters, the equipment reached the end of its own tether, and slung him to a hard stop, nearly pulling his shoulder out of socket.

Standard procedure dictated that one be holding onto the rails inside the press chamber before the door opens, in case there is a pressure deficit in either direction. He hadn't been holding onto anything but his oxygen bottle, and he was fortunate to have gotten that hooked up. His heart was still beating madly, hot blood pumping between his ears, and the last words of Brian Bradley echoing distantly in his memory. *I'm sure you'll be needing what remains of the oxygen and food over there.*

Across the distance, he could see Jonathan just twenty meters from the other ship. Jonathan had come back and switched to oxygen tank, leaving the lifeline behind.

Donnie hung there in the void, a few meters outside the cargo bay of the Atlas. He could pull himself down to the edge and push off real hard, sending himself across the void to the other ship. But even if he did make it to the ship, he doubted Brian would allow him to be let on. So this was his fate? He was doomed to drown in deep space on nothing but a dream of return?

Before, he had been able to see a different side of it all, through the eyes of success and accomplishment. He had been able to see that space really wasn't that giant – despite its never-ending size. He could go places in it. He could be one with it. And now he was one with it, and it was closing in around him like a papoose. It was suffocating him with its scale. His eyes stung with tears.

Gary Grant and Andy Duryea hung close to the edge of the cargo door, just watching. Mike was nowhere in sight. Was he still over there fighting to get into the strange ship as well? Donnie shook. He finally resolved to pulling himself back inside the cargo bay. As he pulled himself down by the hoses, he realized he was staring into an empty crate in the cargo bay. The lid floated nearby, still attached by chain to the rest of the box. It was the same crate he and Mike had investigated only a few days before, when Mike had burned his hand on its frozen surface. They had opened it up to find six large black capsules, a perplexity to them as scientists and astronauts alike. Neither of them could gather a logical idea as to what they were for.

And now they were missing. What could have happened to them? Had someone taken them out? He reached the steel rack that had stopped the equipment, the hoses of which he had been clinging to, and pulled himself down to the storage area where the crates sat, chained to the floor. Looking back through the cage behind that, he noticed several empty spots where crates had once been chained. Their chains still lingered, drifting like the ghosts of space-snakes. *What the hell?* How had so much equipment and crates gone missing?

He pulled himself along the rail toward the press chamber so he could reenter the ship and detach from his oxygen bottle. All along the opposite side of the cargo bay there was evidence of missing crates and equipment boxes. He felt his breathing speeding up again as he reached the door to the chamber and pushed the open button. Gary and Andy were silently making their way toward the opening, as Donnie hovered near it waiting. The door slid silently open. As they all clambered into the empty chamber, Donnie yanked himself inside, then turned to lock the door after it closed. Once the door was locked, the room began filling with fresh oxygen. He turned to look out the window, wondering again what had happened to all the missing crates. Then something slammed against the window and Donnie yelled out in horror, jumping in his suit. His heart threatened to rip itself out of place as it hammered madly in his chest. He looked up at the window.

It was Mike.

| **CHAPTER** *thirty-four* |
reconfiguration

As Donnie opened the pressure chamber door, Mike summoned him out quickly, and turned him to face the direction Mike was facing. Mike made signals with his hands saying *look*. Donnie looked out across the void and saw the engines of the other ship coming to life. There were sparks dancing in the blaster cones. And then it happened. The other ship left the scene. There was a burst of pressure as an explosion occurred at the back of the ship. A large fireball rocked the empty space around it, and Donnie actually heard a thump. The blast of fire and gases it had forced away from the ship had carried with it the sound of its own explosion. It sounded like a firecracker going off under water – a muted and distant *whump* of hot gas – and the ship was gone. It struck off across the darkness like newfound faith.

Donnie and Mike held their breath, knowing the importance of keeping their sites on that ship. They watched it go away, trying to memorize the direction of travel against the pattern of stars, knowing that even if they were off by a single degree here, it would equal millions of kilometers in the wrong direction on the other end. It seemed hopeless, but they hadn't much else to do, and no other hope of getting home. And shortly, it was no longer visible. There, hanging where only seconds before had been a ship, now was a single white speck. It was Jonathan Rodgers and his suit was shredded. Donnie took a deep breath and shook his head. They were now four strong. And it was time to get to work.

They sat inside the EVA control room staring out the window, looking into the cargo bay. The crew had gathered to regroup and discuss their few and fleeting options.

"So were you not going to head over there?" Mike finally said, breaking the silence.

"Mike, he was trying to lure everyone in," Donnie said. "He had no intentions of bringing any of us on board."

"Well he got Jonathan," Mike said. Andy was staring at nothing, eyes wide with tired frustration and perplexity. Gary was chewing his lip, looking at Mike and Donnie.

"So what now?" Mike said quietly.

Donnie breathed deeply. "Look. Look out there in the cargo bay and tell me what you see." Mike looked through the window, and almost immediately, his head straightened, as did his face.

"What the hell happened?"

Donnie shrugged. "It's just gone. Bradley didn't take anything with him over there did he?"

Mike shook his head. "I wonder how long he's been sending shit to that other ship."

Donnie shrugged again. "He might not have. If his mission was to disable this ship, he's probably been going out at night and dumping random crates and equipment."

"That son of a bitch!" Mike said, shaking his head.

"Yeah, well there's nothing we can do about that now. But we need to get this ship going. What can we do to make that happen? Is there anything?"

Mike squinted hard, and started nodding slowly. "I think there is."

They reached the engine room and closed the compartment door. Inset in the wall behind the entry door was a small opening that led to another compartment. Inside that compartment was where all the nitrogen tanks stood. These tanks routed nitrogen to small jets all over the exterior of the ship, used for steering and minor movements. Mike had the grand idea of pulling all the hoses and routing them back to the engine room, where they could effectively regenerate a combustion chamber with which to power the ship. Being resident on a high-tech ship where all the technology had failed, they had to resort to primitive chemistry and weak rudimentary science.

"If we can blow a thousand pounds of nitrogen into the blast chamber and set that shit on fire, it'll give us a pretty good boost, albeit not very quickly," Mike said.

Donnie frowned at this. "Uh, Mike, nitrogen has a flammability rating of zero."

But Mike was smiling that crooked smile that said he knew something. He had not flinched. So Donnie frowned some more and added, "Unless I haven't done my research."

Mike said, "Think of a thunder storm. Lightning breaks away the electrons in the nitrogen and oxygen. Makes nitric oxide."

Donnie was now squinting instead of frowning. But he was also nodding as well.

"Nitric oxide will most certainly combust," said Mike, pointing at Donnie.

It was weak and far-fetched, but anything was better than sitting still. There were over a hundred tanks they would have to work into their program, so it would take a great amount of time, but it could be done. And the worst part was that once they burned the initial flash, they would have to reroute everything back to its proper channel so they'd have the ability to steer. But if it got them home, it would be worth it.

The idea was to flood the combustion area with rich nitrogen, then dump in a load of oxygen from one of the breathing tanks. Then they would fire the anti-matter thrusters, hoping like hell there was just enough left in there to create the kind of annihilation they needed to spark the lightning. And not subsequently blow up the ship. If they timed it just right, it could work.

Donnie spent almost an entire day filling the central blast pipe with nitrogen from the many bottles that connected to the adjustment jets. He would pop the quick-connector off the jet and patch it into the blast pipe, then run off about half of what remained in each bottle. The blast pipe ran directly into the combustion chamber in the back of the ship. When he had run off the desired amount, he would plug the nitrogen bottle back into its corresponding jet, so they would still be able to make attitude adjustments to the ship. He hoped it was enough.

Meanwhile, Mike tried to repair the radar. The actual computer that ran the radar seemed to be fine. It was just the sensors that seemed to be sending bad data to the console. Thus, it was repairable.

When they finally met in the cockpit, eyes stinging red with sleep deprivation and long working hours, they strapped themselves into the thrones and knocked their fists together. This was it. The time of reckoning had arrived. Mike threw the switch that powered on the radar, and they crossed their fingers. It paused a moment, then scripts began running down the screen. And then it beeped, and a bright green spot appeared in the center of the cube matrix. The grid lines spun and settled, and spots started filling in. It was working. They breathed a sigh of relief, and Mike started laughing.

"Oh, thank God! Something works again!"

"Yeah," Donnie said, "now let's just hope the engine will blast us out of here."

Mike pressed a key that historically had been used to enrich the fuel burn. Only now, the other end of the circuit had been attached to a spare oxygen tank. So when the oxygen blew into the pipe, mixing with the nitrogen, it became a different kind of fuel mixture. Donnie pushed the ignition button. Nothing happened. He looked at Mike and had just enough time to widen his eyes, worried that all their work had failed. And then it happened. The long pipe full of the new gas blasted into the combustion chamber, and some small amount of antimatter was ready. There was a loud rocking explosion behind them, and they suddenly felt a sense of movement. It had worked. The ship was now moving with a considerable force in the direction they were facing.

They came out of their seats and embraced, laughing and hollering in celebration. This was the first event worthy of celebrating for either of them in a really long time. Their ingenuity had gotten them going. To what end, they would have to wait and find out. Maybe no end. Maybe a dead end. It might have been, they both knew, a blast toward a point just wrong enough to send them millions of miles into deep space. They would have to wait and see. But for now, they could celebrate.

Gary and Andy had been tasked with redistributing the supplies and equipment in the cargo bay, and dumping the non-essential pieces. They were taking inventory of what was left, and trying to gather all the food and water, medicine and supplies. There were now hundreds of crates hanging about in the cargo, none of which could be of any use in their current predicament. It was all necessary on Mars, but was meaningless in the trip.

After a day of digging around, Gary had come across two large crates full of composite fire logs, which had been allocated for fires on the surface of Mars. These logs were compressed combustibles, soaked with solid rocket fuel. Mike and Donnie and he had dumped them all in the blast chamber. Then they tried once more with the antimatter and got lucky once again. And now they had some serious velocity behind their progress.

The next day, while sitting in the cockpit, Mike noticed the blip on the radar. According to the numbers on the screen, they were ninety thousand kilometers behind the other ship. But they were gaining. Donnie reckoned they'd gotten a better boost than he had originally thought possible. Mike had also reminded him that the other ship was a small rescue-type pod, and wasn't geared for speed or long distance, so it wasn't out of the realm of possibility that Atlas would finally catch up with it. Their hard work had paid off, and they had gotten it just right. For once, something had gone their way.

And thus, the chase was on.

Donnie and Mike had been keeping a hard eye on the other ship in the radar, knowing it was their own and only salvation. Atlas had no means by which to tell their direction of travel any longer, so they were reliant on the other ship's guidance.

During the days that passed, Donnie and Mike had long talks about how they would land the ship once they broke through Earth's atmosphere – if fate were actually to lead them that far. At this point, they had nothing else to believe in, so they spoke of it as if it were a mathematical certainty. It kept them from going insane.

On the ninth day of their chase, Mike was beginning to look frail and sickly. He hadn't slept for more than a few minutes at a time for the last several days. His eyes were tired and bloodshot from staring so intently at the radar screen, waiting, anticipating the closure of that hated distance between the two ships. Donnie could hardly stand to look at him, shaky and disturbed as he was. And it wasn't long until they were grating on each other's nerves. It was of paramount importance that they both maintain an accurate evaluation of the situation, their closing distance, and – most importantly – their direction. This meant they had to share the cockpit full-time. The breaks they took to freshen up and relieve themselves were short and far-between.

They didn't see much of Gary and Andy, and secretly, Donnie began to suspect that they had found their own ways of passing the time. He imagined that on a trip slotted for fifteen months, the allure of sexuality was far more than just desirable. And attractive was the idea of sex in zero gravity. Someone was surely bound to try it sooner or later, he guessed. And the obvious thoughts of Shanna returned on the heels of those thoughts. He was deeply saddened about losing her – she was just a kid. Losing Jonathan hadn't really affected Donnie much at all. He guessed it was because of the stressful events in which it had taken place. But Shanna, his personal assistant for the last few years – and now suddenly an attraction – he felt strange affinity for her, and mourned her loss.

Donnie had taken an interest in trying to repair some of the other failed systems on the flight deck control panels. If he couldn't figure out how to fix them, he reckoned he would at least attain a familiarity with their inner workings. This was something he had before counted on Brian Bradley to handle. There wasn't much he could do, but it kept him busy, and it kept him from watching Mike as he gazed longingly at the radar. And keeping his hands busy with systems about which he knew so little somehow freed his mind to do other things – like ponder the hows and whys that had gotten him stuck in space. Within these new thoughts, he came to terms with some things he had not previously considered. And when he started voicing some of these thoughts, he caught Mike's attention.

"So if they bought our satellite for some other reason than to steal our technology, then why did they pay so much for it? Why did they order it without any attachments? All they can do is navigate and transmit data. Data they can't even collect with no attachments. What the f-"

"Holy shit!" Mike shouted suddenly. He had not only broken Donnie's train of thought, but he almost startled him directly into a heart attack. Mike had pushed off the chair suddenly and was turned facing Donnie. He also had a sudden color about him.

"What? Shit, Mike, don't do that," Donnie said, covering his heart. He had lost most of his color simultaneously.

"Donnie, do you know what you just said?"

Donnie shook his head quickly, but couldn't re-rail the previous train of thought. "No."

"Holy shit, that's it! You're genius, Donnie! That's it!" Mike said, shaking his shoulders.

Donnie couldn't help but feel the excitement in Mike's sudden rush. "What? What is it? What the hell did I say?"

"You said 'all they can do is navigate and transmit data'. That's what you said," Mike reminded him. Then he hung there waiting for a response.

Donnie nodded for a moment. "Yeah. That's right. I was just wondering what Royal would want with non-working pr-" He was cut off again.

"Exactly! They'd have to be stealing our technology," Mike said.

"Well," Donnie frowned, "we've already determined that's not a serious scenario. It can't be. That company is a hundred years ahead of us."

Mike's face got serious. "Maybe they needed it just like they bought it. Plain old vanilla."

"It's useless, Mike. You know this. All the blank models have…" and he caught it. His eyes widened, and his jaw dropped.

Mike nodded approvingly. "And they're not a hundred years ahead of us either." Mike turned and pointed out the cold dark windscreen. "They've only got us by a day."

Donnie and Mike had long since homed in on the other ship, and had silently begun to wonder why they hadn't tried any evasive maneuvers. There could be no doubt that the Bradley crew knew they were being followed. For they had more than just working radar. Maybe, Donnie thought, they just knew the odds of the Atlas being able to do anything more than crash into the ocean. But after two weeks of silently shadowing the rescue ship, Donnie and Mike both began to realize the strange familiarity of their trek.

Some ten days ago, they had made a broad swoop out and down, bringing the sun to high noon above the Atlas, and at that point, it had almost all been lost. Donnie had used a lot more nitrogen on the course change than he had thought it would take, and they were now running on less than thirty percent of the full capacity. They would run out almost ten million miles shy of Earth. In betrayal of any math they could conceive in their minds, there would be no way to steer a ship through an atmosphere without some form of propellant. They would have to catch the other ship and board it for any chance of survival. There was much doubt that would happen, and many were the night that Donnie dreamt of his pursuit, taking a leap of faith and bounding free of Atlas on little more than a breath of air – he and Mike pushing long for the ship they would never reach, and watching it dwindle in their masks as they flailed useless in space like whale and wasp.

But for no other reason than an absolute lack of alternative plan, they carried on. They made tiny adjustments when necessary, cautiously eyeing the gauges, leaning to the left like a superstition in hopes it would get them there. There was simply nothing more for which to aim. It was all or nothing. At least they had a chance in their chase, no matter how infinitesimally small it really was. In the grand scheme of things, they were already dead.

They were still following about fifteen hours behind the rescue ship in order to maintain a margin of safety. In this way, they could make changes to their course and attain a better sense of what the other ship was doing. It also protected them in case the other decided to do something stupid. But most importantly, it gave them the room and time they needed to think. The rescue ship was visible in the windscreen as a bright speck of shining metal, seemingly self-illuminated. It was hard to imagine that it was more than fifty thousand kilometers ahead of them.

The future was uncertain, as was their path. Here they had come to trust their enemy to lead them home. And that strange familiarity began to lose its strangeness as they realized they were again heading away from the sun. Being between Earth and Sol, this would be desirable. But based on the star charts, the

Earth was behind them. Mike scratched it out on paper with a broken pencil, and showed it to Donnie during one of their makeshift mornings, holding it against the windscreen to illustrate his math.

"That's west, Don. There's no denying that turn we took a few weeks back. Had we put the sun beneath us in that context, we would be heading home right now. But we didn't. And until we had a few days to catch our bearings, there was no way we could have noticed. But I have noticed now."

Donnie was shaking his head. "I don't know. I guess I'm just in denial, man. I don't see it."

"Heh. You will, buddy. You will."

And he did. Two days beyond this revelation, they saw the other ship swoop again, but this time it was up against their current orientation. And Atlas was out of gas. They pulled back hard on the yoke, and it gave them a couple of degrees and blew dry. Both of them inhaled sharply when it expired, then they stood watching the other ship rise hard above their field of vision before it disappeared into the darkness that is deep space. Effectively, the other ship had taken the last exit, and Atlas was left heading straight ahead. The last little blast of nitrogen had been enough to nose them up a little, but hadn't changed their direction at all. Their current direction of travel would put them right in the orbital path of the Red Planet. That put Earth's directly behind them. The rescue ship wasn't headed home after all, seemingly still making a mission out of this trip. And when Donnie finally saw it, his heart sank.

Mike sighed as Donnie surrendered himself to the captain's chair. "So what's the plan, boss? Do we bail out now and enjoy our last few minutes breathing space air or just hang on as long as we can?"

Donnie turned to look at Mike, sullenness evident in his eyes. "This is a joke to you?"

Mike sighed again, and shook his head. "No, Donnie, but there's nothing else to do! We're out of gas, we're out of nitrogen, we have no equipment, and ninety percent of our systems are down! We're running on nothing but God's will right now!"

"We've been running on God's will for the last three months. It's a wonder we've made it this far."

"How far *is* this far? Donnie, it doesn't matter how the hell far away we are from anything! We're no better off than when we were leaving the Goddamn galaxy! We might as well throw ourselves into a black hole!"

"Calm down, Mike! Yelling about it's not going to do any good," Donnie said. He was more worried of Mike's attitude than the outcome of the trip at this point.

"Calm down? You don't want me to yell about it? What the hell *am* I allowed to do, for shit's sake? We're on a mission to nowhere, and our arrival is set at never o'clock! We're gonna die out here with nothing but stars around us and the Earth behind us! If I knew we would someday at least crash into the Atlantic, I would be a little more comfortable with our predicament. But in case you haven't noticed, we're alone out here and we might as well be sitting first class on the world's largest paper fucking airplane!"

"That's elegant, Mike. I don't know what you want me to say." Donnie's voice was barely audible in the stillness of the cabin.

Mike breathed in deeply. A long moment passed before he said, "Nothing. I'm sorry I lost my temper. It's just finally settling in."

Donnie looked Mike hard in the eyes. "Well get used to it, champ. Welcome it. I don't know how it will all end, but short of us pulling a double suicide, we're going to witness it." Donnie swallowed and looked away, shaking his head as if to say he didn't believe his own words. "And it's probably going to be sooner than later."

Donnie took his seat and buckled in. "So how long do you think they were following us?"

Mike followed suit, buckling in. "Huh. Ever since we left."

"I should have known not to sell them any satellites. I was just floored by the dollar amount they were willing to pay."

Mike nodded, a wan smile crossing his lips. "I'd have had those same dollar signs in my eyes, chief."

"I just don't get why they wanted to spend that much money just to follow us." Donnie looked over at Mike and raised his eyebrows.

"You mean besides to rescue Bradley? Think about it – they had to have our comm-chip to be able to keep track of where we were. What better way to obtain it than to buy our satellite."

"How'd they know it was the same chip we used in Atlas though?"

Mike shrugged. "Hell, Bradley could have told them. But most companies do it. They'll send out entire fleets of these things all using the same chip. Proprietary design and programming. Why would you change it if it works?" He pointed a lazy finger at Donnie. "Only problem is most companies who make a proprietary satellite comm-chip don't also own shuttles."

"I should have thought of that. We should have designed a different comm-chip for the shuttle fleet," Donnie said, shaking his head.

"Nah. Who'd have guessed we'd have someone trying to reverse-engineer it so they could follow us on a mission to nowhere?"

"Well I just want to know why they want to keep us away from Mars so badly. They spend millions of dollars on a single satellite to steal our technology, so they can track us. They send a man up with us to disable all our shit and shut us down, and send a ship to rescue him. What are they hiding, Mike?"

Mike shook his head, a smirk set on his face. "That, my friend, is the question of the century."

It was five days later that Mike finally fell across a pattern in the stars that told him what was happening. He had long ago discovered that they were shooting straight out from the Sun, and would eventually cross the orbital path of Mars. But it was these additional five days he had buried his head in the charts that brought him to realize the constructive plausibility of their current plight. They would definitely be crossing its path. But if his math was right, there would be a planet there to meet them.

In a frenzy of excitement, Donnie and Mike had gone shooting through the cargo bay and into the trailer to ready the lander. The lander would be their method of descending to the planet's surface while the ship remained in orbit. Then at the end of their mission, they would blast back up into the atmosphere and spacewalk to the Atlas, leaving the lander to drift away.

Instinctively, Donnie reached for the trailer's bay door control console when they emerged from the tunnel. But he stopped short as they looked up at the empty cage, hanging cold and lifeless on the wall of the trailer. The lander was gone.

Mike drew in a breath as they realized what had happened. He then hung his head, cursing under his breath.

"What the hell happened." Donnie wasn't asking.

Mike looked up at him. "He jettisoned the landing pod," Mike said, shaking his head.

Donnie sighed and furled his lips. "There it is. Our last hope."

engagement

In the long light of a distant sun, the shadows had settled on miraculous missteps and the wickedly despondent future of a crew who had been shaven down to only four souls. If ever there were a grim prospect for survival, Donnie Oliver, Mike Thurman, Andy Duryea and Gary Grant had come upon it – bought and paid for. It seemed fate had dealt them a significantly strong hand in attaining pursuit of a ship without the use of standard propulsion, but that same fate had left them dangling on the precipice of the solar system with no foothold for return. There was now a slight chance the Atlas team would confront the Red Planet by mistake alone, but to what end? What good is a space rescue only to bring you safely to a planet you can never leave? For most, dying on Mars wasn't any better than dying in deep space.

He had quit coming into the cockpit altogether. They had no control of the shuttle, no communication with anything living, and no spots on their radar that would otherwise signify hope for encounter. There was, therefore, not much point in sitting front row to the show. Mike, on the other hand, had embraced their destiny – foggy as it might have been, and built himself an armory of hope and courage. Every few hours or days, he would try some of the systems to see if they had been magically restored. There was no distinct separation of time anymore, and he knew no matter what lay ahead, he was only along for the ride.

With most of the systems having long since died, the oxygen had begun to grow stale and scent-laden. It smelled of dust and heat, and burned the lungs when taken in too sharply. They were running out of food, air and water, but Donnie reckoned it was for the best. Why prolong the façade of a glorious subsistence? Within the cloud of disharmony that had befallen them over the last few months, Donnie had reached the point of wishing he had never taken the trip at all. The shuttle Atlas had become a generator for negativity, and it brought its weight down on all who couldn't escape its cold grasp. Donnie's long dream of setting foot on the planet was shadowed only by the disappointment he felt that they might not even live to see it happen.

So separate they stayed, but together they did the only thing they could do: they waited.

That night, Mars became visible in the right-side windscreen, still almost two-million kilometers away but very large and definitely getting closer. Mike had been on the verge of falling asleep when a thin sliver of the Red Planet crept over the edge of the windscreen. It had taken him a few moments to realize what was going on, but as the sliver grew and the planet became more visible, his heart started slamming in his chest. He had never seen anything so amazing in his life. He had grabbed the PA handset and tried to call Donnie to the cockpit, but then remembered the PA was out. It was then he started shouting in excited panic, and Donnie shortly came bursting through the door.

And both men were speechless.

After calling Gary and Andy to the flight deck, they all stood and wondered aloud how a planet as large as Mars could have snuck up on them like that. It ultimately took Donnie penciling out their estimated trajectory in accordance with the star charts to understand what had happened. They had been traveling a little to the left of what they had originally thought, and not straight out away from the sun. Thus, upon arrival within the region of Mars's orbital path, the planet had been coming in from the right rear of the ship. And now the dark side of the giant was looming largely in the full right side of the windscreen – blocking out stars and galaxies from their view.

Over the course of the next six hours, it moved all the way across the windscreen until nothing else could be seen at all. They were now heading straight for it, as its gravity had long ago started persuading their path. It was at once a fantastic sight and an ominous portrait of how their lives would end. It greatly excited Donnie to be so close as to touch the planet he had long wished to visit. But the fashion of their arrival played a sickening affront to his cognizance. There was no getting away from it now, and he would quickly have to come to terms with his fate. Back home where he ran the company, he could make phone calls and arrangements to prepare and resolve potential catastrophes. He could delegate a fall guy if necessary. But here he was powerless to stop the approach of the most significant achievement he had ever made. That is until Mike sounded off behind him.

"Well we're not going to ride this fucker down are we? Let's go!"

Donnie shortly found himself following Mike through the ship toward the trailer that still clung to its aft section. They pulled their way through the long tunnels of the Atlas, thoughts spinning in their minds about the looming planet beneath them. When they had left the cockpit, the calculation was that they would be arriving in an hour. As they approached the aft of the shuttle, Mike came to rest with his hands on the wheel of the exit hatch.

"You ready for this?" he said.

Donnie shook his head, knowing what Mike had in mind. "You think the trailer's going to save us?"

"It's got fifteen chutes that deploy in proximity. It's our only chance, Donnie!"

Donnie snorted. "Chance for what? To live? How the hell do you expect to exist once we get out?"

"Who the hell cares? I would rather die of suffocation walking around the planet than by crashing into it!" Mike shouted.

"A terrestrial collision would be much swifter," Donnie said solemnly.

"You're kidding me! We've made it this far Donnie! What the hell has happened to you? You used to be so adventurous."

"There's just no point anymore." The depression had found its way into his soul, and Mike saw it in his eyes.

"Donnie. Listen. There's a chance we might run into Bradley and his crew."

Donnie laughed out loud. "Come on, Mike! You're a scientist, not a gambler! The chances of that happening are less than a billion to one!"

Mike held his finger up. "But there is a chance. And I'll take that chance." Mike stood staring at Donnie for a long moment before he spoke again. "Besides. Your lifelong dream was to stand on this planet. Live it the hell up."

Donnie nodded, and a smile crept onto his face, for the first time in ages. He knew it was far-fetched that they would survive the crash, but better than anything else he could come up with. They had originally intended to drop the trailer upon arrival and have it soar sweetly to the surface on a series of large parachutes as they made touchdown in the lander. But Donnie had never considered having to rely on the trailer to get them there safely.

"Let's do it," Donnie said, and held his fist up. Then he summoned Gary to help them.

After spending a half-hour in a frenzy of moving potential needs to the trailer, Mike opened the hatch and climbed into the small tunnel that led to the trailer. Once on the other end, he turned and helped Donnie, Gary and Andy come through. They donned their space suits and helmets and closed off the trailer, tightening the airlock. They could sense the acceleration of their approach already. It was beginning.

Donnie took hold of the large steel handle that controlled the emergency jettison system and looked over at Mike. Mike strapped himself into the harness that hung by the hatch and nodded back at him. Donnie pulled the handle with everything he had, and in slow motion, it began to move downward. A loud hiss turned into a sudden roar, and an explosion knocked him away from the wall. His tether caught him dangling, and he quickly yanked himself to the harness opposite of Mike. Gary hung in the webbing beside Mike, and Andy hung directly behind him. He was playing protector to the only woman left in his life.

The trailer was now detached from the shuttle, and freefalling to the planet below.

The rumbling at first seemed to be a distant annoyance – no more than a little turbulence in the dusty atmosphere of Mars. But it quickly grew to an almost unbearable shaking that rocked them violently within their harnesses. Donnie stared wide-eyed and white with fear at Mike, who had his eyes closed against the pressure. Donnie's helmet took a continual beating as it banged against the bulkhead behind him. Gary also had his eyes closed, gripping the webbing with white knuckles and a fierceness that could have crushed steel. Andy was invisible behind him. And within the roaring quake that threatened to breakup the shuttle trailer, Donnie came perilously close to blacking out. And then it stopped, sudden as a hailstorm.

Donnie knew they were now free of the atmosphere, and dropping from the sky. There was a period of silence as they fell with no restriction. Donnie closed his eyes and prayed that the trailer systems wouldn't fail them like the Atlas had. And like a breath of fresh air, he felt a series of jolts as the chutes opened one by one. The repeated *whump-whump* sound was felt rather than heard, but it was more comforting than anything sonic Donnie could ever have imagined.

The Martian gravity had begun suddenly to take effect, and Donnie noticed the weight in his suit again. He felt resistance to the fall as they rocked silently back and forth on the winds of the strange planet. It felt so much like home he could almost taste the air. Being composed of different elements though, they would be bound to their suits and helmets for the whole visit – however short or long that was to be. Excitement began creeping up heavily, and he had the feeling he wasn't the only one affected by it.

The only windows in the trailer were narrow strips set in the curve of the ceiling, and couldn't be seen from their vantage point. Light shone through them though, and though it wasn't as bright as a sunny day on Earth, it was a sun they had not seen in months. It sparkled like freedom through the reinforced glass, creating thick beams of glorious sunshine that beat the bottom of the trailer and briefly spotlighted motes of dust on their trek to new places.

Donnie braced himself for the fall. Tightening all his muscles, he looked up and noticed Mike and Gary had taken a similar posture. They would be landing any moment. The only thing missing was the pleasant female voice coming in over the intercom, welcoming them to sunny Mars, where she hoped they would enjoy their stay.

Donnie wished he could see something – anything by which to judge their fall. It was a sickening feeling of anticipation, knowing they would be slamming down on the surface soon, but not knowing when. He felt much like a boy blindfolded, knowing he's about to be slapped. He noticed his teeth grinding and dared open his eyes to check on Mike. The slam chose that very instant to introduce itself.

Donnie felt as though his skeleton had been ripped from his flesh as the impact brought everything to a sudden halt. The magnificent slam of metal on rocks had been overwhelming, and coupled with the pain and disorientation of being crushed against his own weight, he lost consciousness.

The sound of his breathing was loud and unwelcome as he came to. He opened his eyes, or thought he did, but could see nothing but the red darkness of his eyelids against a screaming sun. It was quickly evident that he was being dragged by his legs, and a cold shiver traversed his spine as he became cognizant of the footsteps surrounding him. There were more than one man could make.

The sensation of being dragged along a warm and sunny coastline was augmented by the sound of the crunching boots on rock and dirt. But that didn't quell the fear that suddenly seemed to be rising in his gut. Donnie forced his eyes open and immediately had to squint against the sun. He saw silhouetted the two figures who dragged him, but the placement of the sound was inaccurate. *There must be more behind me.* He tried to speak, but his mouth felt dusty and parched, unable to formulate words. After a long period of indeterminable time, the motion ceased, but Donnie's stomach kept moving. He felt suddenly hot, and with the swimming of his stomach, had to be sick.

Hot vomit poured into his helmet, by way of his cheeks and ears and he coughed and choked on it as he gasped for breath beneath its presence. With no sense of urgency, he felt someone grabbing both of his arms and hoisting him to a sitting position. He coughed and spit, clearing his mouth, and felt the liquid seeping into his suit down his neckline. For the first time, he came in contact with its smell and almost had to vomit again. He held it back though, and tried to close his nose off to the foul and stinking bile. Through watery eyes, he came to look at the shapes standing before him. His previous assessment had been accurate, as he now sat penitent before a group of strange men. They were human, to be sure, but Donnie was certain he had never met a one of them.

It was immediately clear his position among the men. They weren't his friends. They were established and professional. They belonged here. Donnie didn't. They had at one point made the same trek as Donnie – albeit a little more direct – but it was clear they had gotten here without issue, and intended to leave the same way, when came their time. Donnie had no illusions as he stared aghast at the sight that lay before him. He was no longer in command of anything – not even himself.

Five of them stood some ten meters distant ahead of him, one leaning on a dark and dangerous-looking shovel. They all stood staring emotionlessly at Donnie. He could not see their eyes or their faces – for their visors were black. But he could feel their visage, burning him like the hot sun at his back. To his left were three more, one of whom was squatting and handling small pebbles as he stared at Donnie. And again – all still and measuring. Then there were two ahead and to the right of him who stood beside the prone body of Mike Thurman, who lay in a heap of motionless detachment. Donnie guessed quickly he was dead. And the man who stood directly before Donnie seemed to be in charge. His arms were crossed and he moved red earth around with his foot as he waited silently.

"Who are you?" Donnie managed on a weak voice. The man looked up.

"Your friends are dead. We'll handle the burials. Is there anything you'd like to vocalize before you join them in blissful interment? You managed to defeat the gargantuan odds we placed against your arriving here – the least I can do is allow you to speak." There was no emotion in the man's deep voice – only a functional grumbling that said he would rather get on with it.

Donnie's heart felt wrapped in chain. It seemed he had to will it to beat as it pushed ten-ton blood through his steely veins. He swallowed coarsely and spoke.

"My soul is heavy."

The man sighed. "In your ascendancy to the ability of space travel, you overstepped the boundaries by which you were unwittingly confined."

Donnie swallowed again and breathed in deeply, slowly. On the horizon he saw movement – too distant to discern, but hauntingly familiar. "Who are you?" he asked again. "Who are you to claim this your planet?"

The man laughed, and was chorused by a few of the others. "You're searching for camaraderie. There's a strange leaning toward humanity with other humans when you've left the hive. It's like the boundaries of race that disappear when people of many colors are put together in a stressful situation. Everyone recognizes a certain consonance." The man looked up at Donnie again as he paced slowly, purposefully, back and forth.

"But you're looking in the wrong place for humanity here. We did not simply beat you to Mars," the stranger said. "We meant to ensure your failure. It would be a detriment to our project to allow someone the privilege of gazing upon our achievements. So while we are not claiming it is 'our planet', as you so eloquently put it, we are determined to ensure that what we've established here never becomes evident."

"What are you hiding? Don't you think that man as a whole has the right to take part in the discovery of new things?" Donnie pleaded. But if felt as though he were asking himself for answers more than the stranger.

The movement on the distant hill had settled into a streak, growing in Donnie's vision, and it became evident that it was a rover of some sort – a conveyance that in its wake sent great plumes of dust billowing into the ruddy sky.

"I think you're interested in the wrong things, Mr. Oliver. You've goaled yourself with these apparitions of this brilliant new landscape – a clean slate by which to build a science of discovery. But there's nothing here!" the man said, turning and spreading his arms as if to validate his accuracy.

"Then why the trip? Why travel sixty-million kilometers across space to visit a planet that has nothing on it? What's the fucking point?"

"It's not what we've found here," the man said richly, "but what we've brought." He turned as the vehicle rolled to a stop beside the group of dark-clad men. A man jumped down out of the vehicle hefting a large crate, from the top of which protruded a series of black cylinders, rounded on the ends like monstrous medicine capsules.

Donnie's stomach tightened again and he gritted his teeth.

"Well, thank you for joining us, Mr. Oliver. It was a pleasure making your acquaintance. Perhaps in the next life we can all be on the same side of the table." The man then pulled a pistol from behind his back and went through the motions of checking the chamber, racking the slide and ejecting a cartridge, all for effect. The cartridge hit the dry red dirt with a dead thump. As the man thumbed the catch, the rack flew forward with a metallic slam, and Donnie looked away.

Donnie's eyes grew weak, and his breathing slowed as he tried to come to terms with what was happening. Death, in all her glory, finally appeared to be greeting him. But despite its terrifying grip on his soul, Donnie's mind began to settle. He began to feel that peace for which he had so longed. His thoughts went back to Delilah and her long, cool, black hair. The smell of her skin and his last look into her eyes before he walked away forever. The look of the concrete on the flight line before he climbed into Atlas and sealed the door. The sands of the Arizona desert blowing across the tarmac as they prepared for takeoff on their gigantic mission. The shimmering and hazy red sun of the Arizona desert rising upon a brand new day – the last earthly sunrise Donnie would ever see. His eyes twitched slightly as he realized the tank strapped to his back had just run out of oxygen. Within minutes, the ambient supply within his suit would be extinguished.

"Last words, Mr. Oliver?" said the man with the pistol.

Donnie looked up at him and felt a smile crack his lips. He reached back and took hold of the clasp on his helmet. "Yeah. Fuck you. I made it. I made it, I resurrected Mars." Quickly, Donnie popped the seal on his helmet and threw it to the ground at the strange man's feet. The man stepped back and lowered the pistol, a look of dumbfounded defeat about his posture.

Donnie broke the seal on his gloves and dug his hands deep into the dry red dirt, extinguishing all doubts that he had made it, and staring long into the red desert world that lay stretched before him. Carried halfway across the solar system in search of a reckoning, he had finally found purchase on the surface of an alien planet – though he had never gotten to take steps there. The dry wind stung his eyes and cheeks, but he reveled in it. He nodded his head and looked up at the sky, absently wondering what Martian rain would feel like on his face. As his lungs fought for air that wasn't there, he let the nothingness of the universe greet him with its absent fingers. He leaned back and lay down on the dirt, smiling at the newfound peace in his proximity. With a confidence and comfort he had never before realized, Donnie Oliver let go his final breath and closed his eyes against forever. There was nothing more to see.

| EPILOGUE |

closure

The rain had finally settled into a steady roar. The gutters were all overflowing, and some lower intersections downtown had flooded, giving the appearance that the sidewalks blended right into the streets. In a city not built to handle anything more than a nominal shower, it looked catastrophic. The streets were awash with dirty brown water, having had the dust knocked out of the air, and the buildings were bleeding with the dark runoff. It was as if everything was starting over. In a way, it was.

Callie sat staring out the window, her knees together, her chin in her hands. Her elbows rested on the desk, on either side of a coffee mug that had once held heat. The now-cold liquid within sat untouched since she had taken her last sip almost an hour before. And she had not moved more than an inch in easily as long. There was simply no will left in her to do anything other than stare out the window, watching the water pour in sheets off the roof across the street. The side of the neighbor's house was muddy from the splattering of the flood in the flowerbeds.

Her watch suddenly felt cold against her wrist, and as she straightened it, she realized it was no longer ticking. She unclasped it and dropped it in the drawer and sighed. She then pulled the drawer open and removed the watch to look at it again. On the back was etched the words, "Congratulations on 1 year! The Olivers." Her mouth made the motion towards a smile, but the rest of her face didn't allow it. A tear stung the corner of her eye. She dropped it in the drawer again, and slid it closed.

The Oliver Company had initiated plans to scale back a large portion of their business, and Samson had laid off several hundred employees immediately. He had heard the news of a traitor within the ranks of the workers, and got paranoid – if not a little angry. In the process of scaling back, he had cut funding for a large portion of their research. Callie had been given three months to tie everything up and find another place to work. There was simply nothing left for her to do at the company. She knew it wouldn't be a task to find another job, but the thought that she would no longer be working for the Olivers pained her. She had previously thought of it as her final resting place in the life of her career. She had hoped to retire in fifteen years with a nice pension plan and a plaque commending her twenty years of honorable service. But most of all, she hated moving. It was unlikely she would find another job in her field in Arizona.

Callie leaned back, yawning, rubbing her eyes, and trying to find the willpower and energy just to get up. Her satellite phone shivered in her sweats pocket. Slipping it out, she saw on the display that it was Walter. Typically she would be happy about his calling, but within the well of depression she found herself lately, she knew it would probably be a while before anything would gladden her. Chewing her bottom lip, she answered it.

"Uh huh?"

"My dear lady. I'm so sorry about your loss. You doing okay?"

She chuffed. "Yeah, as well as I can be, I guess."

"Well I have some good news. There's an opening on my team. I thought of you first. Wanna reconsider?"

Callie squinted her eyes against the thought, and sat silent for a long moment. She dropped her hand to her lap, the phone still alive and lighted in her grasp. Walter allowed her the silence. And in that silence, she found the oddest sensation tempting the edges of her mouth. Slowly, it crept into a smirk, and she found herself nodding.

She looked back at the window, the rain outside, the mud on the neighbor's bricks, and the general gloom of the day seemed to be gone. There seemed to be in this want for her, a reconfiguration of her previously conceived ideas about what was depressing. It was a sudden and inexplicable turn to the half-full view of the day – instead of the half-empty view of her foreseeable future. Like grocery shopping while hungry, Callie was decidedly of the opinion that she shouldn't make big decisions on a tired and depressed state of mind. But then there were those exceptions that would break free her depression and allow her some comfort. She leaned forward, elbows on her knees, and chewed on her lip. It was a bad habit she had recently taken.

Was this feeling of lightness a façade? Was she just happy to be getting a call? Was her love for

Walter and her disdain for loneliness propelling her to make a wrong decision? She could, of course, take some time to think about it. But maybe some decisions were best made in the heat of the moment – striking while the iron is hot. Maybe she didn't have a choice to make. Maybe it was already made for her. A thousand thoughts tempted her, but she let go of them easily. She had all the time in the world to relax and recuperate, and plenty of money in savings to allow her the comfort of doing so at home. There was no need for a rush decision, be it made or otherwise.

There seemed to be butterflies in her stomach – an uneasiness in light of the phone call, perhaps? Or was it excitement at the prospect of working with Walter again? She had sworn she would never rejoin the ranks of Royal. They were, after all, the evil that had perpetrated the disastrous events of the failed mission upon which she lost several of her close friends. It was the same disaster that had fueled the fire now burning up her company from the inside. If she took the job, she would effectively be sleeping with the enemy. But at the same time, one had to consider the benefits of working for them. Not just anyone was offered work at RRC. And if she were to continue the investigation she had started into Brian Bradley, what better place to do so than behind a desk in an office at Royal? *From the inside.* So which was it? Callie thought she knew the answer already.

She leaned back in her chair and propped her feet up on the desk, then returned the phone to her ear. "You still there?" Callie lifted the cold mug to her mouth and took a swallow.

9 798990 120013